PUCKING WILD

ALSO BY EMILY RATH

JACKSONVILLE RAYS SERIES

SPICY HOCKEY ROMANCE

That One Night (#.0.5)

Pucking Around (#1)

Pucking Ever After: Vol I (#1.5)

Pucking Wild (#2)

Pucking Ever After: Vol. 2 (#2.5)

Pucking Sweet (#3)

SECOND SONS SERIES

SPICY 'WHY CHOOSE' REGENCY ROMANCE

Beautiful Things (#1)

His Grace, The Duke (#2)

Alcott Hall (#3)

STANDALONES

CONTEMPORARY MM OMEGAVERSE

Whiskey & Sin

ADDITIONAL STORIES

Lemongrass

A Jax Rays Novella, exclusive to the Queer & Cute Anthology

PUCKING WILD

EMILY RATH

KENSINGTON PUBLISHING CORP.
Kensington Books
www.kensingtonbooks.com

KENSINGTON BOOKS are published by:

Kensington Publishing Corp.
900 Third Avenue
New York, NY 10022

kensingtonbooks.com

All Kensington titles, imprints, and distributed lines are available at special quantity discounts for bulk purchases for sales promotions, premiums, fundraising, educational, or institutional use.

Special book excerpts or customized printings can also be created to fit specific needs. For details, write or phone the office of the Kensington sales manager: Kensington Publishing Corp., 900 Third Avenue, New York, NY 10022, attn: Sales Department; phone 1-800-221-2647.

The K with book logo Reg US Pat. & TM Off.

ISBN 978-1-4967-5241-3 (trade paperback)

First Kensington Trade Paperback Printing: March 2024

10 9 8 7 6 5 4 3 2 1

Printed in the United States of America

Cover design by Craig White
Author photograph by Jennifer Catherine Photography

Tropes: Hockey romance, reverse age gap (F33/M22), friends to lovers, accidental roommates

Tags: MF, hockey romance, romantic comedy, instalust, he falls first, reverse age gap, accidental roommates, positive plus size representation, bisexual goddess, dom(me)/sub, toy play, begging for a pegging, someone's always naked, all the Taylor Swift songs on the playlist are Ryan's, one kiss is all it takes

This is for all the thirty-somethings trapped in marriages, friendships, and family dynamics you've outgrown. Set yourself free. Watch how you fly.

Oh, and give pegging a try.

Content Warnings: This book contains some themes that may be distressing to readers including a character who is trapped in a marriage with a narcissistic, abusive partner. She experiences gaslighting, belittling, and attempts at control, shame, and blame. At one point, her partner becomes physically violent, restraining her by the neck (depicted on page). There is reference to other violence perpetrated by him, including on-page depictions of verbal and emotional abuse. His family aids him in gaslighting and controlling her.

There are also depictions of sexism in the workplace, including morality double standards. You will also read about elements of stalking, harassing, and blackmail. The main characters have their photos taken without their consent (they don't perpetrate this on each other).

A character suffers an injury described on the page (no blood or gore). A character also suffers from severe dyslexia and exhibits a range of coping strategies. This same character has feelings of inadequacy linked to their dyslexia that include making self-deprecating remarks. This character is shamed by others for their learning difference (on page).

Aside from the above, this book contains detailed MF sex scenes that include elements of dom(me)/sub, impact play, anal play, bondage, breath play, toy use, pegging, and praise.

Author's Note

This is the second book in the Jacksonville Rays Hockey Series. Book one, *Pucking Around*, is Rachel's story. Here's what you need to know from *Pucking Around* to get the best reader experience in *Pucking Wild*.

- Rachel and Tess are best friends who were living together in Cincinnati when Rachel got a sports medicine fellowship and moved to Jacksonville to join the Rays, the newest NHL expansion team
- Rachel is currently in a polyamorous relationship with two of the Rays (defenseman Jake and goalie Ilmari) and the Equipment Manager (Caleb)
- Ilmari made a rash decision at a fundraiser and donated half a million dollars to a sea turtle conservation nonprofit
- On a visit to Jacksonville, Tess meets Ryan Langley, starting forward for the Rays. They have a meet cute moment on the beach, followed by a secret kiss in Jake's house where Ryan may have seen Tess in her birthday suit (I included that scene here, so keep reading)
- Tess and Ryan haven't seen each other or spoken since beach day

Pucking Around is 200k words long, so a lot more happened, but that's as much as I'll recap here. Go read it. Start with the spicy prequel novella *That One Night*. This story starts on that fateful night in L.A. when Rachel placed her hand on the plexiglass and dared Ilmari Price to earn his new last name. Enjoy!

XO,

Meet the Rays

PLAYERS

Davidson, Tyler "Dave-O" (#65): backup goalie
Fields, Ethan (#94): forward
Gerard, Jean-Luc "J Lo" (#6): defenseman
Gordon, Sam "Flash": rookie, non-starter
Hanner, Paul (#24): defenseman
Jones, Brayden "Jonesy": rookie, forward
Karlsson, Henrik (#17): forward
Langley, Ryan (#20): forward
Morrow, Cole (#3): defenseman
Novikov, Lukas "Novy" (#22): defenseman
O'Rourke, Patrick "Patty": rookie, non-starter
O'Sullivan, Josh "Sully" (#19): forward, Captain
Perry, David "DJ" (#13): forward
Price, Ilmari "Mars" (#31): starting goalie
Price, Jake (#42): defenseman
Walsh, Cade (#10): forward
West, Connor "Westie": rookie, non-starter
Yuley, Kevin: rookie, non-starter

COACHES

Andrews, Brody: Assistant Coach (defense)
Denison, Nick: Assistant Coach (offense)
Johnson, Harold "Hodge": Head Coach
Tomlin, Eric: Goalie Coach

TEAM SUPPORT

Gordon, Jerry: Assistant Equipment Manager
Price, Caleb: Assistant Equipment Manager

MEDICAL SUPPORT

Brady, Brad: Interim Director of Physical Therapy
O'Connor, Teddy: PT intern
Price, Rachel: Barkley Fellow
Tyler, Scott: Team Doctor

OPERATIONS/MANAGEMENT

Francis, Vicki: Operations Manager
Ortiz, Claribel: Social Media Manager
St. James, Poppy: Public Relations Director
Talbot, Mark: General Manager

OTHER NOTABLE CHARACTERS

Ford, Joey: Out of the Net
Gerard, Lauren: J-Lo's wife
Kline, Mike: Ryan's agent
Lemming, Cheryl: Out of the Net
Lemming, Nancy: Out of the Net
O'Sullivan, Shelby: Sully's wife
Owens, Troy: Tess's estranged husband
Owens, Bea: Tess's mother-in-law
Putnam, Charlie: Tess's lawyer

STAR SIGNS

TESS: Gemini (air): playful, curious, passionate
RYAN: Virgo (earth): methodical, committed, kind

RYAN'S TOP FIVE FAVORITE TAYLOR SWIFT SONGS

1. "All of the Girls You Loved Before"
2. "Enchanted" (Live)
3. "Daylight"
4. "Lavender Haze"
5. "I Knew You Were Trouble" (Taylor's Version)

PUCKING WILD PLAYLIST

1. "Flowers," Miley Cyrus
2. "Pretty Please," Dua Lipa
3. "Lose Control," Teddy Swims
4. "Shivers," Ed Sheeran
5. "What Makes You Sad," Nicotine Dolls
6. "Daylight," Taylor Swift
7. "King," Florence + the Machine
8. "Watermelon Sugar," Harry Styles
9. "You & I," Rita Ora
10. "One Kiss," Calvin Harris, Dua Lipa
11. "A Beautiful Mess (Live)," Jason Mraz
12. "The Devil Wears Lace," Steven Rodriguez
13. "Can't Have You," Jonas Brothers
14. "Light My Love," Greta Van Fleet
15. "All the Girls You Loved Before," Taylor Swift

PUCKING WILD

1
Tess

"RACHEL!" I shout, taking another sip of my champagne. "Come on, girl. I'm growing a beard out here!"

"Hold your horses," she shouts back. "The freaking zipper is stuck. I'm afraid I'm gonna break it—*shit*—"

"Well, get out here, and I'll fix it for you," I say, hopping to my feet.

This night has been a total whirlwind. Rachel just had to drop the gauntlet with her sexy little taunt, telling Ilmari she'll marry him if their game against the LA Kings was a shutout. Well, joke's on her, 'cause now I'm standing in her mother's bedroom, waiting as Rachel hunts through her mom's couture gown collection, looking for something suitable to wear to a wedding. *Her* wedding.

That's right, I'm about to be a bridesmaid at my best friend's surprise midnight four-way wedding. God, I love L.A. In true rock 'n' roll fashion, her dad is busy setting his house up as party central. Her brother Harrison is coordinating food, while her mom is downstairs inviting guests and frantically calling in favors to have flowers delivered.

Meanwhile, I'm on dress duty. And I mean to take this job seriously. It's not every day the girl you thought would never settle down decides to marry three men at once. This dress needs to be one for the ages.

I slap my champagne glass down on the dresser. "Rach!" Just as I'm about to dive inside the massive walk-in closet and drag her ass out, Rachel sweeps around the corner and my mouth drops to the floor. "Ohmygod," I gasp.

"Well? What do you think?" she says, dark eyes wide as she takes in my expression.

She stands before me in a floor-skimming, shimmery gold slip dress with barely-there straps. The bodice dips low between her breasts, clinging to her like a second skin. If I was a cartoon, I'd have big hearts in my eyes.

"This is as close as we're getting to a wedding dress," she says, smoothing the dress over her hips. "I'm sorry, but I'm not wearing pink, and all the black ones felt too austere."

"Rachel, is that runway Versace?" I say.

She does a little half-turn, glancing at herself in the mirror. "Umm . . . no, I think it's custom, honestly. Mom wore this to the Grammys back in the 90s. I tried it on once or twice when I was a kid."

Her only jewelry is a pair of heavy pearl drop earrings and the stack of thin gold bracelets she habitually wears. Oh, and her dainty septum ring of twisted gold. Her dark hair is tied up in an artfully messy bun, showing off the delicate curve of her neck. Her makeup is just a little bit smeared under the eye.

She looks perfect.

"Well?" she says with a huff, arms flapping as she does a little half-turn, peeking over her shoulder again.

"Oh, honey," I say on a sigh. "You look so beautiful. They're gonna die."

She smiles back at me before gasping. "Oh—the jacket!" Then she's disappearing back inside the closet. "Get in here and help me," she calls. "Tell me if you think this is too much."

I step through the doorway into the huge walk-in closet to see Rachel fiddling a silver beaded jacket off its hanger.

"Do you think these will look weird together?" she says, holding up the shimmery silver jacket. "I thought it made kind of a cool mixed metals statement," she adds with a shrug. "And the silver at least feels a little more bridal but . . . you hate it. It's too much." She's staring at me again, waiting for my approval.

I swallow back my happy tears. "No, I think it's unique. It's rocker glam and totally you." I step in, taking the jacket from her. "Here, let me help you, honey."

She turns around with a grateful smile, dropping her arms back so I can help her slip into the sexy, shimmery jacket. It's got cute fringe detail at the sleeves that in the right lighting will make it look like she's dripping diamonds.

"I figured I'll take it off after the ceremony," she adds.

I step to the side, taking in the full picture from her signature Rachel bun, following the line of the dress's slit down to her naked toes. With a tip of my head, I purse my lips. "Something's missing."

"I'm not wearing a veil," she huffs. "That would definitely be overkill."

"No, you've got your something old and something borrowed," I say, pointing at the dress and the jacket. "The flowers can be your something new. We need to find you something blue."

She laughs, fiddling with the sleeve of the jacket. "What was your something blue at your wedding?"

My smile falters as memories of the day flash in my mind—the heat of the sun on my shoulders during the outdoor ceremony, one too many glasses of champagne at the reception, dancing until my feet blistered. "My shoes," I reply softly.

"Oh, that's brilliant." Rachel hurries around the corner. "Mom basically has her own shoe warehouse in here," she calls. "Come help me pick out a pair."

The back of Julia Price's designer closet is a room just for shoes, artfully arranged from floor to ceiling on custom lighted shelves. Shoes twinkle in every color and style from Hermès flats to red-bottomed Louboutins. The contents of this room alone are worth more than what some people make in a lifetime.

"Geez," I say, noting the bottom row of stylish leather boots. "Mama Price gets to shop in her own DSW every day of the week."

"I know, right?" She turns, holding up two very different blue shoes—one a strappy heel, the other a tall, pointed-toe pump. "Which one?"

"The strappy," I say immediately. "You'd be kicking those pumps off before you even walk down the aisle."

"Good call," she says, replacing the pump and grabbing the strappy heel's partner.

Taking a deep breath, I glance over my shoulder, grateful to know that—at least for the moment—we're alone. "Listen, Rach . . . "

She pauses, one foot flamingoed in the air as she works the buckle of the strap. "Yeah?"

I step forward and grab her lightly by the shoulders.

She drops her foot to the floor. "Tess, what—"

"Just listen for a sec," I say over her. "I wouldn't be doing my job as your best friend if I didn't ask you this. If I didn't look you in the eye and hear you say the words—"

She groans. "Tess—"

"Rachel Diane Price," I say, my voice louder. "Are you *sure* you want to get married tonight? Because I swear to God, if you give me even a *look* like you'd rather run, I will throw you over my shoulder, linebacker my way down those stairs, and we'll run."

1
Tess

"I need to hear you say it, Rach," I say again.

Rachel smiles, her eyes suddenly watery. "Tess, I love you so fucking much."

"I love you too," I say quickly. "And only my love for you has me asking this now. You deserve an out if you need it. I mean, you haven't known these guys long, Rach. And it's a big freakin' leap. Marriage is . . . well, it's a legal quagmire—"

"Tess," Rachel says again, lifting a hand to cup my face.

I still at the touch.

"I don't need Lawyer Tess with me right now. I'm good," she says with a gentle nod.

I suck in a breath, letting it out. "You're good?"

"I'm really, *really* good," she replies. "Tess, they're the ones."

"They're the ones?" I echo.

"They're the ones," she repeats. "Tess, I've waited my whole life to feel like I make sense. Always searching for the reason. *My* reason. I thought travel was my reason. Then maybe it was medicine. And I do, I love medicine," she adds. "I love healing what's broken in others. Each time I think it heals a little something in me too."

I smile. She's certainly helped heal me. She found me at my lowest and gave me a home and a friendship I wouldn't trade for the world.

"And then Jake found me in Seattle," she says with a smile. "And when he found me, I found me too. I'm who I'm meant to be now. With them, I'm me. Jake, Caleb, and Ilmari, they're my reason. So, I'm not walking down that aisle tonight. I'm running. I'm running to them, Tess. I'm going home."

That word. *Home*. It stirs something deep inside me. I've never had a place that felt like home. I envy her that she's found hers at last, even as I'm so happy for her I could burst.

"Fuck," I huff with a laugh. "We should have written that down." I look around distractedly.

"What are you looking for?"

"Your phone. You just wrote your vows. Say exactly that, and you'll have the whole house in tears." As I snatch up her phone and unlock it, there's a scuffle out in the bedroom.

"Ouch, you're shoving me," Harrison grumbles.

"Well, then, walk," Jake huffs. "Just don't let me see Rachel."

"Jake, you're being a little dramatic right now," says his twin sister from behind them.

Both the guys are dressed to kill in suits that fit them so well it looks like they were poured in. And Amy looks gorgeous in a little black number. She's got Jake's coloring—the dark hair and pretty hazel eyes. But the line of her jaw is more feminine, the features of her face softer. And, of course, he's almost a foot taller.

Harrison calls out, "Rach, we're coming in!"

I block the doorway with my body. "Absolutely not. He's not seeing her before the wedding."

Jake stands between Harrison and Amy, both hands covering his eyes. "I don't wanna see her, Tess. I just need to talk to her. Babe, I need to talk to you! I'm kind of freaking the fuck out!"

My protector mode surges. "Jake Compton, are you having second thoughts?"

"What?" he squawks. "*No*. Fuck no. Get out of my way, and I'll marry her right here, right now. I wanted to marry her the night we met. Rach, tell her I'm not backing out!"

Deep inside the closet, Rachel laughs. "What's wrong, angel?"

"Shit, can I drop my hands?" he says.

"I wish you would," Harrison mutters.

"You look ridiculous," Amy laughs.

Jake drops his hands, blinking at me as he takes me in. Then his face splits into a wide smile. "Whoa, Tess, you look dynamite. Green is definitely your color."

I smile, soaking in his compliment. But I know I look great in green.

And the cut of this dress really does wonders for me. It's got these cute off-the-shoulder sleeves and a structured bust that gives the girls a great lift. The silky skirt flows down to the floor, fluttering around my ankles.

"Nice try, handsome," I say, crossing my arms. "But you're not getting past me."

"I don't want to get past you," he replies. "And I swear I don't want to see her before it's time. I just—Seattle, I need to talk to you about something!"

I glance over my shoulder to see Rachel standing there with a sappy, lovesick look on her face. God, they're both hopeless. "What do you need, Jake?"

"I just talked to Caleb, and apparently he asked Mars to stand in as his best man when Cay and I get married," Jake calls.

"Well . . . I think that's really sweet," Rachel calls back. "Cay's not really close with anyone else but you."

"Yeah, and then Mars asked Cay to stand in as *his* best man when he gets married to *you*," Jake goes on.

"So, what's the problem, angel?"

He groans. "Alright, well, I've got our twins out here because I really think we need to settle this once and for all," he calls, one hand each on Harrison and Amy's shoulders. "Seattle, I know you may want me to be your best man but—"

"What?" Harrison cries, slapping Jake's hand off his shoulder. "No fucking way, asshole. Rachel is my twin. I will literally stab you in the throat if you try and take this from me. I'm best man."

"See, *this* is the problem," Jake calls. "Your brother is threatening to murder me if I'm your best man!"

Inside the closet, Rachel is laughing. "Jake, you know I love you, but Harrison is my best man."

"Damn fucking straight," says Harrison. "You've been a Price for all of three hours. I've been a Price for almost thirty years. You want a job, be their ring bearer."

Jake holds up his hands in surrender. "Hey, man, that's cool with me. I totally agree. You should be her best man. That's what I wanted to say. I'll hold the rings. I'll hold her flowers—"

"I'm holding her flowers," I say, my hands back on my hips. "Best friend holds the flowers."

"Right, Tess holds the flowers," Jake corrects. "Why don't—how about I stand up with Mars, huh? I'll just stand over by Caleb and Mars," he calls out for Rachel's benefit.

Rachel smiles. "That sounds great, babe. Was that your only concern?"

He groans again, glancing to Amy. "Well . . . there's still the issue of who's going to be *my* best man when I marry Cay. And babe, I love you so fucking much—"

"Hey, don't even try it, jerk face," Amy huffs. "I flew all the way from Japan for this. I'm your best man."

"And that's what I want," Jake says quickly. "Am, it's you and me. Comptons for fucking life. I want it to be you, I just—" He sighs, glancing over his shoulder at me.

That's when I finally crack a smile. "You just don't want to hurt Rachel's feelings or make her feel left out. Right?"

"Exactly," he says, relief etched on his face at being understood.

God, this man is too damn precious. He's like if a golden retriever came to life and started wearing bespoke Armani suits. And here I was grilling Rachel about needing an exit. What's the point? No matter where I might take her, this man will just follow us. Jake Compton Price is Rachel's end game. I have absolutely nothing to worry about by putting her happiness in his hands.

"I'm coming out," Rachel calls.

"NO!" Four voices say at once.

Jake slaps his hands back up over his eyes as she steps around me. She moves into the doorway, the tail of her gown whispering across the carpet.

"Wow," Harrison huffs, his dark eyes wide as he takes in his twin for the first time in her rocker glam wedding look. "Sis, you look . . . holy shit."

"That good, huh?" she says with a laugh.

He steps forward, quickly wrapping her in a hug.

"God, this is fucking torture," Jake groans.

"You really do look amazing," says Amy, tears shining in her eyes.

"Thanks," Rachel replies, slipping loose of Harrison's hug. "Alright, we're officially calling this Twin Summit to order," she declares. Then she turns to Jake's sister. "Amy, I would never dream of taking the spot that only you can fill. You're Jake's best man tonight. No question."

Amy nods.

"And H, you're mine," she adds.

"Of course," he replies.

Rachel places one hand on Jake's shoulder. "Angel, look at me."

"No," he replies. "I don't want to jinx us."

"I don't believe in superstitions," she says gently. "Besides, I think Twin Summit rules outweigh wedding superstitions. I want you to look at me."

Slowly, he turns, dropping his hands. The moment he sees her, I swear my heart skips a beat. That look he gives her, it's the look of pure love. His whole face changes from one of anxiety and worry to one of unbridled joy.

"Oh my god," he says, struck breathless by his bride's beauty. "Baby, you look fucking amazing."

"So do you," she replies, sniffing back her tears.

"Fuck, I wanna marry you right now." He cups her face with both hands.

"I love you so much," she murmurs.

"I love you," he replies. "God, my heart's beating a million miles a minute," he adds with a nervous laugh, taking one of her hands and dropping it down to his chest. Her fingers splay over his heart as she gets to feel it beating for her.

Inside my own chest, the dull thumping of my jaded heart echoes in its loneliness. Battered and broken, she beats in survivor mode. It pulses to the cadence of a single word. It's a harsh reality. A life sentence.

Alone. Alone. Alone.

I tune out that sound, focusing instead on my friends. This is their moment.

"H, when you married Somchai, I thought it would change us," Rachel admits, glancing at her brother. "And it did, but now I realize it's *supposed* to change us. Somchai is your person now. He's your number one, not me."

Harrison just nods.

She turns the other way. “Amy, I really hope you’re okay with this, because I love your brother so goddamn much. And I swear, I’m going to be so good to him—”

“I know,” Amy assures her. “I’ve never seen him so happy, Rachel. You and Cay and Mars, you deserve him. And he deserves all the happiness you can give him,” she adds, eyes shining as she smiles up at her brother. “I just want you happy, Jake. It’s all I’ve ever wanted.”

“Then you approve?” Jake says, his hands still holding steadfast to Rachel.

Amy nods again. “Yeah, I do. I defy anyone to see you four and think you don’t belong together,” she replies. “You got everything you ever wanted . . . and a few things you didn’t even know to want,” she adds, and we all laugh.

“God, isn’t that the truth,” he replies.

“So, we’re all good?” Rachel says, glancing between them. “The twins are good?”

“I’m good,” Amy replies still smiling.

“Yeah, I’m good,” Harrison echoes.

“Jake, you’re good?” Rachel adds, her gaze landing on him.

He nods, still calmer being in her arms.

“What about you, Tess?” Rachel calls, glancing at me. “You approve of this chaos? A four-way L.A. wedding?”

I huff a laugh and smile. “I had a feeling we’d all be standing here eventually. You’re too unorthodox for your own good.”

“Well then,” Rachel replies, taking Jake’s hands in both of hers. “Jake Price, I want to marry you. Tonight. But first, I want to watch you marry Caleb.”

3
Ryan

"I'm just saying, don't you think it's all a little weird?" Davidson shuffles in front of me as we take our seats.

Is this weird? Of course, it is. It's our last night in L.A., we're fresh off another win against the Kings, and instead of crashing asleep in my hotel room, I'm standing in my game day suit in rock legend Hal Price's Beverly Hills living room, balancing an Old Fashioned in my hand.

I'd say that's pretty weird.

Oh, and the only reason I'm standing in Hal Price's living room is because I'm about to watch his daughter—who happens to be my team doctor—marry two of my teammates *and* my equipment manager.

Again, pretty fucking weird.

We all had our suspicions about her and Compton, but it was never more than gossip. Then, last week, the truth came blasting out. *Boom.* Compton and Sanford are out as gay. Fucking finally. No surprises there. That news was almost boring in its predictability.

I mean, don't get me wrong, I'm totally happy for them. Love is love. Give me a flag and douse me in glitter. I'm down to dance at a pride parade. And Sanny and Compton were practically already married. That they're rushing down the aisle is a surprise to literally no one. I already bought them nine rounds of His & His golf as a wedding present.

But then, *boom* again. Just as soon as we all settled with the news of their relationship, they flipped the script on us. They're in love with each other . . . and Doc Price . . . *and* they've all been secretly living together practically since the start of the season.

What kills me is that I kind of already knew. When I ran into Tess on the beach, she told me Compton invited her and Doc to stay for the weekend to enjoy the beach. Yeah, she's a sneaky little liar. Tess *knew*. Doc was already living there even then.

But that surprise was *nothing* compared to the final reveal: Kinnunen is with them too.

I won't lie, Kinnunen intimidates the fuck outta me. The man rarely ever speaks unless he's barking out orders on the ice. I don't think he's exchanged even a full sentence with me since I joined the team. So, to watch him stand up in the middle of a crowded locker room and declare himself engaged to our team doctor . . . the doctor we only just learned was living with Compton and Sanny . . . yeah, all our heads pretty much exploded.

Oh, and then they all declared they were changing their names to Price.

How many times can a person's head metaphorically explode?

They've all been tight-lipped about the details, but I get the feeling maybe he's only with her. Like, that's a thing, right? He's marrying her . . . and they're marrying her . . . and each other . . . but he's not marrying them? I think that's what we're here to witness tonight. Again, details are fuzzy.

I take a sip of my Old Fashioned, dropping into the empty chair next to Davidson. The room buzzes with energy as hockey players mingle with Hollywood elites. I don't often get starstruck, but I swear to God, if Al Pacino walks into this wedding tonight, I'm gonna pass the fuck out.

Novy slides into our row and sits in the empty chair next to me, a sly grin on his face. "Guys, I just touched a Grammy."

"What?"

"Hal's Grammy," he replies with a jerk of his head. "It's just over there on the shelf behind the piano. I touched it."

"You didn't," I huff.

Next to me, Davidson cranes his neck, looking to the corner of the room.

"I did," Novy replies.

"He did," Morrow adds, dropping into the empty seat next to him. "He made me take a picture."

Novy grins, flashing me his phone screen.

I gasp. The asshole didn't just touch Hal Price's Grammy, he picked it up off the shelf. He's holding it, smirking like a total douche. "Nov, you can't just take people's trophies off the shelf," I hiss.

"Why not?" He shrugs, slipping his phone in the inside pocket of his suit. "Coley held it too."

"Asshole," Morrow grunts, jabbing him with his elbow. "I told you not to tell."

I just huff again. "You two are idiots."

They squabble under their breaths, arguing over whose idea it was to pick it up.

"Guys, this is *weird*, right?" Davidson repeats, leaning across me to loudly whisper at them. "No one else is gonna say it? I'm the only one?"

Novy and Morrow go still, slow turning to look at Davidson. They're both defensemen, so they each have a few inches on me and, like, thirty pounds of muscle. Novy's got a jagged pink scar zigzagging up his cheek. It's still healing from when he took a skate to the face and had to get one hundred and thirty stitches. The man had already perfected the art of the scowl. He's Russian so they're born with that, right? It's like a factory setting. But now when he scowls, he looks like he's gonna murder you and your dog *and* uproot your house plants just to be a dick.

"You got a problem with all this, Dave-O?" he says, a muscle in his jaw twitching.

I go still, feeling trapped between them.

"Yeah, if you've got a problem being here, there's the door," Morrow echoes, his tone just as hard. It's an odd look for him because, off the ice, Cole Morrow is a super-nice guy. The puck bunnies go crazy for him. His usual charming smile has been replaced with a glare as he waits for Davidson to speak.

"No, I'm cool," Davidson says at last, sinking back into his chair. "This is totally fine."

"Damn right it is," Morrow replies.

"Why don't you just not speak again tonight, Dave-O," says Novy, dismissing him.

Davidson bristles but stays silent. He's only a backup goalie, and he's having a shitty season so far. He can't talk back to a starting defenseman, and he knows it. Not unless he wants Novy to make his life hell whenever he gets in the net.

Novy's an asshole on the best of days, but his defense of our teammates is oddly touching to see. Who would have ever pegged him as such an ally?

"Oh my god," Morrow gasps. He grips Novy by the shoulder, and then they're both turning. They morph into a pair of excited squirrels whispering to each other and shoving.

"Langers, *look*," Novy hisses, slapping my shoulder.

I turn my head, following their gaze to the corner of the room where Hal Price is standing there laughing, his hand on the shoulder of none other than Al Fucking Pacino.

4
Ryan

"I think Langers is about to piss himself," Morrow laughs.

"Shut up." I tear my gaze away from the vision of Hal Price laughing with Al Pacino.

Our captain, Sully, drops into the row behind us wearing a wide smile like a kid at Disneyland. "Guys, Slash is here."

We all turn, following his point to the other side of the room where Slash is most definitely standing next to Alice Cooper.

Yeah, this is fine.

"And to think I was gonna skip this to stay and soak in the hot tub," Sully adds, shaking his head in disbelief.

"Ladies and gents, if you could all start finding your seats," calls a deep voice from the front of the room. "I think we're ready to get this party started."

We all turn. The guy talking is Doc's brother, I think. Rumor is she's a twin like Compton. His sister is here somewhere too. I met her during pregame warmups. No wonder he keeps quiet about her around us. She's a total ten. Apparently, she's a rocket scientist or something cool like that.

"Johnny Depp is here," Poppy squeals, dropping into the last empty seat by Morrow. "Oh, my good gracious, I'm gonna faint." She presses a manicured hand dramatically against her chest.

"Pop, did you see Slash?" says Sully, leaning between the seats.

"No," she gasps, her head turning on a swivel.

"And Al Pacino," Morrow adds.

"Ohmygod," she whines, gripping tight to his arm. "This is just so exciting. I can't believe they said no pictures. I'm dyin' over here."

Of course, our public relations manager wants pictures of the

Rays rubbing shoulders with Hollywood and rock royalty. But the goons at the door were clear: no pictures, no video.

"You know, we're all kind of big deals too," Novy mutters, arms crossed. "Hockey's only a multibillion dollar a year industry—"

"Hush," she says, eyes wide as she looks all around.

I chuckle, clicking my phone into silent mode. Doc and the guys are never gonna live this night down. This is already the coolest wedding ever and it hasn't even started.

It only takes a few minutes for everyone to settle. Over half this room is Rays. I don't think anyone opted to stay at the hotel. Even the coaches are here. Head Coach Johnson is sitting in the back, three seats down from Slash.

Suddenly, some of the guys all start to whoop and cheer. I turn, eyes wide, as I take in Kinnunen walking down the makeshift aisle between the chairs. He's easily one of the best-dressed guys on the team. Tonight, he's rocking a moss green suit and no tie. If I wore that color, I'd look like an idiot. On him, it's effortlessly cool.

"Go, Bear!"

"There he is!"

"Get it done, Mars!"

Morrow leans across Poppy, patting his arm as he passes.

Compton and Sanny walk in right behind him, big smiles on their faces. Compton catches my eye, grinning like a lovestruck idiot.

"Yeah, Sanny," Novy shouts. "Lock him down quick, or I will!"

The guys all laugh as Sanford gives Novy a death glare. He may not have the scar to match Novikov, but it's still intimidating as hell. The guys shuffle around at the front of the room, Kinnunen stepping back to let Compton and Sanford claim the middle spots.

"Aren't we supposed to hold hands?" asks Compton.

"Shut up," Sanford says and we all laugh.

"Come on, asshole. Hold my hand or something," he replies, holding out a hand towards our equipment manager.

"Hold his hand or I will," Novy shouts to more laughter.

With a sigh, Sanford takes it, which makes Compton's grin grow even wider. Damn, I can't help it. I'm smiling too.

Soft music starts playing over the surround sound speakers. Then there's a wolf whistle and we're all turning to watch Compton's sister walk down the aisle. She's smiling wide, the super-hot female version of Compton. It's honestly kind of trippy.

As if we're having the same thought, Novy leans in at my shoulder. "Am I crazy, or does Compton make a very hot girl?"

I want to laugh or give him a shove, but I can't. I can't do anything. I can't even fucking breathe. Walking in right behind Compton's twin is the woman who has single-handedly been haunting all my dreams.

Tess.

Fuck, she's so goddamn beautiful. Compton's sister is in a slinky black dress, but Tess is in emerald green. It sets off the red in her hair and the cream of her skin. My chest feels tight. My hands are clammy. She's smiling wide as she sways down the aisle. She catches my eye as she passes and winks.

Kill me dead.

Compton's twin takes her place just behind him at the front, but Tess sits in the front row next to Doc's twin. Someone else has joined the guys up at the front. I perk up as I place the face with the name. Holy shit, it's John Jay Walsher, original drummer for the Ferrymen. *The* Johnny Jay is going to officiate? This wedding is so fucking cool.

"Please rise for the bride," he calls.

We all stand as the music changes. With a room full of Rays, quarters are cramped. A row of defensemen stand behind me, so I can't see a damn thing. I turn, looking to the front instead. I'm not disappointed by the view. My heart squeezes tight as I see the looks on the faces of Compton, Sanford, and Kinnunen. Holy shit, they're in love. All three of them. It's written all over their faces. Compton is crying. So is his twin. Even stoic Kinnunen looks misty.

I smile. Suddenly this doesn't feel so weird. They all look happy. They all want Doc, and they're willing to share her. It's kind of beautiful, actually. Life's too short to go through it settling for a life you don't want.

With that thought in my mind, I turn, peering between the two rows separating me from Tess. Her eyes are locked on the guys too. I wonder if she sees what I see. Is she happy for her best friend?

I'm distracted thinking about Tess as I follow the lead of the guy to either side of me and sit down. Now I can finally see Doc Price.

She's a knockout in a sparkly gold dress and silver jacket. She takes up a spot next to her twin, smiling wide.

"We're all here tonight to witness the union of these four fine people," calls out Johnny Jay. "The laws in the state of California mean that technically this is a double wedding, but they'd like it clear that they stand now before their family and friends united as one—one team, one family."

"The Fearsome Foursome," Compton says with a smile.

"Don't call us that," Sanford mutters at John Jay.

Around the room, a few of us laugh.

"You two lovebirds are up first," says John Jay, glancing between the guys. "Do you come together of your own free will to be married?"

"Yes," Sanford replies, his eyes locked on Compton.

"Yeah, I do," Compton adds.

"Did you prepare any vows?"

Compton's eyes go wide. "Shit—no. We literally decided to do this three hours ago." He turns to Sanny. "Babe, I don't have any vows prepared—"

"It's fine," says Sanford.

"But—"

Sanford raises his other hand and grabs Compton's shoulder, giving it a gentle squeeze. "I'll go first, yeah?"

Slowly, Compton relaxes and nods.

Sanford drops his hand away from his shoulder. From my seat, I've got a perfect angle on his face. Sanford is a serious guy. Even when he's joking around, he's usually deadpanning. Right now, he's as serious as I've ever seen him, his dark eyes locked on our favorite defenseman.

"Jake, I love you," he declares, loud enough for the whole room to hear. "I've loved you for ten fucking years. I loved you in secret," he admits. "I loved you like a coward. I didn't deserve to be loved by you in return—not until I got out of my own damn way. But I needed a little help. I needed a push."

He glances around Compton to where Doc is standing and smiles. "Four months ago, I got a shove. A hurricane on two legs swept into our lives and knocked us both off our feet. She was my push to love you out loud. To love you as you always should have been loved. So, here's my vow: The coward who loved you in secret is gone. Rachel remade us both into something stronger. I'm here now, Jake. I'm right fucking here, and I'm saying it out loud."

Compton nods, tears in his eyes.

"You've always been my friend," Sanford goes on. "Then you became my lover. Tonight, I make you my husband. You're mine, Jake Price. You're mine, and I'm never letting go."

Damn, am I about to cry in front of Slash and Al Pacino? Next to me, Novy reaches into his pocket and pulls out his pocket square. Leaning across Morrow, he hands it off to Poppy, who is a quietly sobbing mess.

I turn my attention back to the guys as Compton takes a step closer, his eyes locked on Sanford. "So, umm . . . playing hockey has always been about putting myself first—my training, my diet, and my travel and game schedules. Everyone in my life just learned to orbit me. And if my life was too much for them, they flung themselves out of my orbit as fast as possible."

It's like he's describing the personal lives of half the men in this room, myself included.

"Over time," Compton goes on, "I realized I was a sun with no planets, the center of my own universe. I had everything I ever wanted, but I was alone, just me and my career. You were the only one who stayed, Cay. You stuck it out. You let me be selfish and self-centered. You let me put my career first and never once questioned it, never made *me* question it," he adds, a slight tremor to his voice. "You joined me at the center. You don't orbit me like all the others did. You stand resolutely at my side, unmoving. Babe, you are love in suspended motion. The calm in the storm of our lives. You're where everything stops. You're where *I* stop. You are . . . everything," he finishes with a shrug.

As his vows end, the silence in the room speaks volumes. I think everyone is collectively holding their breath.

"Well . . . shit," Davidson murmurs. "That didn't sound weird at all."

No, it didn't. In fact, it sounded pretty fucking perfect. It sounded like Compton and Sanford share the kind of love that all of us search for . . . and so few of us ever find.

5
Tess

"Aren't they supposed to cut that first?"

I gasp, leaning away from the three-tiered wedding cake. "I was just looking at it," I say quickly, spinning around. When I turn, I'm face-to-face with Ryan Langley. His blond curls are slicked back, tucked behind his ears, and those pretty green eyes carry a hint of a laugh.

"Hey, Tess," he says, his All-American smile warming my insides. He looks delectable in that navy suit. He lost the tie ages ago. I can see the tail of it poking out of his pocket.

I ignore the stupid fluttering of my heart. I knew he was here. Of course, I knew. I felt his eyes on me the moment I walked down that aisle. And he kept his eyes on me.

And I ate it up . . . because I'm a terrible friend who wants things she can't have . . . like sweet, young puppy-faced hockey boys with abs for days and a megawatt smile.

Seriously, someone get this boy in a toothpaste commercial already.

"Hi, Ryan," I say, leaning my hip against the table. I'm going for calm and collected. "I saw you earlier."

"And I saw you," he replies, taking a sip of what I think is an Old Fashioned.

The last time he saw me, I was wearing decidedly less in the way of clothing. Nothing at all, in fact. I can't help but feel like this dress is armor . . . or more like a shield against doing something foolish like kiss him again. With the way he's looking at me right now, I have a feeling I'll need it.

I set down the glass of water I'm holding. "I was wondering when you might come talk to me."

"Right now," he replies. He glances from me to the cake. "Were you trying to steal a bite?"

I shrug. "Rachel doesn't really like cake. And I'm sure you guys are all on your crazy hockey diets. And we all know Hollywood types don't eat cake," I add. "This will likely just get thrown out with the morning trash."

"I never say no to cake," he replies. "I'll just add five miles to my morning run."

"Five miles for a slice of cake? That doesn't sound like a very even trade."

"There are other ways to burn off the calories," he teases, and that twinkle in his eye works its way right through to my lady bits.

I feign a gasp. "Ryan Langley, are you trying to proposition me for sex?"

"Get your head out of the gutter, Owens," he replies. Setting down his Old Fashioned, he holds out his hand. "I was talking about dancing."

I glance down at his offered hand, stupid heart fluttering again. "Don't we have to eat the cake first? Otherwise, what calories are we trying to burn off by dancing?"

He drops his hand, realizing his mistake. "Oh . . . right." Then he glances over his shoulder, looking to see if anyone is close by. Moving quick, he snatches up the long cake knife.

I gasp for real. "Ryan Langley, don't you dare." I grab at his wrist as he laughs, trying to wrestle the knife from him. "You can't cut their cake—"

"You just said no one was gonna eat it," he teases, gently pulling away from me. "You said it would sit here all night before it ends up in the trash. We're saving it, Tess. A wedding cake deserves to be eaten. We're helping it fulfill its wedding destiny."

"You can't just cut into it," I cry. "Only crazy drunk uncles and psycho ex-girlfriends cut into a wedding cake before the bride and groom."

He stills, glancing down at me. "What kind of weddings do you go to?"

"Knife down, Ryan."

With a smirk, he sets the knife down, and I drop my hand away from him. In our tussle, I didn't even realize I've pressed myself up against him. I can smell his crisp, sporty cologne. Fuck, he smells good. I stifle my groan as I lean away.

"No one will miss a little frosting," he reasons. "And then we'll dance off the calories. It's the perfect crime."

"Ryan—"

"Oh, look at that," he says, swiping his finger over a rosette at the bottom of the cake. "I slipped. Clumsy me." He holds up a finger thick with white buttercream frosting. "You gonna make me stand here holding the smoking gun? Come on, Thelma, this was your idea."

I cross my arms. "Thelma? Does that make you Louise?"

He just shrugs, still smiling.

"I think you're a J.D. at best," I tease.

"Ouch. You know what, for that—" Lightning fast, he moves his hand, smearing the frosting against my lips.

I gasp again, one hand rising up to ghost over my mouth. "Ryan—"

"Gotta eat it now. Hurry, before Doc comes over here and accuses you of ruining her perfect wedding."

With my hand over my mouth, I lick my lips, savoring the sweet, sugary taste of the cake frosting. "You're an asshole," I say, dropping my hand away.

"Got a little more here," he replies with a grin, holding up his finger.

Ready to beat him at his own game, I lean forward, sucking the tip of his frosted finger into my mouth. Now he's the one gasping in surprise, his body jolting. I suck the frosting off his fingertip with a sexy little moan, giving him a little flick with my tongue before I let him go.

"Holy fuck," he says, breathless.

I smirk. He's almost too easy. We're ignoring the fact that it's working on me too. "Your turn," I say, dipping my finger into the cake to flick off a little frosted rosette. He's right, no one will even notice they're gone. I hold my finger up between us, waiting to see what he'll do.

Surprising me, he ducks his head down closer and sucks the tip of my finger into his mouth, tasting the frosting. His mouth is warm, his tongue teasing. I hold my breath, all senses firing, as his teeth give me a little nip. The sensation races down my arm, across my chest, and zaps me right in the clit.

Oh fuck.

He lets me go, his gaze molten.

I want to kiss him again. I want to feel those soft lips. I want to taste the frosting on his tongue. I inch closer, tipping up my chin. "I thought you said you wanted to dance," I say, my lips parting, inviting him in. "That's good for one song, I think."

A charged moment stretches between us as he leans a little closer, his hand brushing my hip. Those pretty green eyes are locked on me, reading me, asking me an unspoken question.

He's going to do it. He's going to kiss me. I want him to.

But then he lets out a breath and leans away. "Dancing . . . right." Ever the gentleman, he holds out his hand to me. "Tess, will you do me the honor?"

Reeling from the almost-kiss, I put my hand in his and let him steer me across the room towards the dance floor.

6
Ryan

I have no idea what the fuck I'm doing. This woman is so far out of my league. She's smart and funny and so damn sexy. Women like Tess Owens don't pick guys like me. So why is her hand in mine? Why am I leading her onto the dance floor?

I've been watching her all night. I can't help it. I feel drawn to her. It's her laugh. So bright and full-bodied, just like her. The sound pierced straight through me, rooting me to the floor as I stood there like an asshole, pretending to listen to Sully and J-Lo's jokes.

I didn't want to stand in the corner with my teammates. I wanted to be at Tess's side as she laughed, my hand placed casually on her curvy hip. I'd offer her a fresh glass of wine, my lips brushing gently against her temple. It would be quick, like a habit. Then I'd stand there, quietly watching her work the room, just soaking in her essence like a fucking coral sponge.

The music transitions into a slow song, and I thank my lucky stars. It's like God knows I don't want to embarrass myself in front of this woman.

She didn't let me touch her in Compton's kitchen. She let me kiss her, yes, and it was fucking amazing. I felt her naked body press against my bare chest, so warm and soft. But she made me keep my hands to myself the whole time. In the moment, I didn't mind. But as soon as she was gone, I felt oddly bereft that I didn't get to hold her.

I'm changing that right fucking now.

I turn on my heel at the edge of the dance floor, reeling her in against me. She steps in willingly, her full breasts brushing against my chest as I lace our fingers together. Her other hand goes to my shoulder. My fingers glide over the silky fabric of her emerald dress, my palm splaying possessively at the small of her back. She fits snug against me, our toes tapping as we find our footing and start to sway.

"Do you like to dance?" she says after a minute.

I glance down. "With you, yes."

She smiles without teeth. It lifts the rosy apples of her cheeks, making soft creases at the outside corners of her eyes. She's wearing makeup tonight. She's all but concealed the freckles that dot her nose and cheeks. I see them on her collarbones though, peachy and perfect, charting sun-kissed constellations across her skin. Diamonds sparkle at her ears, just simple studs. I imagine she picked her most neutral pair, thinking only of Doc and how it's her night to shine.

But Tess Owens would be radiant in anything. She can't help herself. God, this woman is under my skin. What the hell am I going to do about it?

"You all leave in the morning?" she says, her hand brushing down my arm.

I nod. "Seven a.m. lobby time," I reply. "It's back to Jax for a few days, then we've got back-to-back games in Texas before we head up to the Winter Classic in New York."

"Rachel told me about it," she replies. "The Rays got invited as a first season thing, right?"

"Yeah, we're playing a New Year's Eve game against the Montreal Canadiens at Yankee Stadium. It's like an oldest and youngest League matchup thing," I explain. "Just means we'll get no downtime for Christmas this year."

"Will you at least get to see your family?"

I nod. "I'll spend two days with my mom and sister. They've already made plans for us to spend Christmas Day on the beach. What about you? Any big family plans?"

She hums a noncommittal sound.

I shift my hold on her waist. It's subtle, but now I almost feel like she's tucked under my arm. I'm touching more of her this way.

"You played well tonight," she says, her fingers flexing softly against mine.

I don't mind that she's changing the subject. I'm too busy trying not to hyperfocus on the fact that I was just sucking on those fingers over by the cake table. I can still taste the frosting on my tongue. "You were watching?"

"Of course. You're really impressive, Ryan. You may just be my favorite Ray to watch."

The caveman in me sits up and beats his chest at being complimented by her. Not that I need her praise to know I'm talented. "Careful, Tess," I tease. "Don't go giving yourself away now."

"Giving myself away?"

"Yeah. Clearly, you've got a crush on me."

She scoffs. "You wish, hockey boy."

"Admiring my skill and speed . . . watching my hands as I work my stick down the ice . . . "

She rolls her eyes.

"Can't take your eyes off me," I press, leaning closer. "Can't stop that excited little fluttering of your heart each time I take a shot on goal."

"You're delusional," she deadpans. But I see the little smile at the corner of her mouth.

"It's cute, really," I say, straightening myself out. "I'm flattered."

"I did this to myself. Never compliment a professional athlete," she says with a shake of her head.

"*Always* compliment an athlete," I counter. "It's the fastest way to our hearts."

"I thought the fastest way to an athlete's heart was food," she teases back.

"True," I reply. "There's probably little I wouldn't do for some homemade mac and cheese."

She smiles. "Mac and cheese? Really? Are you twelve?"

"It's the ultimate comfort food," I reply with a shrug.

"Can I at least make it gourmet?" she asks, willing to play along. "I could get on board with a good lobster mac and cheese. Give it a little crispy panko topping . . . maybe a drizzle of black truffle oil—"

"Nope. Kraft blue box. Toss in some cut-up hotdogs if we're feeling fancy."

"You're breaking my heart, Ryan," she replies with a sigh. "And here I thought this was love at first sight. Your hotdogs are ruining the fantasy."

"Ah, but you don't believe in love at first sight," I tease.

She glances up sharply, her hand going stiff in mine. "What makes you think that?"

"*You* do," I reply, giving her hip a squeeze. "You may go around naked in other people's houses, kissing strangers and hugging Al Pacino like an old friend, but you're way too guarded to go falling for someone at a glance. This pretty package piqued your interest," I add, gesturing confidently to myself. "But we're a long way off from you confessing your undying love."

"Oh, but you think we're on the path?" she teases, trying to match my casual tone. "You think you're gonna get me down the aisle, Ryan? Future Mrs. Hockey Boy?"

"Hey, you said it, not me."

"I suppose you don't believe in love at first sight either?"

I shrug again. "I believe people see what they want to see." My gaze drifts left to where Compton is slow dancing with Doc. "Compton believes in love at first sight," I say, nodding his way. "I think he took one look at Doc and just knew."

She follows my gaze. "Yeah . . . I think he did too."

"But Sanford doesn't believe in diving in after one glance. You heard his vows. He tortured himself for years before he could admit how he feels."

She nods, her gaze still locked on her best friend.

"They all found their way to each other in the end," I go on. "It's messy, but it's real. Gotta appreciate that."

"Messy . . . but real."

We're both quiet for a minute, taking another slow half-turn.

"Maybe you can come to another game soon," I say, ready to shoot my shot.

She lets out a soft laugh. "I didn't think the NHL did many match-ups in Cincinnati."

"We don't. But Chicago is kinda close, right? Or you could always come down to Jax again. And tickets are no problem," I add, knowing I'm probably sounding desperate. But I don't care. I want to see her again. "So, what do you think?"

"I think . . . I'd like that," she admits, leaning into me as I do another little half-turn.

I smile.

Her hand brushes down to my elbow as she leans away. "But . . . "

Fuck.

My hand tightens against her back. "No buts. Come on, live a little, Tess."

Her gaze softens as she glances up at me. There's an apology in her look, and I fucking hate it. "Ryan—"

"I know I've been teasing and coming on strong, but I like you, Tess. I just want to get to know you better."

"You don't know me at all," she says. "You just like what you see."

"Well, you're fucking gorgeous, and you know it. I'd be the biggest liar in the world if I said I didn't want you wrapped around me like naked bark on a tree."

That earns me a laugh. The sound warms my chest, making me smile.

"But if you think your beauty is *all* I see, you're wrong," I add.

Her smile falls as she gazes up at me, those green eyes wide. "What do you see?"

"I see *you*," I reply. "I see a woman who's bold and fearless. A woman who loves to laugh. You've got a great laugh, Tess."

She sucks in a breath, a flash of something sparking in her eyes. It's there, then it's gone, and then she's looking down. "What else?"

"I see someone who loves her friends," I go on. "Someone who puts others first. Maybe I like the idea of being the one who gets to put *you* first. I like taking care of people, Tess. And I take excellent care of what's mine."

She smiles, raising a hand to cup my cheek. Her thumb brushes softly against the corner of my mouth. "I bet you do," she says.

Why does this feel like goodbye?

I turn my face, leaning into her hand, and press a kiss to her thumb. "I want to see you again," I admit. "It doesn't have to be at a game. Pick a weekend, and I'll fly you down to Jacksonville. Or I could fly up to Cincinnati—"

"No." She drops her hand away from my face.

Fuck, she's still pulling away. "Tess—"

"We already agreed," she says. "You're a Ray, Ryan. You're Rachel's friend, her patient—"

"Nope," I say, giving her hip another squeeze. "I'm not buying it."

"You're not buying that you're her patient?"

"I'm not buying that as your excuse," I counter. "Rachel is your friend, not your mother or your keeper. I bet she'd have no problem with you dating a Ray if she thought it was really what you wanted . . . am I right?"

"My work is crazy right now," she says, still deflecting. "It was hard enough getting away for this," she adds, gesturing around.

A work excuse? Really? I'm surprised by her lack of originality. "Look, I'm a grown man, Tess. If you don't want to see me again because you're not interested, you can just say that—"

"I do," she says quickly, pressing herself a little closer. Her hand splays against my chest as she leans in. "I *do* want to see you. I like you, Ryan. You're sweet and funny and I'd love nothing more than to see you again. Maybe in a perfect world, I would get to do only the things I want to do," she adds, her voice sounding suddenly tired. "But the truth is that my life is a mess right now. It's not work, it's . . . me. It's complicated."

"I know you're divorced," I say. "Or you're getting divorced. Doc wasn't really clear. She didn't like me being nosy," I admit with a soft laugh.

Her eyes narrow as she looks up at me.

"But if that's what's holding you up—"

"No," she says quickly. "Well . . . honestly, yes. I mean, we're separated. God, we've been separated for almost three years."

"Are you thinking of going back to him? Is that still on the table?" I ask, heart in my throat. No matter how much I may like Tess, I'm not a homewrecker. If her answer is yes, I'll walk away and not look back. But I'm relieved when she says no.

"I am *never* going back to Troy," she adds vehemently.

"So then . . . what's the hold up? Just tell me the truth, Tess. Whatever it is, I can take it."

"The truth?"

I nod, gazing down at her, waiting.

We've stopped dancing. I've stopped breathing. The party swirls around us, but I don't register any of it. There's only her in my arms. There's only us.

"The truth," she says again, her lips barely moving.

"Say it."

Holding my gaze, her lips part. I watch the gentle rise and fall of her chest. I know if I lean close enough, I'll feel her warm breath ghost across my lips.

"The truth is that a sweet guy like you is likely looking to settle down," she says at last. "You may not believe in love at first sight, but you believe in love. You believe your Future Mrs. Hockey Boy is right around the next corner. And you believe good things come to good people, and that if you want something bad enough, you can have it. No obstacle is too high. You're all bright and shiny, Ryan, ready for your life to start."

My breath is trapped in my chest as I take in her words.

She holds my gaze. "You look at me and you see wife potential, don't you? Another prize for your shelf. A game to be won. But I've been someone's wife, Ryan," she goes on, her gaze hardening as she drops her hands away from me. "And I will *never* be a man's trophy again. We can laugh and dance and tease each other all night long. But when that sun rises, you'll see the truth. You'll see me for all that I am. And what I am is a waste of your time."

With that, she turns on her heel and hurries away, leaving me standing there with empty hands.

7
Tess

Heart in my throat, I leave the dance floor, trying to put as much distance between Ryan and me as possible. Honestly, I wouldn't put it past him to follow after me. But I don't look back. Somehow, I fear it might hurt more to see he's *not* following me.

Tears sting my eyes, blurring my vision, as I duck out of the first open door I see. The moment the cool L.A. air hits my lungs, I suck in a ragged breath. "Fuck," I whimper, hating how easy it is for Ryan to turn me into such a mess.

I'm just tired. That's what this is. And I'm probably a little drunk. Nothing some sleep and a few Advil can't fix by morning.

It's quieter out here, the sound of the music dampened by the wall of thick glass. Soft golden light stretches out across Hal Price's manicured lawn. To my left is the open space that leads out to the stage area. To the right is the pool.

I move right, angling for the lounge furniture. I'll just take a minute to sit and breathe. And I'm taking these damn shoes off. Heck, at this point, I feel like throwing them in the pool.

Maybe I'll throw myself in too.

Sink to the bottom.

Count to one thousand.

My pity party is interrupted by the sound of a deep voice. I turn the corner to see another secluded seating area. Soft patio lights hang on the underside of an arbor, casting a twinkling, golden glow. Ilmari paces in his shirtsleeves, phone to his ear. He's speaking low in Finnish.

I studied Latin and Greek in school, and I know just enough Italian to get myself into fun trouble on vacation. My ear desperately tries to pick out even a single word of his language, but Finnish is completely incomprehensible to me.

He turns in his pacing and stills, his eyes narrowing on me.

I give him a little awkward wave.

He surprises me by pointing to one of the empty chairs, inviting me to stay. Then he's turning away, humming something into the phone. He lets out a soft laugh, pacing to the other end of the oversized sectional.

I drop into the closest chair with a sigh. Sticking my leg out the slit of my dress, my tired fingers fumble for the strap of my shoe. I wanna cry when I finally get them both off, kicking them to the side.

Ilmari finishes his phone call and turns to face me. "Sorry about that," he says.

"Not at all. I interrupted you," I reply. "It's a bit late for a phone call, isn't it?"

"Not in Finland. It's nearly one in the afternoon in Helsinki."

"Right. Was that your agent?"

"My adoptive father. I wanted them to hear from me the news of the wedding before word reached them via the press."

"And . . . is he happy for you? Is he sad to have missed the wedding?"

"My aunt is devastated," he replies, taking a seat on the couch opposite me. "She made me promise to bring them all to Finland this summer."

We sit in silence for a moment, the pulse of the music thrumming against the wall. I get the feeling something's bothering him. We'll call it the particular angle of his scowl.

"Is everything okay?" I ask.

He clears his throat and shifts.

"Mars—"

"I fear I may have made a decision in haste," he admits. "I am regretting it now immensely."

My stomach drops out. "Ohmygod. Mars, are you having second thoughts? 'Cause if you walk out on Rachel after three hours of marriage—"

"What? I'm not talking about Rachel—"

I gasp, my hand covering my mouth. "Then is it the guys? If you think you'll pry her away from them—"

"*No*," he says more forcefully. "Will you stop guessing and let me speak?"

"You just said you made a decision in haste," I counter. "Married after only four months to your doctor and two of your teammates feels pretty hasty to me, Mars."

"There was nothing hasty in my decision to make them mine. If you would stop talking, and let me speak, I will explain myself. Christ, you're worse than Jake."

"Rude."

"Prove me wrong," he counters with a glare.

I lean back, crossing my arms over my chest. "Will you just tell me already? Before I freak out or get tired of waiting and jump to the bottom of the pool—"

"I'm afraid I made a bad investment," he says over me.

Well, that takes the wind right from my sails.

"A bad investment?" I echo. "This is about money?"

He nods.

"Well . . . how bad of an investment? How big was your risk?"

"Not that kind of investment," he replies. "A few months ago, I invested in a nonprofit," he explains. "Rachel warned me not to, but I was feeling . . . generous."

I get the feeling the word 'generous' is not what he intended, but I say nothing. "How generous were you?" I ask instead.

"Five hundred thousand dollars."

I narrow my eyes at him. "What kind of nonprofit?"

"They do sea turtle nest monitoring," he replies.

I sit back and blink, confused. "You donated half a million dollars to a group that monitors sea turtles?"

He nods.

"Well . . . *why*?"

"It's complicated," he replies.

"Try me."

He just shrugs. "Call it guilt."

"Guilt? You donated half a million dollars to a sea turtle nonprofit out of guilt? What, did you murder a family of sea turtles? Did you mow them down in a yacht or something?"

"No," he replies with a frown.

"Well, then I don't get it. Why would you give so much money away?"

"Consider it my vain attempt to rebalance the cosmic scales," he replies.

"What?"

"I live wholly unsustainably," he explains. "Private jets, private busses, hotels, single-use containers for every meal—to say absolutely nothing about the scourge of stadiums on the environment. I just felt like I couldn't live with myself if I didn't do something . . . anything."

"Holy fuck," I say on a sigh. "You're telling me you look and sound like that, you play hockey the way you do. I'm sure you fuck like a god," I add. "Our Rachel doesn't settle for anything less than the best. *And* you're environmentally conscious?"

I'm not even surprised when he just nods. Yep, he's the whole freaking package. No wonder Rachel and her boys locked him down so fast.

I shift forward on my lounge chair. "Okay, Mars. Walk me through it. Why do you call it a bad investment?"

He raises a brow at me. "Are you genuinely interested in this? I didn't mean to unload my burdens on you—"

"I asked," I remind him gently. "And of course, I'm interested. Nonprofit management is kind of my jam."

"I thought you were a lawyer. Something corporate, right?"

I laugh. "I'm a lawyer, yes. And 'something corporate' pretty much sums up how interesting my job is. But I also have a degree in nonprofit management. I'll help you if I can."

He looks surprised. "Really?"

It feels good to have something to help focus my thoughts. "Lay it on me, Mars. What's the worry?"

"Well, it turns out the nonprofit is less organized than I would have liked," he admits. "Less well-funded. Less professionalized."

"Uh-oh. How bad is it?"

He frowns. "It's three people and a PO Box."

I snort a laugh. “Fuck, I’m sorry. I don’t mean to laugh. That *is* bad. I bet you made their day with your generous donation though.”

His scowl deepens as he leans back, crossing his arms. “This isn’t funny, Tess. This is not how I wanted to start my marriage. I don’t want the first action I take to be admitting a gross financial failure to my partners. I need them to see me as capable . . . responsible.”

“Okay, if it’s possible, I like you even more now,” I admit. “Are you worried they’ll take the money and run?”

“I’m worried they have no idea what to do with it,” he explains. “They admitted they’ve never handled such a large donation before. And there’s no plan in place for the longevity of the nonprofit.”

“Well . . . it sounds like you need to build the nonprofit from the ground up,” I reply. “You’ve got the cash and you’ve got a few eager volunteers. I think you could build something really cool. I’ve seen nonprofits accomplish more with less. This doesn’t have to be a lost cause.”

He nods, but I can tell he’s not quite convinced.

“What you need is a director of operations,” I explain. “Someone sharp with some relevant experience growing out a brand. And you need to expand out your donor pool immediately. You’d be surprised how quickly half a mil gets eaten up in a budget.”

He gives me an appraising look. “Very well. You’re hired.”

“What?” I cry.

“Director of Operations. You have the job.”

“Mars, I have a job,” I laugh. “A *good* job. High-powered corporate lawyer, remember?”

“Just give me six months of your time,” he says. “Help me get this on the right track. Whatever your pay is, I’ll double it.”

I laugh again. “Oh, you’ll double my current salary?”

He nods and I’m positive he’s totally serious.

“Okay,” I say. “I accept the position.”

His eyes go wide. “Really?”

“Yep.” I lean forward, rubbing my hands together. “Now, as my first act as your Director of Operations, I’m firing myself, effective immediately.”

“Why?” he grunts.

“I’m *way* overpaid.”

"Tess . . . "

"What? Don't try and cover up one bad financial decision with another one. Mars, you don't want me as your director anyway. I don't know a damn thing about sea turtles."

"Yes, but that's not really necessary in the director role, is it?" he challenges. "What's needed is a sound business mind capable of scaling up a brand, you said so yourself."

"I'm flattered," I admit, hoping it shows in my face. "Truly, Mars. And it honestly does sound like fun. But my life is in Cincinnati. My job, my apartment, my . . . family," I add, my voice faltering a bit.

"I understand," Mars says at last.

"You don't know how much I wish I could say yes," I admit. "Six months in Florida, are you kidding? A little beach air in my hair, all that delicious fried shrimp. Not to mention I miss Rachel like a piece of me has been cleaved away. She's my best friend, Mars."

"I know."

"You three better be so fucking good to her," I say, pointing a finger at him.

"We will," he says, getting to his feet.

"You better," I challenge, rising to my feet too. "Or I *am* gonna come down there to Jacksonville. And I'm going to chop you up into tiny little bits and feed you to those damn sea turtles."

He smirks. "Noted." Then he holds out a hand to me. "Come. We've stayed away long enough."

I snatch up my shoes, slipping my finger through the straps. Righting myself, I let out a little breath. He's right. It's time to go back in there. For Mars, it's the start of something new. For me, it's the end. He gets to walk in there and say 'hello' to his new wife. I get to walk in and say a tearful 'goodbye' to my friend, the woman who has been the only home I've ever known.

Reaching out, I take his hand.

8
Tess

"Hey, Tess!" My assistant Rhonda slips out from behind her desk as I approach.

"Hey, girl," I call. "You have a good Christmas?"

"Well, Steve's parents were in town," she replies, which is answer enough.

I unwind my thick scarf one-handed, holding my coffee with the other. "Yeesh. How bad was it?"

"Wendy informed me that she thinks my children are going to hell because I wouldn't let her baptize them when they were babies," she replies.

"Seriously?" I cry, handing her my coat.

"Yep." She hangs my coat and scarf up with hers. "Oh, and she accused me of stealing sleeping pills from her purse. Twice. Turns out she had them in her makeup bag the whole time."

"Oh god. Is she gone, at least?"

"Yes, thank God. They left for Akron this morning."

"That's a relief," I say with a sympathetic grimace. I pick up my bag and coffee from the edge of her desk.

"Hey," she calls as I turn towards my office door. "Your meeting with Dalton Holdings Limited got pushed to 10:00 a.m. Some HR thing was just scheduled at the last minute. You're meeting with them at 9:00 a.m."

I glance over my shoulder, lowering my voice so the other secretaries in this suite can't hear us. "Do we know what it's about?"

"No idea. I just saw your name was added to the meeting invite. Dale is running the show."

I fake a snore, which earns me a soft laugh from Rhonda.

Dale Eubanks is the head of HR for Powell, Fawcett, and Hughes, and a duller man has never drawn breath.

"Give me ten minutes to charge the batteries," I say, gesturing with my coffee hand. "Then you and I can head down together."

"Oh, I have a mandatory accounting training," she replies. "But . . . I can probably get out of it if you need me—"

"No," I say with a laugh. "No need. I'm sure this will prove to be nothing. Probably a mandatory refresher on reporting client gifts. Don't they make us sit through that every Christmas?"

I wave her off as I enter my office. I've only got fifteen minutes. Just enough time to sign one of the contracts stacked on my desk. And just like that, Tess Owens closes another multimillion-dollar deal before nine in the morning.

I take a sip of my iced caramel macchiato with a smile.

FIFTEEN minutes later, I'm on my way down to Human Resources, tablet and coffee in hand.

"Good morning," I singsong as I hurry my way across the seventh-floor atrium. My heels click as I sweep past the pair of girls working behind the desk. They're cute things fresh out of college with matching blonde ponytails.

Oh, and they're both named Katie.

"Morning, Ms. Owens," says Katie One. She always wears a slightly startled look on her face, like she's constantly surprised to find herself sitting behind a desk.

"Are they in conference room B?" I say as I walk past.

"Actually, Ms. Owens, they might not be ready for you yet," says Katie Two, scrambling out of her chair.

"The meeting doesn't start for another two minutes." I walk right past them, angling for the frosted glass door of the conference room.

"Ms. Owens, wait—"

The door whispers across the carpet as I push it gently inward. "Good morning, I—"

I pause in the open doorway, my hand pressed against the cool glass. My gaze darts quickly around the room. Two of the three partners are here. Oh, and Dale, of course.

"I thought I was early," I say. "Did I get the time wrong?"

"Tess, we're not quite ready for you yet," Dale replies from his seat at the head of the table.

"I'm sorry, Mr. Eubanks," calls Katie Two from just behind my shoulder. "I tried to tell her."

"It's fine, Katie," he says with a wave of his hand.

"I don't understand," I say, glancing around.

My gaze lands on Troy sitting to the left of Dale at the opposite end of the long conference table. He's wearing a holier than thou look as he takes me in with those dark eyes.

"What happened?" I say. "Oh god, did someone die?"

"Come in, Tess," says Dale. "Let's get the door shut."

I take two steps in, letting my hand drop to my side so the frosted glass door swings shut in Katie Two's face. "What happened?" I say again.

Something is definitely wrong.

"Why don't we have you join us over here," Dale calls, gesturing to a seat empty by one of the other HR reps. I think her name might be Judy.

"The suspense is killing me here," I admit, dropping into the leather swivel chair. I set my tablet and coffee down on the table. Now I'm seated directly across from Troy. He balances his elbows on the table, his fingers steepled under his chin.

"We were just discussing the ethos of Powell, Fawcett, and Hughes," Dale says as soon as I'm seated. "We pride ourselves here at PFH that we're a company of integrity. We may play in the corporate arena, but we're a family business first, family values. Wouldn't you agree, Mr. Fawcett?"

I glance across the table. Grant Fawcett III is seated next to Troy. He's the second highest ranking partner at the firm after Troy's mother. It was his grandfather who started the company with Bea's father. Beatrice Owens (neé Powell) is the reigning queen of PFH.

"Mhmm," says Grant with a slow nod. "That's what my grandfather wanted. That's what we're all striving to build here."

"And part of keeping family values at the center of our business is adhering to a strict code of ethics," Dale goes on. "We all sign contracts that include a morality clause." Slowly, Dale turns to me. "Tess, did you know you signed a contract that included a morality clause?"

"Yeah. It was pretty boiler plate," I reply.

"It's a bit more than that," Dale says, adjusting his glasses. "As one of the client-facing junior partners at our firm, your conduct must be seen as beyond reproach at all times," he goes on.

I go stiff in my chair. "I'm sorry—has there been a complaint I don't know about?" I glance around the table. "Did one of my clients have a bad experience? Because I swear—"

"This isn't about how you handle clients, Tess," Grant explains. "This is about how you conduct yourself as a junior partner. We're under a microscope here. And we can't allow any conduct unbecoming of a PFH partner. That comes straight from Bea."

My heart squeezes tight in my chest. "Bea knows about this?" I glance sharply over at Troy. "Well, can I please know too?"

Slowly, Dale nods. "Show her."

The woman to my right places a hand on the manilla folder resting in front of her. Slowly, she slides it my way.

I snatch it up and flip it open. My eyes go wide as I take in the image staring up at me. It's printed on glossy photo paper, but the image is grainy, like a blowup from an iPhone. My heart sinks straight out of my chest. It's a picture of me dancing with Ryan Langley at Rachel's wedding last week.

"What is this?"

"You tell us," Grant replies.

Next to him, Troy sits in silence with all the confidence of a judge holding court.

"Troy, what is this?" I say, holding up the photo. My heart is pounding.

There are more under it. I look through them quickly. Four photos of me dancing with Ryan. Each one shows us looking cozier than the last. We're gazing at each other with hearts in our eyes and smiles on our faces. In the last one, his face is turned into my hand as he kisses my palm. I can almost feel the warmth of that kiss.

It's chilled by the Arctic temperature in this room.

"This isn't what it looks like," I say, setting the photos down.

"What it *looks* like is you giving 'fuck me' eyes to another man," Troy counters.

"Ryan is a friend," I reply. "Nothing happened. We just danced. And this was a private event, by the way."

"Which just made these photos all the more enticing for the press to get their hands on," says Dale. "These were posted online a few hours ago with about two dozen other photos from Rachel Price's wedding. They're running on every news site with a string of stories, to include a few headlines about you and your new beau."

The woman next to me slides me the other folder.

I flip it open and see a stack of papers with trashy news headlines—celebrity gossip, sports news, Hollywood inside scoops. There are pictures of Rachel with her guys, several of Rachel's dad and his band, the Rays rubbing shoulders with the A-list celebrities. And then there are the photos of me dancing with Ryan Langley. One of the headlines calls me his newest lady love. Another calls me his girlfriend.

"This is a mistake," I say. "I can request a retraction or a correction—"

"It's too late, Tess," says Grant.

"PFH is officially in damage control mode," Dale echoes.

"Damage control?" I repeat with a raised brow. "What the heck does that mean? Am I not allowed to defend myself here?"

Grant scoffs. "And what defense can you launch to the lead partner of PFH for why you let it look like you're cheating on her son with a 22-year-old NHL star?"

"I was *not* cheating on Troy in the middle of my best friend's wedding," I cry. "And besides, I'd have to still be with Troy for anything I do with another person to count as cheating—"

"We're still married," Troy says. "You're my wife, Tess. Jesus—"

"That's a technicality and we all know it."

"It's a temporary separation. We're working on our relationship," he counters. "And it's private—"

"Ohmygod, are we rewriting history now?" I shout. "Okay, you want to talk about PFH as a 'family first' company?" I say, using air quotes. "What about you, Troy? Where was the conference room shakedown when you cheated on me with your secretary *in your fucking office*? I got to walk in and catch Candace on her knees with your cock in her mouth—"

"Whoa," says Dale, leveling a warning hand at me. "Tess, let's try not to get vulgar here."

I turn to him, eyes wide. I feel like I've stepped into some kind of alternate dimension. "This is so messed up," I say, breathless. "This is so completely fucked. I've done nothing wrong."

"You know as well as anyone that appearance is everything," says Dale. "We can't excuse this kind of negative press when it involves our partners and their families. There has to be consequences for any and all morality clause breaches."

"So, what were *his* consequences?" I cry, waving my hand across the table at Troy. "He fucks anything with tits, he does it *on* PFH property, and yet I'm the one getting my wrist slapped for dancing at a wedding?"

"He wasn't photographed," Grant replies.

"And it wasn't splashed across the AP for all our clients to see," adds Dale.

I just shake my head, actually feeling the moment I lose all faith in humanity. It slips from my body like a puff of smoke, floating before my eyes before it disappears. "So that's it then? One standard for him and another for me? Seems really fair—"

"One standard period," Dale counters.

"So, what's happening now then?" I say. "What's my punishment for daring to emasculate Bea's precious son?"

"Careful," Troy growls. "I pushed Mother to be lenient here. Don't make me change my mind."

"A leave of absence," says Dale over him. "Only temporary, of course."

"Oh my god!" Shoving back from the table, I stand. "A leave of absence? Are you fucking kidding me?"

"Only until this all dies down," he goes on. "Likely we'll have a plan of action that will involve you and Troy doing some image control—a few public functions, some client dinners. And Troy is fully on board," he adds. "We all want this smoothed over as quickly as possible. In six weeks, we can reevaluate."

"Six weeks?" I cry.

Dale just nods. "That's been company policy in the past for administrative leaves."

Across from me, Troy nods too. He's trying to keep his expression solemn, but I can see the faintest hint of a smirk on his lips. *Fucker.* This is what he wants. Any excuse to keep me trapped under his thumb. Never mind that I close nearly *double* the deals that he does. I may be the greater financial asset to PFH, but Troy is the legacy with ties to the company's founder. He's the heir apparent to our current CEO.

Speaking of the queen . . .

"I don't believe for one second that Bea agreed to this," I say. "She wouldn't. She *can't*."

Bea Owens has long been like my guardian angel. My own mother never cared about me. She was always chasing her next boyfriend and hopping from job to job. I lived with whichever family member was willing to take me in for a few days or weeks at a time. But I was always just an inconvenience. Always in the way.

Not to Bea. She saw my talent and drive. She recruited me into PFH and paved the way for me to make junior partner. When everything with Troy and I started to fall apart, Bea helped us try and make it work.

"Where is she?" I demand. "I want to hear from her that this is what she wants."

Troy just scoffs. "Be my guest," he says with a wave of his hand.

"You know she'll take my side. Once I explain everything."

"You think so?"

"I *know* so."

He gives me a grin like he just checkmated my king right off the chess board. "Well, then it should really surprise you to hear that this little plan to rehab our marriage was all *her* idea."

9
Tess

"Tess!" Troy calls. "Stop walking—"

"Just go away," I cry as I hurry my way across the atrium.

"We need to talk—"

"Fuck you," I say, still not slowing.

The Katies sit in shocked silence as I march up to the elevator and slam my thumb against the up arrow.

"Come on," I whimper, watching the lights flash along the top.

Troy sweeps in behind me, his hand on my shoulder. "Tess—"

"Don't touch me," I hiss, spinning to break our contact.

He drops his hand to his side. "You're being so irrational right now. I don't know how I'm supposed to talk to you—"

"Irrational?" I cry, eyes wide. "My career is on the line because you got your fucking feelings hurt!"

"This isn't about me, Tess—"

"Everything is about you!"

Behind me, the elevator doors open with a ding. I spin away from him and step inside. Of course, he follows. I jab my thumb on the number nine and then pepper the 'door close' button.

"You only need to press it once," Troy says from my shoulder.

"Shut up."

"Pressing it again does nothing—"

"Oh my god, you have to shut up," I cry as the doors slide shut. "Please, for once, just fucking shut up so I can hear myself fucking think!"

"God, you're a mess," he mutters. "I think this leave of absence is coming at just the right time for you."

I spin around, taking him in. He's always been handsome—dark eyes, chiseled cheek bones for days. He oozes wealth and sophistication. At 6'2", he's a big guy too. Working out became his obsession the summer before he turned thirty. Now he fills out his suit with those broad shoulders and that well-muscled chest.

But his beauty no longer distracts me the way it once did. Now I see it for what it is: vanity, insecurity. He works so hard to keep his body in shape because he wants other women to find him desirable and men to find him enviable.

And I know there's been so many other women.

Puffing out my chest, I hold his gaze. "Troy, we're done. I want a divorce."

His eyes go wide as the elevator halts and dings, the doors sliding open. I dart out, praying the doors crush him as they close. But I'm not that lucky.

"Tess!"

I launch across the ninth-floor lobby, hurrying towards my office suite. Wrenching the door open, I charge forward, ignoring the surprised looks of the secretaries. I see Rhonda's empty desk and my heart sinks. She's still in her meeting, meaning I have no buffer. It's about to be David versus Goliath, and I left my slingshot in my other pencil skirt.

"Tess! Goddamn it, will you just talk to me?" Troy shouts.

I jerk open my office door, desperate to put a wall between us and the secretaries before he tears into me. I can't bear to let other people see me cry, and I don't think I can hold these angry tears back much longer.

Slamming my tablet and coffee down, my chest heaves as I pant for breath. I look down at my hands splayed against the dark, polished wood of my executive desk. I can feel Troy sucking up all the air behind me as my office door clicks shut. The asshole has the audacity to turn the lock. The sound echoes in my chest, like the bars of a jail cell latching closed.

I spin around. "Unlock the door, Troy."

"I don't want us to be disturbed," he counters, dark eyes narrowed at me.

"And I don't want to feel trapped in here with you. Unlock the fucking door before I scream."

"God, you're paranoid," he huffs. But he unlocks the door. "There, are you happy? Will you stop being crazy now and just talk to me?"

"I want a divorce," I repeat.

"No."

"Troy—"

"Tess, *no*. I'm not going to let you make this decision right now. You're too emotional—"

"You're damn right, I'm emotional! This was *you*, wasn't it? You found those photos and took them to Dale, complaining about this morality clause bullshit—"

He's shaking his head. "This isn't about me. This is about the integrity of PFH—"

"Oh, don't you fucking *dare*," I cry. "This is about your ego and nothing else. What I want to know is why now? Why these photos? Surely you have better evidence—"

"That's right, I *do*," he says, stepping into my space. "I've got enough evidence of your affairs to end you. Out of the goodness of my heart, I was the bigger fucking person and I kept quiet."

I take a deep breath, trying to find my calm. "You know, when everything first fell apart, I wanted a divorce. But your mother encouraged us to take it slow, to work on finding a fix. I agreed to counseling. It was only when I learned that you were still fucking the secretaries that I walked out."

He scoffs, turning away.

"But then your mother came to me again and asked me to consider a trial separation," I go on. I know he knows all this, but he likes to conveniently forget the important details. "She asked me to keep it quiet for the sake of the company, for the sake of the family. I agreed. I'd do anything for her, Troy. You know that. And it didn't seem important to dissolve a paper marriage as long as you were behaving—"

He spins around. "Behaving? Jesus, I'm not some naughty child, Tess. I'm a grown ass man."

"I thought we had both moved on," I press, taking a step closer. "This was business only. It appeased your mother and helped her save face with *her* friends. All our mutuals know it's over. And we were *both* seeing other people—"

"I kept my affairs quiet," he shouts. "That's the difference here,

Tess. Meanwhile, you're splashing yours across page six, making me look like the asshole of the century."

"I told you it was nothing—"

"Yeah, like I believe that," he scoffs.

Righteous indignation surges through me. "I've *never* lied to you, Troy. That's your M.O."

He glares at me, daggering me with his eyes.

After a tense moment, I let out a tired sigh. "Just give me a divorce, Troy. It's time—"

"No. We're not there yet." He shakes his head. "I'm not gonna let you do this to us."

"We are *so* there! We're right fucking there. Troy, this isn't a marriage anymore. It's a hostage crisis!"

"God, you are so overdramatic! I can't believe I thought I could have a calm, rational conversation with you about this. You're chaotic—"

"And you're transparent," I counter. "You think I don't know what this is about—"

"This is about you being a frigid workaholic. *You* pushed me away, Tess. You gave up on us, and you blame me for seeking comfort in someone else's arms? I couldn't live in the shadow of your indifference. You never put me first. So yes, *I* put me first, Tess," he shouts, jabbing a thumb at his chest. "Someone had to."

His words hit me like a slap, and I reel back. "You really believe that, don't you?"

"It's true, and you know it," he replies. "Even if you won't ever admit it."

"I *did* put you first, Troy. I always only ever put you first. I sacrificed everything for you—"

"And what did that earn me except your shitty resentment?" he says, leveling a finger in my face.

I lean away, eyes wide. I'm trapped between him and the desk, the edge of it biting into the curve of my hip.

"You don't get to play the martyr and make me the villain," he says. "I didn't ask you to pick my law school or work for my family firm or fucking smother me—"

"Well, did I smother you, or was I indifferent?" I challenge.

He turns away, cursing under his breath.

"You can't have it both ways, Troy," I call at his back. "Did I put you first or last? Or do you even know? Did you even notice me until I was gone? No, you were too busy with your golf weekends and your client dinners and your girlfriends—"

"Don't turn this around on me. You always do that. You spin my words and make me the asshole. I'm not the asshole, Tess. I'm not the cheater—"

"You cheated, Troy. You were married to me and fucking other people without my knowledge or consent. That makes you the literal definition of a cheater." It's my tone that surprises me. So detached.

I'm numb.

Broken.

Done.

"Christ, I'll never be enough for you, will I?" he says. "I'm always the disappointment. Always coming up short. You never respected me, Tess. Never loved me like I deserved."

I close my eyes, trying to shut out his words. I can't bear this feeling of being trapped in his presence, accepting his gaslighting revisionism of our entire ten-year relationship. "Please, just let me go," I whisper. "Troy, please. I want a divorce."

"And now you want to quit. Yeah, things are tough right now. But you know what? That's real life, Tess. We've got problems to work through. But now you're suddenly just done? I guess I don't know what else I expected. Go ahead and run. That's what you do best." He points at the door, dismissing me from my own office. But I'm not sure if it's a trick. I wouldn't put it past him to chase me out and continue to make a scene in front of our colleagues.

"Are we really done here?"

He just glares at me.

"If we're done, can you please leave?"

"You're the one taking a leave of absence," he needles. "Not me."

Of course, he's not taking a leave of absence. Because he gets to walk through life without ever feeling the negative consequences of his actions. Impervious to blame, immune to criticism. No, consequences are reserved for lesser mortals.

Mortals like me.

Holding the frayed strands of my dignity together, I turn away from him, slipping my tablet into my bag.

"Wait," he says, his voice suddenly softer. He steps forward, his hand brushing my shoulder, and I go stiff. "Fuck, seriously?" He drops his hand away. "I can't even fucking touch you without you flinching away? Am I such a monster to you now?"

He's right up in my space, his large body inches from mine. He overwhelms me, the spicy scent of his aftershave mixed with his cologne. I know it so well. That scent signature is burrowed deep in my psyche. So masculine . . .

The connection has me sucking in a sharp breath as I piece it together.

Of course.

"It's because he's a man," I say, not turning around. "Isn't it?"

He goes still. "What are you talking about?"

Slowly I turn, my breast brushing his arm in our closeness. I gaze up at him, my hand clutching tight to the leather handle of my bag. "You're torching my life now because Ryan Langley is a threat to your fragile masculinity. Hot young NHL star with stamina for days, making his millions, flashing that handsome smile—"

"There's nothing fragile about my masculinity," he snarls. "And I don't care who you fuck." He says the words, but his eyes give him away. There's a fire there, embers burning hot. He's jealous. He doesn't want me; he's made that crystal clear. It was clear even when we were still fucking. We were both so physically and emotionally checked out by the end.

Troy doesn't want me. But he doesn't want another man to have me either.

"I've had a string of lovers since we split," I say. "You know about them all. Erica practically lived with me for half of last year. But since you, all my lovers have been women. You can dismiss a woman. She's not a threat to you or your reputation. But one picture of me with Ryan, and now you're setting my life on fire. Finally, you have some real competition . . . and an excuse to torch me."

"You're delusional. And you're an utterly forgettable lay. I bet he struggled to get off. I know I always did."

His cruel words can't hurt me. I'm completely detached from

my body, floating in space and time. And if my life is already up in smoke, why not fan the flames a little?

I nod, lips pursed. "Well . . . he didn't seem to complain when I was deep throating him on my knees, choking on his cum. His dick is huge, by the way. My pussy still feels wrecked, and it's been a week—"

"Shut the fuck up," he growls, his hand going to my throat.

My hand rises on instinct, wrapping around his wrist. Tears sting my eyes as he squeezes. "Troy—"

He presses me back against the desk. "Don't say another word, you filthy fucking whore," he orders, his lips almost brushing mine in his closeness. "I gave you everything. I pulled you up out of the gutter and gave you this life that you take for granted. You don't deserve my love!"

I breathe through the pressure, holding his gaze. Slowly, I give his hand a squeeze. "Troy . . . "

"I said shut up! You make me fucking crazy when you won't just shut up and listen to me!"

"Troy . . . honey, you're choking me," I rasp, a tear slipping down my cheek.

Slowly, I see the anger recede in his eyes as he traces a line down his own arm, ending at the hand on my throat. With a groan, he drops his hand away and steps back.

I gasp, holding in a sob as I grip to the desk, hand massaging my throat.

Don't panic, I tell myself. *Don't let him see you panic.*

Another tear falls as I watch him pace two steps back.

"Fuck, do you see how crazy you make me? You think I don't love you, but this is what you do to me, Tess. You make me feel like a fucking monster, and I hate it."

"This isn't love, Troy." I massage my throat, praying he didn't leave a mark. "You don't love me . . . and I don't love you."

"You can't tell me how I feel—"

"This is possession," I press, dropping my hand back to my side. "All we do is hurt each other, and it has to stop. We gave your mother her way, but enough is enough. Let me write up the papers. All you have to do is sign, and you can finally be free of me. Please, Troy—"

"God—*fuck*—just stop pushing," he cries. "You know this isn't easy for me, Tess. I'm not a quitter. I don't lose. I—fuck, you just had to go embarrass me in front of the whole fucking world." He steps into my space, and I hold my ground, not letting him see how scared I am, how much I want him to just leave.

"I bet you wanted those photos taken," he says, his face inches from mine. "I bet you posed for them. You wanted to twist the fucking knife in my heart!" He pounds on his chest with his balled fist. The sound sparks panic as I imagine that fist pounding against me instead.

"I didn't, Troy. I swear to you—"

"I don't know how we repair this damage," he says over me. "I don't know how you think you come back from this," he adds, gesturing around my office.

I go still, my heartbeat frozen in my chest. "A divorce would solve everything. We dissolve the marriage and ride out the gossip. This isn't the Middle Ages, Troy. Divorce happens all the time," I soothe, placing my hand on his arm. "People will move on—"

"I don't care about other people," he says angrily, shrugging away from my touch. "I care about you and me. *Us.* How do I work with you after this? There's no escaping your judgmental looks or your shitty, hurt expressions. I can't just let you drag me down and paint me as your cheating ex-husband."

"Troy, I would never do that. I'm a professional—"

"You're already doing it," he counters. "Every day you waltz in here, totally unaffected by our separation. It's so easy for you to make a mockery of me, and I can't have that. I'm rising up the ladder here, taking on more responsibility every day. Soon I'll be full partner."

I lean away, eyes wide. "What are you saying?"

"I'm saying this is bigger than you and me. It's careers and reputations."

I put the pieces of his threat together. "So, you're saying I stay married to you to protect your reputation . . . or you'll have me fired? You'll end the career I spent a decade building over a few grainy cellphone photos?"

"I'm saying you need to think about what matters most to you," he counters, slipping his hands in his pockets. "You've got a reputation, too, you know. I'd hate to see you make an irrational choice. You say I'm the one lighting the fire here, Tess, but that's not true. *You're* holding the match. You've got all the power right now, not me. What you do with it is up to you."

He turns away from me and moves towards the door, ripping the air from my lungs.

I feel empty. Hollow.

"I'll give you a few days to cool off and think everything over," he says at me over his shoulder. "And don't worry," he adds, pulling my door open. "I won't have security escort you out. I'm not the asshole you think I am, Tessy. But you should really go ahead and clear out of here before lunch . . . leave us to clean up your mess."

10
Tess

My keys rattle down on the kitchen island as I stare blankly across the wide expanse of my apartment. It's raining outside. Pouring. Sheets of icy sleet pelt sideways against my wall of windows making a rhythmic *rata-tat-tat* sound. Thunder rolls far in the distance, a deep rumble I feel in my chest.

I lift a hand slowly, pressing it against my wet cheek. The sleet burns so cold, my skin almost feels hot. I'm drenched. I could have ordered an Uber, but there was something poetic about walking home in the freezing rain in utter disgrace, dismissed from my job for daring to dance with a cute hockey player at my best friend's not-so-private wedding.

The only light in my apartment comes from my Christmas tree set up in the corner. The multi-colored lights twinkle on a timer. I love those stupid fucking lights. Troy only ever wanted white lights on our tree. It was my little act of rebellion the first Christmas I lived with Rachel to buy colored lights.

Slipping out of my heels, I kick them aside. My toes are wet inside my black stockings, chilled to the bone. Slowly, I lower my hand from my face to my double-wrapped scarf. Stripping it off, I drop it to the floor with a wet *plop*. Then I undo the buttons of my cream Antonio Melani belted wrap coat, shrugging it from my shoulders.

I become more frantic as I go, tugging at the bottom of the silky blouse tucked into my pencil skirt. My breath comes in sharp pants as I jerk the buttons, popping one clean off. It rattles onto the counter. I need it off. All of it. *Now*. I can't breathe.

I unzip my skirt and shimmy it down my hips, stepping out of it. Then I stretch my arms behind my back, chilled fingers fumbling for the strap of my bra. The clasp releases and I gasp, dropping it from my shoulders. I stand there in my kitchen in nothing but my stockings and underwear. Arms wrapped tightly around my middle, I sob. I'm so angry I could scream. I *do* scream. Loud. It's feral and raw and not nearly enough of a release. The sound is sharp in my throat, stinging in its intensity.

"Fuck," I shout. "Fucking fuck!"

Inside the pocket of my coat, my phone dings. I stand there, chest heaving as I catch my breath.

Ding.

Ding.

I snatch up my coat and dig in the pocket for my phone. Swiping the screen with my thumb, I unlock it. My messenger app glows bright.

RACHEL (11:03 a.m.): Well, the cat's out of the bag.

The messages below that include a few links to some of the news articles about her surprise secret wedding.

RACHEL (11:04 a.m.): It was one of the caterers. Apparently, the little weasel took photos all night and sold them to TMZ. Bitch. I hope she gets hit by lightning.

Honestly, I'm not surprised. They weren't going to keep this quiet for long. Knowing it was a caterer who snapped photos of Ryan and me doesn't do anything to fix my current predicament. I'm on leave, effective immediately.

My phone dings again, and I glance down at the screen.

RACHEL (11:07 a.m.): I let Poppy take a few photos too. Much better quality than the weasel's sneaky, zoomed-in shots. Thought you might like this one.

A picture pops up in the feed. I tap it with my thumb, and it fills the screen. It's a candid shot taken of several of us sitting on one of the living room couches. Ilmari is on the end looking every inch the Finnish bear. What has me pausing is that he's clearly laughing, his mouth open, eyes creased in the corners. His arm is around Rachel who is leaning into him but turned away. I'm next to her, leaning in, also mid-laugh. My hand is slightly raised, like I'm trying to catch my smile before it runs away.

Next to me are two of the Rays, Morrow and Novikov. I think they both play defense. Jake is leaning over the back of the couch, his head down between theirs, as they share a laugh too. The captain, Sully, is perched on the end of the couch, saying something with a smile.

I don't even remember what we were all laughing about. We look so natural, so perfectly at ease. I don't know why, but tears spring to my eyes. I turn my phone upright and minimize the photo to see another message from Rachel.

RACHEL (11:09 a.m.): It's good to see you looking so happy. The boys are ready to make you an honorary Ray.

I tap the photo again, zooming in on each of our faces. I do look happy. I *was* happy.

Glancing around my apartment, a feeling of deep longing settles in me. My gaze lands on the only source of light in the room: my Christmas tree. The Christmas tree I bought and decorated with Rachel. More happy memories—making eggnog on the stove and ruining it with too much nutmeg, dancing in our underwear to Christmas music, eating Chinese takeout on the couch.

I used to be happy all the time. I used to laugh and love out loud. I was wild once. I was free. I've been trying to find my way back to that girl who danced in her underwear. Rachel was helping me find her.

I miss her.

I miss *me*.

Tears slip down my cheeks as I watch the lights on my Christmas tree blink and twinkle—red and blue, green and pink. *Blink. Blink. Blink.*

"Fuck this," I say, my resolve hardening in my chest.

I *am* that girl.

Slapping my phone down on the counter, I march across my apartment and into my bedroom, heading straight for the closet.

Determination burns in my chest like a warming fire as I snatch up my suitcase and haul it into the bedroom, slinging it onto my bed. I drop the throw from around my shoulders and unzip the suitcase.

I'm free, I repeat to myself as I begin to pack. *I'm wild and fun and fucking free.*

"IS this the house, ma'am?" my Uber driver calls from the front seat. It's hard to hear him over the sound of all this rain. It's pounding the car in heavy sheets. His windshield wipers are working their hardest, but the visibility is almost nothing.

I peer out through my foggy window, wiping a circle in the chilled glass with the meat of my fist. "Two more down," I call to the driver. "The tall one on the end with the lights on."

He inches the car forward, rolling it along until he comes to a stop in front of a handsome house framed in dark shadows. Golden light shines out through the rain, illuminating the grass and a large truck parked in the drive.

"This it?" my driver calls.

"Yes," I reply, thumb tapping on my phone to close out the ride.

"Let me just get your bags then."

"Oh no," I cry, patting his shoulder. "Just pop your trunk and I'll get the bags. You just stay dry, okay?"

"Thanks, ma'am," he says with obvious relief. "You know how to swim, right?"

"Sure do," I reply, flinging open my door.

The rain pelts in, making me yelp as I hurry out of the backseat and around to the trunk. I work fast to drag all my bags out of the back. My computer bag is slung over my shoulder, the strap slicing between my breasts. I've got a backpack too, heavy with clothes and shoes. Not to mention my two massive roller bags. I'm soaked to the bone within moments as I wheel them up the driveway, the sound lost to the thunderstorm.

Puffing out a sharp breath, I press my thumb against the doorbell. Inside the house, a dog barks. I wait, my hands clutching to the handles of my bags. Water drips down my neck, between my breasts, off the tip of my nose.

The door swings open to reveal Jake standing there in nothing but a pair of athletic shorts, a bag of Garden Salsa Sun Chips in his hand. "Tess," he cries.

"Hey, Jake," I say, feeling suddenly self-conscious.

Poseidon darts outside, dancing around my legs, his body wiggling in excitement.

"Hey, puppy," I coo, giving him some pats. I smile as he licks my hand.

"Where did you come from?" says Jake, peering behind me as if he's looking for an alien spacecraft or a teleportation device.

"Umm, the airport," I admit with a shrug.

"Did I know you were coming?" he says. Then he gasps, eyes wide. "Ohmygod, did I forget to pick you up?"

"No," I say with a laugh. "No, this visit wasn't planned."

"Oh, thank God," he says, his free hand splayed over his chest like he's trying to keep his heart from jumping through his skin. "Rachel would've made me sleep on the couch for a week if I left her best friend high and dry at the airport . . . well, high and wet," he adds, taking me in from head to toe. "Jeez, get in here." Sticking his free hand out the doorway, he grabs one of my bags and reels it in over the threshold, stepping back to make room for me.

Poseidon dances around my feet as I wheel the other bag in. I step into the bright, spacious entry way, water dripping off every part of me.

"You look like you swam here," Jake teases, tossing his bag of chips down on the entry table. "Seattle's gonna be so psyched to see you."

I go still, hand clutching to my bag. "Is she here?"

"Nah, she and Cay are out for dinner and a movie," he replies. "He's trying the whole 'domestic wedded bliss' thing. It's adorable, like watching a chimp on roller-skates."

I can't help but smile trying to picture Caleb Price being married and domestic. I'm also kind of relieved Rachel isn't here. As soon as I face her, I know I'll lose it. She reads me like a book. She'll have me telling her everything, and I'm not ready for that quite yet.

"Do you want me to call her?" he asks, slipping his hand into the pocket of his shorts. "I'm sure they can cut their evening short—"

"No," I say quickly. "I, umm . . . well, I didn't actually come to see Rachel."

Jake narrows his eyes at me. "Who did you come to see then?"

"Well . . . actually, I came to see Ilmari."

If possible, Jake's eyes go even wider. "Seriously?"

"Yeah. Is he home?" I peer over his shoulder down the hall.

"Hey, Mars," he shouts. "Get over here. Right fucking now!"

In moments, Mars steps around the corner from the living room. Like Jake, he's wearing nothing but a pair of athletic shorts. His blond hair is down, falling to his shoulders. I've never seen him wear it down before. With the beard and his scarred brow, it definitely adds to the whole sporty Viking aesthetic.

Jake Price is fit, but Ilmari Price is literally carved from stone—eight-pack, a tight "V", and pecs that could break boulders. He strides down the hallway, bag of open pistachios in hand. His eyes go wide as he takes me in.

"Did you order a spicy redhead?" says Jake, jabbing a thumb in my direction.

"No," Ilmari replies.

I glance between them. This ball of emotion sitting in my throat might just choke the air right out of me. It's been lodged there since I impulsively ordered an Uber and drove straight to the Cincinnati airport.

"Were we expecting you?" Ilmari says at me.

"No," I reply, suddenly breathless.

Oh shit, here come the waterworks. I fucking *hate* crying. Before I can stop myself, I'm closing the distance between us. I let out a sob as I fling my arms around his neck and press myself against him, crying into his naked shoulder. His hand holding the bag of pistachios gets pinned between us with a soft *crunch*.

He goes stiff, muttering something in Finnish. I don't know which he's hating worse: the hug or the tears.

"What the fuck did you do?" Jake cries at his partner.

"Nothing," says Ilmari, wholly indignant as he awkwardly pats my shoulder.

"Well, she was fine until you got here," Jake challenges. He leans in closer to me, his hand on my other shoulder. "Tess? Are you injured?"

"No," I sniffle, my hands gripping tighter to Ilmari's shoulders.

"Are you on the run from the law? Is this like a hideout situation?"

"Christ, Jake," Ilmari mutters.

"Well, I don't fucking know," he says. "Cay doesn't call her Tornado for nothing. Maybe she spun some shit up, and now she's on the lam. We can't afford to hide a fugitive right now, Mars. We leave for the Winter Classic tomorrow. And I'm sure as fuck not going to prison as her accomplice. Are you kidding me?"

"No one's going to jail," Ilmari replies. "Just give her a moment to compose herself, and she'll tell us why she's here."

"What the hell did I miss?" Jake gestures between us. "Since when are you two such good friends?"

"We're not," Mars and I say at the same time. "Go make yourself useful and get her a towel," he adds, shoving his bag of pistachios at Jake's chest.

Jake takes them with a huff. "Sure, I'll go get a towel. Want me to go fuck myself while I'm at it?"

"*Now*, Jake," Mars orders.

Jake wanders off with the dog chasing after him.

"Take your time," Ilmari says at me, his body relaxing a little against mine.

His permission acts like the opening of a second set of flood gates. I'm a mess as I just cling to him and cry, letting go of everything I've been holding onto all day. One moment I was standing in my apartment, the next I was standing at the Delta ticket counter. I've always felt so safe in Rachel's orbit, since that very first night we met. Her men make me feel safe too. An honorary Ray, she called me. Right now, that feels pretty fucking good.

The dog barks in excitement as Jake returns, beach towel in hand.

I'm a sniffling mess as I relax my hold on Ilmari. My hands drop from his shoulders to his elbows as I lean back, glancing up into his concerned face. His dark blue eyes are locked on me as he waits for me to speak.

Jake drapes the towel over my shoulders as I ask the question I've been practicing since I left my apartment. "Do you still have that job available?"

11
Tess

"Are you *sure* you won't change your mind?" Rachel presses, tucking her tablet into her backpack and zipping it closed.

"For the hundredth time, yes," I reply with a groan.

"Because it would only take a phone call to arrange it," she adds. "Plane ticket, hotel, box seats—the works. New Year's Eve in the Big Apple."

"As fun as that sounds, I really think I just need to take a minute and . . . regroup."

She gives me an appraising look, like she's waiting for me to crack.

I lean my hip against her kitchen island, crossing my arms, and stare right back.

It's the morning after my surprise arrival, and Rachel and her guys are busy packing up Ilmari's truck to head for the airport. They've got the Winter Classic game this weekend in New York City, which means I'll have their house to myself.

Well, me and the dog. He's currently chasing the guys around the front yard as they load all their gear into the truck.

"I promise I'll be fine," I say. "Honestly, I'm looking forward to it. I'll walk on the beach with the dog."

"Yeah, you gotta throw his ball at least once a day or he loses his freaking mind," says Jake, walking up to Rachel and slipping her backpack off her shoulder. "This your last thing, babe?"

She nods at him, and he slings it onto his shoulder, brushing his lips against her temple.

He looks like a dream in his tailored grey suit and black tie. Ilmari is dressed up too. Apparently, all the players have to be in a suit to get on the plane. It's an NHL rule. Rachel says they all change once they get airborne, meaning she gets a sexy strip tease while snacking on peanuts and Diet Coke. That image alone is enough to have me reconsidering her offer to join them.

"I put three pints of Cherry Garcia in the freezer for you," Jake calls. "And the dog food is in the pantry, left side bottom."

"Thanks, Jake," I reply. "Cherry Garcia is my favorite."

"He knows," Rachel and Caleb say at the same time.

With a smirk, Jake shoulders Rachel's bag and heads back down the hall.

Caleb lets him pass and then sweeps into the kitchen. He's dressed in his Rays polo and athletic pants. His tattooed arm stretches out across me as he reaches for a banana from the fruit basket. I gasp, leaning back, as he turns and tosses it wordlessly to Ilmari, who has quietly joined us.

I feel so in the way. They have a life here, and now I'm daring to just set up camp for the next . . . who knows how long. Days? Weeks? I told Ilmari I would help him get his nonprofit off the ground. It's not like I have anything better to do while I face the bullshit terms of my temporary leave.

"What?" says Rachel, reading me like a damn book.

"Nothing," I say, flashing Caleb a smile as he steps wordlessly past me.

"It's not nothing," she says. "Did you change your mind about coming with us?"

"No," I say, watching as Ilmari steps out too. "It's just a little weird, right?"

"What's weird?"

"Me being here. It's weird, right?"

She huffs a laugh. "Tess, we lived together for almost three years. I know your habits better than I know theirs."

"But that's my point," I press. "Rach, you *just* got married. You're all still figuring each other out. I'm in the way—"

"Don't," Rachel says, stepping around the island. "You're not gonna do this. You're not going to talk yourself out of staying."

"Rach—"

"I've been praying for this moment of clarity to hit you for three freaking years. And now that it has, we are *not* going backwards. Do you hear me? You'll go crawling back to Cincinnati over my dead body."

"Babe, we gotta go," Jake calls from the entryway.

"I'll be right out," she calls back. Then she's focused on me. "Listen, if you feel that weird about staying here, I have another place you can stay."

"Another place? You a real estate mogul now, Rach?"

She smirks. "No, it's Ilmari's old place. Cute little bungalow about fifteen minutes from here. Right on the Intracoastal—"

"I can't do that," I cry.

"Why not?"

"Well . . . because it's *his* house. Staying here with you and your guys feels weird but staying in Ilmari's house feels . . . weirder."

She slips her hand into her pocket. "It's not like he's using it. He lives here now, remember? He just hasn't sold it yet. Here—" She works a small silver key off her keychain and holds it out. "Consider it part of your package deal, Ms. Director of Operations. Keep in mind that free housing comes with obligatory dog-sitting . . . you know, when you're not turtle-sitting."

I can't help but smile as I reach out and take the key.

"I'll text you the address once I get in the car," she says.

"Thanks, Rach," I murmur, annoyed that stupid tears are stinging my eyes again. I'm going to make it one day without tears this holiday season, or I'll walk into the ocean and join the turtles permanently.

"Hey," she says, placing a hand on my shoulder. "I love you."

"I know," I reply with a watery smile. "What's not to love?"

"Exactly. That's what I've been saying for three years. You are a goddess, and you deserve to be worshipped and adored. Altars, burning of incense . . . maybe some ritual orgies."

"Will you just go?" I laugh, giving her a shove. "Or Mars is gonna drag you out."

"Are you staying?"

I close my fist around the key and nod.

"Good." Finally, she moves towards the door. "Oh, and hey," she calls over her shoulder. "There's a sauna out on the back patio, and it's divine. Give it a try."

I follow her through the kitchen and down the hall, narrowing my eyes at the back of her head. "You guys fucked in it, didn't you?"

"No comment," she replies with a laugh.

I just sigh. "Yeah, you fucked in it. 'Cause you're a horny little horndog who can't get enough."

"Can you blame me?" she teases, tugging open the front door. "You get yourself a hockey player and see if you can ever get enough."

"Is that an invitation?" I tease right back.

"Down, girl. The Rays are off limits, remember?"

My heart stutters a bit as I think of my dance with Ryan, the kiss I wanted but didn't get. Just as she's about to step out the door, my hand is reaching out, brushing her arm. "Hey—do you really mean that? Is it like a hard line in the sand for you?"

She turns, her gaze leveled at me. "Oh, Tess, what did you do?"

"Nothing," I cry, feigning indignation.

"Tess . . . "

"Nothing," I say again, laughing this time. But then I squeeze my boobs together and give her a saucy wink. "Yet."

"I fucking hate you," she says, shaking her head.

"You love me, remember? You just said it."

"When do you move out again?"

"Today. And I'm taking the dog with me," I tease.

"Just give him back on Sunday night or Caleb will cry," she says pulling the door shut.

Poseidon dances at my feet, drawn to the only company he has left. I'm flattered he thinks I'm more interesting than his overflowing basket of toys. He blinks up at me with those pretty blue eyes, his black and white tail wagging slowly side to side.

"What do you think, bubs? You ready to go on a little drive with me?"

That sets him off like a firecracker. He's a yipping, howling mess as he chases me up the stairs. I have no idea what the heck I'm doing with my life, but coffee and a beach walk with the dog sounds like enough of a plan for now.

And maybe I'll try the sauna tonight . . . after I disinfect it first.

11
Ryan

"Hey, man, can you put this up there?" Cade Walsh sticks his arm out towards me, reaching across the airplane seat to hand me his backpack. He's a third string forward and a rookie, but he keeps his elbows to himself and always travels with good snacks, so I let him be my seat mate.

I wordlessly take his backpack, shoving it into the overhead next to mine as my phone pings in my pocket. I reach for it as Novy shoves his way past behind me. "Jeez, asshole," I mutter, glaring at the back of his head.

"'Scuse me," says Morrow, sliding past too.

They've both been so weird since L.A. Novy is usually a big prankster, life of the party, even if he's also a moody asshole. And Morrow is one of the nicest guys on the team. Right now, their shoulders are set in frustration as they take opposite seats in the same aisle, crossing their arms like lovers in a tiff.

Whatever. Their bullshit is not my problem.

I open my messages app and tap the top message. It's from my agent, Mike Kline. Heart in my throat, I drop into my seat. I tap the new voice memo and listen.

"Hey, Ryan. I know you're probably already in the air," comes his bright voice. "But you can listen to this when you land—"

"Hey, Langers! Wanna play Mario Kart?" Sully shouts from two rows up.

"We're gonna smoke your ass!" says Perry from just behind me, punching my shoulder.

All around our section of the plane, the guys call out.

"I call Yoshi!"

"Give me a sec, and I'm in."

"You always play Yoshi, asshole—"

"Make him play Toad—"

"*Shh*," I rasp, ducking my head down. I tap the button on the side of my phone, turning the volume up all the way, and start the voice memo over.

"—already in the air, but you can listen to this when you land. You—"

"Dude, why are you in my lap?" Walsh gives me a shove.

"Shut up." I tap the little blue 'keep' so this message doesn't disappear.

MK is still talking. "—you can always call when—"

"Dude, come on. It looks like you're giving me a blowie. Get up," says Walsh, shoving me again.

"Langers, you in or out?" says Perry, peeking his face around the side of my seat.

"Fuck!" I launch to my feet. Spinning on my heel, I race down the aisle towards the back of the plane. I march right past the support staff, nearly tripping on the strap of Poppy's purse, before I'm in the galley.

"Sir, you need to find your seat," says the flight attendant.

"I gotta piss," I say, shoving at the lavatory door.

"Sir, you'll need to wait—"

I don't let her finish. I just squish myself inside the tiny lavatory and snap the door shut. Staring at my own reflection in the mirror, I replay the memo for a third damn time.

"Hey, Ryan. I know you're probably already in the air, but you can listen to this when you land," comes MK's voice through my earbud. "You got it! The endorsement deal is all yours, my friend. Nike is sending over the preliminary contract later today. You're looking at a tidy one mil before taxes, paid out in installments, of course. I sent over all the particulars in an email, but you can always call me when you land. Congrats!"

The message ends, and I just stand there, looking at my reflection. My white dress shirt is unbuttoned, collar loose. My blond curls are tucked behind my ears, slicked down with styling gel. I haven't shaved in a couple days—too busy with my mom and sister in town for the holidays—but I like the effect.

I look older. When did this happen? I used to look in the mirror and always just see a young hockey bro. The tourney t-shirts and backwards caps, the stupid shaggy flow.

I smirk. The man in the mirror smirks back at me. He has my eyes. A man with a multi-million-dollar NHL contract. A man who wears a bespoke suit and Tom Ford shoes with a TAG Heuer Monaco-style chronograph on his wrist. A man who just landed a million-dollar endorsement deal with Nike.

My smile widens as I feel my heart race.

"I did it," I say at my reflection.

I'm *doing* it. I'm living my dreams. Since I put on that first pair of skates at six years old, I've been climbing this mountain. I fought and sacrificed and trained for so long. And it hasn't been easy. Every card has been stacked against me from the beginning. We needed government aid to get me through school, charity to pay for my hockey equipment, scholarships to make it onto the right teams.

But I did it. I put in the work and sacrificed damn near everything to become a Division I athlete. Then I was named a first-round draft pick to the San Jose Sharks. Now I'm a Ray . . . and a Nike spokesperson.

We won't mention my brief stint as a shampoo model.

Ever.

My smile widens. Who am I kidding? The guys rag on me all the time. Two weeks ago, Novy played my commercial before the coaches rolled our game tapes. Everyone laughed and touched my hair. Let's see if they're still laughing when I tell them about this endorsement deal.

Knock, knock.

"Mr. Langley, you have to return to your seat," calls the flight attendant. "Now."

"Coming," I shout, tucking my phone in my pocket. I give my reflection one last look in the mirror before I make my way back to my seat for takeoff.

13
Ryan

Yankee Stadium is electric tonight as forty thousand hockey fans celebrate New Year's Eve. It becomes like a cage of white noise as I try to block everything out beyond the plexiglass, staying in the zone. The freezing winter air burns my lungs, sharp and metallic in my throat.

We're halfway through the second period and we're down by one. The Habs are playing like lions tonight. Their forwards are throwing elbows and making hard checks. It's bullshit because this is an exhibition game. There's no reason these guys need to be out here checking us so hard. If they don't back off, someone is gonna get hurt.

I'm puffing like a racehorse as I get into position for the face-off. Sully takes the center spot. Karlsson skates into position across the circle and gives me a nod. The player to his left is the worst one out here. I can see from the set of Karlsson's shoulders he's had enough of the rough play too. A word from us, and our defensemen will start bringing the heat. Let's see how much No. 82 likes getting smashed into the boards by the Novikov freight train.

The ref skates in and we all tense, ready for that puck to drop. My gaze is laser-focused on his hand. I grip my stick, breathing deep, counting the seconds.

Focus. Speed. Control.

It's my mantra. Focus on the puck. Move fast. Control your stick.

Eyes up.

The puck drops, and Sully just barely wins control of it, shooting it back to me. As soon as it hits my stick, I come alive, bursting with speed as I try to lose my shadow. But he's right on top of me. I can hear him breathing like a mastiff around his mouthguard, thick and slobbery. He shoves his stick in, nearly tripping me, trying to wrestle the puck away.

Fuck, you're gonna lose it.

I have to get it away from me. He's herding me towards the boards. He won't be gentle, and I can't take another hit. My hips and shoulders are already screaming from the beating I took in the first period. I need this shift to end. Now.

Eyes up.

I scan the ice and slap the puck hard. It flies across the ice to Karlsson, and I'm saved a slam into the boards. I scramble down the ice, following Karlsson and his aggressor as they chase the puck over the blue line. A defenseman is ready to apply pressure, and Karlsson has to think fast. He slips the puck between both players, a clean shot back to Sully, who brings it around the back of the net.

I know what he's doing, and I'm ready for it. He wants to pass it to me and offer me a corner shot on goal. But a blur of red comes blasting in from behind me, cutting off Sully's pass to me. We lose possession of the puck, and it goes hurtling down the ice out of the defensive zone.

The Rays defense is ready. Morrow and Novy are a pair of Canadian moose, and Mars is our Finnish bear in the net. Novy wrestles the puck away right in front of the crease and sends it screaming down the ice towards Karlsson.

Focus. Speed.

I push with everything I have, cutting up the ice with my blades to make my mark so Karlsson can pass it to me. I'm faster than my shadow. I tear down the ice, breaking free of him. I glance back just in time to see Karlsson get boxed in. He drops the puck back to Morrow.

Eyes up.

I turn my gaze to the plexiglass, and a head of red curls with a wide smile stops my heart in my chest. Her hand is pressed to the glass as she screams, eyes locked on me. She's here? How is she here—

The sudden flash of camera phones blind me, reflecting off the plexiglass and I blink, looking sharply away.

Focus—

"Langley!"

"Ahhh!"

Time stops as my body registers two things at once. First, I'm airborne. I float in suspended animation, the milliseconds slowing down, my legs swept out from under me. Second, I'm in a ton of fucking pain. It radiates from my knee, up my hip, down my shin. Fuck, it zaps me like lightning.

I clench down on my mouthguard hard enough to crack my teeth as I brace for impact. My helmet smacks the ice right at my temple. Shoulder. Hip. Knee. I cry out again, rolling to my side, my stick forgotten as I place both gloved hands on my knee trying to stabilize it. If something is broken, I need to hold it in place.

"Fucking asshole," I shout as the Habs forward scrambles to his feet.

"Sorry," he says as he skates off, chasing down the puck.

Panic swirls with my adrenaline. Both work to numb the pain as my knee suddenly forms its own heartbeat, radiating pain out in waves.

Not the knee. Please, God, not my fucking knee.

Without hockey, I'm nothing. My family needs me. My sister, my mother—I'm their only support. And hockey is the only way I'm ever gonna earn. If my knee is busted . . . this is the end . . .

Panic is winning out over adrenaline as I hear the whistle. They've finally noticed I'm down and not getting up. I know it's only been a few seconds. Somewhere beyond the plexiglass, Tess is watching me lie here on this ice. Was it Tess? Did I hallucinate her? I don't even know. Can't think about it now—

"Langley!" Sully gets to me first, sliding to a stop and dropping to one knee, his hand on my shoulder. "Langers, you okay, man?"

"What happened? Where is he hurt?" I hear Novy's voice, but I don't look up into the blinding stadium lights. They're all standing around me, casting my prone body in shadows as I pant, my hot breath making steam against the sheet of ice at my cheek.

"Oh fuck, it's his knee—"

"Langers, can you get up?"

Someone's hand is on my hip. He wants me to roll over onto my back. But I'm frozen, letting the pulsing pain in my knee paralyze me.

"Don't fucking touch me," I cry with a voice not my own.

"I'm so sorry," comes Morrow's voice. "I thought you had it. I'm sorry. It was a bad pass—"

"The asshole took you out at the fucking knees," Sully growls.

Yeah, I know. I was fucking there.

"Let's give him some space, fellas," calls the ref, ready to push my teammates back.

"Langley!" calls a new voice.

Doc and Assistant Coach Andrews are hurrying across the ice from the bench. Doc has her medical bag on her shoulder.

An EMT beats them to me. "That was a nasty hit, but you're okay," she soothes. "Where does it hurt? Your knee?"

A big guy in a matching EMT jacket is at my head. "We should stabilize his neck."

"Langley," Doc calls again.

Coach Andrews drops down on one knee next to her. "You're alright, Langley."

"Coach, the asshole fucking clipped him," Sully says.

"I know," says Coach. "We all saw it. Let's let the EMTs work."

"Let me look at it, Langley," Doc says.

I breathe out through my mouth in sharp pants as I drop my hands away, giving her leave to touch me.

"What's your pain level?"

"*Ungh*—seven," I groan. But then she presses in with her thumb, and I practically levitate off the ice. "Ahh—*fuck*—ten," I gasp. "It's a fucking ten. Don't do that again." My arm flails as I react instinctively, just wanting the pain to stop.

"Okay, it's okay," she soothes, catching my arm before I can hit her. I'll apologize to her later. "His left knee took all the impact of that hit," she says at the female EMT.

"And his head hit the ice first in his fall," the male EMT replies. "How you feeling, sir? You feeling dizzy at all? Look at me, please. Follow the light."

He shines a light in my eyes, and I groan.

"We need to get him off the ice," says Coach. "Can he walk off?"

"You got this, Langley," one of my teammates call.

But Doc shakes her head. "With that hard of a hit, we need scans to be safe. We need to rule out a break."

I let their medical talk float over my head like snowflakes caught in a flurry. I gaze up, my eyes focusing beyond the lights to the haze of the sky overhead. I'm flat on my back on an ice rink . . . in the middle of Yankee Stadium. Forty thousand people are watching me lie here.

"I can walk," I hear myself say. "Doc, help me." I rock forward with a groan, trying to sit up.

Her gentle hands push me back down. "Easy, Langley. You're getting a ride off the ice this time, okay?"

"Hang in there, Langers," says Sully, his face visible over the shoulder of Coach Andrews.

"You got this," Novy calls.

It's the work of moments before they have me on the stretcher and strapped down. I groan as the hydraulic lift shoots me into the air. I've never in my career been wheeled off the ice. It's humiliating, like I'm lying here naked instead of clothed in my full hockey kit.

"Where's my stick?" I mumble.

"Don't worry about it," says Coach, patting my padded shoulder.

I'm missing a glove. When did it come off? I feel the sharp winter chill on my fingertips. It stings so cold it burns. As if she can sense my problem, Doc steps in next to me, her bare hand taking mine. "It's okay, Ryan," she soothes. "I'm right here, okay? I'm going with you to the hospital."

This all happened because I lost focus for a split second. I saw a pretty face, and my brain skipped like a scratched vinyl record.

"Tess," I mutter. "She's here, right?"

Doc leans down over me. "What? I didn't hear you."

My head rolls to the right, and my vision goes hazy. I blink to clear it and peer through the plexiglass, looking for a freckled face and red curly hair. Tess is here. She distracted me. She's under my skin. She—

The pretty redhead at the glass wearing the Rays jersey looks stricken with worry as I pass by on my stretcher. Not *my* redhead. Not Tess. No, the woman behind the glass is too short, too thin. Dark eyes, not green.

But the mind sees what it wants to see.

"Not here," I mumble, turning away. "She's not here." My eyes close, and I feel like I'm sinking through the stretcher into warm water.

"Hey—Langley, stay awake for me, okay?"

Doc's voice sounds far away. Her grip on my hand is my tether. I'm a hot air balloon floating above the stadium, watching it all from on high. She calls at me from the ground, her hands cupping her mouth as she shouts through the din.

"Ryan, stay awake . . . "

I groan, wanting to do as she says. I'm a team player. I always do what I'm told. Doc says stay awake.

"Ryan . . . "

I'm a hot air balloon, and I'm floating . . . floating . . .

14

Ryan

Monitors beep and hum all around me, their lights blinking in the semidarkness. The IV in my arm itches like crazy. I want to scratch at it, but that will likely work it loose. Again. I already did it once tonight, which annoyed the nurses.

Yeah, I'm a terrible fucking patient.

And I hate hospitals even more than I hate airplanes.

I spent half my life in one as a kid, watching my dad fight a slow losing battle with cancer. It's hard to unpack the trauma associated with a place that gives life as often as it takes it away. For the longest time, I just had the memories of a grieving nine-year-old to inform my impressions. Time and distance have lessened my sense of primal fear, but there are some memories that embed themselves deep within the DNA.

Like the fact that all hospitals have the same smell. As soon as my stretcher rolled through the doors of the emergency room, I felt like that scared nine-year-old again. It's the faintly metallic smell of medical-grade cleaner that lingers on every surface. Mix in the scent of starched hospital sheets, add in a whiff of stale coffee, a whisper of drying paint, and you've got the hospital bouquet.

It's noxious.

Stifling.

Triggering.

I have to get the fuck out of here.

I look down at my left knee. It's wrapped up in a brace and propped from below by a pillow. My right leg is hidden under the thin hospital blankets. The bare toes of my left foot stick up, pointing to the ceiling. Apparently, I'm supposed to sleep like this, lying on my back with the brace on. I never sleep on my back. I don't even know if I *can* sleep on my back.

This night is gonna suck.

At least they've assured me I'll be discharged in time to join the team on the return flight to Jax. I don't want to be left behind. This night has been traumatic for me beyond the knee injury. I don't want to be alone.

As if in answer to an unspoken prayer, there's a knock at my door and Sully enters.

"Hey, there he is," he says with a wide smile. "How you feeling, man?" He steps around my bed to drop down into the empty chair.

"Whoa, you look like shit," Morrow says from the door, following him in. His words are teasing, but his eyes are hardened, his mouth set in a frown rather than his usual smile. He's still blaming himself for the bad pass that got me clipped.

"I'm fine," I reply to Sully's question, looking at Morrow. "Tired but fine."

Jake comes through the door last, my backpack slung on his shoulder and my overnight bag in his other hand. "My darling wife sent me with gifts," he says, holding up both bags. "Jeez, you look like shit, man. Probably smell like it too. Want your deodorant?"

He doesn't even wait for me to say 'yeah' before he's dropping both bags onto the other empty chair. He goes digging through my backpack, pulling out my Old Spice and tossing it over to me. I freshen up my pits as Sully helps himself to the pitcher of water on my bedside table.

"How's the leggo?" says Sully, gesturing to my swollen, aching knee.

"Doc says I have a second-degree sprain of my MCL," I reply.

Jake helps himself to a seat at the end of my bed. "What does that mean exactly?"

"How long are you off the ice?" Sully rephrases.

I shrug. "Doc says I'm looking at about four weeks of RICE. We don't want the tear to get any fucking worse."

We've each had enough injuries between us to know the RICE regimen: rest, ice, compression, elevation. I have to control the swelling. The rest is just pain management while the body heals itself.

Doc walked me through it all twice before she left, which I appreciated since they slipped me some good pain killers down in the ER.

Sully gives my shoulder a squeeze. "Four weeks is nothing, man. Easy time."

"Yeah, we'll hardly even get the chance to miss you," Morrow adds, the relief etched on his face. "The rookies will be at your beck and call. And you know the WAGs will fix you up with enough meals to last you through the rest of the season. It'll be like a vacation—"

"Wait, doesn't your place have like a shit ton of stairs?" says Sully.

I just shrug. "I mean, yeah. But I've managed on crutches before. It's really not a big deal."

"Dude, that dump you rent is a split-level," adds Jake. "There are stairs fucking everywhere. It's a death trap. You're not staying there."

"Guys, I'm fine. Four weeks, remember? And nothing's even broken—"

"Maybe a rookie can just take him in?" Sully says over me at Jake. "Walsh?"

"Walsh rents a one-room apartment and has a live-in girlfriend," I reply.

"Perry, then," Jake offers.

"Or Dave-O," counters Sully.

"Surely times aren't that desperate," says Morrow with a scoff. Then he sighs, shaking his head. "I mean . . . I guess you could stay with me. It's only four weeks, right?"

Both Sully and Jake turn to him with matching frowns.

"Wow. Heartfelt," Jake deadpans.

"Yeah, you had about as much enthusiasm as if you just offered to let him jizz in your shampoo bottle," says Sully.

I snort a laugh. "Thanks, but no thanks, Coley. I can only guess what kind of weirdness you and Novy get up to over there."

"Nov is moving out," he mutters, crossing his arms.

We all turn to him.

"Wait—what happened?" says Jake, eyes wide. "Did you guys break up?"

Sully chokes on a laugh.

"Shut up, asshole," Morrow snaps. "It's none of your business."

"Wait . . . *did* you?" Sully presses. "Like . . . are you two secretly a thing?"

"No way," Jake cries. "Hey, Cay and I aren't the only ones." He raises a hand like he's seeking a high five, but Morrow just groans.

"It's not like that, assholes. It was always meant to be temporary. You know, while they did the renos on his house," he adds with a shrug.

Novy bought a big bachelor pad of a beach house a few blocks down the street from Jake. They both have multi-year contracts with no-trade clauses. They can afford to put down roots and invest in things like kitchen renovations.

We all wait for Morrow to say more but he just glares. "It's just—look, this is about Langley's problem." He gestures back at me lying in the hospital bed. "He's the one who needs a place to stay."

"Oh god," Jake laughs, smacking his forehead. "I'm such an idiot."

"What?" asks Sully.

Jake looks to me. "I've got the perfect place you can stay. Furnished, close to the practice arena, and not a single stair."

"Where?" I say.

He slips his hand into his pocket and takes out his keys, working one off the ring. "Here, man."

I shift forward, taking the silver key from his hand. "What's this?"

"Key to Mars's house," he replies.

The three of us stare down at the key like it's a rare, unearthed treasure.

"I've never been to Mars's house," Morrow says, his tone almost reverent.

"Me either," says Sully. "I don't even know where it is. How do you have that?" he adds, eyes wide as he takes in Jake, like he's suddenly recalculating him and his potential.

Jake just laughs, then frowns. "Wait—are you assholes serious?" When none of us respond, he huffs again. "We got married, remember? In L.A.? You were all fucking there?"

"But . . . I thought it was like a 'Doc in the middle' kind of thing," Morrow says.

"Yeah, we didn't know you had a key to his place for . . . you know, just like . . . just you," Sully adds.

Jake scoffs. "You guys really need to brush up on your polyamory. I'm not fucking Mars, alright? And he's not fucking me," he adds, pointing a finger at Morrow who swallows his retort. "He's my metaphor."

Sully and I share a quick glance. "Your what?" I say.

"My metaphor," Jake repeats. "It's a polyam term."

"I really don't think it is," Sully says, trying to contain his smile.

I'm doing the same. I drop my gaze to my knee, which sobers me right up.

Jake crosses his arms over his broad chest. "I think I should know what I call Mars in our own marriage."

"Dude, a metaphor is like a figure of speech," Sully says. "Like 'life is a highway' or 'I'm so hungry, I could eat an elephant.'"

The corner of Jake's mouth quirks. "You're bullshitting me right now."

"Nah, man. I'm pretty sure that's right," says Morrow.

With a glare, Jake pulls out his phone. His thumb taps the screen, and we soon hear a dial tone as he puts the call on speaker.

"Fuck—what?" comes Sanford's voice. "I was asleep."

"Hey, solve something for us really quick. What's a metaphor?" Jake asks.

Sanford grunts, and there's a rustling sound like he's sitting up in his hotel bed. "What?"

"A *metaphor.*" Jake enunciates each syllable. "I'm sitting here with Langers and the guys at the hospital tryna tell them Mars is my metaphor, and they don't believe me that it's a real polyam thing so . . . "

There's a pause so pregnant you could feel it kick the air between us.

"Jesus fucking Christ," Sanford says at last. "Babe, a metaphor is a figure of speech like . . . fuck, I don't know . . . 'life is a highway'—"

Sully and I choke on our fists, trying to quiet our laughter, as Jake launches off the bed, taking the phone off speaker. "Well, then, what the fuck is Mars?"

It's all we can do to hold it together as Jake paces from my bed to the door. I don't dare look at the other guys. I just focus on my busted knee.

"Uh-huh," says Jake into his phone. "Yeah, alright, fine—okay, will you just chill? I'm on my way back, jeez." He drops the phone from his ear and hangs up. "Such a bossy asshole," he says under his breath. With a sigh, he glances up and looks between us. "So uhh . . . it's metamour. Not metaphor. Mars is my metamour."

"That's cool," says Sully. The man looks like he's about to give himself appendicitis from how hard he's trying not to laugh.

But Morrow has no such reserve. He just looks at Jake and shakes his head in stunned disbelief. "You must give the best fucking blowjobs of all time."

That breaks us. Sully and I roar with laughter. I laugh so hard it gives me a headache worse than the one I already had. Pretty soon I'm groaning, a sharp pain stabbing me behind the eyes.

"Oh, you have no idea," Jake says with a grin, taking it all in stride.

"Come on, Mr. Metamour," says Sully, pushing himself up out of the chair and moving around the end of my bed. "You too, Coley. Let's give Langers time to rest."

"You can't call me Mr. Metamour," says Jake with a glare. "Only Mars gets to call me that."

"I have a feeling hell will freeze over before Mars Kinnunen calls you Mr. Metamour," Morrow says with a laugh, scooping his soccer ball up off the floor.

"It's Mars *Price*, asshole," says Jake, punching Morrow's shoulder hard.

"Ouch—*fuck*—" Morrow turns on him, ready to take his own swing. The defensemen are always more physical with each other than us forwards.

"Easy," says Sully, stepping between them. "Save it for the ice, guys."

"Hey, what am I supposed to do with this key," I call to Jake's retreating form.

"Use it," he replies. "Until you're back on your feet."

"I'll have Shelbs alert the WAGs," Sully adds. As team captain, his wife Shelby is queen of the wives and girlfriends. I'm about to be buried under a mountain of homemade soups, cookies, and casseroles.

"But I don't even know where Mars lives," I call as Jake pulls open the door. "What's the address?"

Jake glances over his shoulder. "1006 Harbor Road. Oh, and he's got this awesome sauna thing out on the patio. Might help you loosen up that knee," he adds with a nod to my leg.

"See you tomorrow," Morrow calls, walking out the door first.

"Get some sleep, man," adds Sully. "We'll come bust you out of here first thing in the morning."

Get some sleep. Right. Lying on my back in a fucking hospital? With a sigh, I stretch out over the side of my bed and reach for my backpack. Pulling it onto my lap, I dig in the front pocket and take out my Nintendo Switch.

It's gonna be a long fucking night.

15
Tess

"Come on," I say, fussing with the settings on my phone.

The sauna on Ilmari's back patio has built-in speakers that let you connect via Bluetooth. I just have to get it to recognize my device. I've pressed the reset button twice. Now I'm trying to reset my phone too.

"Stupid piece of—*aha*—" I cut off my insult as I hear Dua Lipa's "Levitating" pulsing from inside the sauna.

Ilmari has a great patio. Like most Florida homes, it has a cage extending from the edge of the house and out over a micro pool with a stone pool deck. The only light out here comes from inside the pool, which glows an eerie pale blue.

I've done the odd steam room before, but until last night I'd never tried a sauna. It's safe to say I'm a convert. There's something about the smell of the wooden walls as they heat. It's the best kind of aromatherapy. I left the sauna last night feeling almost high. It was amazing. I've been waiting all day to do it again.

Well, the dog has been walked, I've got chardonnay chilling in the fridge, and I made myself an epic salad I intend to devour after this pamper session. I'll sit on Ilmari's super comfortable couch and watch his TV, and tonight I'm sleeping in his bedroom that looks and feels like an IKEA showroom.

This is my life now. New year, new Tess.

But first . . . the plunge.

"You can do it. In and out. Quick like a cat."

I've got my hair tied up in a messy bun and a beach towel wrapped around me as I eye the steps of the pool.

"Do it," I say again, nerves firing all over my body. "3—2—1—"

Dropping the towel to my feet, I squeal like a little girl and rush down the steps naked. I sink into Ilmari's freezing cold pool. There's a privacy fence that juts out to either side of the condo, blocking me from view of the neighbors. And I didn't turn any of the patio lights on, so even a creeper with binoculars wouldn't get much of a show.

"Fuck—*ahh*—this is the worst," I cry, teeth chattering. Tears sting my eyes as I feel my nipples sharpen to deadly points. In moments, I'm laughing, stumbling up out of the pool.

Leaving the towel on the ground, I wrench open the sauna door and step inside. The interior lights glow softly as the heater hums. I shut the door behind me, taking a deep breath of hot air. That scent of cedar fills my lungs as I close my eyes, loving the glorious sting of the heat as it kisses every inch of my dripping wet skin. I turn and sit on the soft, white towel I set out on the wooden bench. I stretch my arms out to the sides and then up, reaching for the ceiling.

The past two days, I've been doing sunrise yoga on the beach, and my body aches. It feels strange to have the time for yoga. My job is demanding, to say the least. Between the long hours, the travel, and the mandatory socializing with clients, exercise has always felt like a luxury I can't afford.

I hum along to the music for a few minutes before I start to get that dizzy feeling of overheating. Taking a deep breath, I hurry out of the sauna and walk straight back into Ilmari's pool. The cold water tingles against my burning skin, and I get that rush, that high that has me smiling ear to ear. I wade in the shallow end for a minute or two before I step out and hop right back in the sauna.

I continue my cycle of hot sauna and cold pool for three more songs before I feel ready for a glass of wine. Leaving my towel behind, I saunter naked into the condo and head for the refrigerator. The heat from the sauna all but dried the water off my skin, so it's not like I'm dripping wet.

And look, I'm a girl of simple tastes. I like cheap wine and expensive cheese. I've got four bottles of chardonnay chilling in the fridge that I picked up at Publix on a buy-one-get-one sale. They've got the screw top caps and everything. I don't need a cork slowing me down.

I can just barely hear the music outside as I sway to the beat, pouring myself a glass of the chilled wine. The only light on in here comes from above the stove, casting out a soft yellow glow.

I glance over my shoulder to the living room to see Poseidon passed out on his checkered donut pillow. I kept him busy all weekend with trips to the beach and the coffee shop. He's been a good—

I gasp as he suddenly leaps off his pillow, wide awake and barking his head off, his teeth bared.

"Sy, what—"

My words stop short as I nearly drop my glass of wine. My gaze is locked on the wall of glass leading out to the patio. A man is standing there. He's wearing a dark hoodie with his hood pulled up, his face in shadow. I'm looking at him and he's looking at me while the dog barks like crazy. His reflection wavers as he moves, and I realize Sy is facing the entryway, not the glass wall.

That's when I scream.

The man isn't out on the patio. He's *inside* the house.

16

Ryan

I'm staring at the reflection of Tess Owens in the glass wall, my heart frozen in my chest.

A *naked* Tess Owens.

Fuck, why is this woman always naked? And why is she here of all places?

We paint an odd picture in the glass. The lighting is just right to show me standing in the middle of the entryway on my crutches and her standing in the kitchen holding a glass of wine. We're separated by a wall that stops just a few feet ahead of me.

She sees me and I see her and that's when she screams. The dog is already barking, and its pandemonium as I watch her reflection spin around, no doubt looking for a weapon. I wouldn't put it past her to come around the corner swinging a frying pan.

"Tess!" I shout, shuffling forward on my crutches.

Meanwhile, the dog keeps barking.

"Get the fuck out!" Tess screams, still lost to her terror as she spins around holding a kitchen knife. "I'm calling the police right now!"

"Jesus—fuck—" I grunt, swinging down the short hallway. "Tess, put down the knife. It's *me*. It's Ryan."

I turn the corner and fumble with the crutches as I free one hand and jerk my hood back, letting my messy head of blond curls free.

She's standing there in all her naked glory, brandishing a knife, looking fierce as a red-haired warrior goddess. I have no doubt she'd tear me apart with that thing. Fuck, why is it making me hard? It's gotta be the pain meds. My dick is drunk on codeine and thinks she's the most beautiful thing we've ever seen.

She *is* the most beautiful thing. Those wide green eyes are locked on me with all the ferocity of a she-wolf. Her curls are tied up in a big bun on her head and her perfect skin is flushed an angry shade of red. It's splotchy across her chest, down her arms, her thighs.

What the hell? Was she sunbathing in January? It's like fifty degrees outside.

No, she's sweaty like she was just working out. Naked?

And then it hits me.

Oh, fuck.

She's not alone.

I glance over my shoulder, waiting for whatever hotshot she's here with to come strolling in from the bedrooms looking full of himself and satisfied. I hate him.

"Oh—Ryan," she says, her voice cracking with relief. But it quickly turns to anger. "You scared the fucking shit out of me," she shrieks. "How the hell did you get in here? How do you *always* get in?"

"Through the front door," I reply, my voice raised to match hers.

"It was locked!"

"I have a key—"

"How?" she cries, tears in her eyes. Fuck, I really did scare her. She's shaking with it. I'd try to comfort her, but she's still holding that damn butcher's knife.

"Jake," I say simply. "He gave me a key. It's in my pocket if you want to check," I add, nodding down to my right front pocket of my grey sweats.

I try to avoid looking at her peaked nipples, but I can't help it. They're so pink and perfect. Was Mr. Hotshot touching them? Surely, he got a taste—

Stop.

The anger fades in her eyes, replaced quickly with concern as her gaze settles on my crutches. Then the knife goes clattering down to the counter. "Oh god, what happened to you?"

I'm oddly stung by her unintended dismissal. She doesn't know. She wasn't at the game. She didn't even watch it on TV. Which means she didn't see the hit. She didn't see me lying on that ice—

Actually, now I'm glad. I don't want her seeing me like that.

"I'm fine," I say.

"You're not fine," she retorts. "You're on crutches, Ryan. What happened?" She steps closer, her nakedness now within my reach.

I grip tighter to the handles of my crutches. "I got clipped during the game," I explain. "It's nothing. Just a knee sprain—"

Her eyes go even wider, her brows arching high. "A knee sprain?" She reaches for me. "Let me help you."

I stiffen, readying myself for the feeling of electric shock that is her touch. "M'fine," I mumble, not daring to watch her hand glide up my arm.

"Stop saying you're fine. You look dead on your feet, and you're swaying like you're about to fall over. Come sit down on the couch."

"I'm just tired," I admit, letting her lead me over to the living room.

It's been a hell of a long day, starting with a night of no sleep and an 8:00 a.m. hospital discharge, followed by a two-hour mechanical flight delay in New York and a weather rerouting over Virginia that added an hour to our flight time.

I wanted to just go home, but the guys wouldn't hear a word about it. Morrow dropped me off here. Two rookies are at my house packing up some of my shit to hand off to Jake, who will come over with a grocery delivery later. Then Sully's wife will be here tomorrow to finish stocking the fridge. They've all settled it. All I get to do is just let it happen.

Tess helps lead me over to the couch, and I sink down onto it with a groan. Big mistake. Now the world's most gorgeous woman is standing over me naked, her pussy right in my eye line. My gaze locks on the soft thatch of trimmed curls pointing down like an arrow.

This is cruel and unusual punishment.

Tess seems wholly unbothered. "Why are you here, Ryan?"

"I could ask the same of you," I counter, putting a hand up as if I can block her pussy from view. Fuck, I'm too tired to deal with this right now. And Mr. Hotshot will probably come swaggering out here any minute. I bet he's using Mars's shower like he owns the place. I fucking hate him.

"What are you doing?" she says, looking down at my raised hand.

"Could . . . umm . . . can you maybe cover with something?"

"Cover?"

"Yeah, you're a lot of naked, Tess."

She smirks down at me. "You didn't seem to mind it last time. In fact, I got the rather distinct impression you liked seeing me naked."

"Yeah, well, last time you weren't slicked with the sweat of some other guy," I say dropping my hand down.

She goes still, her smile switching to a glare. "Excuse me?" Then she huffs, crossing her arms over her breasts, one hip cocked to the side. "What exactly do you think is happening here? You think I'm hiding a guy back there?"

"Well, you look like you just got fucked six ways to Sunday," comes my muttered reply. Maybe if I wasn't on so many painkillers, I could finesse this better. No, fuck finesse. I'm too upset. She's under my skin. The thought of her with someone else has me seeing red. "You're wandering around Mars's place like you live here—"

"I *do* live here," she snaps. Then she's stepping forward, putting herself between my spread legs. She grabs my chin, tipping my gaze up to meet hers. "And let's get one thing crystal fucking clear. You don't own me, Ryan Langley. We've kissed and we've danced, and we've flirted, but I am my own fucking person. I'm not beholden to you or anyone. And this shitty jealousy is a huge turn off for me. So, I suggest you pack it away if you *ever* want a snowball's chance in hell of seeing me naked again."

Her speech over, she drops her hand away from me and leans even closer, her breasts swaying in my face. I can smell something aromatic on her skin, like incense or an herbal soap. As quickly as she's there, she's gone, jerking something off the back of the sofa from behind my head. It's a sofa blanket. She takes it and quickly wraps it around herself like a toga, flicking the tasseled end over her shoulder.

"There. Happy?"

"No," I groan, sinking back against the cushions of the couch. I can still see every inch of her curves. Now they're just artfully draped. And those damn nipples are still perfect peaks, poking against the soft fabric of the grey blanket.

"And for your information, there's no one else here," she declares. "I wasn't getting fucked, Ryan. I was in the sauna. Now, if you'll excuse me, I left my phone outside. I'm calling Rachel and figuring out what the hell is going on."

She steps past me in her blanket toga with all the confidence of a queen. Opening the sliding glass door, she disappears out onto the patio. The dog follows her. The door whispers shut, leaving me alone in Ilmari's house.

Awesome. This is just fucking perfect. I've been here two minutes, and I've already upset her. That has to be some kind of record, right?

I glance around the condo, my eyes quickly taking in all the clues I missed during our surprise exchange. It's easy with Mars's minimalist decor to note what is out of place. There's the bottle of wine on the counter, fresh flowers in a vase on the kitchen island, snacks lined up under the microwave. There's also a laptop set up on the kitchen table. A legal pad rests next to it. All the evidence of someone taking this place and making it their own. Tess *is* living here.

Wait—why is Tess living here? Doesn't she have some big, high-powered job up in Cincinnati?

Well, it was a good idea in theory, but it looks like I won't be staying here after all. After the way I just showed my ass in front of her, I'm not surprised she's upset. I could blame it all on the painkillers, but that would be a lie. My irrational jealousy was real. It surprised me as much as Tess. She doesn't owe me anything. And I've never been the territorial type before.

What the hell is happening to me?

I know what's *not* happening. I'm not moving in with Tess Owens. Life simply isn't that cruel . . . or that kind.

17 Tess

I stomp out onto the back patio, my entire body humming with nerves. That's twice now that Ryan Langley has caught me off guard. Don't get me wrong, I like being naked, but I don't typically show my body off to men I've just met. Now Ryan has seen me naked, not once, but *twice*.

What's that saying? Third time's a charm?

"Yeah, good luck getting a third time out of me, buddy," I say to no one at all.

The look in his eyes just now was a total surprise. In Jake's kitchen, there was only want and hunger. He liked what he saw. He craved it. If I wasn't battling a sandy ass crack and sunburned shoulders, I may have even taken things further than a kiss. He's sweet and cute and so ridiculously fit I want to cry . . . or beg. I mean, you could cut glass on those sexy hip bones.

But tonight, there was a different look in his eyes. Possession. Need. *Anger*.

That last one threw me for a loop. The anger rolled off him like a surging storm. He thought I was wandering around the house, freshly fucked, flaunting myself in front of him.

I'm done with possessive men who think they get to own me. If Ryan keeps up this attitude, he'll see me fly before he ever sees me naked again.

Unless he's your roommate.

The thought flashes through my mind and I bat it away, glancing down at my phone.

RACHEL (7:45 p.m.): MISSED CALL

RACHEL (7:50 p.m.): MISSED CALL

RACHEL (7:51 p.m.): Girl, answer your phone. Major crossed wires happening over here!

RACHEL (7:54 p.m.): MISSED CALL

RACHEL (7:55 p.m.): Please don't freak out, but apparently Jake told Langley he could stay there too. He didn't know you were already there.

RACHEL (7:56 p.m.): Don't worry, I'll fix this. OMW

I sigh, shaking my head. At this point it's all just par for the freaking course. I glance up to see Ryan still sitting inside on the couch. He's in profile, not looking my way. He looks exhausted and miserable. And he's hurt. A knee sprain, he said. I didn't even ask him how bad it is or how long he'll be off the ice. Hockey is the only thing these guys care about. It's their whole world. He has to be reeling a bit too.

The doorbell rings, and both he and the dog jump with surprise, their heads turning towards the front door. Ryan reaches for his crutches, wincing as he tries to get up.

I launch into motion, pulling open the patio door. "I'll get it," I say. "It's just Rachel."

He sinks back onto the sofa with a groan, not looking my way.

I hurry across the living room, the tail of my blanket dress dragging across the floor. Poseidon dances at the front door, whimpering with excitement, like he knows who waits on the other side. I pull open the door, and he darts past me, yipping for joy to see his family again.

Mars and Jake are here too. Rachel looks anxious, Jake looks guilty, and Mars is pissed. As one, they take me in, three sets of eyes trailing from my face, down across my blanket dress, and back up.

Jake's face splits into a grin. "Well, that happened fast." He glances to his partners. "I guess we have no problem here then, right? So, everyone can just stop being mad at Jake now."

"Hush," Rachel says with a wave of her hand. "Tess, oh my god, what did you—"

"Will you get your head out of the gutter? I wasn't having sex," I cry indignantly. "I was in the sauna." I spin on my heel and march back into the house. Ignoring Ryan, I sweep into the kitchen and snatch up my glass of wine, taking a deep swig.

The Prices say their 'hellos' to him as I step up to the edge of the sofa, not sitting down. The three of them stand there, Rachel and Jake in front, Ilmari framing them from behind with his arms crossed over his barrel chest.

"So apparently we got our wires crossed a bit here," Rachel begins. "Tess, I gave you a key when we left and said you could stay here as long as you needed." Her gaze shifts slowly to look at her husband. "Apparently, Jake said the same to Ryan without telling anyone—"

"Oh my fucking god, don't get me started again," Jake huffs. "You did the same thing, babe. You didn't tell anyone you gave her a key—"

"It just hadn't come up yet," she retorts, hands on her hips. "We were all a little busy with the Winter Classic, remember? It didn't seem necessary to chase you out onto the ice and horse-collar you just to tell you I gave Tess a key to a house none of us live in—"

"Horse-collaring is a football tackle," he shouts. "In hockey it's called 'holding'—"

"That is so far beyond the point—"

"It *is* the point! You're married to three hockey players—"

"Enough," Ilmari barks, his gaze darting between them. "How did either of you get a key? That's *my* question."

"Caleb," they say at the same time.

"He made us all keys just in case we needed them," Rachel explains.

"Yeah, what's yours is mine now, asshole," Jake adds. "Metaphors, remember?"

"Ohmygod, it's *metamour*," Rachel cries. "We can't keep correcting you—"

"Fuck! I hate that fucking word." He glares at Mars. "I hate calling you a metamour, Mars. It's weird and confusing and I just—I fucking hate it."

"I never asked you to call me that," Ilmari replies.

"We gotta pick something better," Jake presses. "Why can't I just call you my husband?"

"I never said you couldn't," he says softly.

Jake sucks in a sharp breath. "Wait, oh my god, are you serious right now?" He looks to Rachel, all the anger blown from his sails. "Babe, is he serious?"

"He's always serious," Rachel replies, her anger receding, too, as she glances between them.

"It's my factory setting," Ilmari adds, slowly crossing his arms again.

"No way. Don't fucking do that," says Jake. "Don't make a joke now. Mars, are you serious? Can I call you my husband? I might cry in front of these guys if you say yes," he adds, gesturing with a wave at me and Ryan.

We share an awkward glance. Maybe Ryan and I should just go wait this out in the sauna.

"Call me whatever you want," Ilmari says at last.

"I mean, Cay's my husband," Jake says. "Like, my *husband* husband. Like, we're legally married."

"I know," says Mars. "I was there."

"But you could be my husband too," Jake says gently. "In a purely friends way," he adds.

"I said call me whatever you want," Ilmari repeats with a shrug.

Jake gazes at him for a minute. Finally, he breaks away with a shrug of his own. "Nope. Not happening. I'm not calling you my husband until you beg me for it. We'll find another word to use as a placeholder."

Ilmari's scarred brow lifts slightly. "A placeholder?"

"Yep," Jake replies. "'Cause the day *will* come when you'll beg me for it. Could be tomorrow, could be ten years from now. I'm patient. I'll wait."

"Is that a threat or a bet?" Ilmari replies, smirking.

"Ooookay," says Rachel, holding up both hands between them. "Let's continue this at home, yeah? We gotta deal with this," she adds, gesturing to me and Ryan. "I mean, I hate to do this, but Ryan, Tess *was* given a key first so . . . "

"It's no problem. I'll go," says Ryan from the couch. "I'll call Perry or Dave-O and have them come pick me up."

"You're not rooming with Davidson for the next four weeks," Jake counters. "We shack you up with him, you'll kill him inside of two days. The guy may be a sieve, but he's our sieve. We need him."

"For now," Mars adds.

"Perry, then," says Ryan. It's his voice that hooks something deep in me. He sounds so tired, so physically and emotionally drained.

"It's fine," I hear myself say, my hand clutching to the front of my blanket dress.

They all glance over at me, even the dog who stands dutifully at Rachel's side.

"Seriously?" says Jake.

"Tess, it's not a big deal," says Rachel. "There are plenty of other places he can stay. We're just trying to find him someplace with minimal stairs while he's on the crutches."

"I told you, I'm fine," says Ryan.

"And I told *you* to shut up," Jake counters. "This is happening. Deal."

"He can stay here," I say.

"Tess . . . " Rachel says in warning, shaking her head.

"What, there's two bedrooms, right?" I say with a shrug. "And he's already here. And he's tired," I add, glancing down at him. His exhaustion is written in every line of his face. My poor sunshine puppy from the beach is now looking like a stray left out in a box in the rain. "As long as he doesn't expect to get fucked six ways to Sunday," I add.

He groans, looking away. I'm glad he's embarrassed. It means the sweet puppy is still in there. He was just momentarily possessed by a junkyard dog.

"Won't be a problem," he mutters.

"Tess, you're an angel," says Jake with a relieved sigh. "It'll be so much easier if we can just keep him here. It's close to the practice rink and the rookie apartments. And you won't have to do a thing," he adds quickly. "The rookies and WAGs will take care of everything."

"WAGs?" I repeat.

"Wives and girlfriends," Ryan explains, not looking at me.

"Yeah, Queen Shelby will be here in the morning to stock the fridge," says Jake. "All the WAGs will prep his meals. And I bet you can ask them to clean up a bit too," he adds, glancing around. "Or leave it for the rookies. We'll have someone check on him every day and drive him to PT until Seattle clears him to drive himself."

"Which will be when?" Ryan asks, his tone pleading.

"Give yourself a week," Rachel replies. "Just rest, ice, and elevate."

"I've got all your stuff out in the truck," Jake says at Ryan. "I'll go get it. Mars, make sure the guest room has sheets on the bed," he calls over his shoulder as he jogs off.

Mars just sighs. I can only imagine how much he likes being bossed around in his own house. He flashes Rachel a long-suffering look and she smiles, giving his hand a squeeze as some unspoken agreement passes between them. Ilmari wanders off in the direction of the bedrooms.

"I'll get you an ice pack," Rachel says, heading to the kitchen with Poseidon on her heels.

That leaves Ryan and me alone in the living room.

"You don't have to do this," he says softly. "Really, I can go."

I place my hand on his shoulder. "Stay. I want you to stay."

With a heavy sigh, he leans into my hand. After a moment, he tips his face up slightly, letting his lips graze the inside of my wrist. It's not a kiss, but it's not nothing either.

I try to ignore the way it makes my heart beat faster.

18

Tess

Rachel and her guys clear out, taking the dog with them. I give Ryan his space once I see that he's set up in the guest room, his leg balanced on top of a pillow, a bag of ice perched atop his knee. He's playing some kind of game on his phone that makes loud go-kart racing sounds.

It's odd, but just knowing Ryan's here is bringing me comfort. I'm going to log this away under the label 'Gemini Problems.' It's the extrovert in me. I don't like being alone. I spent so much of my young life alone by nature of my circumstances—abandoned by my mother, ignored by my relatives, too poor to join the cool after school clubs, and too embarrassed to invite friends over when I didn't know whose couch I'd be crashing on from week to week.

I think that's why losing Rachel has been so hard for me. I try not to say anything because I know how happy she is now, but going from having her in my life every day to staring at the void of her empty room has been awful. She told me to rent it out, but I just couldn't bear to think of someone else sharing my space.

What can I say? I'm an extroverted introvert with truly impressive trust and abandonment issues. But man, do I know how to pick a quality cheese.

Now Ryan is here, and it's unsettling me that I don't mind. What is it about this hockey boy that I keep letting him in? I let him flirt with me, let him kiss me. Now he flashes me one glance of those hurt puppy eyes, and I let him move in across the hall.

I lean over in my kitchen chair and glance down the dark hallway. A soft strip of golden light glows at the bottom of his bedroom door. It's been a couple hours since he got here. Checking the time, I'm shocked to see its nearly midnight.

What is he doing in there? Shouldn't he be asleep by now? He was dead on his feet hours ago. And I heard Rach walking him through his pain management routine before she left. He's got enough pills on his bedside table to drop an elephant.

He's probably asleep, too tired to turn out the light.

He's a grown man, Tess. Leave him alone.

Righting myself in my chair, I turn my attention back to my glass of wine and my show. Ryan Langley is not my problem. He's the solution to my problem . . . he just doesn't know it yet.

TO my credit, I last about fifteen minutes. That's ten minutes longer than I would normally last, thank you very much. I finish my episode of *Bridgerton*, and then I'm up out of my chair, snapping my laptop shut.

Ignoring the bossy voice in my head telling me to leave him alone, I inch down the dark hallway. His door is cracked open. I take a step closer and peek in.

Ryan is shirtless, sitting up in bed. Holy mama, I forgot how ripped he is. His boyish blond hair is mussed. It's the hair that ages him so young. He's in his early twenties, but his college frat boy hair gives him a look like he isn't old enough to order a shot of Jäegermeister.

I shift my weight, and the floor creaks loud enough to wake the dead. I duck back, but it's too late. He glances up sharply, his eyes locking on mine.

"Tess?" he calls out.

I wait a beat and then push open his door. "Hey," I call, keeping my voice soft. "Just checking on you. I figured you fell asleep with your light on. I was gonna turn it off," I say, gesturing at the lamp in the corner.

"You can turn it off if you want," he replies.

I step into the room, leaving the comfort of the dark hallway. "Why are you still awake?"

"Can't sleep," he replies.

"Aren't the pain meds supposed to help with that?"

He shrugs. "I'm not taking them."

I drop my hand away from the lamp. "Why aren't you taking your meds? You've gotta be in pain, right?"

"I don't like the way they make me feel. The pain's not so bad compared to the stomach cramps from the meds."

I put my hands on my hips. "Am I gonna have to tell Rachel that you're being noncompliant with her rehab routine?"

"I *am* being compliant," he replies, gesturing to his knee. "Look. This is me being fucking compliant, and I'm fucking miserable about it, okay?"

"Are you uncomfortable? Do you need another pillow?"

"Of course I'm uncomfortable," he huffs. "I can't fucking sleep like this. It's been two fucking days."

"You can't sleep with the brace on? Does it hurt or—"

"I can't sleep on my back," he corrects. "I can't—I don't ever sleep on my back. But all the docs say I have to keep my leg like this to protect my MCL from any pressure or twisting. So, I can't fucking sleep."

He looks so perfectly miserable. I don't even realize that I'm crossing the room towards him. "Oh, Ryan," I say with a sigh, reaching out to brush his messy hair back from his brow. "What are we gonna do with you?"

"Put me out of my misery."

I smirk. "I don't think things are quite that dire."

"I'm going out of my fucking mind," he admits, a slight catch in his voice. The poor man is past the point of exhaustion.

Alright, it's time for someone to take charge of this situation. Geminis love a good problem to fix. "Well, okay," I say, hands on my hips as I glance around the room. "I don't think it's a matter of you not being able to sleep on your back. I think we just have to set you up for success."

"Tess . . . "

"Step one, turn off the video games," I say, plucking his phone off his lap.

"Hey—"

"Studies show that phone use before bed disrupts your sleep cycle."

He crosses his arms over his bare chest and glares at me. "Oh, yeah? Name one."

I turn away from him, searching the bedside table for his phone charger. "Johnson and Bernstein 2002. It was a sleep study done up at Mayo. Groundbreaking stuff." I turn off his game and plug the phone in.

"You totally just made that up."

"Of course I did. I'm a corporate mergers and acquisitions lawyer, Ryan. Not a sleep specialist."

"So, you admit you have no qualifications to help me fall asleep," he presses, a glint in his eye. He's liking this. Truth be told, I am too.

"Sit up," I reply. "We're gonna get you horizontal."

He laughs. "And now to distract me from your lack of qualifications, you're trying to use your feminine wiles to get me horizontal. Are you gonna have your way with me, Tess?"

I jerk the pillow out from behind his head.

"Ouch—*shit*—" He catches himself before he falls back and hits the headboard.

"Sweet puppy, you listen to me now," I tease. "If you think you have what it takes to ride this rollercoaster, you are sorely mistaken. In your current state, you wouldn't make it up the first hill. There will be no having my way with you tonight. There will only be sleep."

Now he's smiling. "Not tonight . . . but tomorrow is another day. And I'm game if you are."

"You have to live to see tomorrow," I counter. "And at this rate, you're about to fall dead from exhaustion. Now shimmy down a bit and lie down." I help him situate, fixing the pillow under his knee as we get him into a much more relaxed incline. "How do you sleep on all those planes?" I ask, unfolding the throw blanket and laying it over him.

"I curl up on my side," he replies, his biceps flexing as he pokes and prods the pillow into shape under his head. "I sleep best on my stomach, though. So usually, I just don't sleep. I play video games and listen to audiobooks and stuff."

Stepping over to the corner, I click off the lamp. "Better?" I say into the dark.

He's quiet for a minute. "Yeah," comes his soft voice.

"Think you can sleep now?"

"I—yeah," he says quickly.

"What?"

"It's nothing. It's dumb. I'll try to sleep."

"Come on, Ryan," I tease. "You've seen me naked twice now. I have no secrets from you. Don't keep secrets from me."

He shifts on the bed. "I, uhh . . . your voice is soothing," he admits. "Could you maybe stay a bit longer and . . . maybe talk to me a little?"

I can't help but smile. He's just so damn sweet. "There's no chair in here," I reply. "And Tess Owens doesn't sit on hardwood floors. Let me go get a chair from the kitchen—"

"That's dumb. Just sit on the bed," he replies, pushing up on his elbows to try and look at me through the dark.

"You're on the bed."

"It's a queen-sized bed, Tess. There's room for both of us. What if I promise to keep my hands to myself?"

"Do I have to promise the same?"

I don't even know what made me say it. The banter just pops out around him. The same thing happened at the wedding. It's like each time we meet, he gets more comfortable in his own skin, more comfortable with me too. The fumbling boy I met on the beach is gone, and in his place is this flirty man who asks for what he wants. I like it. I like the idea that he's different once you get to know him.

He lets out a strangled sound from the bed, flopping back onto the pillow. "No," comes his soft reply.

Poor hockey boy is in agony, wanting something he can't have.

And that something is me.

Stupid butterflies flutter in my chest. I stomp those bitches down hard and fast. "Okay, Ryan. Here's the deal. I will sit on this bed with you for exactly fifteen minutes, and I will talk at you, and you will not respond. You are to be trying to fall asleep, understood?"

"Yeah, that's totally cool," he says, unable to hide the eagerness from his tone.

"Don't get too excited. I'm gonna walk you through my hair routine in excruciating detail. We're talking hair masks, keratin sprays, detanglers, leave-in curl products. And I will not touch your dick or any part of you remotely close to your dick," I add, my tone firm. "So let go of that fantasy right now."

"Got it. Yeah, I won't say a thing. And no dick touching."

I step around the other side of the bed and crawl onto it, careful not to jostle him too much as I lie down. I curl on my side facing towards him and he turns his head too, looking at me.

"Let's start with my weekly routines," I say, keeping my voice soft. "So, once a week, I deep condition my curls with a moisturizing hair mask. And I treat my scalp to a coconut oil massage, which helps promote good blood flow and strong hair follicles."

"Hmm," he says, his head turning away as he closes his eyes. "That's it."

"That's what?"

"The scent that's been haunting me since beach day," he replies, his words slurred by fatigue. "In my mind I was calling it piña colada. It's coconut. My coconutty dream girl."

My heart stops, and the butterflies all take a knee. Dream girl? I wait for him to say more, but he doesn't. He just breathes in and out, his body relaxing into the bed.

I lean closer to him. "You realize you lasted exactly seven seconds after swearing to a vow of silence, right? I have no choice but to leave. We can't have you thinking actions don't have consequences—"

"Stay," he says, reaching out to grab my hand. He laces our fingers together, pulling my arm across his stomach. "You were talking about scalp massages."

"Mhmm," I reply, swallowing down the emotion in my throat.

"I've never had a scalp massage."

"Give me my hand back," I whisper.

His fingers tighten around mine. "No. You'll leave."

I smile. "I won't leave. Give it back, and I'll pet your head."

He lets go of my hand, and I brush it up his bare chest, letting the tips of my fingers graze his warm skin. Using a gentle touch, I stroke my fingers over his soft hair. I scrape lightly along his scalp with my nails.

He groans, following my touch. "Keep talking. Hair mask."

I curl my other arm under my head, continuing to pet him as I talk him through my hair mask routine. He doesn't last five minutes before he's crashed out asleep.

19
Ryan

The sound of my phone buzzing on the side table wakes me up. Each vibration sends it skittering along the dark wooden surface. I snatch for it one-handed. I don't even pause to read the caller ID.

"Hello," I grunt, my voice hoarse with sleep.

"Good morning! How's it going, Langley?" comes the way too chipper voice of Shelby O'Sullivan.

"Morning," I reply.

"Oh, did I wake you?"

"S'fine," I mutter. "I should be up anyway."

On the other end of the line, she laughs. "Sounds like someone had a long night."

Her words kickstart my brain. The events of the previous night come rushing back to me, and I almost give myself whiplash with how quickly I turn to look at the other side of the bed.

Tess is gone.

Of course she is. Did I really expect her to spend the night with me? Still, it was so nice to fall asleep to the sound of her voice, the feel of her gentle touch. I don't like how much I'm frustrated not waking up next to her too. I've gotta deal with this crush before I do something truly embarrassing like beg her to hold me. Maybe Doc will let me sweat it out in a brutal PT session today.

Fuck, Shelby is still talking at me a mile a minute. She's been talking this whole time.

"—about ten minutes out from the house, and I just thought I'd call ahead to make sure you had time to get yourself ready to open the door."

I sit up, feeling stiff all over. "Ten minutes," I echo.

"I've got all the goodies here for you, and some of them are even nutritionist-approved."

"Sounds good."

Outside in the hall, I hear a door shut. Tess is up and moving around. I don't want to miss her if she's about to leave. I jerk the blanket off me and swing my legs off the side of the bed, reaching for my crutches.

"—and Josh arranged to have Lauren Gerard come pick you up for your PT at 9:00 a.m.—"

"Yeah—hey, Shelbs," I say, raising my voice. "I need to hop off here and go ask my roommate something really quick."

"Oh, I'm sorry—wait—roommate? Is Mars staying at the house still? Did he move back in? Ohmygod, is something wrong between them already?"

The speed at which this woman flips from unbothered to unhinged is truly astounding. One whiff of gossip, and all the WAGs pounce like a pack of feral hyenas. It would be easy to complain, but we all know the actual players are even worse.

"No," I say, wobbling on one foot like a drunk flamingo. "It's not Mars, Shelbs. The Prices are fine. More than fine. They were here last night. You'll meet her when you get here—"

"Wait—*her*?"

Shit.

"Ryan Langley, do you have a puck bunny in that house?"

"I'm hanging up now."

"—can't believe you. Don't think I won't tell Josh. Your first priority should be your recovery, not adding notches to your bedpost—"

"Okay, byeeee," I say, drawing out the "e" as I hang up on her.

I tuck my phone into my pocket and swing forward on my crutches, not bothering to get a shirt. I hurry into the main room and look around. She's not out here, but she was. The kitchen smells like fresh coffee, and there's a few new dishes drying on the rack. Her laptop and legal pad are stacked beside a leather backpack on the table.

From back down the hall, I hear the unmistakable sound of a hair dryer and I breathe a little sigh of relief. She's still here.

I peer into this fridge, taking note of the items Tess purchased—yogurt, salad stuff, fresh pineapple, a pack of turkey, and some cheddar cheese. What I don't see is a pale blue pitcher of freshly brewed iced tea.

My housekeeper Yolanda knows just how I like it. She's this awesome Cuban woman I met at the practice rink. She was one of the janitors there, and she was always so nice to me. I made her an offer she couldn't refuse, and now she works for me two days a week, stocking my fridge with the most amazing food. She makes me iced tea each week too. I don't know what magic she puts in it, but it's delicious—not too sweet, with just a hint of lemon.

The doorbell rings, and I close the fridge, swinging over to the front door. I see Shelby's outline through the fogged glass. "Who is it?" I call out, just to be a dick.

"Open the door, Langley. The ice cream is melting!"

That has me on the move, twisting the bolt on the lock to let Shelby in.

She sweeps past me, her hands full of bags, big sunglasses framing her face. She's tall and skinny, built like a volleyball player. In fact, I think she may have played in college. Her long, dark ponytail swishes as she walks.

I follow behind her, turning the corner just as she sets all her reusable shopping bags down on the counter. Immediately she turns, flicking her sunglasses up to the top of her head. "You look like shit, Ryan," she says in greeting. "Have you even showered since the Classic?"

I just shrug. "I'll get around to it eventually."

She squares off at me, hands on her hips. "You'll do it today, or I'm gonna hose you down in the front yard. Don't think I won't. And if you're entertaining bunnies in here, I'll do the sheets at the same time."

"Nice to see you too, Shelbs."

Remembering her manners, she sweeps forward and wraps me in a hug. "Oh—" she stiffens in my arms.

"I'm sorry," comes Tess's voice from behind me.

Shelby pulls away and peers around me.

I glance over my shoulder, my gaze feasting on Tess wearing curve-hugging black leggings and a cropped Ferrymen top. She's layered it with an open fleece zip-up in a soft grey color. Her red curls frame her face, her freckles on full display.

"Well, you don't look like a bunny," says Shelby in greeting.

"Excuse me?" says Tess.

"You're Doc Price's friend." Shelby steps around me, holding out a hand. "It's Tess, right? Hi, I'm Shelby O'Sullivan."

"The team captain's wife," Tess replies, looking at the hand but not taking it.

"'Til death do us part," Shelby says with a laugh, dropping her hand back to her side. "Langley here was just telling me about you. He says you're roommates now?"

"I wasn't," I say, leveling my gaze at Tess. I don't want her to think I'm gossiping about her. "I didn't say anything about you."

"It's temporary," Tess replies, her gaze still on Shelby. "I'm only in town to help Mars with his nonprofit."

"Oh, that's right," says Shelby, making herself at home as she starts unloading all the groceries. "Sea turtles or something like that, right? Josh told me a bit about it."

Tess nods. "Rachel offered me use of this place while I'm in town. Seeing as they're all newlyweds, I thought it best I not be underfoot."

Shelby laughs. "Yeah, I can imagine it's a bit chaotic over there."

"And I'm only here because of this," I add, gesturing down at my braced knee.

"Well, then it's kismet," Shelby replies. "You're welcome to any of this food by the way," she calls over to Tess.

"I'm fine," Tess says, moving towards the coffee maker. Her phone on the kitchen table lights up.

"Tess, your phone is ringing," I say.

She ignores me . . . and the phone.

"You don't like me," Shelby presses, leaning her hip against the fridge, her gaze following Tess.

"Shelbs . . . " I say in warning.

"You don't know me," she goes on. "But you don't like me."

"I'm just having an off day," Tess replies, closing the lid on the coffee maker. "An off decade," she adds under her breath.

Her phone lights up again with another call.

"Tess, your phone—"

"Leave it," she snaps at me.

"It's fine," Shelby says. "Most women tend not to like the WAGs. They usually have a lot of ideas about us. We're all silly bimbos looking for a sugar daddy or we trapped our men with babies and now they're stuck with us. Trust me, I've heard it all."

"I don't have any ideas about you, Shelby," Tess says. "I'm just having a bad day."

Shelby glances at the clock over the stove. "It's barely 8:00 a.m."

Tess slips her fresh cup of coffee out from under the drip spout and transfers it to a travel mug. "Yeah, and I'm already this level of done. So, trust me when I say that it's not you, it's me."

Damn, where is the fun flirty Tess from last night? The Tess that teased me and laughed as she held my hand? What's wrong with her? Why is she so on edge this morning? There's something she's not saying.

"Tess, your phone," I say for a third time.

"Fuck's sake, Ryan," she cries, snatching it off the table. "If I wanted to answer it, don't you think I would?"

A chill seeps down my spine as I take in the haunted look on Tess's face. Her sudden appearance here in Jax is making more sense by the minute. "Who's calling you so many times?" I need her to say it. I need her to confirm my suspicions.

"Mars is almost here," she says. "I gotta go." She slips the phone in her pocket unanswered and tucks her laptop and legal pad into the leather backpack. "You two have a good day." Not waiting for either of us to say another word, she ducks around me. I hear the front door shut with a snap.

It only takes a few seconds before Shelby lets out a whistle. "Jeez, she's kind of a capital B bitch, huh?"

My gaze lingers on the window as I watch Tess climb into the passenger seat of Ilmari's big silver truck. "No," I hear myself say. "She's just going through some tough shit right now—and no, I won't elaborate," I add, giving her a glare.

The corner of Shelby's mouth twitches with a smile. "You like her."

"I don't know her," I admit, and fuck if that's not the truth. Tess hasn't told me a damn thing about what's happening to her and why.

"Be careful with that one, Ryan" Shelby warns.

"Why?" I hear myself say.

"Because she's not a bunny," Shelby replies.

"You think I don't know that? Women like Tess don't end up with guys like me."

Shelby tips her head to the side, appraising me. "Why do you say that?"

I go still, not realizing I said that out loud. "Come on," I say, forcing a laugh. "Tess Owens is a total ten. She's gorgeous and so fucking smart. She's a high-powered corporate lawyer, Shelbs. She runs non-profits and saves endangered animals, and I'm . . . me," I finish with a shrug.

Now Shelby is laughing. "Yeah, and you're *just* an NHL superstar. You're smart and funny and handsome as heck. Oh, and in your free time, don't you volunteer to coach youth hockey?"

"Sometimes." I feel my cheeks heat at her praise. "I mean, when I can, I do."

"Tess may be a ten," Shelby goes on. "But I'm not convinced she's WAG material."

I glance sharply her way. "Well, if she's not a bunny and she's not a WAG, what is she?"

Shelby just gives me a knowing look. "She's a cataclysm."

I blink. "A catawhat?"

"Chaos walking," she replies. "I have a feeling your Tess is a runner. She's the kind of woman who loves you and leaves you in the same breath."

"How do you know that?"

"I see the signs," she replies. "You want my advice?"

I just shrug, knowing she'll give it either way.

"Stay away from her, Ryan . . . unless you're ready to suffer an epically broken heart."

10

Tess

It's all I can do to jerk the door open and climb inside the cab of the truck. My heart is racing, and I feel like I'm choking on air. Wow, this is all hitting me all at once. My body is a swirling vortex of thoughts and emotions.

"Good morning," comes a deep voice.

Ilmari sits behind the wheel, his blond hair tied up in a knot. He wears a T-shirt and shorts like it's not January and 55 degrees outside. Apparently, Finnish hockey players can't feel the cold. Meanwhile, my tits are freezing. I should have added another layer.

I pull the door shut and drop my backpack down between my feet, choking on a sob. I can't cry in front of this man. Not *again*. Losing it on him the other night was bad enough. Jake is still walking around on eggshells like he's afraid I'll crack. He keeps offering me ice cream.

Ilmari's eyes go wide. "Tess, what—"

"Drive," I gasp, flailing wildly for my seatbelt as tears fill my vision.

"Tess—"

"Ilmari, drive!"

He doesn't push me again; he just shifts the truck into reverse and pulls out of the driveway. In moments, we're meandering through his quiet neighborhood, his gaze locked on the road.

I switch between crying and sucking down air as my phone buzzes in my pocket with more missed calls. I can't stand the feel of it touching me. It's as unwanted as Troy's actual physical touch. Even from such a distance, he can still force his way on me.

Jerking the phone from my pocket, I drop it down into the

cupholder where it continues to softly buzz. The sound is muted by the truck's engine and the quiet hum of the radio.

"When you're ready," Ilmari says, still not looking my way.

We drive for a few minutes in silence. He turns left out of his neighborhood, headed for the beach. We're meeting his crew this morning, the three volunteers that form the core of his nonprofit. I can't face them if I'm a sobbing mess. I have to let this go. I have to give it a voice.

"She looks like her," I say at last. "I remembered seeing her on beach day, but she had a big hat and the kids and the dogs. I didn't focus on it too much then. But this morning she really did look just like her. It took me by surprise is all," I finish, sniffing back my tears.

"O'Sullivan's wife. She was at the house," Ilmari intuits.

I nod, dropping my hands to my lap as I recover my breathing.

After a minute of silence, he asks the obvious next question. "Who does she look like?"

"My husband's secretary," I reply, my mind flooding with the memories I try so hard to keep locked away. "They had an affair for almost a year. I caught them together . . . more than once. By the end, they weren't even trying to hide from me."

Candace was only the first woman I caught him with but there were so many others.

The silence stretches between us as my phone continues to buzz in the cupholder.

"Is his infidelity the reason your marriage ended?" Ilmari asks.

"One of the many reasons," I admit. "It certainly sped things along."

Ilmari glances down to my buzzing phone. "Your phone is ringing."

"I know," I reply, gazing resolutely out the windshield as I watch the palm trees flash by.

"It's him," Ilmari intuits again.

"Yes."

"Rachel told me today might be difficult for you, though she didn't say why. She's given me strict instructions to bring you home with me."

"I'm fine, Mars," I reply with a weak smile.

He flicks on his turn signal, following the signs for the beach. "Fine you may be, but I do as I'm told. You're not leaving my sight until I deposit you safely in my wife's arms."

I close my eyes, breathing deep. I know with a surety marrow-deep that *this* is why I got on a plane to Jacksonville. I wanted to be close to Rachel as I made this leap. I wanted to freefall knowing someone would brave any element to catch me. Rachel will do anything for the ones she loves, just like me.

But now she has three men to catch *her* from falling. Ilmari Price doesn't take leaps of faith. He is the steadfast rock that moves but is never shaken. Same with Caleb. Jake might be more of a cliff jumper at heart, but even then, I'd rather know he's at my side, helping me swim back to shore.

I'm safe here with Rachel. I'm safe with her husbands. I'm safe with the Rays. I've set all the pieces of wood on this bonfire. Signing the divorce papers and delivering them to Troy was the kerosene. It's time to light the match.

I turn to face Ilmari. It feels oddly right that it be him. My quiet protector. I want to stand now in the shadow of his strength.

"Hey, Mars, will you do something for me?"

He glances my way, keeping one eye on the road. "What?"

Slowly, I reach forward and pick up my phone. A half-dozen missed calls and a string of text messages light up the screen. Troy is in rare form this morning, desperate to hurl his insults and cut me down.

I hold out the phone towards Ilmari. "When this rings again, will you answer it?"

He glances down at it with a frown. "Why is he calling you?"

"Because before I left, I signed divorce papers," I reply. "A courier delivered them to him this morning."

His brow furrows. "I thought you were living apart. Years, it's been. That's what Rachel told us."

"Yeah, it's been three years since we shared any semblance of a life or a marriage."

"And yet you stayed married to him. Why?"

"It's complicated," I reply. "Mostly it was about his family, about making them happy . . . and about my fear of abandonment. Plus, it didn't seem important to have a formal dissolution so long as we were cordial with each other."

"So, what changed?"

Ilmari's good at this. He's careful with his words and he doesn't look my way, giving me the space to answer or not, and in my time. I'm usually the kind of person that seeks to fill an awkward silence, but with Ilmari I find myself wanting to lean into it.

"I think I changed," I reply, giving him the simple truth. "Through every stage of our relationship, I was always the one changing. I changed to please him so many times. I changed my habits and my likes, my sense of humor. Hell, I even changed my coffee order. I'm not even convinced I *like* coffee. I drink it because he does," I finish with a shrug.

We're both quiet for another minute.

"And now?"

I let out a breath. "And now I've changed again. I'm stronger, I think. Resigned to my fate."

"And what fate is that?"

"To survive," I reply.

"What does that mean?"

"Not everyone is meant to thrive, Ilmari. Some of us are born merely to endure. It took falling in love with Troy and falling back out again to realize how adept I am at survival. And I want it, Mars," I whisper, heart in my throat. "I want to survive on *my* terms and by *my* strength. Troy wanted me to think I was weak. He wanted me to be malleable clay he could make and remake in his image."

Ilmari glances my way. "And are you that clay, Tess?"

"No."

"Then what are you?"

Taking a deep breath, I hold it in my lungs, letting it fill me. "I am the fire that forges the clay into something stronger."

Ilmari is quiet as he considers my words. At last, he glances my way and says, "It sounds to me like you need to answer the phone for yourself."

As if on cue, the phone begins buzzing in my hand. I glance down to see the name on my caller ID: DEVIL SPAWN.

"What will you do?" Ilmari asks, his tone so calm and quiet.

I gaze down at the phone, feeling the buzz of it in my hand. "I should answer it. I should let him have his say, right? That's all he ever wants is the last word. He can scream at me and rage, and then we can be done with it. He won't sign otherwise. He'll never let go if he thinks I'm somehow winning in all this."

"So, you want to answer the phone," Ilmari summarizes.

"No," I say quickly. "I don't want to answer. I don't care if we never speak again. He's a monster, and his words are nothing but poison."

"I think you may be overlooking one of the important nuances of human communication," he replies.

I glance his way, the phone still buzzing in my hand. "What?"

Ilmari just shrugs, his gaze on the road. "No answer is still an answer."

I let that truth sink deep. *No answer is still an answer.* I don't want to answer my phone. I don't *have* to answer my phone. So, I won't.

Breathless with nerves, I jam my thumb down on the automatic window switch. The tinted window rolls halfway down, and the cab of the truck is suddenly blasted with icy air as we climb the bridge stretching across the water. With a shriek, I fling the buzzing phone out the open window, watching it sail over the guardrail and out of sight.

I'm on autopilot as I roll the window back up and turn slowly to look out the front. I can still feel the chill of the wind on my face. "There," I say at last. "He has his answer."

Reaching across the center console, Ilmari pats my arm. "Good girl."

I let out my breath, shoulders sagging, as fresh tears sting my eyes. But these aren't tears of feeling anxious or trapped. These are happy tears. I feel giddy, like I swallowed a freaking rainbow. Troy will likely find a way to make me pay, but in this moment, I swear to God I don't care. In this moment, I'm free.

I place my hand over Ilmari's on my arm. "So, tell me about these sea turtles. Have you ever actually seen one?"

21
Ryan

I'm in the car with Lauren Gerard and her two little girls, the four of us rocking out to Disney songs, when my phone rings in my pocket. The front lights up with a picture of my sister and me from Christmas, stretched out on towels at the beach.

Lauren turns down the music, and I answer the phone. "Hey, Cass. What's up?"

"Hey, bro," she replies. "You got a sec?"

I groan. My sister Cassie may be thirteen months older than me, but since our dad died, I feel like I stepped in to fill his shoes. It was little things at first, like scaring off her douchey boyfriends and being her DD at parties. Once I got drafted, I became her main financial support. Right now, I'm putting her through the last two years of her PhD program in Comparative Literature.

Yeah, Cassie got all the brains. She just doesn't know how to turn that bookish cleverness into a job that pays. Oh, and she's a slob . . . and she forgets to do things like pay her cell phone bill. But she's my only sister, and Mom can't really help her on her meager nurse's salary.

So, Cassie leans on me. And damn it, but I let her. It's always all been on me. She's only calling now because she wants money.

"What do you need, Cass?" I say.

"Well, hello to you too—"

"I'm in the car, so spit it out."

"Fine," she huffs. "The deadline is approaching for this really cool opportunity to study French in Bordeaux this summer. I talked to my advisor, and she says it'll be a quick way to complete my language requirement for my program."

I sigh, glancing over at Lauren. She gives me a weak smile and a shrug. "It's for your program?" I press. "Like, it gets you credits to graduate on time?"

"Yeah, totally."

"How much?"

"Umm . . . it's only like nine thousand dollars. And it's all-inclusive."

"And there's not a scholarship or anything?"

"God, Ryan," she huffs. "If there was a scholarship, don't you think I would have applied? If nine thousand dollars is really that big a deal—"

"I never said that," I say, bristling at her tone. "But this isn't going to be like the summer you spent drinking and riding bikes with your sorority sisters across Tuscany, right? You're actually going to school? You're like, learning and shit?"

I can practically hear her eye roll through the phone. "Yeah, Ryan. I'm learning and shit. Want me to send you the website link?"

My hackles rise higher at what I know is meant to be a jab. "You know, since you're the one asking me for the favor, you could try saying something that sounds a little more like 'please.'"

"Please," she says quickly. Her voice softens a little. "God, you know I hate having to lean on you like this all the time. Please, Ry? My program is almost done. This is my last summer, so this is, like, the last big thing, I swear."

I sigh, looking out the windshield as we head over the bridge into downtown. "When do you need the money by?" I say at last.

"Tomorrow."

"Fuck," I mutter.

"Mommy, he said Daddy's bad word," Estelle calls from her booster seat in the back.

Lauren glares at me, and I flash her a look of apology. "Fine, Cass. I'll transfer the money over tonight, okay?"

"Thanks, Ry," she chimes. "You're the best."

We hang up, and I glare down at the phone.

Lauren smirks. "I can't wait to see you as a girl dad someday. You'll be worse than Jean-Luc."

I groan, dropping my phone in the cupholder as I crank the tunes back up. I was already in a shitty mood because of the weirdness with Tess earlier and Shelby's warning. Now it's a hundred times worse. But it's nothing a little "Hakuna Matata" can't fix.

22
Tess

Mars and I pull up at an all-but-empty beach parking lot. He parks the truck in the front row and we open our doors at the same time. A sloping sand dune cuts off my view of the beach, but I can feel the sea air and smell the salt on the breeze.

A young man waves us down, jogging over in a pair of board shorts and a half-zip pullover. “Hey, there he is! Mars Attack, lookin’ good, man.”

I glance over at Ilmari. “Mars Attack?”

“Do not encourage him,” he says as he slips out of the truck.

I can’t suppress my smile as I hop down too. Mars quickly steps around the front of the truck and comes to stand by my door.

The young man swaggers up to us in bare feet. His hair still looks wet and sticky with salt from his morning surf. He’s maybe in his mid-twenties, his face already deeply lined and weathered by the sun. Behind him, a beat-up, yellow Jeep sits stuffed with several surfboards.

“How’s it goin,’ Mars Mission?” He says, offering out his hand to Ilmari. “Whoa, who’s the duchess?” he says, looking at me.

“Your new boss,” Mars replies, shaking the surfer’s hand.

“Awesome,” Surfer Joe replies, nodding like a bobblehead.

“Mars Attack?” I say with a smile. “Mars Mission? Are those his nicknames?”

“Oh yeah, totally,” Surfer Joe replies.

“May I ask why?”

Surfer Joe slings an arm around Ilmari’s broad shoulders as he flips the sunglasses on his head down onto his face and says, “‘Cause this guy is out of this world.”

The pained look of tolerance on Ilmari's face is giving me life. Surfer Joe may just be my new favorite person. "You know, I'd have to agree," I tease, flashing Ilmari a grin.

"I said don't encourage him," Mars mutters.

"Oh, come on now, Rocketman, where's the fun in that?"

Mars gives me a look clearly meant to convey sentiments of deep hate and loathing. Then he gestures at me. "Tess Owens, this is Joey Ford. He's the current head of the organization."

Surfer Joe's name is Joey? I nearly choke holding back my laugh as I eagerly shake his hand. "Joey, nice to meet you." His hand is rough as sandpaper and his grip hard as iron.

"The king is dead, long live the queen, eh, duchess?" Joey says with a grin. "I don't know the first thing about running a nonprofit. I'm just here to give the turtles a fighting chance."

"And behind you are Cheryl and Nancy Lemming," says Ilmari at my side.

I turn to see a pair of smiling older ladies walking up to us holding hands. They, too, look like they just came from the beach. Their bare toes are sandy, and their cheeks are flushed from the wind.

"Hi," I say with a wave.

"Oh, Nance, she is so pretty," coos the one who must be Cheryl. She's tall and willowy with kinky grey curls. Meanwhile, her partner is shorter and more pear-shaped, with dark hair and eyes. "Honey, you are just the prettiest thing."

"Thank you," I reply with a smile.

They close the distance and shake my hand, then Ilmari's.

"We're so excited to meet you," says Nancy. "Mars said you were a wizard with nonprofits."

"I'll admit, we're new to this game," chimes Cheryl. "But what's the proper sports vernacular? Put us in, coach," she says, and they both laugh.

"We're willing to do the work," adds Nancy.

I glance up at Mars. "Are we waiting for anyone else?"

"No," he replies. "This is it."

I glance around at the four of them: the goalie, the surfer, and the lesbian nature lovers.

And now me.

"All present and accounted for," chimes Joey, wrapping an arm around my shoulder. "Welcome to the Northshore Turtle Crew."

AN hour later, I've forgotten all about the cold. I'm sweating and panting, my feet sinking in the sand as we walk along the base of the dunes. We're nearly back to the parking lot now. I can see the patio of blue umbrellas marking the entrance.

I don't know what I expected for my first meeting with the Northshore Turtle Crew, but it certainly wasn't a grueling hike in deep sand while Joey, Nancy, and Cheryl rapid-fire explained absolutely every aspect of sea turtle conservation and dune restoration. My mind is spinning as I try to hold it all in my head and remember to breathe at the same time.

Fuck, I'm outta shape.

Meanwhile, Mars Attack looks almost bored as he strolls barefoot, his hands in his pockets, easily keeping pace. The crazy Finn is wholly unbothered in his shorts and T-shirt, the wind whipping at his hair.

"So that's pretty much it," says Joey, gesturing with both hands at the expanse of beach in front of us. "Any questions?"

We all slow to a stop, and I place a hand to my chest, trying to catch my breath. My Achilles heels are screaming at me, unused to the stretch and pull of walking in this deep sand.

"Umm—I guess—well, I guess I need to know what you all want," I get out at last, using rooted tree pose to open my chest and take deep breaths.

"We want to save the turtles," Cheryl replies.

The other two nod fervently. Mars does nothing, standing slightly back from the rest of us.

I look to him. "Mars? I need to know what you want from me here."

"We want to save the turtles," he echoes.

I huff a laugh. "Well, you guys just downloaded an hour of data into me and the long story short is that the options seem to be endless." I gesture around at the quiet expanse of beach. "I mean, is this a conservation group? Beach walks and clean ups and 'save our oceans' rhetoric? 'Cause you're already doing some of that."

They glance around at each other.

"Or is this a citizen science group where you're tagging and monitoring turtle nests? 'Cause you're doing that too. Do you wanna raise awareness about turtles and their nesting grounds for the general public? Or is this a civic action group? Are we taking the fight to local lawmakers and beachfront property owners, fighting for change?"

"Well . . . can't we just do it all?" says Joey with a shrug.

"Yeah, it all needs to get done in the end," Nancy adds with a nod.

"In my experience, the fastest way for a nonprofit to fail is for it to try and do too much at once," I explain patiently. "I just listed off enough work for like five different organizations to tackle over the next ten years. You can do one of those things really well and two of them well enough. If you try to do all five, you'll just flounder and fail."

"But they're all interconnected," says Cheryl. "We certainly need the conservation education just as much as the citizen action."

"I don't disagree," I reply. "But it's about specializing." My gaze lands on Ilmari. "Take Mars Attack here for example," I tease, flashing him a grin. "He plays hockey, right?"

They all nod.

"Well, to play hockey you need people passing the puck, right?"

They nod again.

"But you also need guys protecting the other players," I go on. "And you need someone standing in the net. When Mars gets on the ice, he doesn't play all the positions. He has to trust that other people will fill those roles. He does his job and *only* his job, and he does it well. We gotta think of this the same way. We need to specialize."

"I say that's what we do, then," says Cheryl, smiling up at Mars. "Let's all play goalie."

"What do you mean, honey?" says Nancy, glancing at her wife.

Cheryl gestures around at the expanse of dunes. "This is our net. This is our home, Nance. *Our* beach. And we're going to protect it for those turtles. I say we're dune defenders now. Let's step out of the net and take the fight to all the bullies and the businesses who want to tear these dunes apart. If they want a piece of this beach, they'll have to get past us first."

"Yeah, goalie power," says Joey. "I'm in."

"Save the turtles by saving the dunes," Nancy says with a smile. "I like it."

I smile too. "It's perfect." I glance back at Mars. "And I think Cheryl just gave us a name for the rebrand."

Ilmari raises that scarred brow at me.

"What, no more Northshore Turtle Crew?" says Joey, glancing between us.

"Nope," I reply. "With NHL superstar Ilmari Price as our key patron, a goalie-themed name feels very on-brand. The fans will love it. Thanks, Cheryl."

Cheryl looks from me to her wife. "What did I say?"

I grin wide. "Folks, welcome to the first official stakeholder meeting for Out of the Net."

13
Tess

After our beach walk, Ilmari treats us all to lunch at this lovely little oceanfront restaurant. We chat over bloody marys and vegetarian tacos. I learn Cheryl and Nancy are retired architects who live on the beach. They have a little bungalow and some dune property that they've turned into a green energy oasis. With nothing better to do, they seem ready to make Out of the Net their new obsession.

I name Cheryl our new Chief Financial Officer, while Nancy is officially our Project Manager. Joey gladly accepts the title of Volunteer Coordinator. And Mars is, well, Mars. He's present in all our conversations, quietly listening. But he doesn't engage much. I can see the wheels of his mind turning, but he offers virtually nothing to us except his polite presence.

After lunch, Mars takes me to a car dealership so I can pick up a rental. Next to the car dealer is a cellphone shop. I duck inside and pick up a prepaid phone. As much as I don't regret my impulsive decision to chuck my phone out the window, I feel naked without a means of communication.

Standing out in the parking lot, I make Ilmari plug his number into my new phone. As soon as he hands it back to me, I dial his number, holding the phone up to my ear.

"There," I laugh. "You're officially my first call. New phone, new Tess."

Smirking at me, he sends the call straight to voicemail.

"Hey, what are you tryna say?"

Slipping his phone back in his pocket he holds my gaze. "Nothing."

I laugh.

Slowly, he cracks a smile too. "It feels good to say nothing sometimes, doesn't it?"

I nod. "So fucking good."

BY the time I get back to the bungalow, I'm exhausted. It's only 9:00 p.m., but I feel ready to crash asleep. The house is quiet, all the lights off except the light to Ryan's room. Not knowing if he's asleep in there or not, I tiptoe around, slipping my laptop out of my leather backpack and carrying it to my room.

Staying as quiet as possible, I do a quick rinse-off in the shower, scrubbing away the sweat of the day. My lower legs are going to be killing me tomorrow thanks to that beach march. As I stand under the hot water, steam filling the shower, I drag the loofah slowly up and down my arms and across my chest. I like the smell of this body wash. I'm just using whatever was in here in the girliest bottle. I'm assuming it belonged to Rachel. It's something soft and floral, with a hint of jasmine.

I glance down to see the way my nipples are peaked, droplets of water streaming over them. The heat feels so damn good. And I'm wound so tight from the stress of the day. A little release would feel good too. I drag the loofah down over my stomach and drop it between my legs, turning my back to the shower's spray.

Dropping the loofah at my feet, I let my hands roam down my body, over my breasts, skating along my hips, before I dip one hand down, slipping my fingers between my pussy lips. My clit is begging for some attention. I can't even remember the last time I got myself off. I stand under the spray, letting the steam fill my lungs as I work myself slow with the fingers of my right hand, my left tweaking my nipple.

I need more—more friction, more attention. It's one of the reasons I like sex so much; I usually need a helping hand. Some women might be able to O on command, but that's never been me. I have to work for it, especially when I'm alone. I prefer the rush of being with another person, riding the high of their energy as we crash and burn together.

Turning off the water, I snatch up my towel and wrap it around myself, stepping out of the shower. I move into the dark bedroom and head straight for the large suitcase I've yet to unpack. The lid is flipped open, and it already looks like a bomb went off inside. The only light comes from above the vanity mirror in the bathroom, but it's enough to see by.

I dig down on the left side of the suitcase and tug out a lumpy pink packing cube. Tossing it on the bed, I work the zipper one-handed, dropping my towel to the floor. Inside the packing cube is my treasure trove—vibes and dildos, a few butt plugs, my trusty strap-on.

I snatch up my favorite green bullet and climb onto the bed on my hands and knees, facing the end. I always get a better O on my knees when I'm getting myself there. Bracing my weight with one hand, I turn on the bullet with the other and tuck it between my legs, humming low in my throat as I feel that first vibration tease my clit.

"Fuck," I whimper, hardly making a sound.

I shift my knees a little farther apart and glide the bullet back and forth over my clit, teasing the entrance of my pussy to get it wet. I groan as I feel the toy get slick around my fingers. Getting wet has never been my problem. I can do panty-dripping arousal all day long. It's getting *off* that takes work.

"Come on," I moan, pressing in a little harder with the bullet, circling my clit clockwise, then counterclockwise. The vibration feels amazing, setting off a fire that warms as it spreads, racing down my legs, leaving my toes tingling. My breath catches, and I know I'm close. The heat blooms across my chest, curling and fluttering.

"Yes—*fuck*—please, God," I whine. My breasts sway as I work the toy, biting my bottom lip. "Yes—fuck me," comes my all-but-soundless plea to the heavens.

For the love of God, will someone please just fuck me?

Lost to my own pleasure, I don't hear the knock at the door. I definitely don't hear it open. But I do hear a man's voice.

"Tess?"

24
Tess

I gasp, bolting upright on the bed to see a wide-eyed Ryan standing in my open doorway, leaning on one crutch.

"Jesus—*fuck*—" I cry, slipping off the side of my bed, vibrator still buzzing in my hand. "What the fuck are you doing?"

"Oh my god." Yep, he's just realized what I was doing. The poor boy blushes red as a tomato as he backs into the doorknob with his hip and hisses. "Fuck—Tess, I'm sorry—"

Indignation surges through me. "What, it's not enough that you barge into houses unannounced to catch women naked, now you're just walking right into their bedrooms?"

"I didn't know you were home," he counters, looking anywhere but at my naked, flushed body. *Again*. "Why didn't you announce yourself when you got in?"

"I thought you were asleep," I cry, clicking off the bullet and tossing it on the bed.

Big mistake. That draws his eye down and now he's looking at my open treasure trove. The puppy's eyes go, if possible, even wider as he feasts upon my colorful sex toy collection.

"Oh . . . fuck."

I flip the bag shut. "Eyes up here, Ryan," I say, pointing to my face.

He groans, his gaze going from my face to the abstract painting on the wall. "Tess, could you—"

"Nuh-uh," I cry, hands on my naked hips. "No way. If you're about to ask me to cover up in my own damn bedroom, I'm gonna have to insist that you go fuck yourself with your hockey stick. Just because you think I'm not home, you think it's okay to waltz in here? What were you looking for?"

"Nothing—"

"Then why barge in—"

"I heard a noise! And then I saw a strange car in the driveway. You weren't answering your phone, so I didn't know what the fuck to think. I thought maybe someone broke in."

"That's my car," I explain. "It's a rental. And I don't have my phone anymore. I threw it in the ocean today."

"You—what?" That gets his eyes back on me. "You threw your phone in the ocean?"

"Well, it was whatever that stretch of water is just before you hit the beach," I reply.

"The Intracoastal?"

"Yeah. I threw my phone out the window of Ilmari's truck."

Ryan holds my gaze. "Why?"

"Because it wouldn't stop ringing."

There's so much left unsaid in that statement. I'm almost convinced he means to ask me about it. He's going to push me. He's finally going to ask about Troy. It looks like the words are right on the tip of his tongue. But then his gaze softens.

"Why didn't you let me know you were home?"

"I thought you were asleep," I repeat.

His eyes narrow. "No, you didn't. You saw the light on. You were hiding out in here. Why?"

"You don't need me mothering you, Ryan. You've got a line of WAGs and rookies ready to take care of you—making all your meals, driving you around. You don't need me in the way. Especially after . . . you know, after how I behaved this morning," I finish lamely.

Hobbling further into my room, he leans his hip against the dresser. "Something with Shelby had you spooked. I was hugging her when you came in. Was that . . . did it upset you?"

"No," I reply.

"Because she's married," he goes on. "I'm not—I mean, we're not—I'm not into Shelby."

I smile softly. "I know that, Ryan."

"Well then what was it? Can you please tell me?" He looks so damn earnest. He genuinely wants to know. And damn it, but I feel like telling him.

I cross my arms over my bare tits. “She looks like my ex-husband’s mistress.”

His pretty green eyes go wide. “She—what?”

I drop down to sit on the edge of the bed. “Shelby bears a shocking resemblance to the secretary who used to pleasure my husband under his desk at work . . . and *on* the desk . . . and in my house in my bed,” I reply darkly. “In fact, I know on at least one occasion he was trying to slip her out the back door while I was *in* the house.”

“Jeez.”

“Today was just a lot for me, okay? I signed my divorce papers, and Troy got them this morning. He was the one calling me nonstop, looking for a fight. The marriage has been over for years, but I never bothered with all the legal drama, and this is why. My ex is a grade-A narcissist with a god complex. Pepper in a dash of crippling incompetence and a pinch of toxic male privilege, and it makes him vindictive . . . and dangerous.”

Ryan goes still, his breath tight in his chest. “Tess, does he know where you are?”

“No.”

He steps closer, leaving the support of the dresser. “But can he track your phone to Jacksonville? Because if he can track your phone to Jax, the Prices will be the first place he looks for you. He knows about your friendship with Doc, right?”

I nod. “Yeah, he knows.”

He lets out a breath, glancing around the trappings of Ilmari’s minimalist bedroom. “You shouldn’t stay here. We need to get you situated somewhere else. Somewhere he wouldn’t think to look. You could go stay at my house,” he offers quickly. “I can give you the keys.”

I blink back the sharp sting in my eyes, trying to flash Ryan an unconcerned look. “So, what, are you secretly a cop or something?”

“No,” he replies. “But my dad was until he had to medically retire. Some of his buddies were always around when I was growing up to . . . you know . . . be around,” he finishes with a shrug.

I don’t miss his use of the word *was*. A father’s friends forced to step in and help raise a young man? I’m sure there’s a sad story there.

He turns away like he’s about to leave.

"Ryan—wait," I call, getting to my feet.

He stops at the door and glances over his shoulder.

I cross the room over to him. "Where are you going?"

"To get you my keys," he replies.

I reach for his arm. "Don't," I say. "It's late already. And I don't want to go to some strange house and stay there all alone," I admit. "I want to stay here . . . I want to stay with you." I lower my gaze to where my hand is touching his bicep. The muscle underneath his T-shirt is corded and strong. I brush my hand down his arm to his elbow. Now I'm touching skin, my fingers grazing along the soft hairs of his forearm.

"Tess," he groans, eyes shut as he holds still. "Please . . . "

"Am I safe with you, Ryan?" I step in closer until my peaked nipple grazes his elbow. I watch goosebumps shoot down his arm.

"Yes," he says, voice tight.

I brush my lips against his shoulder in a featherlight touch as my fingers trail down his arm to his wrist. "Will you protect me, Ryan? Will you make me feel good?"

"Tess . . . "

"Tell me you don't need it too," I say, my forehead pressed against his shoulder. "Tell me, after the stress of the last few days, that you aren't aching for some relief. Tell me you don't want to feel something right now . . . just for a moment. Tell me—"

I don't finish the words as he turns in my arms, our lips colliding in a fevered kiss. He claims all my air, opening my mouth and plunging in with his tongue. I nearly forgot how good he was at this. I want to savor him this time. I want to brand the memory of his kisses against my lips.

His crutch clatters to the floor. When we kissed before, I made him keep his hands behind his back. Now he's got his hands on my shoulders, brushing up my neck to cup my face.

I arch into him. "Touch me. Please, God, finish what I started."

My plea unleashes him. With a desperate groan, he digs one hand into my hair, tipping my neck back as he devours my mouth with kisses. His other hand follows the curve of my breast. He curses softly against my lips as he palms me, barely getting a handful.

"If I had to see you naked one more fucking time and not touch you, I was gonna die," he whispers against my mouth.

"Touch me," I order. "Ryan, please—touch me anywhere. Everywhere—"

I'm left panting for air as he drops his head down, sucking my nipple into his mouth.

"Oh god—" I cry, both my hands digging into his hair. I hold on as he flicks and teases with his tongue, driving me crazy. Meanwhile his left hand works my other breast, pinching the nipple between thumb and forefinger.

My pussy is soaked. I can feel the heat growing between my legs. I'm desperate for more. I need friction. I need his warm tongue and fingers and the rub of his stubbled cheeks on my thighs. Fuck, I need *him*.

"Ryan," I whimper. "I need . . . "

"Say it," he says, his mouth still on my breast.

"I need it," I beg, feeling incoherent as he winds me up tight. My whole body is shaking with anticipation and the aching desire to feel this release.

"Tell me." He bites down on my nipple.

"Ahh—*fuck*—I need to come," I cry out, my hands tightening in his hair. "Please, Ryan—please, baby, I need to come. I need to come so fucking bad," I whine, pulling his face up and pressing his lips back to mine.

His right hand wraps around my nape, holding me secure, as he drops his left hand down. With no preamble or teasing whatsoever, he works two fingers right through my slick pussy and shoves them up inside me.

"Fuck—*god*—" I practically scream, clenching around his fingers.

He works his fingers in and out, his thumb joining the effort on my clit, eagerly trying to bring forth the soul-shattering orgasm I'm so desperately craving. I hold his shoulders as we kiss, sucking and biting each other's lips like crazed animals.

"You're so wet," he groans. "Tess, I'm dying—"

I squeeze my thighs around his hand. "Get the toy," I say breathlessly. "The bullet, the green one—"

"I don't need a fucking toy. I can make you see stars all on my own."

"Sharing is caring," I tease. "There is no "I" in team—*ahh*—"

He nips my neck right over my hammering pulse point, which shuts me up.

I drop my hands back to his shoulders. "Ryan, please."

He pulls his fingers from my cunt, leaving me clenching on nothing. Both his hands cup my face, the fingers of his left hand slick with my arousal. I feel it against my cheek.

"Don't get me wrong," he says with a smirk, those apple green eyes blown black with hunger. "I have no problem with toys. But I'm not giving away my first shot with Tess Owens. I'm not taking the assist. This orgasm is *mine*. Now, get on the fucking bed."

25
Ryan

Tess gazes up at me, her eyes glassy and her cheeks flushed. "Who are you and what have you done with Ryan Langley?" she teases, her lips glossy with my kisses.

We're both panting like we just survived a set of suicide sprints. Fuck, she spins me up unlike anything else. Her kisses are explosive, like little tastes of dynamite on my tongue. My hands frame her face while her hands are wrapped gently around my wrists. Heart pounding in my chest, I hold her gaze. "Am I surprising you?"

"A little, yeah. You've just always seemed so sweet."

I frown at her. In my experience, 'sweet' is the kiss of fucking death. "What, did you think I'd come to your bed wearing a propeller hat and Ninja Turtle undies?"

She laughs, biting her bottom lip to hold the sound back. "Honestly, I don't know what I thought . . . but I like it," she adds, her smile falling as she gazes up at me. "You're a really good kisser, Ryan."

"You're not so bad yourself," I reply. The fingers of my left hand glisten with her arousal. I'm on autopilot as I take those fingers and brush them against her parted lips.

She sucks in a breath of surprise. Ducking down, I chase it, my lips claiming the arousal painting her lips. She whimpers, her naked body melting against mine as I tease her again with my tongue. She's holding nothing back. It's fucking intoxicating. I'm drunk on kissing her.

"Fuck," I groan, pulling away. I need more. As she watches, I suck both my fingers into my mouth. The taste is muted, but sweet. I clean her essence from my fingers, loving how she squirms with need, her cheeks flushed.

"Ryan," she murmurs, her mouth barely moving.

My name on her lips is fucking everything. I need to taste her. I wasn't kidding, I need her spread out on that bed. I intend to bury my face in her cunt and never come up for air.

I'll admit, I don't often go here with girls. Putting my mouth on a pussy feels too intimate for a first time, and I pretty much only have first times. I can count on one hand the number of times I've given a girl a second date. When I've felt comfortable, we've gone there, and I've enjoyed myself. In a few cases, it was the girl who didn't want to go there.

And I'm not a total asshole. If I don't go down on them, they don't go down on me. Which means most of the time, my hookups are little more than a rushed make-out session and some hot and heavy pounding, my dick wrapped in a condom.

I'm not out here trying to win awards for "world's best lover." My sole focus for the last fifteen years has been scoring goals, winning trophies, and making it to the NHL. Sex was more of a biological imperative. I did it to survive. More often than not, my hand has sufficed.

But now, with Tess in my arms, her taste on my tongue, all my careful boundaries are slipping away. I don't *want* to put my mouth on her pussy, I *need* it. I'm craving her like I crave air. The rational part of my brain is telling me to slow down and get some distance. But my heart is pounding out of control, and he wants us to see this through, even if we only have tonight.

"You're getting on that bed," I say, pointing to it. "I'm not done with you yet."

With a smirk, she turns, showing me her beautiful body as she walks over to the bed. Tess is no slender waif. She's all woman—big breasts, thick thighs, a curvy midsection, and that ass that can't seem to quit. I am weak for this woman. Fucking weak.

I nearly pass out when she crawls onto the end of the bed, putting that perfect ass on full display. Fuck, I want to mark her dimpled skin. I want to claim it—with my teeth, my hands. I've never really explored the darker side of my interests in the bedroom. Again, who has the time? But right now, Tess is kneeling next to her bag of tricks, and I saw some of what was inside. I have a feeling this woman is more than a match for me.

My dick is so hard it hurts, but he needs to wait his turn. I'm only just getting started. "Turn over," I call to her. "Lie down and spread your legs, beautiful. Show me your pussy."

She turns over in the middle of the bed, a soft smile on her face. It's dark in here, the only light coming from her bathroom. The strip of golden light stretches right atop her stomach and thighs. Dropping back to her elbows, she holds my gaze as she brings her knees up. So fucking slowly, she drops them open, exposing her shiny pink cunt to me.

My soul leaves my body as she lets out a little laugh, the sound making her breasts jiggle.

"What's the matter, puppy?" she teases. "You just gonna stand there?"

And because she really wants to leave me for dead, she shifts her weight, dropping her left hand down between her legs to finger her own clit. She makes the sweetest little whimpering sound that burrows its way through my rock-hard dick, straight to my fucking heart.

All coherent thought leaves me except one word: *mine*.

No one is gonna touch that pretty pussy tonight except for me. I take a step towards her, my only desire getting to her, feeling her, sinking into the warm scent of her skin. I want the sweet nectar of her arousal on my tongue.

So, I take that first step closer . . . a step on a bad knee.

"Ouch—mother—*fuck*—" I cry out, stumbling as I quickly regain my balance, shifting all my weight back to my right leg.

"Ryan," Tess cries, sitting up. The lust in her eyes is instantly replaced with concern. "Ohmygod—" And then she's up, slipping off the side of the bed and rushing to my side. "I'm so sorry, I wasn't thinking. I completely forgot about your knee. Are you hurt?" She wraps an arm around my waist, trying to help me bear my weight.

"I'm fine."

"Here, let me help you," she says. "Come sit."

"I said I'm fine—"

"You're not fine."

We cross the five or so steps to the bed and I turn, sinking down onto the end. Immediately, my hands go to her, cupping the thick curves of her hips as I pull her closer to me. I bring her naked flesh right up to my face, inhaling deep against her floral-scented skin, my nose brushing just above her navel. I don't bother suppressing my groan as my dick twitches in my shorts.

"Ryan," she sighs, her hands going from my hair to my shoulders.

I could delude myself into thinking she wants me to continue, but I can feel the tension in her hold. "Is the moment over?"

She shifts her weight to one hip as she combs her fingers back through my hair again. I chase the touch, moving my head with her hand. "Ryan, what are we doing?"

"I thought that was obvious," I reply, giving her naked ass a gentle squeeze.

Her eyes flutter closed, but I feel the increased tension in her arms. Fuck, this woman is a master at pulling away. Shelby warned me, I just didn't want to believe.

"Tess—"

"We need to stop," she says, stepping away from the bed . . . from *me*.

I let her go, my hands brushing the dimpled skin of her thighs as she backs away.

Fuck, what did I really think was about to happen here? We had one conversation about her controlling ex, and that switched my damn hindbrain into overdrive. I wanted to protect her. I wanted to make her feel good. I wanted her to feel safe, comforted, desired.

"I'm sorry," I say, raising my hands in defeat.

"Ryan, no. You did nothing wrong. Please don't think you did."

I nod, suddenly feeling self-conscious about being in this room with her still naked. I drop my gaze to the floor. "Could you please put something on?"

For the first time since we met, she doesn't fight me or laugh off our mutual embarrassment. Stepping around me, she moves silently into the bathroom. In moments, she steps out again, tying the knot of a little pink floral bathrobe at her waist. The damn thing is barely long enough to cover her pussy, and the deep "V" exposes the heavy swell of her full boobs.

But I mean, I guess it's something, right?

"I'm sorry," she says, her soft voice cutting through my mental self-flagellation.

My gaze darts up sharply to her face. "What?"

"I'm sorry," she says again. "I swear I wasn't trying to be a tease or lead you on or—"

"Tess, *stop*," I all but growl. "You did nothing wrong either."

"I pushed you," she admits. "I wanted to . . . to not feel so alone." I can hear the tears catching in her throat. "Ryan, I've been so alone—"

Her voice breaks, and I'm on my feet. I pull her to me, my arms wrapping around her shoulders as I just hold her. "It's okay," I say against her temple, a few of her soft curls brushing my lips. "I've got you. You're okay."

After a moment, she relaxes, her sobs muffled by my shirt as her hands skim around my waist. Then she's clinging to me. We're relaxed, but firmly together. It feels nice. Compared to her smooth curves, I'm all hard edges.

"I'm sorry," she hiccups, pulling back. "I'm such a fucking mess."

"New house rule," I reply, brushing my thumbs under her eyes to wipe away her tears. "No more apologizing for this," I say, gesturing between us. "We're attracted to each other. I can admit it. I think you can too. Tess, you're fucking magnetic. I don't think I can stay away, even if I try . . . and I don't want to," I add with a smirk.

She gives another little watery laugh. "I'm not trying to push you away. I'm just—such a goddamn mess—"

"House rule number two," I say, cutting her off. "No more self-deprecation. You're not a disaster or a pain or an inconvenience or any of the four-hundred and fifty other terrible names you probably have rolling around up here," I say, tapping her temple. "Be nice to my friend, Tess. Okay?"

Her mouth quirks with a smile she's trying not to let loose. Slowly, she nods.

"Let's press pause on this," I say, gesturing between us. "Bad timing now isn't bad timing forever, right?"

She nods, her eyes still glassy with unshed tears.

"Hey, I have an idea," I say. "How about you put on your PJs, and I'll make us some popcorn. We can watch whatever you want on the TV in my room."

She blinks up at me. "In your room?"

"Sometimes it helps me to fall asleep with the TV on. I bet you'll pick something girly, and then I can just kind of zone out and maybe actually fall asleep."

Her eyes flash as she pops her hands on those hips—which should be a crime because it just pulls on the opening of her silky robe, showing me more of her breasts. "You want me to pick the TV show so you can zone out to a stupid chick flick?"

"That way we both win, right?" Ducking down on one leg with the balance of a pro hockey player, I snatch up my crutch from the floor. "Meet me over there in five," I call over my shoulder, not giving her a chance to say no.

AND that's how I found myself eating three bags of popcorn and staying up until 2:00 a.m. rewatching the first four episodes of *Sons of Anarchy*. I lost Tess somewhere early in episode three. She passed out on my bed, her arm curled around the empty popcorn bowl, green jelly eye patch things stuck to her cheeks, with fuzzy llama socks on her feet.

Clicking off my bedside lamp, I settle down into the pillows and try to get comfortable. Doc assures me I won't have to wear this stupid brace for much longer.

Next to me, Tess shifts. I lie still, curious to see what she wants, what she craves even in her sleep. She inches closer, unknowingly using the sink of the mattress to roll gently into me, our bodies connecting from the shoulder down. The smell of her coconutty hair oil fills my senses and I breathe deep. If I turn my face, my lips will practically be pressing against her forehead.

I don't turn. I don't breach her trust by taking something that wasn't freely offered.

But I think about doing it. I think about casually kissing her the way I want. I think about holding her, entwining our legs together, feeling how all the soft parts of her fit the hard parts of me. I think about knowing her and letting her know me. All of me. The parts I share and the parts I hide away. Would she still want me? Would she care?

I think about sharing the quiet touches of such a casual intimacy until sleep takes me.

And when I wake, Tess is gone.

Again.

26
Tess

"Well?" I say, spinning around in a circle. "What do you think?"

I've got my iced caramel macchiato in one hand while the other gestures to the empty office space. Sure, the carpet has some stains that we'll have to strategically cover with furniture. And the walls need a bit of a repaint, but the view looks out on downtown Jacksonville.

Ilmari and Caleb stand in the doorway, glancing around with confused looks on their faces.

"What am I looking at?" Mars mutters.

"If I had to guess, I'd say this is a modern art installation titled 'Dreams Unchased,'" Caleb replies, taking a sip of his coffee.

"Okay, A, fuck you," I say at Caleb. "You weren't even invited. You're officially crashing a business meeting right now."

"Mars invited me," he replies with a smirk.

"You invited yourself because you wanted to get out of taking Jake to the dentist," Mars replies.

"Can you blame me?" says Caleb. "You think he's a prima donna about his sheet thread counts? Go with him once when he has to get a cavity filled and see how quickly you wanna file for divorce."

I just roll my eyes. Ilmari was strict with me that we only had until 10:00 a.m. to get this done because they leave for an away game this afternoon. "Guys," I call, snapping my fingers their direction. "Focus here. Look at the space, Mars. Yes or no?"

"You haven't explained why we're here."

I glance between him and Caleb. "I can never tell when you're serious."

"He's always serious," Caleb teases.

"Mars, why the hell else would I be dragging you downtown at 9:00 a.m. on a Thursday morning?" I cry, gesturing around again. "We're picking an office space for Out of the Net."

"That name is fucking adorable, by the way," says Caleb, taking another sip of his coffee as he does a half-spin. "Do I know why you guys need a physical office space?"

"Uhh, maybe to conduct business out of," I say, not even bothering to keep the incredulity from my tone. "You need a space to meet with clients, train volunteers. Not to mention that if we want to be taken seriously by local government officials or the conservation orgs, we have to have an identifiable presence. Plus, it's just kind of nice to have a place to send the mail."

"And you think this place is the right fit?" asks Caleb, glancing around.

"I think it's the right *price*," I correct. "And anything can be the right fit with a little polish."

While Ryan and I were up late watching TV last night, I was feverishly looking up ideas for simple office makeovers. I've already got a few things ordered, and as soon as Mars gets back from this trip out to Vegas, I'll drag him over to IKEA to help me pick out some furniture pieces.

"Trust me," I say. "You give me a week, and you won't even recognize this place."

"I'd hope not," Caleb replies.

I glare at him. "You wanna take the stairs back down to the car, or you want me to push you out this window? 'Cause I'm not picky."

Still wearing his smirk, he slips behind Mars, using him as a shield.

I turn my attention to our patron. "Mars, what do *you* think? I have all the specs right here," I say, whipping out my phone. "I can walk down the leasing terms with you if you want. I've already asked the landlord for a couple adjustments. He was charging a huge fee for phone lines, and who needs that when we can just use a cellphone? Want me to email you the rental contract or—" I huff when I glance up and see he's walked right past me and is now looking out the window. "Or I guess I can keep looking for locations," I call over to him. "But Mars, we really need to get this ball rolling so—"

"I hired *you* to make these decisions, did I not?" he says at last, his tone icy.

I go still, eyeing him warily. "Yeah, but I just thought you might want to—"

He turns sharply around. "Don't bother me with this kind of thing again, Tess. If you think it needs to be done, do it. I put you in charge for a reason."

Even Caleb looks surprised as he stomps past us, heading for the door.

"So, you just don't care, then?" I call after him, flapping my arm in exasperation. "You're gonna front all this cash, and then just wash your hands of all of it?"

He stops at the door, shoulders tense, not turning around.

"I suppose you don't care about Joey or Nancy or Cheryl either," I shout. "No, frigid Mars Price, Mr. Man of No Freaking Words, has *zero* opinions about how the nonprofit he's single-handedly funding will operate. You don't want anything to do with *any* of it—"

"I *can't* have anything to do with it," he shouts, spinning around. He glares from Caleb to me. "What the hell am I going to do?" he says, glancing between us again. "I have no college education, Tess. I never even graduated secondary school before I went pro. You're all pushing me to think about what comes next after I retire, but there is no next. I play hockey. It's the *only* thing I know. I have no expertise in conservation or dune restoration. Caleb is more qualified to assist than I am," he says with a wave of his hand. "At least he has a degree in chemistry."

Caleb blinks at his partner. "Mars—"

"Don't" Ilmari glares at him. "Don't make light of this."

"I would never," Caleb says gently.

"I am useless to you in this endeavor," Mars says at me. "I gave you the only thing I can offer: capital. The rest is up to you."

"Mars, you have so many gifts, so many talents—"

"Don't patronize me," he snaps. "I don't need your pity."

"Mars, I don't—"

"I hired you to do the work I am wholly unqualified to do," he says over me. "I need you to do this for me. Will you?"

Slowly, I nod.

"Good. Then, moving forward, you need not include me in every detail of your planning. Agreed?"

I nod again.

His gaze darts to Caleb. "Come. We must go." Not waiting for Caleb's reply, he spins on his heel and leaves the office.

Caleb glances at me, his usual asshole smirk firmly tucked away. "We knew he was stewing about something, but we didn't know what or why. Don't be angry with him?"

I shake my head. "No. No, never."

"I'll talk to him," he says, crossing the few feet of carpet to my side. He wraps me in a side hug, kissing my temple. "You good?"

I nod. "Yeah, it's fine, Cay. Really."

He gives me a half-smile that quickly falls. "Please just . . . don't stop trying to be his friend, okay? He'll never admit it, but he needs one."

"We all do," I reply.

He nods. "See you later, Tess."

With that, he turns and follows after the brooding Finn, leaving me alone in the new head office of Out of the Net.

A few hours later, I'm leaning out the window of my car, ordering some fast-food on my way to the office supply store. A pierced kid with green hair takes my credit card, thrusting a large iced tea out the window at me. I'm juggling my drink and the bag of food as the kid tries to hand me back my card and a straw, which I promptly drop out the side of the car.

"Shit—sorry," I call up to the kid.

He wordlessly hands me another straw as my phone starts to ring, buzzing in the cupholder.

I juggle everything into place, plopping the tea in the other cupholder and tossing my bag of food on the passenger seat. The car behind me honks, clearly incensed that they're having to wait 3.7 seconds too long for me to move out of the way.

"Hold your fucking horses," I shout out my window, snatching for my phone.

The name on the front of the phone glows: CHARLIE PUTNAM.

Shit, my lawyer is calling. Never a good sign.

I answer the phone, turning it on speaker. "Hey, Charlie. Can you hear me? I'm in the car on the prepaid."

"Yeah, honey," he calls in his thick Kentucky drawl. "I can hear you real good."

Charlie Putnam is a peach of a man born and bred near Elizabethtown, and he has the accent to prove it. He stands all of 5'0", and I think his bowties are surgically attached to his body. But he's a shark in the courtroom, and he doesn't nickel and dime me, which I appreciate.

"Did he sign yet?"

"What's that, honey?" he says. "Oh, no, not yet. His counsel has ten days to respond to our request, remember? It's only been five."

I don't even bother to let myself feel surprised or disappointed. "Why are you calling me, then? Don't get me wrong, I love the sound of your voice," I add, and he chuckles.

"Well, honey, it's like this. I'm getting a lot of calls to the office demanding to know where you are and why you can't be reached. Frankly, it's reaching the level of harassment."

My stomach drops out as I turn quickly into a gas station. "Oh, Charlie, I'm so sorry. I hate that you're in the middle." I pull up and park in front of the ice box at the end of the gas station mini mart. "What is he saying?"

"Well, he's saying he's gonna go to the police and declare you missing," Charlie replies.

I huff. "That is such bullshit. Have you told him I'm not missing?"

"Oh, yes. I've made it clear we've been in regular contact."

"And you haven't told him where I am?"

"Of course not," he replies. "Though he did ask me to make an offer to you. We'll call it an informal mediation."

I sigh, rubbing a tired hand against my temple. "What does he want, Charlie?"

"Well, he wonders if you'll take a call from his mother."

My heart stops. Shit, this is unexpected. "Bea wants to talk to me?"

"Oh, yes. She's been desperate to get ahold of you too," Charlie replies. "I've been asked to arrange a call."

I stare out the windshield at the sign taped to the ice box

advertising tackle bait. This could be a trick on so many levels. I could think I'm connecting to Bea and really, it's him. I could connect with Bea but he's in the room. They could find a way to track the call—

No.

I try and shut down those thoughts. I don't want to act paranoid.

"When does Bea want to arrange a call?"

"I'm sure she'll drop whatever she's doing to take the call."

"Do it."

"Okay. Well, when would you like to—"

"Now," I say, unbuckling my seatbelt. "I want to do it now. Call her and connect us."

This is the only way. If we plan it out in advance, it gives Troy time to act, time to get involved. And as much as I love Bea, Troy has always been her weakness. If a single word of what I have to say gets mediated to her through him, he'll taint it, and I'll lose her.

She's probably already written me off as the daughter-in-law she used to love. The loss of her respect and support hurts more than I can bear. I blink back my tears, trying to center all my heavy emotions and sink them down deep to the bottom of my chest.

"Are you sure, honey?"

"Yes. Please connect me with my mother-in-law."

"Okay. Give me a minute to chat with Shirley, and we'll have you on the call."

My free hand clenches the steering wheel. "I'm ready."

27
Ryan

It's travel day for the Vegas away game, and I'm not getting on that plane. Hell, I'm not even getting on the bus to go to the airport. I'm just standing here in the loading dock, watching as my team gets on the bus without me.

As I stand here, Brayden Jones, the farm team guy who gets to dress to fill my hole in the roster walks past, bag in hand. He'll be a fourth line guy and probably won't see a minute of action on the ice, but he's officially wearing a Rays jersey and going to the Show.

Watching him excitedly load the bus eases my anxiety. I know this injury is only temporary. As soon as I'm rehabbed, I'll be back out on that ice, and poor Jonesy will be sent back down. That's just hockey.

"Hey, we'll miss you, man," says Jake as he walks past, giving my shoulder a tap with his fist. "Look out for Tess while we're gone, yeah?"

"Yeah," I say, nodding his way.

"You're a good guy, Langers," he says with a smile. "A good friend. We know we can trust you to take care of her and not take advantage."

Fuck.

Does he need to know that I'm just an average guy who actually slept with Tess last night? She pumped the breaks hard on the sex, but we did *technically* sleep together.

"Everything okay?" says Jake.

Now Mars is standing at his shoulder.

"Nope," I say with a smile, and they both frown at me. "Uhh—nope. I mean, like, yep. Nope, all good here. You know, 'cause why wouldn't it be good? Tess and I are just roommates . . . and it's only temporary . . . and I mean, our schedules couldn't be more different, so I never really even see her."

They're both just looking at me.

"But you know, when I *am* at the house, I'll keep both eyes on her," I ramble on. "I mean, unless she's doing something where I should be looking away, and then I definitely will . . . like if she's naked again—"

Shut up. Shut up now.

Jake just smiles and waves as he walks off.

"She's very important to us," says Mars, giving me his best Finnish death glare.

I swallow. "Yeah, I'm getting that."

"Hurt her, and I'll end you," he adds before turning away, which really feels like beating a dead horse.

His warning rings in my ears as I watch him load the bus. I'm still thinking about it as I make my way back inside. I'm on my way up to the gym to hop on the exercise bike when Vicki finds me in the hallway.

"Oh, Langley, there you are," she says, fanning herself with the manilla folder in her hand. "Can you believe this heat in January?"

"Yep, it's warm out there," I say, making the smallest of talk.

Vicki Francis is our Director of Operations, and a bigger ball-buster you'll never find. Hearing that she's been looking for me instantly has me on edge. She's one of the only people on the team that can get us all bouncing like trained seals.

"What can I do for you, Vic?"

"Oh, it's not what you can do for me today," she says with a distracted wave of her hand. "It's what I can do for you. Or I should say what the GM can do. He's in today, and he was asking to see you."

I go still. Mark Talbot is here? I've never actually had a conversation with Mark in my life, though I've seen him enough times at games and team events. He's this billionaire tech guy born and raised in Jacksonville who returned here when he all but retired at forty years old, having sold off most of his companies. He used some of his endless wealth to buy an NHL franchise and set it up here in Jax. Other than the fact that he looks like a *GQ* model, I don't know a thing about the guy.

"Hello? Earth to Ryan," Vicki teases, waving a hand in my face.

I blink, refocusing my attention on her. "I'm sorry, Vic. What?"

She laughs. "I said if you have a minute, you may want to go up and have a quick word. He'll be in his office for only another hour or so."

"Yeah, sure. I can do that—"

"Wonderful," she says. "I'll walk with you."

I have no choice but to get myself turned around on the crutches and hobble my way back down the hallway towards the elevators, Vicki at my side. We ride up to the fourth floor together and she directs me down the hallway towards the owner's suite.

A pretty young black woman sits at a secretarial desk. "Can I help you?" she chimes.

"Yeah, uhh, I'm here to see Mr. Talbot. It's Langley—Ryan Langley," I correct. "I'm umm . . . a player," I finish lamely.

She gives me a very patient smile. "Yes, I'm well aware of who you are, Mr. Langley. If you'll have a seat, Mr. Talbot can be with you in a moment."

"Actually, it's kind of easier to stand," I admit, gesturing to my crutches.

She just raises a brow at me, her fingers already clack-clack-clacking away on her ergonomic keyboard.

"Not that I *can't* sit," I go on, because apparently I have to say every single thing I'm thinking out loud today. "I mean, I *can* sit. I just don't feel like sitting right now. You know, because I've just been sitting a lot and—"

"Mr. Langley?" she says, cutting me off.

"Hmm?"

"You can go in now." She gestures at the door over her left shoulder.

"Thanks," I say, hobbling forward on my crutches.

I try to open the door on my own, but I nearly drop my crutch down and she has to hop up and hold the door for me. I glance around his office as I swing in, taking note of all his sports memorabilia.

"Langley, come on in," calls Mr. Talbot. He crosses the dark carpet towards me and holds out a hand.

I pause and awkwardly shift around until I can shake his hand. "Nice to meet you, sir."

He laughs. "Jesus, that's not a great start, is it? I came in here ready to offer you a contract extension, and you come out of the corner swinging with a 'nice to meet you, sir.' I take this as proof of all the ways I'm failing as a team owner."

"Sir?" I say with a raised brow.

"I've clearly not been doing enough here in town to grow my team if one of my star forwards can dare to utter the sentence 'nice to meet you' halfway through a season."

"Oh, sir—I didn't—"

"Not your fault, Langley," he says. "Let's get you off your feet, huh? Then we can talk contracts."

I go still, glancing around the empty room. "Umm . . . sir, shouldn't the agents be here?" I ask, my panic rising. I can't do this. Not like this. I need MK here. He negotiates all my deals for me. "I've only ever done a contract negotiation through my agent—"

"No need to panic," Mr. Talbot says with a raised hand. "We'll get the blood-sucking lawyers involved from tip to tail, don't you worry. In fact, I believe Taysa has already sent over the preliminary contracts to your agent. You're working with MK, right?"

"Yes, sir," I say with a nod, still feeling on edge. I don't see any stacks of papers ready for me to peruse. Maybe he really does just want to talk. The vise grip my panic holds on my chest eases slightly.

Mr. Talbot slips around the other side of his desk, gesturing for me to take a seat. I sink down awkwardly into one of the two chairs on my side of the desk, resting my crutches against the opposite chair.

"How's the knee?" he says, pouring me a glass of water.

"Coming along," I say, accepting the glass as he slides it over. "Right now, it's just about managing swelling and hoping the tear doesn't get any worse."

"Damn. ACL?"

"MCL," I correct.

"Right. I saw the hit. Nasty stuff. But you're strong," he says. "Built to last."

"Yes, sir," I reply, taking a sip of my water.

"Well, I spoke to MK yesterday," he goes on. "He told me all about your new endorsement deal with Nike. That's impressive stuff, Langley. That's just the kind of attention we want brought to this team. Well done."

"Thank you, sir," I say, perking up in my chair. "I'm surprised he told you about it when the ink isn't even dry."

"Oh, these things always take quite a bit of time to iron out," Talbot replies with a chuckle. "Leave it with MK to chew on for a bit.

Speaking of contracts," he adds, leaning forward a bit, elbows on his desk. "You only have a one-year contract here, correct?"

"Yes, sir."

"I wanted to ask you how you're liking it here with Rays. I know new teams are tough and not everyone likes the trade, but how do you feel? Is there anything you'd like to see done differently? Anything we could improve?"

My heart is in my throat. I'm not sure what I'm supposed to say here. MK always handles negotiating salaries. Do I play it cool? Try to tell him what he wants to hear? Or should I just speak from the heart?

As if he can sense my dilemma, Talbot leans back in his chair. "How old are you, Langley?"

"Twenty-two, sir," I reply. "My birthday was back in September."

"Damn," he says with a laugh. "To be twenty-two again. Prime of fucking life. You feel unstoppable. Isn't there a Miley Cyrus song about being twenty-two?"

"Umm, I think it might be Taylor Swift," I reply, hiding my smirk behind my water glass. I *know* it's Taylor Swift. I keep it quiet around the guys, but I'm a total Swiftie. You try growing up in the same house as my sister and all her friends and not like Taylor Swift.

"Right, well twenty-two is an exciting age, Langley. A young guy like you, with the right combo of talent, looks, and drive, you can pretty much write your own ticket."

The truth is that I've never really felt young. You don't get to feel young when you partially raise your sister while your mom pulls double shifts at the hospital to pay for your hockey. You don't feel young when you leave the house at fifteen to compete in the Junior League. You don't feel young when you become the breadwinner at eighteen, negotiating multi-million-dollar contract deals while most kids your age are saving up to buy their first car.

But Talbot doesn't want to hear my thoughts on growing up too fast. So, I just nod, taking another sip of my water.

"And look, I'm a rational guy. Maybe all you want is to earn some time on the ice, get some pucks in that net, and you'll be looking to trade up. Any team would be lucky to have you. Is that what you want? Do you want to see how high your rocket can climb?"

I'm flustered as I set my glass down. "I—"

"Because I'll be honest with you, Langley. If what you want is to make it to the playoffs every year and earn a fighting chance at the Stanley Cup, the Rays might not be the best fit for you. This is a different team in a different stage of life. We're in the building stage. I intend to build something that will last. That takes time, and it takes cultivating the right kind of talent."

"Yes, sir—"

"And I'll tell you this right now. The kind of talent I *don't* need hogging up my ice is the kind who only sees the Rays as a springboard onto bigger and better teams."

"Of course, sir—"

"First season is tough all the way around," he admits. "We're dealing with the trades, and building a team, and all the hiccups of running a new staff and facilities. It's been a nightmare."

"Yes, sir," I say again.

"But we can't get complacent," he goes on. "I'm already looking to next season, and the season after that. Hell, I'm looking ten years into the future here. A few of the guys have already locked themselves in to four- and five-year contracts with no-trade clauses. They intend to stay here and help me build an NHL team worth playing on."

I sit forward in my chair. "Sir—"

"So, what I want to know from you, Langley, is where do you see yourself in five years—"

"*Sir*," I say again, and I realize too late I'm practically shouting at him.

He blinks at me, those dark eyes narrowing slightly.

"That's what I want," I say into the silence.

"What?"

"Everything you just said," I reply with a wave of my hand. "I want everything, and I want it here in Jacksonville. I know I'm young, and I've still got a lot to learn, but I've also been in this game for fifteen years. It's been my whole life since I was big enough to tie my own skates. To play on an NHL team . . . to be part of a team," I clarify. "That's what I want."

Talbot sits back, surveying me.

I dive into the silence. "Are there guys out here showboating, content to get traded from team to team, only thinking about getting pucks in the net? Yeah, sure. And sometimes you need those guys on the team. But I'm not that guy."

"What kind of guy are you?"

I let out a little breath, searching for the right words. "I'm the kind of guy who sticks," I reply. "Sir, I'm sticking. You give me a chance, you give me some security, some hope of knowing my jersey is safe, and I will help you build a team that doesn't just consistently make it to the playoffs, we bring home the Cup."

He smirks at me. "Those are some big words, Langley. Big promises. You really think you can turn all that talk into action?"

I just shrug, flashing him a smirk of my own. "I'm twenty-two, remember? I'm unstoppable, sir."

He barks out a laugh, pressing his hands flat against his desk as he stands. Taking it as my cue, I stand too, reaching for my crutches.

"You're a good man, Langley," he says, stepping around the desk. "You're a team player. The coaching staff, the captains, the support staff, they all say the same thing: Ryan Langley is the kind of guy you want on your team. I want you in that Rays jersey. If I have my way, I'll keep you in it. But I won't freak you out by discussing the details now," he adds with a laugh. "Give MK a call today. I sent him everything already."

"Thank you, sir," I say, feeling breathless. I take the hand he offers, shaking it again. But when I move to let go, he holds on, his grip tight as iron.

"Don't let this shake your confidence," he says, gesturing with his free hand down at my knee. "You're still the prize, Langley. Rest and recover. The ice will still be there whether it's two weeks from now or two months. Return to us whole."

"Yes, sir."

"Good man." He drops my hand and walks with me to his door. As he opens it, he cuffs my shoulder. "And hey, if that number doesn't work for you, don't hesitate to let me know."

My senses are spinning as I try to imagine what number might be written on an NHL extension contract with my name on it. This all feels too good to be true.

"Fight for what you're worth, Langley," Talbot says in parting. "Always fight for what you're worth."

28
Tess

My heart is in my throat as I hear Charlie's secretary on the other end of the line. "Ms. Owens, we're ready to connect your call through to Ms. Owens. Would you like to connect?"

"Yes," I say. "Thank you."

"Connecting now," she says in her Southern sing-song voice.

I let out a breath as I wait. The only other sound is the humming of the AC unit in my rental car. That sound is broken by the trill of a dial tone.

It dials once. Twice. Three times.

Then the click as we connect.

"Tess, darling?" comes Bea's smooth, alto voice. "Tess, are you there?"

I'm flooded with emotion at hearing the clear note of concern in her tone. "Yes—Bea, it's me. I'm here."

"Oh, Tess," she cries. "You've had us all scared half to death. Your apartment looked like it was ransacked. I was ready to call the police until Troy said he finally heard from your lawyer that you were alright."

"Bea, I'm so sorry—"

"Where are you, darling? Let me come to you. Wherever you are, it's not home. Let me bring you home," she pleads.

I shake my head, knowing she can't see it. "I can't," I say. "I have no home there anymore."

"That's nonsense. Tess, you listen to me now. All of this has been blown so completely out of proportion. I simply cannot believe that Dale chose to handle this situation as he did. I swear to you, when they told me about that god-awful HR meeting, I saw red."

I blink back my tears. "So, you didn't know? You didn't approve them putting me on administrative leave?"

"Are you kidding me?" she cries. "What is this, a Nathaniel Hawthorne novel? We don't punish our best and brightest junior partners for dancing at a wedding, Tess. It's ridiculous."

I breathe a sigh of relief, even as my gut churns. All this means is that Troy lied. *Again.* He lied to everyone, convincing us all that Bea was the mastermind, wielding the company's morality clause like a cudgel to break and silence me.

"You know who *should* be put on administrative leave is Dale," she adds with an irritated huff. "I simply can't believe that after ten years with this company, he thought *this* was the best way to handle what was so clearly a private family matter."

I go still, heart racing as I put together the pieces. "Bea, wait . . . who do you think is responsible for putting me on administrative leave?"

"Dale," she cries. "I swear, that man is a menace. I'd fire him if I could get the other partners to all agree."

Everything stops.

I close my eyes, taking a deep breath. "Bea, this was Troy."

"Of course, Troy is upset," she says quickly. "He's been beside himself wondering where you are. He said he walked you out of the office mid-day on Monday and hadn't heard from you since. We had to have the fire department let us into your apartment, and we found it in such a state. We were sure you'd been taken in the night—"

I can't do this. I can't listen to her spew back his lies.

"—and then there's all this nonsense about the divorce papers. Troy was blindsided, Tess. Devastated. This was never in the plan—"

"Bea, *enough*," I shout. "It's my turn to talk now, okay?"

"Tess—"

"No, *I* need to talk, and I need you to just listen for a minute, okay? I have to get this out. I feel like I'll die if I don't get this out," I say, putting every ounce of feeling I have into the words.

"What do you need to say, honey?"

Where to even start?

"Look, I know you don't want to hear this, but Troy is lying to you. He's lying to everyone. He didn't 'walk me out' of the office last week," I say, miming air quotes. "He *kicked* me out. He threatened to have security escort me out if I didn't go quietly—"

"No," Bea says, and I can practically see her in my mind, shaking her head, the little pearl drops she loves so well dangling from her ears. "Troy would never."

"Troy is the one who arranged everything with that bullshit HR meeting," I go on. "He's the one who assembled the partners without you. He called in Dale and gave them all the photos of Ryan and me dancing at Rachel's wedding. He shoved this stupid morality clause down my throat—which, by the way, if *anyone* in this family is guilty of breaking the company's morality code, it would be your precious son. Did you forget all the women he fucked on company time, in company offices? Because I sure as hell didn't."

"Tess, you're rehashing old history now," she says with a tired sigh. "I'm fully aware that my son has made many mistakes. He apologized. He tried to make it right with you. He went to counseling—"

"He was fucking his secretary the whole time," I cry. "I caught Candace on our security footage stumbling through the bushes in my backyard when I was in the goddamn house!"

"Again, that was in the past," Bea rationalizes. "What happened then must surely still be painful to you. I won't deny it still brings me pain to know the things he's done. But it's not like you hold no blame for what happened," she adds, her tone icy. "It always takes two people to break up a marriage."

Oh, fucking spare me. If one more person dares to give me this particular piece of sage wisdom, I'm gonna punch them right in the cunt, I swear to God.

"I'm not saying I judge you for your choices either, Tess," she goes on, filling my stunned silence. "You chose to put your career first. You *chose* to stop making his happiness a priority. But have I ever judged you for your mistakes? Have I loved you any less?"

"No," I say, eyes closed. "Bea, we're not doing this. I am not to blame for Troy cheating on me. That was a choice *he* made. I can't force another person to cheat. He alone is responsible for his actions. And, honestly, that's not even the main reason our marriage failed."

"Well, you certainly bring it up often enough to justify my being confused," she counters.

I just sigh. This conversation is going nowhere. It's time to redirect. "Bea, I know you love him, but can you really deny that Troy exhibits a pattern of selfish and manipulative behavior? Your son is a narcissist—"

"That's enough," she snaps. "I'm not going to let you turn this into a diatribe of all Troy's faults. You want to talk of choices? You've clearly chosen to hate him. You've chosen to see only the worst in him, and that will be your cross to bear. But I answered this call to talk about *you*. I answered because I was worried about you, Tess. As a valued employee and a loved member of this family, you deserved nothing less."

"I'm not a member of this family anymore," I reply, suddenly feeling so tired. "At this point, I'm just a hostage."

There's a deafening silence.

At last, Bea says, "I never thought you of all people could say something so unspeakably cruel."

Tears sting my eyes again. "No, Bea. Do you know what's unspeakably cruel? Do you want to know what the last thing was that your son did to me before he forced me out of my office last week?"

"Tess—"

"He put his hand around my throat, and he squeezed. He choked the air out of me while I begged him to let me go—"

"Stop," she pleads.

"Why would I stop for you when he wouldn't stop for me?" I press, indignation lacing my every word. "He called me a whore, and he choked me. This was all after he threatened to ruin me. Do you really think there is *any* universe in which I wouldn't ask for a divorce after that? Would *you* stay legally chained to a man who chokes you, Bea? A man who breaks his vows and fucks other women in your marriage bed? A man who belittles you and lies to you? A man who stalks you and scares you and threatens your job, your reputation—"

"I can't bear this—"

"If I can bear it, you will too," I shout. "This is *your* son, Bea. You think this is about the infidelity? No, your precious boy *hurts* me."

"Please, stop," she whispers, and I know she's done. If I push any harder, she'll hang up on me, and I need her. We're both crying, our emotions exposed like two raw nerves. Finally, she breaks the silence.

"Tess, darling, come home. Just come home, and I can help you work through all of this. We can't fix this if you won't come home."

"No," I say again. "I won't put myself within physical reach of Troy ever again."

Another choked sob echoes through the phone. "So . . . what then? You're just done with me too? After thirteen years of a shared life, we just never see each other again?"

"You don't have to break ties with me just because I've broken ties with Troy," I explain, manifesting my hope into the universe. *Please, God, let her not forsake me as all others always do.* "I've tried to make that clear for the last three years. I love you, Bea. You're the mother I never had. I've always loved and admired you, and I want you in my life but . . . "

"But you want never to see or speak to my son, the alleged wife-beater, ever again."

She summarizes it so coolly, with such an air of resignation. And it's in that moment that I know I've lost her. The pain tears through me, ripping me apart. I'm barely holding it together.

"Bea," I whimper into the phone, knowing it's pointless. Maybe part of me always knew.

"Can you just tell me where you are?" she asks again. "I just need to know that you're safe."

"No," I reply, tears streaking down my face.

"You won't tell me?"

"No," I say again, my voice catching. "I can't."

"Why not?"

I speak the truth we both know. "Because I can't trust you not to tell Troy."

We sit in the silence of that truth. I watch as a pair of men casually open the ice box and pull out a few bags. They walk in front of my car, ready to load their cooler, as if inside this vehicle my life isn't going up in flames.

"What happens from here?" Bea says at last.

Finding my voice, I make my plea. "If you ever truly loved me, you'll help me convince Troy to sign the divorce papers. This doesn't have to be contested."

I sense her indecision. "Divorce is such an ugly word," she replies. "And the press, our clients, our friends—"

"There's a way out of this that doesn't involve a PR crisis for the family or the firm," I say, ready to silence her doubts. "But you need to know this, and you need to *hear* it, Bea. Take off your mother hat and put on your CEO hat. Troy means to detonate us both. If you side with him in this, you will be left holding the grenade when he pulls the pin."

"You certainly paint a bleak picture."

"You're the one who's always cared about appearances," I counter. "You want the public face of your family *and* your company preserved? Then help me. Just this once, set aside your blind loyalty to Troy. I have an idea of how we spin this into a positive outcome for everyone, but if you won't help me, then Troy wins . . . and we will all burn."

Whether she can admit it out loud or not, Bea Owens knows the truth about her son. If she has to bet her family's name and her company's reputation on my conduct or his, I can only pray she'll make the right choice.

After a moment's consideration, I hear the resignation in her tone. "Fine. We'll try this your way, Tess. Just tell me what you want me to do."

I smile as the smallest kernel of hope blooms in my chest. It's weak, and so terribly fragile, but it's there. "Get him to sign the papers. Without the divorce papers in hand, the rest of my plan falls apart."

She sighs. "I'll see what I can do."

29
Tess

When I pull up to Ilmari's condo, I pump the brakes in surprise. There are two cars parked in the driveway. I swallow back my frustration as the truth hits me: Ryan is home. I should have realized that the team wouldn't make an injured player travel across the country just to *not* play in a game. After the epic shitstorm that was this day, I really have to go in there and pretend I'm not crushing on my roommate?

And did I mention the cars? He has company. So, after surviving my fights with Mars and Bea, I now have to put on an Emmy-winning performance as the thirty-three-year-old hot mess of a soon-to-be divorcée who is most definitely *not* picturing her roommate naked.

Awesome. Love this journey for me.

I huff, glancing up and down the street, looking for somewhere else to park. Finding a spot a block down, I parallel park and trudge down the sidewalk towards the condo, readying myself for my performance.

The last several days have been oddly nice having Ryan Langley for a roommate. He behaves like a perfect gentleman, helping where he can, given his limited mobility. He helped me with groceries yesterday, swinging around on his crutches with the bags on his wrists.

He always asks me if I want anything if he's ordering in food. And he sends me little voice memos throughout the day. Yesterday he was bored doing his PT, so I got a string of rambling voice memos where he's panting into the phone, rank ordering his favorite *SOA* characters.

At night I've been helping him get comfortable so he can fall asleep. Sometimes we lay on the bed and chat or watch TV. Twice now it was me falling asleep before him.

Everything with him feels so easy, so natural. We joke together like we're old friends. God, he's such a big flirt. But he does it in a cheesy way that is so completely disarming, like his little pickup lines at the beach. He's so charming that you can't decide if you want to kiss him or slap him. You could almost write it all off as a tease . . . until you catch the heat in his eyes.

He wants me. Whether he wants more than sex is unclear. But I won't deny that something about Ryan makes me nervous. It has since that first meeting on the beach all those months ago. He quite literally took my breath away. Part of that may have been the blow to the head with that stupid soccer ball, but it was at least a little bit due to him.

Rachel may be the bigger zodiac girl, but I know enough to believe that certain signs are drawn to each other. They share an energy. I googled Ryan after beach day, and he's a Virgo, which means both our signs are ruled by Mercury, the planet of communication. Is that why I find him so easy to talk to?

I wanted to dismiss our connection, this feeling of opposites attracting, but then Ryan went and called me magnetic. I think he feels it too. He's drawn to me, and I'm drawn to him. Part of me questions if we're not meant to collide.

Taking a deep breath, I swing the door open and step inside. I'm immediately met with the thumping sound of loud rock music. I'm greeted by a scene like something out of a low budget frat boy porno. There are five buff shirtless guys lounging on all the furniture. A few have game controllers in their hands, their eyes locked on the TV, including Ryan. Two more are on their phones, manspreading in those sexy workout shorts that give a generous glimpse of cut thighs.

I'm just gonna say it—whoever is in charge of approving the designs for NHL team apparel deserves a raise.

The guys are so engrossed in their video game and their phones that they haven't even noticed me yet. I turn, glancing over to the kitchen. "Oh my god."

Heaven only knows what look of horror has just crossed my face. It looks like a bomb went off in here. There are dirty dishes everywhere. Someone made a mess using the blender. Scrunching up my nose, I count not one, not two, but *four* empty boxes of Kraft Mac and Cheese. A big silver pot shows the telltale signs of being used to make a vat of powdered cheese noodles.

Lady boner gone.

"Tess—" Ryan's eyes go wide as he takes me in. "Flash, cut the music," he calls over to Mr. Tall, Dark and Handsome stretched out in the reading chair.

The music cuts, leaving the video game as the only sound. I glance to the TV and see a split screen with all the Mario characters in little race cars. I was never hip enough to own or play video games growing up, but I'm pretty sure this one is called Mario Kart.

"Hey, you're home early," he calls, reaching for his knee brace that rests forgotten on the coffee table.

"Am I?" I say, suddenly noticing the mess on the kitchen table too. Someone ate cereal out of a mixing bowl and left out the milk . . . and the cereal . . . *and* spilled some of it.

"Don't worry, we'll clean up the mess later," calls the freckled redhead sitting next to Ryan.

"The guys just came over to make sure I was sticking to my PT routine," Ryan offers.

"It's fine," I say, giving them all a little wave. "Hi, everyone."

A round of deep hellos chorus back at me.

Ryan is distracted, strapping on his knee brace before he gets up. "Uh, guys, this is Tess," he says gesturing at me. "Tess, these are just some of the rookies. That's Flash in the chair there," he says, pointing out the black-haired guy.

"Flash?" I repeat with a raised brow.

"Yeah, my last name is Gordon," he replies with a grin.

I smile. "Cute."

"And this is Yuley and Westie," Ryan adds point to the two guys on the couch. They're both cute, with soft baby faces that contrast with their cut man bodies. Goodness, they look like they might still be teenagers, which makes me feel a little pervy for calling this a porno set.

"And I'm Patrick," says the giant sitting in the chair closest to me. He gets up, unfolding what has to be his 6'4" frame, and turns.

Holy fuckballs.

My eyes go wide. He can't be more than twenty years old, but he's got the body of Apollo. And I swear to all the gods, he's actually glistening right now. Like, baby oil glisten. It's catching in the fucking sunlight. This must be his post-workout glow.

"Nice to meet you, Tess," he says in that deep voice, dripping with the confidence of youth.

He gives me a once over, and it feels like he's undressing me with his eyes. I clear my throat, dropping my gaze away from him. The cocky asshole smirks. Oh yeah, he *wants* me to look. He practically screams "fuckboy." I bet he has exactly two things in his pocket: his car keys and a condom.

"Go bench-press something, Patty," Ryan says, stepping past him in a deliberate way that puts himself between us. "Hey, you have a good day?" he says at me.

His question is all it takes to catapult my mind back through time, reliving the utter chaos of this day. I feel suddenly breathless. But I'll be damned if I'm gonna cry in front of Patrick Abs-for-Days McHockey Boy.

"Yep, all fine," I lie, quickly turning away from him. I fake looking for something in the fridge, though I'm not hungry or thirsty. It gives me a chance to just swing open the door and shove my head inside, taking a hit off the cold air.

"Hey, Tess, can you bring us some sodas?" calls one of the boys from the couch.

I jerk upright, slow turning to look that way.

"Fuck you, Westie," Ryan says before I can respond. "She's not your fucking maid. Get your own damn soda."

"She's standing right there," he replies with a shrug, turning back to his video game.

"I'm sorry about all this," Ryan says, facing me. He looks worried, nervous even. "I didn't invite them over. This isn't my scene, I swear."

"It's fine, Ryan," I say, reaching out to touch his bare shoulder. My fingers barely brush his skin before I drop my hand away. "You can have your friends over. It's none of my business," I add with shrug.

"They're not my friends," he says, his voice lowering. "And they invited themselves over. But I gotta be there for them, you know? Guide them along a bit."

I glance around at the mess on every surface of our previously clean house. "And this is you guiding along the next generation? Teaching them how to make boxed mac and cheese?"

"Don't forget the cut-up hotdogs," he replies with a smirk.

"No, we can't forget the cut-up hotdogs," I deadpan. "The cheese powder needs enough surfaces to congeal to."

"God, I love it when you use words like congeal," he teases, leaning in a bit closer.

I smirk, shaking my head as I snatch out a sparkling water from the fridge and finally shut the door. "When are you gonna let me expand that palate with some creamy lobster mac drizzled with black truffle aioli?"

"Wait—are you asking me on a date?" he replies, his tone more serious. "Is this an invitation to a stay-in date with *the* Tess Owens?"

My heart flutters before I roll my eyes. "In your dreams, hockey boy. If anything, it's an intervention. Clearly, you need one," I add, gesturing around at the mess.

"This place will be spotless, I promise," he replies. "They just got a little carried away."

"It's really fine," I say, placing my hand on his arm again.

We both follow the line of my arm with our gazes, ending at where my hand is touching his bicep. I leave it there a second too long before dropping it away again.

"Is it weird that I'm not used to seeing you with clothes on?" he says, trying to break the tension.

I laugh. "I think it's about time the tables were turned. Why don't you give us a little spin?" I tease, twirling my finger.

The corner of his mouth is tipped up in a smile as he obliges me, making a ridiculously cute one-legged hop circle, keeping his weight off his bad knee. Like the other guys, he's dressed only in those Rays logo workout shorts. He's long and lean, built for speed more than making hard hits. Jake is the one with the body of a defenseman, and Shiny Patrick over on the chair.

"Those shorts should be illegal, by the way," I say, unashamedly ogling his hockey butt.

It's his turn to laugh, but I can see the heat in his eyes. "You like what you see, Tess?"

"It's fine, I guess," I reply with a disinterested shrug. "You're not quite as impressive as Shiny Abs McBuff Boy over there," I add with a nod to the living room.

The heat burns darker in his eyes. He steps in closer until I feel my hip press against the counter. "Oh, yeah? Well, which one of us has a starting spot on an NHL team, huh? Which one of us just got offered a four-year extension contract with a three million dollar signing bonus?"

I blink, eyes wide. "Ryan—wait, what? Ohmygod, that's amazing! When did this happen?"

"Today," he replies, smiling wide.

"Ohmygod!" Setting my drink can down on the counter, I step forward, arms wide, and wrap him in a hug. "That's so great, Ryan. Really, I'm so happy for you."

He hugs me back, his arms going around my waist. He drops his head down, tucking it in at my shoulder, his breath warm on my neck. I don't miss the way he breathes me in. It raises the hairs on my neck and makes my stomach flutter.

I pull back, and he lets me go. My hands slide down his arms to his elbows. He cradles my elbows, too, and we stand there touching, enough space between us like we're at a middle school slow dance.

"Well, are you taking the offer?" I say.

He nods. "Yeah, I think I am. My agent is going to negotiate a few terms, but I've honestly been waiting for something like this for a while."

I give his arms a squeeze, still smiling. "That's great news." Then I glance around at the mess all over the kitchen. "Well, this is just silly. You can't celebrate life-changing news like this with boxed mac and cheese and cut-up hotdogs. Let me take you out."

He goes still, one brow raising in question. "Like . . . *out* out?"

I snort another laugh. "God, you are incorrigible."

"I prefer relentless," he says with a wink.

"You know what, fine," I reply, flashing him a smile. It feels good to smile after the day I've had. "For one night, and one night only, yes,

Ryan Langley. I'm taking you out on a date. Let's go celebrate your big contract news."

He just gazes down at me, his hold tightening slightly on my elbows. "You better not be fucking with me," he warns.

"Puppy, go find some clothes," I say, dropping my hands away from him. "I can't take you out in public like this," I say, gesturing to his short shorts.

He flashes me that All-American bubblegum smile, and then he's turning away from me. "Guys," he shouts into the living room. "Fun's over. You gotta go."

"Five more minutes," Patrick calls without turning around. "I'm kicking Yuley's ass on Mount Wario—hey—"

As he spoke, Ryan snatched up the remote, turning off the TV. He rattles it down, giving them all a death glare. "You assholes have ten minutes to get this place looking spotless, and then you're leaving. And if my girl finds even one Cheerio on the carpet later, I'll be dragging you all over here to vacuum every inch of the floor with your mouths. Got it? Good. Get up and get out."

The guys grumble, but they immediately start cleaning up.

I glance over at Ryan, not bothering to hide my smile. I love myself a cinnamon roll boy, but life is all about the sweet *and* the spice. Something gives me the feeling that Ryan thrives on control. One could even go so far as to call him bossy. I'm taking that little nugget of knowledge and storing it away on the shelf for later . . . right next to the memory of him calling me his girl.

30
Ryan

"Whoa," I say, eyes wide, breath caught in my throat. "Tess, you look . . ."

She walks past the kitchen table over to where I'm standing by the couch, the full skirt of her dress swishing with each step. "Ravishing? Divine? Clean?" she adds with a teasing smile.

"All three," I say with a stunned shake of my head. I keep the words I was actually thinking to myself.

Gorgeous. Fuckable. Goddamn desirable.

As soon as the guys started cleaning up the place, Tess disappeared into her room. That was over an hour ago. Now, the place is spotless, and she's standing in front of me with her red curls tumbling around her face. She's rocking a smoky eye and red lipstick that makes the freckles on her cheeks pop.

But I can barely pay attention to her beautiful face because she's wearing the flounciest, girliest bubblegum pink dress with puff sleeves and a plunging "V" cut that perfectly shows off her breasts. As she steps closer, I see that the dress is covered in little pairs of bright red cherries.

Fuck me dead.

I don't even bother suppressing my hungry groan. This woman is going to be the death of me.

"You look great, too, Ryan," she says, taking me in.

She never said what this date entailed, so I'm just dressed in a pair of jeans, a white button up, and a half-zip sweater. I've got a more functional knee brace on under the jeans and Doc told me to start bearing weight, so I'm going without the crutches tonight.

She fumbles with the little clutch in her hands, pulling out a few cards and a lipstick from her other wallet and tucking them safely inside.

"So, what's the plan?" I say, slipping my hands in my pockets.

"Hmm?" She keeps her eyes down, still rifling through her purse. "Oh, I have some ideas." She glances up, flashing me another smile with those red-painted lips.

Okay, fuck her plans. I want to stay here. If I'm only getting this one night and this one date, I want to sit on the couch with her on my lap in that dress. I want to feel the way the soft tulle bunches in my hands as I pull it up, reaching under it to graze my fingers up her bare thigh, seeking out that heat between her legs—

"Is this the new contract?"

I blink, pulling my attention away from Tess's ass and back to her face. She's standing at the bar now, glancing over her shoulder at me, a packet of papers in hand. I refocus on the papers. "Oh . . . yeah, that's it."

She sets her clutch down on the bar and starts flipping through the first few pages. "Wow, I've never seen a professional sports contract before. This all seems pretty complicated. Have you taken a look at it yet?"

I shift uncomfortably. "Well, I have an agent to help with all the contract stuff, so . . . "

She turns back to the contract. "Agents are great, but it's always good to read a contract for yourself just so you know all the particulars—"

"Hey, Lawyer Tess?" I tease, reaching over her to splay my hand across the page she's reading. Our fingertips brush, and I feel her go still next to me. Fuck, standing this close to her I can smell her perfume. It mingles with the smell of her coconutty hair oil to make a fruity, floral bouquet. It's like she's a damn walking tropical paradise. My very own Sex on the Beach.

"Hmm?" She turns slightly to glance up at me.

I push on the contract and she lets me lower it to the bar. "I was promised a date with Tess Owens. I'd prefer we not spend it pouring over contracts."

She purses those red lips at me. "Some might consider it foreplay."

"What, are you gonna read aloud my bonus payout schedule line by line so we can both get hard over how much money will be pouring into my account?"

"Mhmm," she says, the sound a hum in her throat. "A quarter million upon signing. Five hundred thousand will transfer on March first . . . "

Fuck, how is that actually working? Am I getting hard right now? Her eyes narrow like a sexy feline, and I know she knows. "Oh, fuck you," I say with a laugh that morphs into a groan as I drag my hand down over my face. "You're a goddamn she-devil."

She laughs too. "You are too easy."

"And you're too cruel," I tease back.

Somehow, I know the moment I've said the words that they were the wrong words. Something stutters behind those pretty hazel eyes. It's like a broken TV with static as I see things I know she doesn't want me to see—fear, anger, sadness, frustration. I blink and she's back to smiling, but it doesn't reach her eyes.

"Let's go, handsome," she says, ignoring the contract as she snaps her clutch shut. "I'm driving."

THIRTY minutes later, I'm seated across from Tess at a small, candlelit table in a busy fish camp restaurant. Tess ordered a glass of rosé, and I ordered a beer, and we clinked our glasses to my new contract. A half-eaten shrimp cocktail sits on the table between us.

I can't take my eyes off her. She's distracted and present at the same time. I know she's enjoying my company, and I made her laugh in the car the whole way here. But she's lost in her own head too. I wish she would open up a little more.

"Can I ask you something?" she says, her thumb absently brushing up and down the slender stem of her wine glass.

I perk up. "Yeah, anything."

"Why are you really crashing at Ilmari's house?"

I tap the table, gesturing below it to my knee. "Busted knee, remember? The place I rent is a split-level with, like, four sets of stairs. Sully and the guys were being ogres about wanting me in a place without stairs while I rehab."

She takes a sip of her wine, considering my words. "But why are you renting a split-level? Why are you renting period? If that contract I saw is any indication, you could be living in a much nicer situation. It doesn't make sense that you're mooching off Mars when you can clearly afford to take care of yourself."

Shit, she wants to get deep tonight, doesn't she? I guess that's the way things are with Tess. She's an 'all or nothing' kind of woman. Maybe if I share my truth with her, she'll reciprocate and be more open with me.

"I'm sorry," she says. "That's probably too personal for a first date, right?"

Fuck, she's pulling away again. She's shutting off.

"I'm a planner," I blurt, diving headfirst into my reply. "I don't know, I've always been that guy that wants a plan. I like organization, and I like things being in their proper place."

"Well, that makes sense, seeing as you're a Virgo," she replies, taking another sip of her wine.

I narrow my eyes at her. "You're saying my birthday has something to do with why I like plans?"

Her head tips slightly to the side as she surveys me. "You don't think so?"

"No. That's just dumb."

She laughs. "I'm sorry—" She dabs at her chin with her napkin. "That was a very Virgo thing to say."

I just roll my eyes.

"You were talking about liking plans," she prompts. "Please go on."

I sigh, trying to think of the right way to explain it. "There are parts of hockey that are perfect for me because I have so much control, you know? The structure is there, and I just get to thrive inside it—meal plans, workout plans, practice schedules, game schedules, travel itineraries. Everything is orderly and organized and so crystal fucking clear. Does that make sense?"

"It does."

"So, while I live my life under this constant weight of endless organization, there is one singular piece of this life that creates chaos."

Her eyes brighten, and I know she's already guessed it. "Contracts."

"Contracts," I echo with a nod. "You have guys out here picking up and moving their entire life every single season. If you only sign year to year, you have no idea where you'll be next. There are even some guys, like the guys who play in the minors, that can get called up and sent down multiple times in a year. That's what's happening to Patty right now."

"Oh, you mean Mr. Tall Broad and Glistening?" she teases.

I give her my best mock glare. "Call him that while you're on a date with me again, and I'll take you over my knee and spank you."

Her eyes go wide as we hold each other's gaze. It only lasts a moment before she busts out with a laugh. "Ohmygod, that was so fucking hot. But I can't tell if you actually mean it." She drops her glass down to the table and leans forward, eyes alight. She lowers her voice, her tone oozing sex. "Is that what you wanna do, Daddy? You want to take me into the bathroom, bend me over the sink, and spank me for being a bad girl?"

I lean back in my chair, eyes wide. "Holy fuck."

She laughs, leaning back too. "No, you're a good boy, aren't you. My sweet, lost beach puppy without a home. Man, when I nail it, I really nail it," she adds, almost to herself. "So, Ryan Langley, Mr. King of Organization, is organized in every aspect of his life except his living situation," she summarizes.

"It's where all my chaos reigns," I reply with a shrug. "I've never cared where I live, or whether the house is a dump, or if the windows even lock. It just doesn't matter to me, not until I have some control over my fate. So, I rent a shitty split-level over by the practice arena that the guys all affectionately call 'the death trap.' When the injury happened, I think Sully and the guys took it as their chance to rescue me."

"And now what will you do?" she says, plucking a shrimp from the silver dish and dipping it in the cocktail sauce. "Now that star forward, No. 20 Ryan Langley, has a four-year contract and a three-mil signing bonus, you finally gonna invest in some curtains?"

I grin from ear to ear. "You know my number."

She rolls her eyes. "I've watched you play, remember? I was in L.A."

"Oh, I remember," I reply, holding her gaze. "At the wedding, you told me I was your favorite Ray to watch."

"Hmm," she hums, popping the shrimp cocktail in her mouth. "You must have misheard me."

"I didn't mishear anything," I reply, unable to look away. She's just so goddamn gorgeous.

I'm saved the embarrassment of saying something regrettable like "sit in my lap" by the arrival of our meals.

OUR conversation takes a more fun, casual turn as we eat. We fight over the check—her demanding that this was her idea and thus her treat, and me arguing that I never let a lady pay on a first date. I only get her to relent by promising that she can buy me ice cream.

By the time we leave the restaurant, it's dark outside, but this part of the beach is hopping with night life. The restaurants are all packed, with people milling around outside waiting to be seated. It's a bit chilly, but not too bad that more people aren't strolling with dogs and kids.

There's a line out the door at the little ice cream shop. Tess pouts when she sees it, glancing around the other shop fronts looking for an alternative. "Hey, let's walk over to the beach," she says, pointing to the ghostly white stretch of sand that marks the hilly dunes. "The line will die down in a few minutes, and we can come back. Can you manage without crutches?" she adds, gesturing to my knee.

"I'm not sure," I reply with a grin. "I may need you to wrap your arm around me . . . you know, for balance."

"Oh, well that was happening anyway because I'm cold," she replies, slipping herself right up next to my side and wrapping an arm around my waist.

I blink in my surprise as my arm goes automatically around her shoulders. I'm not actually sure what it is that we're doing here. She called it a date. More than once. But she's also distracted and sad and something definitely happened to her today.

Fuck, I just need her to let me in. She's gotta give me something. Anything.

Sure, I want sex. I want another taste of her so badly. But this has already moved so far beyond sex for me. I want . . . *her*. I want her laughter and her curious questions. I want the way she explains about the nonprofit and building out a donor base. I want foreplay as we talk about the environmental scourge of geotubes and compare our favorite plot lines of *SOA*. I want the smell of her coconutty hair on my pillow.

The truth is that I'm falling hard for this woman, and from everything I see and feel, she's just . . . falling. And I don't know how to catch her. I don't know how to make it stop. And she won't give me a goddamn clue. It's driving me insane.

"Let's stop by the car," she says. "I think I've got a beach towel in the trunk."

"Are we sitting out on the sand?"

"No," she says with a laugh. "I'm gonna use it as a blanket."

We hurry over to the car—well, as fast as I can go in my current state. She pops the trunk and whips out a big striped beach towel.

"Aha," she says with delight, shaking it loose of sand. "Get over here. There will be better body heat with both of us—and hold my phone."

She tosses her clutch into the back, and I shut the lid of her trunk. Tucking her phone in my pocket, I let her drape the extra-large beach towel over my shoulders. Then she tucks herself against me, wrapping the other end around her shoulders. I hold one end, and she holds the other, and that's the way we walk down the boardwalk to the beach. I'm not even cold but fuck if I'm gonna tell her that.

"Oh god, it's so beautiful," she says with a sigh, looking up at the dark, starry sky.

The moon is out tonight, large but not quite full. Only a few clouds dot the sky. There's quite a bit of light pollution down this stretch of the beach, but you can still see a few stars. I gaze out at the quiet ocean. The surf is strong, the white caps breaking once, twice, as the water inches towards us.

I've always liked seeing how the ocean can change day to day. Some days you'll come out here and the beach will stretch out for almost a hundred feet before you hit ocean. On a night like tonight, with the tides rising high, there's really not much further we can go off the end of the boardwalk.

Another couple slips past us with a dog on a leash. Losing their shoes in the sand, they walk hand-in-hand along the dune. Next to me, Tess shifts her weight, her hand under the towel brushing my hip.

"Can I ask you something?" I say, borrowing her line from the restaurant.

She nods, even though I see that wary look in her eyes.

Braving my fear that she'll shut me down again, I ask the question I've been pondering for weeks. "When did you know your marriage was over?"

31
Tess

I want to kiss him.

That's the mantra I've been chanting in my head for the last ten minutes. Holding him close, sharing his warmth, basking in the feel of his absolute attention.

I want to kiss him. I want to kiss him. I want to kiss him.

And Ryan Langley is a damn good kisser. Beyond the obvious mutual attraction, he makes me feel safe. He makes me laugh. It's almost like he tries to pull them out of me, like he *wants* to hear me laugh. It's endearing . . . and, quite frankly, a little disorienting.

I'm standing here, with no other witnesses except the sand and the sea, and I'm actively *not* kissing Ryan Langley. I want to fix this. Immediately. Fuck what I said earlier about keeping my distance. We should always only ever be kissing.

I shift my weight, inching closer to him. This towel was both a genius idea and a terrible one. Because now I can smell the crisp, clean notes of his aftershave. That scent is coiling deep in my senses, setting a little light in my core. It flickers hopeful, growing stronger.

But then his hand stiffens on me. And then he's turning, a question in his eyes. "Can I ask you something?" he says. And I know it will be about Troy. He must have questions. Any man would. He's been honest with me tonight. Can I bear to do the same?

Slowly, I nod.

"When did you know your marriage was over?"

"Wow." I'm surprised by how poignant the question is. He's not asking *if* it's over. He's not even asking when it ended. What he's asking is a much more sophisticated kind of question. I'd expect nothing less from my cerebral Virgo hockey boy. He wants to know when I was done. When did I check out? When did I know there was nothing left?

I swallow down the lump of emotion in my throat, clearing my voice. "Umm . . . I think it would have to be about five years ago," I admit.

"So, two years before you actually split?"

I nod. Of course, he remembers the timeline. I've given him so little to work with, it practically fits on a Post-it. I bet he has it memorized.

"Yeah, it was that Christmas," I explain. "Christmas dinner, actually. His mother always throws these beautiful, extravagant holiday parties. She loves showing off the family and pretending like we're all happy, you know?"

He nods, listening as I speak.

"She'll invite clients and old family friends. They're always these big to-dos. But they're intimate too," I add. "We sing carols and do a gift exchange, and there's usually always an ugly sweater contest." I smile, picturing Bea in a gaudy reindeer sweater with blinking Christmas tree lights wrapped around its horns.

"What happened?"

I sigh, looking out at the ocean. "We were at dinner, and Troy was seated next to me. We'd only just sat down, and we were all shuffling the plates, you know, passing the relish tray and the breadbasket, asking your neighbor for the salt and pepper."

He nods, still listening.

"Someone passed Troy the basket of dinner rolls," I explain. "He took two, set them on his plate, and then he passed the basket across me to his cousin sitting on my other side."

Ryan goes still.

"Look, I know it sounds dumb," I say quickly. "The wife sitting at Christmas dinner knowing her marriage is over because her husband doesn't give her the breadbasket. It sounds crazy . . . but so often that's how he made me feel," I admit. "I sat there in that moment, letting the breadbasket pass me by, and I knew it was over. Either this man that I loved was choosing to ignore me, or he was purposefully withholding choices from me. Worst of all was the question that plagued me the longest: Did he even see me at all?"

"Tess, I'm sorry," Ryan says. "I'm sorry that happened to you."

"Do you have any idea what that feels like?" I glance up at him. "Have you ever felt invisible?"

He considers for a moment before shaking his head. "No. Maybe it helps that I'm tall," he adds with a soft smile.

"I'm glad for you," I reply, genuinely meaning my answer. "It's the worst feeling in the world, not being seen . . . walking through life like a ghost."

"It's happened before," he intuits, his gentle gaze still locked on me. "You've been invisible before."

I nod.

"Tell me when."

"All my life," I whisper, breaking our gaze to stare out at the blank expanse of dark ocean instead. "It's all I've ever known. Everyone who was meant to love me, people I needed to care, people I needed to protect me . . . they all closed their eyes." My eyes close too as a tear slips down my cheek. "They didn't see me, Ryan. I was just a child, and they didn't care."

Ryan turns us until we're practically face to face. With his hand still holding the end of the towel, he tips my chin up, forcing me to look at him. "Listen to me, Tess. I don't know who you were before. All I know is who you are now. And from the first moment we met, not five hundred yards down this exact stretch of beach, you have been the *only* thing I see."

I suck in a breath, eyes wide as I gaze up at him. "Ryan—"

"I see you, Tess," he says, dropping his end of the towel to cup my cheek. "I *see* you. I can't stop seeing you—your wit, your beauty, your grace. You're so goddamn graceful. These fingers," he adds, reaching down to take my hand. "I watch the way they dance through your hair, taming your curls away from your face."

Lifting my hand to his lips, he kisses each of my fingertips, his lips soft. Each kiss lights me up inside, fanning the flames of my desire for him.

"Maybe you are a ghost," he goes on, splaying my hand against his chest. "Because your laugh . . . it fucking haunts me. At the wedding, it was like I couldn't think, couldn't *breathe*, because you were everywhere all at once, laughing and chatting with everyone. I followed you across the party, Tess. I had to be closer to you, to that sound—I needed to be near you—"

"Ryan," I murmur, tears brimming in my eyes. "Please . . . "

"Tell me what you want," he says, his voice catching as he gazes into my eyes with such depth of feeling.

He's so good, so kind—*too* kind. I'll break him. I'll ruin this—

"No." He cups my face with both hands. "Tess, no, goddamn it. Don't pull away again. I see it in your fucking eyes. They give you away every time. There's something you're not telling me. You feel this between us too. I know you do. But something is holding you back from me. Stop pulling away, and let me in." He drops his forehead down to mine and whispers, "Give me something, baby. *Please*."

Throwing all caution to the wind, I hold him by the hips and give him my truth. "I'm only here because of you."

31
Ryan

Tess is crying in my arms, and I only want to make it stop. I want to hold her and heal her and be what she needs to move on. Whatever control I thought I had on my emotions, it's gone. The woman I'm falling for is falling apart and I can't pick up these pieces on my own.

"Give me something, baby," I hear myself beg. "*Please*."

She goes still in my arms, her hands clinging to my hips. "I'm only here because of you."

The words hang in the air between us. Instantly, my mind tries to puzzle out their meaning. Which word carried the most emphasis? She's only here *because* of me? Or she's only *here* because of me?

She glances up. "Ryan, I'm only in Jacksonville because of you, because of the pictures taken of us dancing together at Rachel's wedding."

"Pictures?" I repeat, totally confused.

"One of the caterers was sneaking pictures all night," she explains. "They sold them to TMZ, who published them all, including several pictures of you and I dancing together looking . . . well, we don't look miserable," she admits. "You really didn't know? No one told you?"

I rack my brain, trying to think back to the days after the wedding. "I mean, maybe MK mentioned I was in the press a bit, yeah. But I didn't really think anything of it. The wedding was a big deal. No one mentioned you or pictures with you, that's for sure."

"Well, Troy saw the pictures, and he used them to get me put on administrative leave."

My heart fucking stops. "He what?"

She drops her hands away from me, wrapping the towel tighter around her shoulders. “Yeah, breach of morality clause. He got HR to argue that my behavior with you was indecent enough to warrant a temporary leave. I’ve got six weeks before they’re going to reevaluate, which basically means Troy is giving me six weeks to decide what I want more: a career and a reputation I’ve spent a decade building . . . or my freedom.”

“Oh, fuck. Tess, I’m so sorry. I’m so . . . that’s fucking crazy. Over one dance?”

She just shrugs. “I think Troy has just been waiting for the right opportunity. He came down hard. He twisted up the other partners and used the employee contract to force HR into making this move against me.”

“What can I do?” I say. “I could write something—a letter of support or-or some kind of witness statement that nothing happened. Hell, that night I went back to the hotel with the guys and fell asleep on the couch in Morrow’s room. There were witnesses—”

“No. Ryan, you’re sweet to offer, but at this point, it won’t change anything.”

“How can it not? I’ll call MK in the morning. We’ll have them issue a retraction that nothing was going on between us at the wedding—”

“It won’t matter,” she says over me.

“Why not—”

“Because I told Troy it was true.”

We stand there, two feet apart at the end of the beach boardwalk, our eyes locked on each other. The wind whips a few strands of her red curls across her face. She flicks them back, not breaking our gaze. I don’t know what emotions are showing on my face. Her only look is guilt, and it’s tearing me apart.

“You told him what was true?” I say at last.

“I told him we were together that night. I told him we fucked. I told him it was all true.”

I groan. “Jesus, Tess.”

“You don’t know him,” she says, her voice almost pleading. “You don’t know how vicious he can be. I tried denying it at first. I denied it to HR and the other partners, but that only seemed to make him happy.”

"Jesus."

"Don't you see? He *wanted* me to deny it," she explains. "He wanted to watch me flail. He wanted to watch me tell the truth and suffer for it. That's what he does. He twists me up and makes me think that lies are truth and that his version of reality is the only version. He did it our whole marriage."

Okay, I know I haven't met every person in the world, but in this moment, I'm pretty confident that Troy Owens is the worst one. He's at least top fifty.

She steps in closer, taking both my hands in hers. "Ryan, please believe me that I didn't intend to hurt you or drag you in deeper to all this mess. But I told him the lie. I told him we were together. He wanted to burn me down, so I gave him the match."

My mind works in overdrive as I piece it all together. "Walk me through the timeline. The wedding pictures broke after Christmas, right?"

She nods, letting go of my hands.

"So, after Christmas, the pictures get leaked online. What happened next?"

"I went into work, and Troy already had it all arranged," she replies. "He blindsided me with an early morning HR meeting. They had the pictures and the bullshit song and dance about morality. The coup was already over. They put me on leave, and I left. I came here."

It doesn't add up. "You're leaving things out. Pieces are missing."

"Ryan—"

"If I'm in this with you, I'm in it," I press. "I have to know the timeline. Start again. You go to your HR meeting, they show you the photos and put you on leave, yes?"

She nods.

"Then what happened?"

"I came here," she replies.

I glare at her. "You're fast-forwarding."

"Ryan—"

"Between the HR meeting and you arriving here in Jacksonville, what else happened?" I say over her. "You don't just pack up your entire life and get on a plane. You don't throw your phone out of a moving car—"

"Maybe I do," she counters with a scowl. "You don't know me, Ryan."

"You've called your ex controlling, vicious, and dangerous. You're scared of him, aren't you? I see it in your eyes. He gave you a reason to be scared. What did he do?"

She shakes her head. "Please, don't. It doesn't matter—"

"What did he do, Tess?"

"I went back to my office. Troy followed me. We argued."

"You argued about me."

"We argued about a lot of things," she says, her gaze lowering to somewhere around my left shoulder. "I wanted to understand why—after years of separation and both of us seeing other people—*why* would he suddenly care if I was with you? That's when I realized . . . "

I raise a brow at her, waiting.

"It's because it's *you*," she says at last.

I mull that over for a moment before admitting, "I don't understand."

"You're everything he wishes he could be," she replies, finding my gaze again. "You have a career of your own, not one your mother hand-selected for you. You're rich, handsome, athletic. You're the whole package, Ryan. And you're a man."

My brow furrows in confusion. "What does my being a man have to do with anything?"

"I'm bi," she explains. "After Troy, I swore off dicks, literally and metaphorically," she adds. "For the last three years, I've pretty much only dated women. And Troy is just enough of a misogynistic asshole to delude himself into thinking my girlfriends were just that, girls who were friends. But the moment I'm pictured with a man, he suddenly sees red. It's just so typical. And so deeply disappointing."

"You say he saw red . . . "

She gives me a warning look. "Please, don't push this."

But I can't help it. "Tess, did he hurt you because of me? Because of those pictures?"

She shakes her head, but the look in her eyes is giving her away.

"Tess, did he put his hands on you?" Tears burn my eyes at the thought of this person I care for—any person—being abused.

"I'm fine," she soothes. "He choked me a little and he pushed me around, but I calmed him down, okay? I got him to stop."

I feel gutted, sick. "Tess . . . oh, baby, I'm so sorry. But—did you report him? Did you call the police—"

"No," she says quickly. "Ryan, I'm not getting the police involved. That is not the solution here."

"Not the solution?" I repeat. "He fucking choked you, Tess. Was that the first time? Has he hurt you before?"

She doesn't answer and I know I'm gonna kill him. But he's not my priority right now. Tess is. I take her by the shoulders. "Look, I'm not trying to scare you here, but this all sounds really fucking serious. You're describing an escalating pattern of violence, triggered by you threatening to leave him. You need to get a restraining order. And that's just for a start. You need to document the attack too. You need a police record. I can help you. I have contacts—"'

She pulls away from my grip. "I need you to let me handle this my way, okay? I'm not out here trying to be another statistic. I know this man. I know what he's capable of. I've got my exit strategy in place, okay? My way will work. And this is not your burden to carry or your problem to fix."

My outrage simmers. "You're telling me your psycho ex is using me to ruin your fucking life. You're telling me he hurt you because you said you were with me. Forgive me if that feels like my problem too."

"I'm sorry." Her hand brushes my shoulder again. "Ryan, I'm so sorry. I never meant for any of this to happen. And I was never going to tell you—"

"What?" I inch away from her hand. "What was the plan then? You would just keep living with me and flirting with me and driving me fucking crazy while your psycho ex withholds a divorce because of me? What kind of fucking plan is that?"

"I don't have a plan!" she cries. "You're the Virgo who runs around organizing your life down to your damn calorie counts. I'm loud and chaotic and terrified of being alone. That's why I came. There was no plan, I was just so fucking terrified of being alone. *Again*."

Fuck, my heart is breaking for her. I reach out but she pulls away.

"I couldn't stay there another second," she goes on. "So, I went to the one place I've always felt safe, the one person. I came home to Rachel. Only she's married now, and her priorities are different—and I love that for her," she adds quickly. "But I am fucking terrified. I begged Troy for a divorce. I told him I'd give him anything. Everything. He can use any evidence he wants, and I'll agree to it. I'll say I was the one cheating this whole time—with you, with anyone. He can be the injured party. I won't contest a thing. I just want to be free."

"Tess, I'm so sorry," I say, reaching for her again. "Please, let me help—"

"You're not listening," she cries. "Ryan, I was going to use you. I *am* using you. Stop being so nice to me!"

I drop my hand back to my side.

"You deserve so much better than me. You want things that I can't give you. In this moment, I feel like all I can do is take. I'm in survival mode, and I'll only drag you down with me."

I consider her words. "And how do you survive? What did you hope would happen here, between us I mean?"

She takes a deep breath, holding my gaze. "I had every intention of using you to set Troy off. I wanted him to find me living with you," she admits. "I wanted the idea of you touching me and kissing me and fucking me—whether it was true or not—to haunt him. And I wanted him to come at me hard. I wanted him to torch my entire life. At least then I'd know that the pieces of me that survived are strong. And with those pieces, I would finally start over."

This is a lot of information to process all at once. I feel like I've just gone through a car wash in a convertible with the top down. I'm angry, I'm hurt, and so damn confused. "You were using me?"

She nods.

"And you're still using me now?"

She shakes her head. "No, I can't now."

"Why?"

"You know why."

"Tell me anyway," I say, needing her to say it.

She holds my gaze, and I see such hurt there, such loneliness and resignation. "Because you're my friend. And I don't use my friends."

Yeah. Friends. We'll fucking see about that.

33
Tess

Ryan is quiet in the car the whole ride back to the house. Neither of us were in the mood for ice cream when we left the beach. Then it started to rain the minute we got in the car. Now I'm just sitting in this oppressive silence, the only sound the faint squeak of the windshield wipers and the soft patter of the rain on the roof.

I hate that I ruined this night for him. We were supposed to be celebrating him, not rehashing all my bullshit. But I wanted to kiss him, and I know he wanted to kiss me back, and I just felt like I couldn't go there with the weight of an elephant sitting on my chest. I hate secrets. I'm no good at them. And I don't use people. Even just the thought of using Ryan feels like enough of a betrayal—of him as my friend, of myself and my principles.

Admitting the truth out loud, I feel gross, like I need a shower to scrub all the negative energy away. But he deserved to know, and I stand by my decision to tell him, even with my shitty timing. He deserves to make whatever decisions he needs to make now.

I drive us all the way home and practically moan with relief as I jerk the car into park. We open our doors at the same time and climb out. He moves with his stiff gait towards the front door, keys jangling as he pulls them from his pocket.

I follow wordlessly behind him, my discarded heels in my hand. I take in his frame, cast in shadow by the porch light. Are we just never going to speak again? The silent treatment is a fate worse than death for a Gemini.

He opens the door and steps back, wordlessly gesturing to let me in.

Oh, fuck this. I'm going straight to my room and drawing a bath in that big soaking tub. Then I'm going to dunk my head under the water and scream. I step past him, saying nothing. Behind me, the door shuts. The bolt clicks.

"Tess."

I pause, heart in my throat, as I hear my name spoken from his lips. One word. Slowly, I turn. He's still facing the door, one hand pressed against it. "What?"

His hand drops to his side as he turns too, his heated gaze setting me on fire with a look. The keys drop from his hand to the floor with a loud clatter. "Use me."

"What?"

"You heard me."

My mouth is suddenly dry. "Ryan—"

"But we're changing the rules of the game," he says, taking a step closer. "Old rules said you used me to make your ex jealous. Well, fuck him," he curses, his eyes flashing with anger. "He doesn't deserve one more moment of your precious time or consideration. We're playing this game with new rules. There's only one, actually: Use me to feel good."

My heart skips. "Ryan, this is . . . "

He takes a step closer, both hands going to the bottom of his powder blue sweater. He pulls it off and drops it to the floor, his blond curls mussed. "Do you want to feel good, Tess?"

"I don't want to hurt you," I admit.

His hands are working the buttons of his shirt from the top down, exposing his tanned chest. "Does your pussy have teeth? I didn't feel any before . . . not that I got much time to explore."

I bite my lip to keep from smiling. This is crazy. This is such a huge mistake. "No, it doesn't have teeth."

"Good, because I'd like to taste you with my tongue, and I want to survive in one piece," he says with a smile.

"Ryan—"

He stops, his green eyes locked on me. "All I thought about the whole ride home was how beautiful you are in that dress and how much I want to fuck you in it."

And now my heart has stopped. I can't think. Can't hold thoughts. I can only feel. And what I feel is a sense of deep, aching want.

He jerks his shirt loose from his pants, flashing me his washboard abs. Then he does the sexy man move of working open his wrist buttons. Fuck, I go weak for a man removing his cufflinks. It's probably the sexiest article in a man's wardrobe. Ryan's not wearing cufflinks, but the visual is the same, and the kitty is officially purring.

He drops the crisp, white shirt from his shoulders, and now he's standing in just his jeans and shoes. Oh, this beach puppy isn't lost at all. He knows *exactly* where he's going tonight.

He stops right in front of me, close enough to reach out and touch. "The rules are simple: We're friends who fuck to feel good. You can't offer more. I'm not taking more. I'm asking you, as your friend, if you'd like to orgasm on my face. Say yes, and I'll even let you pick which episode of *SOA* we watch after."

Oh my god, I'm dead. Here lies Tess, passed away from too much sexual tension.

"I don't want to hurt you," I repeat. "Your knee," I add, glancing down.

He reaches out a hand, his fingers gentle under my chin as he tips my face up. "I made you an offer. Come on, Lawyer Tess. I thought this was foreplay for you," he adds with a teasing smile. "The terms are simple enough for you to understand, right? Orgasms, then *SOA*."

"This is crazy," I say out loud. My clutch is still tucked under my arm, my discarded heels in hand.

"Yes or no, Tess."

Holding his gaze, I lift my free hand, trailing the tips of my fingers over his skin from his wrist to his elbow. I watch his expression heat as he clenches his jaw, holding himself back. He wants me. He's burning up with the need to touch me, please me. This is all inevitable, right? I blame Mercury. The Virgo and the Gemini, we were always meant to collide.

I drop my heels and clutch to the floor, not caring where they land. "Yes."

My soft word of assent, spoken into the heated space between us, drops like a lit match onto a haystack. The flames of our passion erupt, and then we're in each other's arms. Our bodies press together, and he groans, muttering a curse. The hand at my chin wraps around my nape and tips back my head, his fingers digging into my hair. I feel that delicious sting of his pull, and my lips part for him. He crashes his needy mouth against mine.

We haven't even made it past the entryway. We stand here, entwined together, our hands working feverishly to touch and caress. I love the feel of him in my arms. He's strong but gentle, his hands guiding me where he wants me to go. I flow with him, dropping my hands down to his hips so he can cup my face. Then his hands travel lower, fingertips brushing my exposed breasts before he's cupping them over the tulle.

"I didn't even want to go out tonight," he says against my lips. "I wanted to sit on the couch with you in this dress and fuck you 'til your cheeks turned as bright as these cherries."

"God, do it," I moan, breaking our kiss and tipping my neck back in invitation.

He takes it, sinking his open mouth onto my fevered skin. He sucks and teases my pulse point, the sensation traveling straight through my body and zapping me in the clit. I suppress a shiver, working my fingertips along the top of his jeans until I'm slipping them inside to cup his firm ass.

He groans, dropping his face lower to kiss the swell of my breasts. "I need to taste you again. Tess, I want a taste—"

"Do it," I say again.

Not waiting to be told a third time, he grips me by the arms and pushes me up against the wall. I gasp, head bumping, as he presses into me with his hips, claiming all my air in another fierce kiss. My hands go to his hair as I scrape my nails along his scalp, which earns me a groan of approval.

"Spread your legs," he says against my lips. His right hand drops down, working the tulle at the bottom of my dress.

I shift my weight, widening my stance as he shifts too, his hip pressing into mine as he makes way for his hand. I can feel the hard length of his erection. I want to touch him, but he seems singularly focused on my pleasure first and, hey, I'm never one to complain.

He breaks our kiss, his forehead pressed against my temple as we pant for air. "What color are your—" He goes still, and I know why. I smile like a Cheshire Cat as I feel his fingers brush over my bare pussy. His body coils tight. "Tess . . . where are your goddamn panties?"

His tone sends my core fluttering as I give him a fake innocent look. "I didn't think I needed any with this outfit."

He swoops down to kiss me again, biting at my bottom lip with a sound somewhere between a groan and growl. "Are you trying to kill me here?"

"No, I'm trying to get that tongue-fucking you promised me," I tease.

"Fuck, you're trouble," he says against my lips. "You drive me crazy." As he speaks, he flips his hand and rubs it over my pussy, cupping me.

I gasp, pressing my hips forward, desperate for more friction.

His fingers delve between my slick folds. "God, Tess, you're so fucking wet."

I bite my lip, head tipped back, as I sink into the feeling of him touching me. He circles my clit, sending the warmth spiraling out across my hips. I hum low in my throat. "That feels good."

He dips his fingers back inside me, drawing out more of my arousal to tease my clit. "What do you like?" he asks, peppering kisses down my neck. "What makes you feel good?"

"Mmm—I—I hate having my ears kissed," I admit, distracted by his perfectly pleasurable shoulder kisses. "And don't you dare touch my feet with anything but your hands."

"Same." He kisses up my neck, avoiding my ear. "No feet for me. Hard pass. And don't tickle me either."

I go still in his arms, opening my eyes to glance up at him.

He goes still too, his fingers still inside me.

"Tickle you?" I say with a raised brow, fighting to contain my smile.

"Yeah, a girl thought it was foreplay or something," he replies. "I fucking hated it."

I laugh. "Noted. Hey, Ryan?"

"Hmm?"

"Keep teasing my pussy."

"Yes, ma'am," he teases, and I laugh out loud. My mind is instantly flooded with images of the day we met on the beach, and he hit me with that damn soccer ball. He called me "ma'am" then, too, and Rachel and I teased him.

I sink back against the wall, letting the waves of warmth wash over me as he works me with his fingers and thumb, alternating between pumping inside me and massaging my needy clit. It feels wonderful, but I need more. I sigh, brushing my hands through his hair as I steal another kiss. "That feels amazing... but I think I'll need your mouth to come."

"Say no more," he replies, pecking my lips before he drops down on his good knee, his bad one bent inside his knee brace.

"Ryan," I cry, trying to pull on his shoulders. "No—let's go to the couch or a bed or—"

"If you think I'm going to suffer through an entire night of you in this dress and not get a taste of you just like this, you're fucking crazy," he says, already bunching the tulle with both hands.

"But—"

"Woman, let me work," he shouts. "I will take you to the couch and finish you there. And if you're very good, we may just end in the bed. But I'm tasting you right here, right now, before I quite literally die of thirst. Now, spread your legs and hold onto something."

I'm smiling from ear to ear as I fling a hand out, reaching for the edge of the console table. I gasp, my grip on it tightening as Ryan ducks under the tulle skirt, his head disappearing beneath the pink fabric dotted with cherries.

"Ryan—"

He presses his face against my pussy with a hungry groan and I melt. He hasn't even touched me with his mouth, and I already have jelly legs as he peppers kisses across my thighs and belly, his fingers still working my clit.

I gasp again as I feel him part me with two fingers and flick his tongue against my clit. "Oh—fuck," I whimper, shifting my weight. Exquisite heat flashes through my core, and I instantly feel wetter. He'll have me dripping by the end. I only pray I can relax enough to come.

He hums against my pussy, teasing with his tongue, spreading me wider to lick along my slit. "You taste so fucking good," he says, his breath hot against my skin.

One hand grips the console table and I drop the other down to his head, hidden beneath the tulle of my skirt. "God, that feels good," I say, my head tipped back.

His right hand continues to hold me open so his mouth can play. His left traces patterns up my thigh, circling around to squeeze my ass. He flips his hand around, his middle finger spearing me while his pointer and ring finger hold me open as he sucks on my clit.

"Fuck—god—" I try to hold still. My hips want to grind. I want more friction. "Ryan, baby, please . . . "

"What do you need?"

"More."

He kisses my pussy one more time, and then he's ducking out from under my skirt and climbing to his feet. My hands smooth down his chest to his stomach and land on his jeans as I pull him closer, tipping my head up in invitation.

He leans down, his glossy lips parted like he means to kiss me. Remembering himself, he pauses, sucking in a breath, eyes locked on me. "Is this okay? Can I kiss you?"

I smirk, tipping up on my toes to reach him better. "I'm bi, remember? I love the taste of pussy too."

His brain short circuits as he processes that new information, and then he's smiling, a flash of hunger in his eyes. "Fuck, why is that so hot to imagine?"

I laugh, kissing my taste off his lips. "Let's work up to the girl-on-girl action. Right now, I need you to finish me, Ryan."

He digs his hand in my hair, pulling me back to break our kiss. We're both breathless as he gazes down at me. "Go to the couch."

He lets me go, and I slip around him, the tulle of my skirt swishing as I walk into the living room, my eager puppy walking right at my heels. I like our chemistry with this too, the natural push and pull. He's dominant but responsive, curious, thoughtful. We're turning sex into a conversation, and like all our conversations, it feels easy and natural. It's like we were made to speak each other's language.

I step between the chair and the coffee table, moving over to the couch. I sink down on it, and he immediately follows, turning to me at once, his hands going to my skirt as he bunches up the tulle again.

"Lie back," he says against my lips, still teasing me with kisses. "Spread these legs for me. You want me to go fast or slow?"

I shift, tipping backwards towards the end of the couch as he helps me bend my leg up and around. He guides me by the ankle, tucking my leg in against the couch so he's sitting between my spread thighs. My other leg drops off the side of the couch, foot flat on the floor.

His hands smooth over my bare knees as he smiles down at me. "Lift this skirt for me. Show me where you want me."

I'm loving his quiet, bossy tone. So methodical, so patient.

It's turning me all the way on. I grab for the tulle around my hips, scrunching it up, loving the silky flow of it pooling around me as I expose my thighs to him.

His hands rise with each inch of exposed skin, fingers splayed against me until he reaches my hips. "Beautiful," he says, dropping his gaze down my body from my flushed face to my pussy.

I hold the tulle back with one hand as I drop the other between my legs, dipping my fingers into my entrance. I sigh, sinking back against the pillow as Ryan watches me touch myself with hunger in his eyes.

"You're so fucking beautiful," he says.

Desire pools in my core as I arch my hips, spreading myself wide for him. I'm basking in his focused attention. He's not missing a thing.

"You like it slow like that?" he says, watching me tease my clit.

"Sometimes," I reply, dipping two fingers back inside. "And sometimes I like it hard and fast. I like getting fucked, Ryan. I like friction and the feel of a man's body on top of me, weighing me down, owning me." I watch his expression and know he wants me to keep talking. He's my processor, my planner. He's logging this all away.

I smile, reaching for his hand. "Fuck my cunt while I tease my clit."

He obliges, his left hand holding firm to my hip as he sinks two fingers inside me, curling his hand around to rub his fingers along my inner wall. The combination of both our hands on me has me sinking into bliss. Yes, this. More of this. Then his tongue. Then euphoria.

"What else?" he asks.

"I like doggy style," I reply. "And anal—oooh, and doggy style with anal. Fuck, that's amazing. Especially if the toy in my ass buzzes."

He blinks down at me. "You like toys in your ass?"

I smile, dipping my fingers lower to brush against his. "Mhmm. I love toys. Didn't you see my collection the other night?"

"You know I did," he replies, his gaze locked on my pussy.

"Mhmm. You don't miss a thing." Arching my back a bit, I slip two fingers in with Ryan's, loving the feeling of fullness.

"Fuck," he says, holding his fingers still inside me.

"Toys are amazing," I go on, sinking deeper into my building orgasm. "They treat you to sensations that are entirely new. But I don't need to tell you that, right?" I gaze down my body at him, willing him to look at me. "You said you like toys too."

It only takes a beat of silence before he curses and pulls away, his fingers slipping free of my cunt. "Fuck," he mutters, sitting back. "I lied, okay?"

I control my features. "You lied? About what?"

"I've never used toys before. It's never—I—it's just never come up," he admits, a faint blush staining his cheeks.

"I know," I reply.

He glances sharply over at me. "What? How can you know?"

"Because I'm good at reading people," I reply. "I read the lie on you the moment you said it. But would you like to try toys sometime? Do you want to know the life-changing magic of fucking a girl doggy style while she has a vibrating dildo in her ass?"

"Jesus," he says on a laugh, tearing his gaze away with a shake of his head. "You are too much for me."

"Oh, don't say that now, puppy. We were just getting started."

His gaze darts back to me. "Are you ever gonna cool it with the 'puppy' crap?"

I smirk, my hand going back to my clit. "Do you want me to stop calling you that?"

He considers for a second before he's smirking too. "No. But just between us, okay?"

"Okay. Can this stay just between us too?"

He raises a brow at me. "Can what stay?"

I hold his gaze. "The fact that I want your dick in my mouth. I told Troy you gagged me with your monster cock and choked me on your cum. I'd really like for that to be true. It feels like the journey I'm meant to take tonight."

Now he's the one smirking. "That's what you told him happened between us?"

I nod.

He considers again. "Well, we can't have you living a lie, now can we?"

"My thoughts exactly."

He leans between my spread legs, his arm bracing the back of the couch as he presses his weight against me. I arch up enough that our lips touch in a gentle kiss. He pulls away first and speaks against my lips, "But first I'm eating your pussy until you come on my face."

34
Ryan

I don't give Tess any more chances to derail this train with talk of kinks or buzzing butt plugs. I want her coming, and I want it in my mouth. It feels like my body is shaking with this hunger, like I'm a Transformer low on energon and she is my source. I need more. I need *her*.

Only the kitchen light is on. The soft white light pools over the back of the couch, keeping her mostly in shadow. But I can see well enough. I drop down to my elbows between her legs, using my hands to spread her thighs wide as I lower my face over her glistening pussy. Parting her lips, I expose her clit and blow a little air on it.

She shivers, goosebumps rising along her thighs as she arches her hips. "Don't make me beg," she whispers, such a tone of need in her voice.

I drop lower until my warm breath fans over her pussy. Sucking on my tongue, I drop a dollop of saliva onto her clit. With my finger, I rub it in, loving that it's me making her wet.

"Ryan—*god*—"

Wasting no more time, I drop my mouth over her clit and suck. This angle is much easier than on my knees against the wall. I use my leverage to press her thighs open, sucking and teasing all parts of her.

Her hands grab my head, her fingers digging into my hair, and I fucking love it. I groan against her clit as I learn her, probing my tongue at her entrance.

"Yes," she pants. "There. Fuck me. Please, please, fuck me—"

Her begging makes me feral. I plunge my tongue inside her, deep as it will go, loving the feel of her heat surrounding me, her hands holding tight to my head. Once she starts working her own hips, thrusting against my mouth, I know I'm a goner. She tastes too good, and I've wanted this for too long.

"I'm right fucking there," she cries. "Put your fingers in me. Suck my clit. I'm gonna—fuuuuck, I wanna come on your hand—"

I adjust as she asks, shoving three fingers up inside her and twisting them around until I can press up and in along her vaginal wall. I tease her clit, flicking my tongue up and down, humming against her. Then three things happen at once: her hands tighten in my hair, her thighs clamp down around my face, and her pussy pulses and squeezes tight around my fingers.

"Ahhh—Ryan—" she shrieks, her body bowing forward in a half-curl as I take her orgasm from her. I tear it from her, body and soul. I claim every quivering, pulsing moment of it, drinking it in from start to finish.

As she sinks back against the cushions with a whimper, her arousal slicks my fingers, pooling a little in my palm. Like the heathen I am, I duck down, slurping her essence from my skin. She tastes like heaven—sweet and simple, like cantaloupe juice.

She's weightless beneath me, still coming down from her high. Her hands slip away from me as she drapes them off the back of the couch. "That was good," she says on a dreamy sigh.

I lean over top of her, lifting my wet fingers to her lips. "Here, pussy lover," I tease. My dick twitches as I watch her smile and suck my fingers into her mouth, eagerly tasting herself. She makes a little sexy sound in her throat.

I groan, cock aching for a taste of that mouth.

She lets my fingers go with a soft little pop, a sleepy smile on her face. "That was lovely, Ryan. Thank you."

I kiss the top of her knee.

"I think it's your turn now, right?"

I smooth my hand down her leg. "You're tired, Tess. It's okay."

She goes still, glancing down her body at me. "You don't want it?"

"I . . . never said that."

Though, this feels like a trap. Am I allowed to tell her how much I want it? I glance her way, curious to know what she's thinking. She's looking sedately back at me, waiting. Fuck, she's gonna make me say it. "I . . . want it."

"You want what, Ryan?"

"I want your mouth on me."

"Where?"

"My dick."

She smiles. "Glad to know we're on the same page. Where do you want it?"

I blink at her. Is this a trick? "I . . . do you think I have a shoulder dick or something?"

"Are you that stressed out talking about this right now? I'm asking you *where* in the house do you want me to suck your dick?"

Oh god, I am such a fucking idiot. This is worse than when I called her 'ma'am.' She's gonna leave. She's gonna pack her bags and go suck Glossy Patty's monster nob.

"I'm not going anywhere," she soothes, and I swear to fuck she has ESP. She's done that more than once. "Let's try again, shall we?" she offers with a smile. Sitting up, she inches forward, her hands smoothing over my bare shoulders and down my arms. "Do you want it here on the couch? Want to be standing with me on my knees? The shower—"

"Here," I say. "And I want you on your knees." I blink in surprise that I said the second sentence out loud.

Her gaze warms with desire. "Yes, sir."

Sir?

I groan, dragging both hands through my hair as she slips off the couch and slides the coffee table back a few inches. As she stands in front of me, her hands go to the zipper under her arm. "I know you're a big fan of the dress, but it's dry-clean only. Plus, I really like the mental image of me being naked between your knees with your dick in my mouth. Would you mind terribly?"

I just blink up at her, unmoving. She's actually trying to kill me. I'm convinced. She's going to use this casual dirty talk to end my life before I can come in her mouth. It has to be her master plan . . . if she was the kind of girl to make plans.

"I . . . " That's it. That's the best I manage.

"I'll take that as a no," she says with a flirty smile. "Why don't you get more comfortable too? Lose the shoes . . . and whatever else too. Though I do kind of like the idea of you keeping the briefs on. There's something so sexy about a man exposed but not undressed."

She wants me to keep the briefs on? Done. At this point, she could ask me to wear a scuba mask and a cowboy hat, and I'd say yes.

I kick off my Sperry sneakers, my gaze locked on her as she drags down that zipper. Then she's pulling the dress off over her head, getting lost in a sea of pink tulle before she tosses it onto the chair.

She stands in front of me in a white, strapless corset-looking bra and no fucking panties. Her little triangular thatch of soft hair points down to the pussy I just devoured. Reaching around behind herself with both hands, she arches her shoulders back, working the clasps of her bra. In moments, it clicks open, and she breathes a sigh of relief, dropping the bra to the floor.

"Whew, that first free breath always feels good," she huffs with a little laugh.

My gaze trails down her body from her face to her full breasts, now hanging naturally, unsupported by the corset. She's got faint red lines marring her skin at her ribs and above her hips. I reach out on impulse, my fingers tracing delicately over the red mark above her left hip.

"They fade quickly," she says, brushing her fingers through my hair.

"I don't want this skin marked." Then I glance up, holding her gaze. "I don't want you hurt. Ever."

There's a softness in her gaze. "You would never hurt me, Ryan."

I swallow the emotion in my throat. "It's important to me that you know that."

"I do."

I pull her to me as I stand. Then we're kissing again. I think, at this point, we should just always be kissing. Friends who kiss. And fuck. And maybe keep living together.

Her tongue dances with mine as she works loose the button of my jeans. I cup her breasts, loving the feel of her hard nipples grazing my palms. She tugs down the zipper, and then her fingers are wiggling their way inside the top of my boxer briefs. I brace for impact, heart stopping as she slips her hand down, cupping my hard dick.

She hums another one of those impossibly sexy sounds against my lips as her fingers wrap around my shaft, stroking me from root to tip. She sucks on my bottom lip as she pulls away, leaving me breathless as all my senses now focus on her hand.

"You kidding me with this, puppy?" she teases. "Please tell me you know how to use this masterpiece to ruin a woman."

"I think so," I manage to say, my brain still buffering.

She smiles up at me, her thumb brushing over the tip of my dick, spreading my precum.

"Fuck," I groan.

She smiles up at me. "This game has only one rule, remember? Feeling good. Let me make you feel so good, Ryan. I want to taste you . . . please you—"

I silence her with my mouth. It's the only option. She has to stop talking before I lose all control, drag her to this floor, and fuck her to pieces. She twists me up with a look and spins me out with a smile. I'm fucking mad for this woman.

Before now, sex has always been procedural for me. I have urges, and I satisfy them. I want the women I'm with to feel good. I want it to be fun for both of us. I want us both satisfied. But mainly I just want the screaming urge to ease so I can refocus on my game.

Control at all times. Body and mind.

With Tess in my arms, I'm quickly losing that control. I *want* to lose control. Sex with her doesn't feel biological. It doesn't feel like satisfying urges. It feels fucking spiritual. We're connected somehow. She reads me. I think she sees me, sees what I'm hiding. She knows I'm curious, knows I want more. Would she let me have it? Would she let me explore all it means to worship her?

She gives my jeans a sharp tug, so they drop down my thighs. The left side catches on my knee brace. Breaking our kiss, she drops her head down, kissing my chest, her hands smoothing over my hips and around to my lower back. She has her way, kissing down my body until she drops to one knee, her face right in front of my tented boxer briefs.

But her attention isn't on my dick. She focuses lower, gently sliding my jeans down from around my knee brace. Ducking down, she brushes a little kiss to my exposed thigh right at the top of the brace.

From her knees, she looks up at me. "Why don't you sit down? Get comfortable."

I step out of my jeans and sit on the couch, my gaze locked on her as she inches forward, spreading my legs. She settles herself between them, her gentle hands brushing up my thighs.

"Take your dick out, Ryan. Show me how you like to touch yourself. Let me watch you play."

I'm breathless, aching for her attention, as I drop my hands to my briefs and tug them down my thighs, freeing my dick.

Her heated gaze takes me in, trailing from my bunched-up briefs to my dick, up my chest to my face. "You look like a king," she says, the want shining in her eyes. "You're so beautiful like this, you have no idea."

"Keep talking to me like that, and this will be over before it begins," I warn.

She smiles. "Do you like praise, puppy?" Her hands dance over my thighs as she teases me, alternating between the soft pads of her fingertips and the sharp glide of her nails. "I think you could be perfect for me," she goes on. "Such a sweet, good boy. I think you like when I talk to you. You like when I narrate my thoughts out loud. Do you want to know what I'm thinking right now?"

I swallow. "Will I survive it?"

She drops her head to press kisses along my inner thigh. "I'm thinking about how beautiful you looked with your face buried in my cunt. There's nothing more powerful than a man on his knees, drawing forth the pleasure of his partner." As she talks, she smooths her hand up my right thigh, stopping just before she gets to my dick. "I told you to touch yourself," she says, her tone firm. "I want to watch you fuck your hand."

My hands are currently splayed on either side of me, bracing against the couch cushions like I'm readying for an earthquake. My right hand moves robotically, wrapping around my dick and I stroke myself, my eyes locked on her.

"Look at you." She watches my hand stroke up and down. "How does it feel?"

"Like my hand is rough," I reply through clenched teeth.

She leans over me, pressing between my legs until her face is floating above my dick. All I see is a sea of red curls. I flinch as I feel a cool drop of something touch the top of my dick.

"Work it in," she says. "I want you wet."

I stroke up my dick and groan, my head sinking back against the couch as I work her saliva over my tip. My entire body is firing with the need to come.

Not yet. Too soon. I need to last. Control.

She does it twice more and pretty soon my dick is slick with her saliva from root to tip. She sits back, watching me work myself, her gaze taking all of me in as she looks from my face to my chest, my dick, my arms. Every moment she watches, I feel my desperation mounting.

"Are you aching yet?" Those hazel eyes watch me lose control.

"Yes," I grit out.

"Do you want my mouth, Ryan?"

"Yes."

"Do you want it fast or slow?" she teases, using my words.

"Both."

"Will you help me hold my hair back? I don't mind if you get a little rough," she adds. "If I need up for air, I'll tap your leg twice, okay?"

Holy fuck. Up for air?

Both her hands go into her hair as she works her fingers through the curls, pulling it up to the top of her head. The movement puts her full breasts on display, her perky nipples pointed right at me. If I'm a king, she's a fucking queen. She oozes confidence. She knows exactly what she wants, and I'm going to let her have it.

She holds her hair up with one hand, pressing in between my legs until her knees hit the base of the couch. She taps my hip with her free hand, and I shift down a little, reclining back against the cushions. "Take my hair, Ryan," she directs.

My left hand sweeps up to wrap around hers at her crown. She slips her hand out and now it's me holding her hair back so she can choke on my dick. It twitches in desperation, ready for her. Her hands smooth up my thighs one more time, and then she's holding me at the base, her tongue teasing my tip. I groan, eyes shut tight, as her wet mouth sucks on my tip. I know this is just a tease. She's barely getting started. I mutter a curse as she takes a little more of me into her mouth.

"Fuck, that feels good." Both my hands are in her hair now, bracing her head as she bobs. She sucks and teases, fluttering her tongue.

"Mmm . . . " She hums against my tip, and I feel the vibrations shooting straight through me to my spine. "You taste good. I want you to give me more. Give me everything. I'm swallowing."

Oh my fucking god, she has to stop talking.

Also, she better never fucking stop.

Both.

Neither.

I can't fucking think—

"Let go," she murmurs. "I feel you holding on so tight."

"I don't want to hurt you," I say, echoing her words from earlier, my hands soft in her hair.

She pulls back, glancing up at me. "You won't. I refuse to succumb to death by dick. But I love the thrill of being used. Now, fuck my mouth the way you're dying to, and come down my throat."

"Fuck." My hands tighten in her hair. "Suck it. Put it in your mouth. No more fucking talking."

With an eager smile, she does as she's told, and the dopamine hit of her obedience has me feeling high. She wraps her mouth around me and sinks down, finally giving me more than a little teasing suck. I shift my hips, inching forward so I have better leverage. My hands move with her head, fingers digging into her curls, as she bobs up and down.

Desperate to give her more, I give a little practice press of my hips, moving against her mouth. She groans her approval, her hands smoothing over my hips. I do it again, my brain scrambling as the only sound that fills the room is her humming and moaning as she sucks.

"Feels so fucking good," I pant, my hips moving in time with her. "Baby, I want more. Can I—god—I want—"

She drops her face lower, her nose all but brushing my trimmed pubes as my whole body is flooded with the sensation of my dick tapping the back of her throat. I can't breathe as she gags herself on my length and my tip is squeezed in her throat.

“Oh fuck—*fuck*—” I cry out, my hands tightening in her hair.

She lifts up, panting for air as her saliva coats me from tip to root.

“Again,” I beg. “Do it again—*please*—”

She does, and I ride with her this time, my hands ready as I grip and pull, thrusting with my hips until it’s me doing the work, tapping the back of her throat with my dick until she gags and pulls back.

“Fuck, Ryan,” she whimpers, wiping her mouth as she glances up at me. Her eyes are watering, her mascara is smeared, and she looks like my every fantasy. “I’m so close,” she says up at me. My left hand is still holding her hair, though several of the curls have come loose, framing her freckled face. “I’m gonna work my clit and go again and we’ll come together, yeah?”

I nod. It’s all I can manage. I certainly can’t manage words right now. I don’t think I’ve ever come with a woman at the same time before. It’s always just been her then me. I’m on fire with the need to see this through. I feel like I’ll hold mine off for a lifetime if it means we come together.

She drops her hand down between her legs, fingering herself. I can’t see anything with the angle of the couch, but in moments, she opens her eyes, her chest flushed as she lifts her fingers. I look down at them, seeing how they glisten.

“See what you do to me?”

“Give it to me,” I order, my voice low as I tug on her hair.

She leans forward, holding up her fingers for me to taste.

I suck her fingers into my mouth, savoring her sweetness. I let her go, and she drops her hand to my thigh. “Come with me,” I pant, reeling her in closer. “My queen, my fucking goddess. Claim me. Take everything.”

She smiles, slipping her hand back between her legs. She sucks in a sharp little breath, and I know she’s just fingered herself. It’s so fucking hot.

“Get on my dick,” I say, pulling her forward by her hair. “Baby, I need to come. Don’t stop ’til I come.”

She keeps one hand on her clit and the other wraps around my base, holding me in place as she sinks her mouth back on me. That moment of connection, her tongue pulsing along my shaft as she takes me deep, has me seeing stars. I grip her hair with both hands, watching every second of her swallowing me.

"I'm so fucking close. Tell me you're close. Come with me. *Please*—Tess—come with me, baby—"

She moans around my dick, the sound making the sweetest vibrations that I feel all over my body. I watch the movement of her arm, her fingers rubbing hard over her clit. She's claiming that friction she says she craves.

She pops off my dick, panting for air as she cries out. "Ohmygod—I'm right there—*ah*—"

I silence her cry, pulling her back onto me. I brace my shaft with one hand and guide her head with the other, arching up with my hips as I gag her, coming down her throat. I cry out, too, head tipping back as my hips shake. I feel like I'm bursting open, like everything that is me is leaving me through my dick. I'm giving it to her. She's taking it. Both. Everything.

Her body rocks against mine as she rides out her own orgasm. We share a moment of connection as we release, two people becoming one. It's unlike any orgasm I've ever had. I'm utterly spent, and yet I never want to stop. It's fucking cosmic.

After a moment, I sink back against the cushions, my body humming, as my hands loosen in her hair. I lift her off me and she's breathing deep through her nose, swallowing what I gave her. Her body is unsteady as she sinks down in a heap at my feet, her face resting on my inner thigh.

I let go of her hair, and it flops over my right knee. I pet her with smooth strokes. I feel like I just finished a game with three OTs. I'm light as a feather and heavy as stone. I don't think I could stand right now if I tried.

Her hands slip around my calves as she holds onto me. She sits at my feet, entangled in my legs, saying nothing. We're beyond words in this moment. I know she feels it too.

I gaze down at her, this rare beauty. Her makeup is smudged, and her freckled cheeks are flushed. I know if I taste her right now, she'll taste like me.

Before either of us can speak, there's a soft buzzing on the floor. Someone is calling.

She sits up as she looks around, her eyes still glassy.

"It's your phone," I say, too relaxed to move.

"My phone?"

"In my pocket."

She digs in the pocket of my discarded jeans and takes out her little prepaid cellphone. Glancing up at me, she puts a finger to her lips, her meaning obvious.

I'm not here.

She puts the phone to her ear. "Hey, Rach, what's up?" she says, her tone falsely bright. "Kinda late for a phone call. I—" She goes still, her gaze shooting up to me as her eyes go wide.

I sit forward, immediately on alert. Something's wrong. I watch as her blissed-out smile falls, replaced with confusion, then horror.

She scrambles naked to her feet. "Ohmygod, *what*?"

35
Tess

"It's just so degrading and humiliating and so patently false," I cry, marching down the sand in my bare feet.

"I know," Rachel says at my side.

The team got back super late last night from their away game, and I showed up at the Price house bright and early with coffees, dragging Rachel out for our morning beach walk. The guys were already all out to the gym.

"How are you so calm about this?" I say, turning to face her. "Rach, they posted photos of me with Jake, and they're saying he's cheating on you!"

"Because it doesn't matter when we all know it's not true," she replies with an indifferent shrug.

When she called me the other night, I could hardly believe it. Then she sent the links. The headlines were like something out of a bad teen drama. "Trouble in Paradise?" "The Price of Betrayal." "The Price of a Lie."

The pictures linked to all the stories are just as ridiculous. Apparently, paparazzi have been watching their house since the wedding. Someone actually managed to get pictures of my late-night arrival. They snapped photos of me on the porch in the rain. My back is turned, but Jake is standing there shirtless, letting me in so it looks like I'm his new sneaky link.

The articles also include a few shots snapped from the morning we all went for coffee and a walk on the beach. And by *all* of us, I mean me, Rachel, her guys, even the damn dog. But they only posted the photos of Jake and me together—walking, laughing, throwing a stick for Sy.

"They literally cropped you out," I huff. "You were right behind us the whole time. I mean, where is the journalistic integrity?"

"I know," she says again.

"And Jake and I were only waiting outside the café because of the dog. You were inside getting the coffees—"

"Tess, you *have* to let this go. This happens, okay? I'm fine. Jake is fine. We all know it's bullshit. We all know it's a pack of lies. But this is the life," she adds. "This is what they do. Frankly, this is tame. Did I ever tell you about the time some paps took pictures of me in a hot yoga class, and they said I was in a Wiccan cult?"

I laugh. "No."

"Yeah, it was like the Witch Trials all over again. Someone actually approached me in a Whole Foods and asked if I wanted to hire their services to exorcise my demons. Honestly, I almost said yes just so I could say I've been exorcised."

I reluctantly laugh, which I know is what she's going for. Then I sigh. "It's just so embarrassing. I'm sorry. You know I would never hurt you like that, right? I would never touch any of your men inappropriately . . . except for maybe a pinch on the butt on St. Patty's Day,"

"I know," she says solemnly.

I see her smirk, though, and I breathe a sigh of relief. I would never do anything to jeopardize our friendship. At this point, she's the only thing like family I have left.

She glances my way. "Our only worry in all this has been you. Tess, this is the absolute last thing you needed right now—"

"I'm fine," I say quickly, not wanting to make this about me.

But she's not buying it. "What are the chances he just doesn't see it?"

"Zero," I reply, watching as a pair of pelicans take flight out of the surf and cross our path.

It was inevitable that my location would leak back to Troy. I just didn't expect it to leak on the front page of *The Sun*, implicating yet another Ray as my not-so-secret lover. If he was livid over pictures of me dancing with a Ray, what will he do with news articles that paint me as their new favorite booty call girl?

God, this is such a disaster.

Not to mention I found out while in a post-orgasm haze, sitting naked at Ryan's feet. Yeah, that was awkward. And now the energy between us feels so strained. He still wants me to file a restraining order against Troy and order a retraction from *The Sun*. I just want to pretend none of this is happening and plan a donor gala for my sea turtles.

What should have been a blissful moment of connection was ruined. We argued. I stormed off. It was only after I cooled down that I peeked in his room to see him on his back in his clunky knee brace playing Mario Kart. Glancing over at me with a frown, he flipped the covers back on the open side of the bed. I tiptoed in, slipped under the covers, and fell asleep next to him. We didn't touch or speak.

When I woke in the morning, he was gone. Apparently, a rookie picked him up early for PT. He stayed out late, too, not coming home until I was already in bed. I pretended to be asleep. Without 'waking' me, he crawled into my bed and fell asleep. I waited for him to kiss me . . . touch me . . . anything.

But again, he didn't.

"Troy only has a few days left to reply to your request, right?" Rachel asks, pulling me back to the present.

"Yeah, three."

"And if he doesn't sign?"

"Then we go to court. But I never expected him to sign on his own," I admit. "He was always going to fight. I'm putting all my hope in Bea that she can talk him around."

"And you really think she'll help you? When has she ever helped you before?"

"None of us want a long, drawn-out legal proceeding as we fight over lamps," I reply. "Bea wants it all swept under the carpet. If getting him to sign uncontested protects her and the firm from any embarrassment, she'll apply the pressure. I don't care how she manages it; I just want it done."

"I know you do, honey." She wraps an arm around my shoulders.

Rachel and I continue our walk in silence, our bare feet sinking into the sand, our hands gripping to our warm cups of coffee. It's blustery for January, and we're both bundled up with polar fleeces.

The beach is quiet. Only a few surfers are out in the water. The surf is icy cold on my toes, but it feels good.

"And you're sure Jake is okay?" I say, glancing over.

"Honestly, he seems thrilled about it all."

I raise a brow, flicking a windswept curl out of my face. "Why?"

"Because now he gets PDA from us as we smooth this over," she replies with a grin. "He already planned a date night over at Top Golf for Caleb on Tuesday. And unless I can talk him out of it, I think he's gonna make me try indoor skydiving. So, thanks for that," she adds.

I laugh out loud at the mental image of Rachel floating in one of those wind tube things. "Oh god, I want pictures of you fake skydiving so bad. Give those to the paps. They'll be frame-worthy for sure. I'm thinking entryway."

"We'll blow them up and hang them over the bed," she adds with a laugh.

I cackle, grabbing her arm. "Ohmygod, and Mars will have to see Jake's stupid wind tunnel face every time he does you doggy style."

I make the face, and then we're both dying, laughing so hard we're crying.

"Tess!"

As if laughing about him is a summons, we both turn to see Ilmari marching down the sand towards us. He's got his blond hair pulled up in his characteristic messy bun. And while he's wearing workout pants and shoes, the man is only in a Rays tech T-shirt. It's 50 degrees outside.

"Does he even own a jacket?"

"I don't think so," Rachel replies. "Kulta?" she calls. "What's wrong, baby?"

He ignores his wife, glaring at me. In his hand is an envelope, and I think I know exactly what this is about. I square off at him, one hand on my hip as I casually take a sip of my coffee.

"Morning, Mars Attack."

"What is this?" He holds up the envelope.

Rachel's eyes go wide as she glances between us. "What's going on?"

"I assume you're referring to the invitation I sent you?" I say with a fake smile. "So glad you got it."

"It's an invitation to me *from* me," he barks.

"So, you'll be RSVPing 'yes' then, right? And you'll notice, I gave you a 'plus three.' So, Rach, you can come too," I add, flashing her a wink.

"Tess, what is this?" he says again. "I told you to keep me out of it—"

"No. You *very* specifically told me to keep you out of the decision-making process, which I did."

Rachel glances between us. "What the hell is happening?"

"This is a punishment for the way I behaved at the office," he says, not looking at her. "You know I'm sorry for that. I apologized, and you accepted. I thought we moved on."

"Wait—what behavior? What apology?" Rachel says, eyes wide.

He's not lying. He *did* send me an apology email. A stiff, formal apology of three sentences. I was about to call him and chew him out when a delivery person arrived at the office with an edible arrangement of chocolate covered fruits and a massage gift card—both from Mars.

I square my shoulders at him. "Yeah, and don't for one second think I don't know you went to Jake to help you make that apology," I counter. "That's the reason I forgave you, Mars. Because you showed yourself a big enough person to lean on your partners and ask them for help when you're clearly out of your depth."

His anger softens, the muscles in his shoulders relaxing slightly.

"You're out here giving me all this sage advice about being myself and taking control? Well, congratulations, the lesson stuck," I say, waving my hand at the envelope.

He bristles again. "This is *not* what I meant!"

"It's perfect," I shout back.

"Well, I'm not doing it. Get Jake to do it. He loves being the center of attention."

"Oh, yes, you are. Everything has already been arranged. You can't back out now, Mars Mission."

"Back out of what?" Rachel cries. "Someone better tell me what the hell is going on."

Slowly, Mars holds up the envelope. She snatches it from his hand, pulling out the super cute invitation I designed. It's got a watercolor motif of sea turtles and coral at the top. She reads it over quickly, her panic fading to confusion, which gives way to a smile.

"This is . . . amazing," she says at last, looking up at Mars. "Kulta, why wouldn't you do it? This is what you want, right? To attract donors? To help Out of the Net grow?"

"Yes, but the right kind of donors," he counters, clearly exasperated. "People who care about the environment, people who want to see legislative changes, better protections for the dunes. Not . . . *this*," he says, pointing at the invitation.

"Look, Mars," I say, gently plucking the invitation from Rachel's hand. "We'll get those donors too, trust me. Plenty of people will be drawn to the work of Out of the Net because they care about the sea turtles. But do you know what *else* pique's people's interest? Stupidly handsome, two-time Stanley Cup-winning NHL goalies with an intoxicating air of mystery."

He huffs, crossing his arms over his barrel chest.

"You wanna know how you help this organization? Be yourself. I've never asked you to be any different, Mars. We don't need the help of marine biologists and conservation specialists right now. We need attention. We need money. We need donors. You are the perfect person to get us all three. So, I present to you: A Night with Ilmari Kinnunen Price."

He mutters a curse in Finnish.

I wave the invitation in the air with a flourish. "It's a black-tie gala where you are the star, and you get to shine your light onto your favorite pet project and ask for donations. You'll mix and mingle and be yourself, and the donations will flood in, I promise you. And you won't be alone," I add. "We're having reps from some of the other turtle orgs come in. Cheryl and Nancy are arranging it all. We might even have an animal ambassador program. Real live baby sea turtles." I glance to Rachel with a grin. "Can you imagine?"

"Oh god, Caleb will literally pop a lung trying to play it cool around baby turtles," she says with a laugh. "I really think this will work," she adds, glancing up at her husband. "Fans and friends will donate just because it's you doing the asking."

"It is not my way to put myself forward and ask for things," he admits, letting a bit of his insecurity shine through again.

And goddamn it, but I love him more for it. I know I'm asking a lot of him, but I also know he can do it. He's more than just hockey. They all are. And he doesn't need a fancy degree to impress people with all he knows about dune restoration and wildlife conservation. Citizen science exists for a reason. He's perfect just as he is.

He just needs to see it too.

Next to me, Rachel smiles, and I know she's thinking the same thing. "You asked me to sit next to you on the plane."

He goes still, not looking at her.

"You asked me for that kiss in the street," she says, stepping closer, putting her hand on his arm. "You asked me to wear your jersey. You asked me to be yours. When you want something badly enough, you're good at asking for it. Why should this be any different?"

He glares down at her. You could cut this sudden sexual tension with a butter knife. "You don't fight fair."

"Have I ever?" She tips up on her toes to kiss his bearded jaw.

"Look, Mars Attack, it's time to get you outta the net too," I say, stepping in before they forget I'm here and start banging in the sand. "You told me to make all the decisions. Well, this is my decision. You're going to the gala, and that's final. You're hosting, and that's final. I will see you on Sunday two weeks from now at seven o'clock, and you better look un-fucking-obtainable. We've got a lot of sea turtles to save."

36
Tess

After a long day of event planning with my Out of the Net team, I arrive home to see a new car parked in the driveway. It's a flashy red two-seater sports car with a convertible top and Florida plates. Snatching up my bags off the passenger seat, I prepare myself to go inside.

I don't want to fight with Ryan. I don't want to exist in this awful bubble of unspoken worry and resentment. I want things to be fun again. I want us both to feel good. I want us to laugh and flirt.

Fuck, we need to have a grownup conversation. What am I always telling Rachel? Communicate, communicate, communicate. Look, I'm great at advice. I'm the queen of giving good, thoughtful relationship advice. I can dish it out all day.

Apparently, I just can't take it.

I enter the house to find chaos waiting within. Ryan's mix of rock music is pumping from the speakers, practically shaking the walls. The music isn't the problem; it's the smoke.

"Ohmygod," I cry, dropping all the shit in my hands.

The moment I take a step forward, the smoke alarm starts going off, beeping in time with the music. Over the din, I hear Ryan shouting and cursing. Pots rattle and smash.

I dart around the corner to see smoke billowing out of the oven as Ryan uses mitts to drag something out. He's coughing as he snatches for it, slamming it down on the stove top. Whatever was in that baking dish is burned all to hell, which accounts for the horrible smell.

It looks like a bomb went off. There's cutting boards and cheese graters and mixing bowls, spilled flour dusting the counter, measuring cups in every size. The milk is out . . . and a Costco-sized supply of panko breadcrumbs . . . and a plastic tub of prepared lobster meat.

"Oh my god," I say again, coughing into my hand, eyes burning.

Ryan slams the oven closed and snatches for a baking tray, waving it in the air to try and clear the smoke. He turns as he swipes and jumps a foot off the ground when he sees me standing there. "Fuck—Tess—Don't just stand there, help me," he bellows, panicked eyes wide.

I launch into motion, ducking under his pan, flailing arms to reach the stove. I turn off the broiler, no doubt the culprit in this fiasco, and glance down into the baking dish to see the remnants of what I can only assume was supposed to be homemade lobster mac and cheese.

Tears sting my eyes for a whole new reason as I slip behind him and hurry over to the sliding glass door. Flipping the latch, I drag the door all the way open, letting a burst of January air in to clear the smoke. I spin around, leaning against the glass as I watch him flail for another thirty seconds.

The smoke alarm finally shuts off, leaving us standing on opposite sides of the living room, chests heaving, eyes wide, as rock music pulses all around. Ryan blinks twice, then he drops the baking tray down with a clatter and snatches up his phone. In seconds, the music cuts, leaving a ringing silence in my ears.

"How long were you standing there?" he asks.

"About two seconds. I just got in when the alarm went off. What were you making?"

"I—nothing," he says, a blush blooming in his cheeks. "Well, nothing now since I fucking ruined it." He turns away, snatching up things off the counter and dropping them unceremoniously into the sink.

I inch closer. "Ryan, were you trying to make lobster mac and cheese?"

He goes still, not looking at me, his hands on the glass mixing bowl. Slowly he looks up. "Yeah, well, it was supposed to be a surprise . . . and it was supposed to be actually fucking edible." He turns away, rattling the mixing bowl down into the sink.

I step up to the kitchen island and survey the mess. "What happened?"

"I don't know." He glances over at the burned mess on the stove. "My mom gave me the recipe, and I swear I tried to follow the instructions, but I may have missed a step or . . . I don't—I'm not good at cooking, okay? I can't always follow the steps or, like, sometimes I skip them . . . "

"You turned the oven on broil instead of bake," I say gently.

He spins around. "What?"

I point to the stove. "You had it on broil instead of bake."

"What's the difference?"

I hold back my smile. "Only about two hundred degrees. And all the heat comes from the top-down when you broil. That's why it burned."

"Fuck." He peers down at the stove, looking at the dials. "Where does it say that?"

I inch around the island, coming to stand beside him. "See this one here?" I point at the oven dial. "You just turned it to broil instead of bake."

He narrows his eyes. "So, one click to the left is broil and one to the right is bake?"

"Yep." I brush my hand over his shoulder. "It's okay. It's a mistake anyone could have made."

"Yeah . . . anyone," he says, wholly dejected by his failure.

I lean my hip against the counter, crossing my arms as I glance over at him. "Why were you trying a recipe as adventurous as lobster mac?"

He looks like such a sad puppy that I'm actually struggling to restrain myself from petting his hair. "For you," he admits softly. "It was supposed to be my 'I'm sorry' peace offering."

"Peace offering?"

"Yeah—Tess, listen." He turns to face me, his hands bracing my shoulders. "I'm sorry, okay? I was totally out of line the other day."

My heart skips as I hold his gaze. "Ryan—"

"No, let me get this out, okay? I'm sorry. I was a jerk. I was projecting what I would do and how I feel onto your situation, and I was pushing you, and I wasn't being your friend. I was being . . . well, I was being like a macho boyfriend, and that's not fair to you."

"You were just trying to look out for me."

"I think we both know you can look out for yourself." He reaches up, flicking a curl back from my face. "You're so fucking strong. And you're smart. You're seriously like Wonder Woman. You've got the brains and the beauty and you just . . . you fucking floor me. And I want to be your friend, and I want to earn that friendship, and this was me saying sorry, but I fucking ruined it," he finishes in one breath, gesturing again to the burned casserole.

"You didn't ruin anything," I reply. "I love my peace offering. It's perfect."

We both glance down at it, and then we're laughing. His deep laugh mixes with my higher notes and I smile, liking the sounds we make together. It makes my heart flutter all over again.

Letting out a deep breath, he shakes his head and opens his arms. "Come here."

I eagerly step into him, my arms wrapping around his waist as his go around my shoulders, locking me against him. I turn my face, resting it against his chest. One hand curls up and he brushes his fingers over my hair, cradling my head to him. We fit together.

Tipping his head down, he kisses my brow, just a quick brush with his lips. "We promised that the rule of this game would be feeling good, yeah?"

I nod.

He leans away slightly, tucking a finger under my chin to tip my face up. "You make me feel so fucking good, Tess. And I don't want to ruin it. Let's just . . . can we maybe try and quiet all the other noise—when it's just the two of us, at least? And not that I don't want to hear your problems, or be there for you as a friend," he adds quickly. "You can tell me anything and I'll listen. But I think if our goal is feeling good, that should maybe be a part of the house rules."

I nod again, my entire body flooding with relief. Of course, I don't have to march in and sit Ryan down to have the grownup conversation about boundaries. We're already on the same page. Our writing styles may be a little different, but we're trying to tell the same story.

"That sounds perfect," I say. "You make me feel good too. I'd like to keep feeling good with you."

His gaze heats as he looks down at me, his hands holding me firmly against him. "What would feel good? Say it, and it's yours."

Standing in this mess of a kitchen, our clothes stinking of epically burned lobster mac, I flash him a teasing grin. "Oh, I know *exactly* what I want."

37
Ryan

"So . . . what? Now we just sit here?" I glance skeptically around the dark interior of Mars's private, at-home sauna.

"Mhmm," Tess replies as she leans back against the wall and drapes a wet washcloth over her forehead, covering her eyes.

This is all her fault. She helped me clean up the kitchen and said we needed to give the house time to air out. Her big idea was for us to strip naked and shove ourselves into a human oven while we wait for the nasty smells of the food oven to dissipate.

So here I am, naked and sweating my ass off next to her, not touching her. This feels like a punishment.

"Ryan?"

I turn her way. "Hmm?"

"Stop thinking."

"What?"

"You're thinking, and it's distracting me from not thinking. We're in here to relax, remember?"

"I guess baking alive just doesn't quite relax me." I cross my arms over my chest.

"It will if you let it," she replies. "It's science."

"What kind of science says this is supposed to be relaxing?"

She heaves a deep sigh. "The heat from a sauna helps relieve muscle and joint pain. It detoxes the body, improves sweat performance, relieves stress, and can even improve the quality of your sleep. So, maybe if you sit in here for a half hour, you'll actually be able to sleep tonight, and you won't need me to talk you through my morning flossing routine."

"Maybe it's not your boring routines that put me to sleep. Maybe it's just the comfort of having you close to me. Did you ever think of that?"

She goes still. Yep, I totally just said that out loud.

Well . . . fuck.

She drops the washcloth down off her eyes and glances over at me. "Ryan—"

"Kidding," I say, forcing a smirk.

She rolls her eyes. "No, you're not."

No, I'm not.

"If you're really that bored, I brought something that might help distract you," she says.

"More distracting than the drop-dead gorgeous naked woman currently glistening like a sun goddess on the bench next to me?"

She smiles. "Honestly? Maybe."

I look around this tiny box. There's nothing but a stack of towels at the end of the bench. "What did you bring?"

"The puppy is curious," she say, eyes still closed as she leans against the wooden wall.

"Tess . . . "

She laughs, sitting up as she slings the wet washcloth over her shoulder. Her curls are tied up in a bun on top of her head. The heat has her skin flushed pink, growing pinker. It spreads across her chest, over her shoulders, blooming in her cheeks. This is what I saw the first night I arrived at the house. She had this same glow. It lit her from the inside out.

Maybe there *is* something to saunas . . .

"Do you trust me, Ryan?" she says, flashing me a sexy smile.

I go still. "Unclear."

"Do you trust me to make you feel good? That's the only rule, right?"

I narrow my eyes. "Babe, we can't fuck in here. I'll stroke out."

"Aren't you a professional athlete at the literal peak of physical performance?"

"Yeah," I reply, drawing out the 'e.' "But you do remember I play my sport on *ice* right, not the surface of the fucking sun?"

She laughs again. "I think you'll survive. In fact, I think this might just make you a sauna convert. Who knows all the ways we could convert you tonight?"

Curiosity is about to kill this cat. "Tess, just tell me."

She flips over the towel at the end of the bench.

"Oh, what the fuck is that?" I say, eyes wide.

She holds up the little pink toy. "It's a butt plug, Ryan. And look how cute it is." She turns it over, showing me the pink, heart-shaped gemstone bedazzling the top of it.

I hold her gaze, heart pounding in my chest. "Tess Michelle Owens, are you asking me to do butt stuff with you in Ilmari Price's sauna?"

"I—wait—Michelle?" She raises a brow at me. "Where the hell did you get Michelle from? That's not my middle name."

I shrug. "I made it up. This felt like a middle name moment. Do you seriously want me to put that in your ass?" I say, pointing to it. "That's what's gonna make sauna time more fun?"

She giggles, biting her bottom lip in a way that has my dick twitching. "Not exactly. Actually, I wanted to put this one in *your* ass."

Heartbeat gone.

"*This* is the plug I want you to put in my ass." Flipping the towel over the rest of the way, she reveals a red plug almost twice the size and length of the pink one.

Soul exiting body.

"Oh, and they vibrate," she adds. "And we'll each have a remote, so we can play with the settings. I'm thinking, to spice things up a little, I'll take your remote and you take mine."

"Tess—" The sound comes out all strangled. "You—what the fuck?"

"Do you trust me, Ryan? Do you want to feel good?"

"Yes, but—"

"Have you ever done any prostate play before?"

"No," I cry, scooting away down the bench. "I've never had anything in my ass before. I don't—things go out, they don't go in. Right?"

"Oh, sweet puppy," she says with a shake of her head. "Allow me to paint a picture for you, shall I?"

"Please don't," I beg, fearing it and wanting it at the same time.

She scoots closer, her sweat-sheened breast brushing against my arm. "Imagine a fullness inside you . . . it's deep and rooted," she says, using that voice that draws me in like a siren's call.

I shut my eyes tight, holding to the solid wood of the bench. I can't block out the sound of her voice . . . and judging by my dick's reaction, I don't want to.

"You center yourself in the feel of it," she goes on. "It anchors you. And then . . . suddenly . . . a spark of life. It's humming, the vibrations moving outward, consuming you until all you feel is waves of warmth cascading through you and over you."

I groan, my dick twitching against my leg.

"And while you take your pleasure, you get to feel like a god knowing you're controlling mine."

I go still.

"You'll have my remote, Ryan. You'll decide whether I simply moan through my release . . . or come screaming. Either way, I'll be choking on your dick as I do it."

"Fuck." I grab her by the neck, pulling her to me. Our wet flesh presses together, sticky with sweat as we kiss. I devour her, kissing her deep, teasing with my tongue, biting her lip. She pants against me, her hands going to my chest, splaying her fingers flat.

"Trust me, Ryan. Let me make you feel so fucking good."

"Do it," I say against her lips, my left hand dropping down to tweak her nipple. She gasps, twitching in my hold, and I laugh. "But you're going first. Nothing is going in my ass until I watch you take yours."

She smiles, pulling back from me, a wicked gleam in her eyes. "I'm already wearing one. I have been this whole time."

My eyes go wide as I glance down her body. "What?"

"Well, yeah. You can't just take a torpedo like that and shove it in your ass, Ryan." She gestures to the red plug. "Anal play takes prep work. That's rule one. I've been sitting on my plug for thirty minutes, getting things nice and stretched out."

"Show me," I say, heart in my fucking throat.

Like the goddess she is, she stands up and turns for me, exuding confidence as she places both hands against the wall and bends over.

My hands react like magnets, smoothing over the dimpled flesh of her ass as I part her cheeks. "Holy shit." A little white diamond winks at me from her asshole.

"Cute, right?" she says, glancing over her shoulder at me.

"I'm not sure cuteness matters with this kind of thing," I reply, my hands still smoothing over her curvy ass. Fuck, she's distracting. She should always be naked, and I should always be touching her.

"You like what you see?" she teases, wiggling that ass in my face.

"You want to take control of my pleasure? We can sit here, relaxing in the heat, letting our bodies detox. And then we'll play with our remotes until we climax. It'll be fun, I promise."

"The things you say." I shake my head. "You slay me dead, Tess."

"Don't die yet. Wait until you've had your first prostate O. Your soul will leave your body as you come for days . . . all over my tits."

I stand up, pulling her face to mine for a kiss. "You are so much fucking trouble," I say against her lips.

"More than you know. Now, bend over, hands on the bench."

Not quite knowing what the fuck kind of twilight zone I've stepped into, I let Tess boss me around. She sets the pink sparkly butt plug down on the bench and snatches the small bottle of lube she also had hidden in the towel.

"Anything else under there, Tess? Rubber chicken? Coordinates to Atlantis?"

"Just the remotes," she replies with a shrug. She steps in close to me, brushing her lips against my shoulder. "Bend over, Ryan. Show me that cute hockey butt."

"Fuck." All my nerves hum as I bend over.

"This ass makes me weak," she says, smoothing her hand over my hip. "Am I a total wanton hussy if I admit your butt was the first thing I noticed on the day we met?"

I smirk. "No."

"You bent down to fetch your soccer ball and it was right there, so full and tight. I wanted to bite it."

I glance over my shoulder at her with a raised brow. "You want to bite my ass?"

She nods, lust clouding her eyes. "Haven't you ever been so drawn to a person you wanted to devour them? You want a piece of their essence. You want to mark them, claim them as your own."

My dick hardens as I look away. "Maybe . . . once or twice."

With you.

She leans in with a low hum, her naked flesh pressing against mine. "You've thought it about me, haven't you?" she teases, pinching my ass cheek.

I twitch, biting my lip and she laughs. "Yes," I admit.

"Good," she says in my ear. "I want you to mark me, Ryan. I want to wear it knowing you put it there in a fit of passion. And I'll mark you too . . . but not tonight." She pulls away and it feels like she takes all my air with her.

I groan, shifting my weight to my good knee. "Are we doing something here, or am I just bent over for fun?"

"Pick a safe word," she says, opening the bottle of lube and squeezing a dollop into her hand.

I glance at her again. "What?"

"You need a safe word, Ryan. This is new play for you, new sensations. You may not like it. You may need it to stop. I need to know when you've reached your limit. Pick a word that you'll only say when you need it to stop. No judgement, no questions, no hesitation."

My mind scrambles to think of something—anything. "Uhh . . . Yoshi."

She giggles. "Yoshi? That's your safe word?"

I smirk. "Yeah. It was the first word I thought of."

"Yoshi it is," she replies, kissing my shoulder again. "Don't say it again unless you mean it, okay?"

I nod.

She steps in behind me, her hips pressing against mine. "Just relax, okay? I promise, if you trust me, this will feel amazing."

I nod again, swallowing down my nerves. "I trust you."

Her lubed hand snakes around my hip and closes around my shaft, stroking from root to tip in one long, luxurious pull. I groan, body sagging as all my blood rushes straight to my crotch.

"What are you doing?" I say, head sagging between my shoulders as she does it again.

"Relaxing you," she replies.

Her chest is bent over my back, her full breasts pressed against my fevered skin. She moves her hips a bit, fucking me with her hand as she rocks into me from behind. It's intoxicating. I love the feel of her wrapped around me like this.

Just as I'm about to say so, she shifts until her pussy is pressed against my right hip, exposing my ass. Her hand on my dick stills, holding me tight, as the fingers of her left hand trail down the small of my back, between my cheeks, until just one finger presses over my tight hole.

"Fuck," I gasp, my body lighting up like she flipped a damn switch.

"Puppy, we're just getting started," she teases, rimming me with that lubed finger. "You know what to say to make me stop?"

I nod.

"Do you want me to stop?"

"No," I grit out. "Keep going."

I'm too curious to stop now.

"Relax," she says. "Deep breath . . . and exhale."

As I exhale, I feel pressure at my hole. I try not to clench as she presses in.

"Look at you." Her voice is full of praise. "So, beautiful with my finger in your ass. You're gonna be a natural, aren't you? Just wait until I'm fucking you in the ass while my tits bounce in your face—"

"Jesus—Tess—*stop*," I bark, my cheeks clenching around her finger.

"Stop as in—"

"Don't fucking stop, just stop the fucking dirty talk. I didn't safe word yet, but I'm about to come if you don't stop turning me the fuck on. Stretch me out and put in the plug. And then you're fucking next."

"Yes, sir," she teases, bending over to kiss the middle of my sweaty back.

I shiver, all senses firing as I'm wracked with new sensations.

Her right hand drops away from my dick and she holds my hip for support as she works her finger in and out of my ass. I hold tight to the bench, trying to keep myself relaxed.

"I'm adding a finger," she murmurs.

I nod, groaning as I feel the tightening of a second finger pressing in. The lube feels strange, but my whole body is slicked at this point. She works those fingers against me. I feel full, but not overly full. It's an odd sensation, but not as weird as I thought it might be. It's even pleasurable. It's almost like—

"Oh, holy fuck," I squawk, my cheeks clenching around her fingers.

"There it is," she sings.

She touched something inside me that felt like a zap of electricity. It zinged through me, straight to the fucking heart. My dick twitches, the tip leaking precum.

"Oh my god," I say, fighting the urge to whimper.

"That's your prostate," she says, curling her fingers up and in to touch the spot again.

I try to stop my knees from shaking.

"Such a good boy," she soothes. "You're gonna love this. I'm going to put the toy in now. Are you ready?"

Am I ready? Is there such a thing as being ready for this? "Yes," I grit out.

She removes her fingers from my ass, and I feel empty. Then she steps away, and I feel like I'm fighting the urge to whimper. I want her against me, all around me, holding me, shoring me up. I watch as she puts lube on the butt plug. Then she's right back behind me, tapping at my hole with it.

"This is going to feel tight at first," she explains. "Maybe even too tight. The pain will fade as your muscles adjust. You trust me?"

I nod for what feels like the hundredth time. "Do it."

She's gentle as she presses in, her hand smoothing over my lower back. "Deep exhale," she says.

I curse under my breath as I feel the stretch and the sting.

"Too much?"

"No," I grunt. "Is it in?"

"Almost," she replies. The burn fades to an aching fullness as she settles the plug in my hole. "It's in."

I take another deep breath. "Now what?"

"Now you put mine in for me," she replies. "Then we play."

I'm still bent over, hands on the bench. "I just . . . what do I do?"

Her hand brushes up my back. "Honey, just stand up. It's not a bomb. It won't explode."

I straighten my back, feeling the way the toy shifts a little in my ass. "Now what?"

She hands me the red plug. "Lube that for me."

I pick up the bottle of lube and squeeze some in my hand. I probably use too much as I wet the plug all over. When I turn to her with the toy, she's already taken the other plug out.

She flashes me an excited smile. "You ready, handsome?"

I nod, stepping closer, toy in hand.

"I'll tell you if I need you to stop," she explains. "Just go slow and work it in."

"What's your safe word?" I ask, stepping around to stand behind her.

She huffs a laugh, bending forward with her hands on the bench. "Honey, I don't need a safe word for a little butt plug action. This is a bored Saturday night for me."

I shake my head, totally in awe of this sexual creature before me. She's so confident, so empowered. It makes me wonder what I've been missing all these years. How much fun could I have been having if I treated sex less like a chore or an item on my to-do list?

I step in behind her, smoothing my hand over her ass and up her lower back. "Ready?"

"Mhmm."

I prod at her entrance with the toy, and she widens her stance, pressing into me until the toy begins to disappear.

"Ryan, have you ever done anal?" she says, glancing over her shoulder at me.

"Once," I admit. "It was college, and I was pretty drunk though."

"I love anal," she hums, bearing down as I sink the toy in deeper. "Mmm, keep going. Push it all the way in." She shivers as I force the red plug the rest of the way into her ass. As soon as it's all the way in, she gives a little shaky laugh. "It's been a while since I played with one this big. Maybe I was being over ambitious."

"Should we stop or—"

"Hell no," she replies, pushing off the bench. "This is gonna feel amazing." She reaches under the towel and takes out two small remotes, one pink and one red. She hands me the red one. "Come on, let's go dip in the pool and cool off. Then we'll play."

Apparently, we're walking around wearing butt plugs now. What the hell is happening to me? I follow her out of the sauna into the chilly January night.

She walks right over to the pool, plug hidden between her cheeks, and walks down the steps, sinking into the icy water. "It'll feel good, I promise. Cool off now, and we'll warm up in the sauna," she adds with a flirty wink.

Taking a deep breath, I walk down the steps of the pool, the plug only slightly uncomfortable. As soon as I'm waist-deep in the water, a vibration shoots up my ass, straight to my heart. "Holy—*fuck*—" I gasp, spinning around to glare at Tess. As soon as the vibrations start, they stop.

"Just checking to see if the remote works," she says with a grin.

I wade towards her. "Oh, you are in so much trouble—"

"Ryan, no," she shrieks, wading away. "Dunk me in this pool, and I'll turn your plug up to ten!"

I drop my hands away from her, letting her slip away, up out of the pool. She's halfway up the stairs when I click her remote on. She gasps, grasping for the handrail as I quickly click it twice to up the vibration.

"Oh god," she whimpers, hurrying up the stairs with it still vibrating.

I follow her with a grin. Okay, I can see the appeal of this. We go back into the sauna, and she surprises the hell out of me when she takes her folded towel and sits down.

"Are—do you—doesn't that hurt?" I manage to get out.

"No," she replies with a shrug. "Come here, baby. Come sit by me, and we'll relax." She pats the bench next to her. "Part of the fun with this kind of play is the anticipation."

I'm trusting this process. If she says I can sit with a sparkly butt plug in my ass, I'm going to do it. She sets my towel out and I sit down, wincing slightly as I find an angle that doesn't put pressure right on the plug.

She reaches over with her free hand, placing it on my thigh. "Just lean back. Relax and close your eyes. Breathe in the smell of the cedar. Try to let go of all your worry and anxiety."

Okay, this is starting to feel like a yoga session now. I'm not mad about it. And the juxtaposition between the hot-cold-hot *is* refreshing. I can feel my muscles and joints loosening up. I guess I just expected this to be—

"Oh, fuck," I cry out, bending over, elbows on my knees, as the plug goes off, hammering my ass with strong vibrations. Changing angles was a fucking mistake. I practically squeal as I flop backwards. The buzzing plug hits me right on my prostate. My dick hardens, all the blood rushing from my head to my crotch.

She doesn't keep it on long before I'm given a reprieve.

Not to be outdone, I fumble for her remote and turn it on. Next to me, she hums. Tess is much more relaxed than me, leaning back against the wall, eyes closed. She's almost serene as she just lets the vibrations rock through her.

I click it higher.

No change.

Higher.

"Mmm, that feels good," she says.

Slowly, she lifts her hands to her breasts and starts to touch herself, lazy and languid. She tweaks her nipples, and I've decided I fucking love this game. I duck down, eager to taste her. As she pinches herself with a seductive sigh, I close my mouth over her fingers and her nipple, sucking on them both.

"Fuck, yeah that's good," she whimpers. She pulls her fingers free, digging them into my hair as she holds me to her breast, demanding that I keep sucking on her. With her free hand, she works my remote, turning it on again.

The vibration is higher this time, and I can't suppress a full body shiver.

"You like it?"

"Yeah," I reply.

"You want more?"

"Please," I hear myself say.

The vibration intensifies and I gasp, all my muscles contracting around the little toy. I look down, watching as the tip of my dick leaks precum. This is surreal and amazing. She doesn't even need to touch my dick. I really think I could come with no contact, which would be a fucking first.

"Turn mine up," she whimpers. "Ryan, I need to taste you. I need you to tease my pussy as I suck your cock."

"Get over here," I reply, clicking her toy up higher.

She shifts until she's on her knees on the bench, ass pointed away from me. She crawls forward, cheeks flushed, eyes glassy. I cup her face, stealing a kiss, but then she's pulling away, her head dropping to my crotch, and she sucks the tip of my dick into her mouth. The moment her lips close around me, she turns up the goddamn toy.

"Fucking hell—" My hips kick forward, ass lifting off the bench as she sucks me deeper. The combination of sensations has me feeling like I'm being pulled apart. The plug is full in my ass, and the vibrations send a sharp tingling all over my body, like I'm being licked by fire. Her mouth on my dick is a dream, so wet and warm.

She snatches for my hand, whimpering as she moves her hips on air. She takes my hand and puts it between her legs, and I take over, my fingers seeking out her needy clit. I make contact, and she arches into me, humming around my dick.

"Tess—*god*—babe, I'm not gonna last long if you don't—*ahhh*—ohmygod—fucking fuck—" I drop my hand away from her pussy as she turns the remote up to what better be the highest fucking setting. I need to come so bad I think I might cry. A tremor starts deep in my groin and rockets up my spine.

I shift my hips a little, and that has me seeing stars. The point of the plug sits right on my prostate, the buzzing rocking me from head to toe. I have an out of body experience as it feels like all my muscles contract at once. I bend over in a half curl, my hands tightened into fists, as I come harder than I've ever come in my life. I don't know what the hell kind of feral sound I'm making. Can't think. Only feel.

Tess had no warning, but she takes it like a champ, holding her mouth open as my cum pumps out of my tip, hitting her lips, her chin, her greedy tongue. I make a mess of her as I just can't stop coming.

"Oh my god," I moan, my body suddenly losing air like a popped balloon. I fizzle, all energy leaving me, as I collapse against the bench. Tess turns off my plug, and it's like flipping a switch. Lights out. I'm dead. Done.

She reaches across my lap for the red remote that I don't even remember setting down. She takes control of her own orgasm, clicking it up and working her clit. "Watch me," she pants, her breasts jiggling in the most seductive way as she fucks herself. "Ryan, watch—"

As if I can look at anything else? I watch my queen take her pleasure, riding out her climax, her sweet moans filling the small room. Her skin is flushed, her head tipped back, body glistening as she makes herself come. It's fucking breathtaking. She finishes, turning the toy off and dropping both remotes. They clatter to the floor at our feet. Then she slumps forward, catching herself with one hand, her forehead dropping to my shoulder.

"How was that?" she says after a moment.

"So fucking good," I reply. "I'm officially a convert to butt plugs."

"I knew you'd like it." I don't need to see her face to know she's wearing her sleepy smile.

"I'm still not convinced about the sauna," I admit.

She just keeps smiling, turning her face to peck my chest with a kiss.

I manage to lift a hand, digging it into the hair at her nape. I tip her head back, kissing her lips, not caring that she tastes like me. In fact, I think it turns me the fuck on. She's mine and I'm hers. Nothing we could ever share could be bad or wrong. I want to taste like her, smell like her. Bring on all the coconutty hair oils and strawberry lip gloss.

"Am I corrupting you, Ryan?" she says. "Should we stop while we're ahead?"

"You're a she-devil," I say against her lips. "My goddess." I give her a kiss. "My queen. You fucking own me." I kiss her again. "Do anything, take anything. It's yours."

"Hmm," she says on a sigh, kissing me back. "As much as I love the idea of taking you for everything you have, I'm starving." As if in evidence, her stomach lets out a low grumble, and we both laugh. "Why don't I order us a pizza while you go get cleaned up?"

She kisses the tip of my nose, and then she's moving away, as if her bones weren't just liquified by the most intense orgasm of her life. Perhaps I need to try harder next time.

Towel under her arm, she glances over her shoulder at me. "You coming?"

"I don't think I can get up," I admit. I'm not even sure I remember how legs work.

She laughs again, crossing back over to me and holding out a hand. "Come on, sweet puppy. We really gotta work on your off-ice stamina. Give me a few weeks to toughen you up, and I'll have you coming like that all night long."

A few weeks? This woman can have more than that. She can have months. Years. Hell, if she'll only give us a real chance, a chance to be more than just friends, I'll be her sweet puppy for the rest of my fucking life.

38
Tess

I spend the whole of Thursday morning running around like a chicken with my head cut off. Between helping Joey set up for a volunteer clean-up event over at the beach and playing phone tag with two city council reps, I somehow manage to bake two dozen of my famous triple chocolate chunk oatmeal cookies.

Apparently Shelby O'Sullivan is hosting a huge birthday party tonight, and I promised Rachel I would make an appearance. All the Rays will be there, which should make for a wild and crazy night. I'm hoping Shelby will accept my cookies as a peace offering.

Her party has a "favorite fictional character" theme, and I've been putting together an outfit all week. Is it funny and on theme? Yes. Will I look hot? Double yes. Is Ryan going to lose his freaking mind? Obviously, my entire point.

The doorbell rings just as I'm putting the finishing touch on my lipstick.

"Shit." I glance at myself in the mirror. I'm wearing my sexy devil costume, complete with red leather skirt, lacy bustier top, black fishnets, and little black horns peeking out the top of my head. My makeup looks flawless—a dramatic smoky eye and cherry red lips.

Tossing my lipstick down with a soft laugh, I saunter off towards the front door. Whoever it is better be ready for a bit of a jump scare. I peek out through the fogged glass of the front door and see a mail truck driver hop back in his truck and drive off.

Opening the door, I glance down. A smallish box is perched in the center of the welcome mat. I pick it up and read the label and my heart stops.

It's addressed to me.

No one has this address except a few of the Rays and my lawyer. And no Ray would send me something by mail when they could get it to me in person. It's certainly nothing to do with Out of the Net. My list of suspects narrows down to one.

"Well . . . fuck."

I slam the door shut and throwing the bolt. Then I carry the box like a bomb into the kitchen and set it down, glaring at it.

"What's your game now, huh?" I say at the box.

Snatching a knife from the block, I stab into the flaps of the box, aggressively cutting through the tape. Whatever waits for me in here, it's not going to be good. Dropping the knife down with a clatter, I tear the flaps and fold them back.

The box is full of confetti—no, shredded paper. He dumped the contents of a paper shredder into a box and mailed it to me?

And then it hits me.

"Oh my god." I pick up a handful, inspecting it more closely. Yep, these are printed pages. I can just make out some of the words. He shredded the divorce papers and mailed them to me unsigned. Tears sting my eyes as I open my fingers, letting the confetti fall back into the box.

"Goddamn it," I say, my voice catching.

I shift the confetti a bit and see a small envelope. Bracing myself for the worst, I pull it out and flip it over. He didn't bother sealing it. I take out the contents, unfolding the papers. My heart sinks out of my chest. It's printed screenshots of the bullshit tabloid articles featuring Jake and me. He scrawled a message on the top page. I recognize his sloping cursive:

Whores don't get to make demands

"Lovely."

My fingers shake as I delicately fold up the papers, slipping them back inside the envelope. I set the envelope down on top of the shredded divorce documents and pick up the box, taking it to my room. I leave it on my dresser as I go into the bathroom and snatch my phone. Flicking through my short list of contacts, I press Charlie's name and dial.

"Hey, honey, how you doing today?" comes his cheery tone.

"He didn't sign, Charlie," I say in greeting.

"I—well, I haven't heard back from his counsel yet, but they *do* have till end of day—"

"He didn't sign," I say again. "I know he didn't sign, because I have the contract right here and it's unsigned."

"You have it? How—"

"He shredded it unsigned, and mailed it to me," I explain. "Charlie, how did he get my address? You are the only person up there who has it."

"Well, I would never—"

"I'm not saying you gave it to him," I add quickly. "I'm asking you, as someone who deals in family law cases, how would he get ahold of my address? I'm in a different state. He doesn't have my phone number; I'm not returning his emails. How would my ex-husband know where to send me mail?"

Charlie sighs into the phone. "My best guess?"

"Yes, please."

"He's got someone following you."

My heart stops.

"We knew with all your tabloid drama this might happen," Charlie goes on. "He must be paying someone to track you down."

"What should I do? What *can* I do?"

"Look for any signs that you're being followed and document them if you can," he explains. "Curious cars on the street, people going through your trash, someone taking pictures without your consent. Document every time he makes contact, and throw nothin' out, do you hear? Keep that box of shredded papers. Keep all screenshots, all emails."

"Okay." Tears sting my eyes again. I hate the idea of this box poisoning my air with its negative energy.

"Honey, as your attorney, I have to ask—do you believe you're in danger? Should we start the TRO process?"

"No," I say quickly. "No, I don't think we're there yet. Let me . . . " I let out a deep breath, trying to get my brain to unscramble.

"Are we moving forward with the divorce? Should I request the court hearing—"

"Wait. Let me just make another call, and I'll get back to you, okay? I'm not ready to give up on this yet. Let me try one more thing."

"Okay, honey."

"I'll call you back, Charlie."

"I'll be here 'til around seven, and then I've got a dinner, but you leave me a voicemail and I'll get back to you."

"Thanks, Charlie."

I hang up, taking a deep breath. As soon as I feel centered again, I march out into the bedroom. Glaring down at the offensive box, I tap a number into the keypad I know by heart. Then I press the green call button. Holding it up to my ear, I wait.

On the third ring, it connects.

"Hello?" comes my mother-in-law's voice. "Who is this?"

I don't respond.

"Hello?"

Taking a deep breath, I charge ahead. "Bea, it's me."

"Oh—Tess?" Her tone shifts from authoritative to surprised. "Darling, what's wrong?"

"You know what's wrong," I reply. "What I need to know is what you plan to do about it."

She sighs, and I can almost imagine her slipping her readers off and setting them on her desk, pinching the bridge of her nose. "What happened?"

The time for coddling her is over. "He shredded the divorce papers and sent them to me in a box with a note calling me a whore," I reply.

"Tess, this is all so distasteful. It's such a complicated business—"

"Then uncomplicate it. Make him sign—"

"Is *he* the one making things complicated, or are you?" she challenges. "You hurt him with your latest publicity stunt—hurt all of us, Tess. I'm doing my best to clean up this mess, but thrusting yourself back into the spotlight isn't helping anyone—"

"Those are tabloids," I cry. "It's bullshit, Bea. I'm not with Jake Price. It's trash reporting—"

"It's fuel for this fire," Bea counters.

"And Troy means to watch me burn, right?" I challenge. "Are you going to help him? Is that what you want too?"

"He's angry and upset," she replies. "Justifiably so. You're asking him to uproot his entire life, to end a relationship that's lasted over a decade. He's not taking any of this lightly."

I shake my head, blocking out her attempts to minimize and deflect.

"Perhaps if you'd just agree to speak with him—"

"No." My palms are suddenly sweaty at the mere idea of another encounter. "That's not happening. Bea, I'm done. I'll give him *one* more chance to do this uncontested. You write up the papers this time and get him to sign."

"Tess—"

"You get him to sign, or I will see him in court," I shout, a tear slipping down my cheek. "And then every awful thing he has ever said or done will become a matter of public record—the cheating, the abuse, the isolation, the harassment. I will drag your precious son into this fire with me, and we will burn together, so help me God."

"Now your true colors begin to shine," she says, her tone cold, distant.

I take a deep breath, eyes closed. "This all stops when he grants me my divorce. Only he can do it, Bea. Only he can set us both free."

She's quiet for a moment. "I need more time."

"Well, I have no more time to give," I reply, wholly resolved. "So, are you helping me or not?"

39
Ryan

"Come on," I mutter, hands balled into fists as I watch Sully, Jonesy, and Karlsson skate down the ice, passing the puck. They had to reshuffle the forward lines with me missing, which means Jonesy is practicing with the starters this morning. He's playing like a hotshot, making fancy stick moves and hogging the puck.

"Come on," I say louder this time. "Just pass it, Jonesy!"

Sully is open and waiting, but Jonesy keeps it, trying a backhand flick that gets blocked by J-Lo. He bats the puck away and sends it down ice, leaving Jonesy scrambling to chase after it.

"Stop showboating and pass the damn puck," I shout as he skates past me. This is the worst part about being injured: the watching. I launch to my feet, grabbing the top of the boards. "Pass it, Jonesy! For fuck's sake—"

"Yoo-hoo, Ryan!"

I spin around, watching as Poppy St. James comes sauntering down the row of seats, her heels clicking as she walks. Does this woman ever not wear heels? She's our public relations manager, but don't let her Barbie looks fool you. She's sharp as a tack and ruthless.

Her gloomy shadow Claribel walks in her wake. Poppy is loud and bright in a lavender pantsuit and blazer, while Claribel is a goth girl with dark eye makeup and dyed hair.

"Hi, Ryan," Poppy chimes. "You got a minute?"

I stifle my groan. Whenever Poppy asks for a minute, she really means an hour. And if Claribel is involved, it means I'll be doing something stupid like slapping a teammate in the face with a tortilla or answering questions about my favorite books and music.

It was one of her stupid viral TikToks that outed me as a Swiftie.

Don't get me wrong, it's a good nickname for a forward. But now the guys up in the sound booth are having too much fun with it. The last time I scored a goal, they played "22" as my goal song.

"What's up, Poppy?" I say, giving Claribel a nod. She barely acknowledges me, her eyes on her phone.

Poppy flashes me a smile. "We're looking for one more Ray to help us with this commercial spot, and you're perfect. Come on." She doesn't even wait for my answer, she just spins around.

"Well—wait," I call.

She glances back, one brow raised.

"I—well, I can't leave," I say, gesturing to the ice. "Coach wants me watching practice."

"This will only take a few minutes. Now come on, handsome. The camera crew is waiting."

Camera crew?

I groan audibly this time, following after her with a slight hitch in my step. I'm feeling my morning PT already. Doc says I'm doing great, and I'll be back on the ice soon. Not soon enough for me.

"What are we doing?" I say as we clear the end of the bleachers and exit the rink.

"We've partnered with the Jacksonville Humane Society to shoot a pet adoption promo," Poppy replies, leading the way through into the other smaller ice rink.

Mars, Davidson, and Coach Tomlin are out on the ice now. It looks like they're finishing up. Mars already has his mask and gloves off, leaning against the boards as he watches Davidson scramble in the net. Tomlin is merciless, shooting pucks at him left, right, and center.

"Good," Tomlin shouts. "Recover."

At the other end of the rink, a Jax Rays media display has been set up on the ice. The cameras are ready, the crew just standing around.

"I found one," Poppy calls with a wave, hurrying her steps.

I glance around at the scene. Novy and Morrow are on the ice in their street clothes. Morrow is beside himself, laughing like a kid as a tiny yellow puppy licks his chin.

"Nov, look," he says. "Look, I think he likes me."

Novy just glares at him. He's holding something that looks like an alien in a frizzy wig. I get closer and see that it's a dog. A tiny, hideous, hairless dog with a poof of white fluff on its head.

"Come on, this is bullshit," he says as Poppy passes. "You know I'm allergic to dogs."

"Which is why I gave you the hypoallergenic one," she replies dismissively.

"Dude, I told you, that's not a dog," says Morrow. "It looks like that thing that sits on Jabba the Hutt in *Return of the Jedi*."

I choke on a laugh. It totally does.

"Ryan, come take your pick," Poppy calls. "We've got a cute little bulldog over here, a few kitties—Oh, sweet heavens—look at the way she's looking at me," she coos, bending over to stick her finger in the front of a cat carrier. "Claribel, tell me I don't need a cat," she whines, clearly lost to the little grey and white kitten sniffing her finger.

"You don't need a cat," Claribel deadpans, her eyes still on her phone.

The bulldog with an underbite peers up at me with watery eyes.

"Can we hurry this up?" Novy shouts. "This thing is hairless, and this is an ice rink. I think it's getting frostbite."

"Hold your horses," Poppy huffs, flicking her long blonde ponytail off her shoulder. "And it's not a *thing*, Lukas. It's a dog. A very rare breed of dog called a Chinese crested."

"It's shivering, and it can smell my fear," Novy snaps.

She huffs and turns away.

"So, uhh, what's the deal here?" I say, glancing around at the smiling volunteers and the camera crew.

"We're shooting a short commercial for the Humane Society," Poppy replies. "It will go on all our socials too. Just pick an animal and take the card on top of their cage. Then you read out what's on the card in front of the camera," she says, gesturing to the little white cards attached to each cage and carrier.

My heart stops. "You, uhh . . . you want me to read what's on the card?"

"Mhmm." She snatches one off the top of the bulldog's cage. "So, this one says her name is Gracie and she's a five-year-old American bulldog. She's house-trained, loves kids, blah, blah, blah. Just read the card."

She foists it at me, and I feel my hand reach out and take it.

"Colton, you're up first," she calls, spinning away from me.

"Dude, I swear, I'm gonna adopt this little guy myself," Morrow says, still laughing as the puppy squirms in his arms.

"At least yours has fur," Novy replies. "I feel like I'm holding a raw chicken."

I don't hear the rest of their banter as the three of them wander off towards the cameras. I glance down again at the card in my hand. Fuck, it's hand-written. The font is so damn small, and some genius used colored pens for each section. My heart races faster as I glance around, looking for some point of exit. Gracie the bulldog just peers up at me through the bars of her cage, judging me.

"Hey, can you stop slapping pucks for five minutes," Poppy calls down the ice at the goalies. "You can stay in the shot, but we need some quiet for this."

"You realize this is a hockey rink," Coach Tomlin shouts back. "And this is a hockey practice!"

"I reserved this rink for 11:30," she yells back. "You were supposed to be done a half hour ago. Now, clear off my ice, or I'll drag you *all* in front of the camera. Yes, I mean you too, Eric!"

The goalies grumble, but they move off. Poppy may be all of 5' tall, but she's a force of freaking nature. The woman always gets her way.

Which means I'm about to be standing in front of a camera holding the leash of an ugly, fat bulldog, looking like a jackass as I try to read this stupid card. Fuck, this is the worst part about being a pro athlete. Why can't I just play hockey? I'm actually good at that. I don't mess it up.

"I can't do this," I say at Claribel, holding the card out to her. "Can you find someone else?"

She slowly looks up, glancing from the card to my face. "You wanna tell that to Poppy?"

I groan, my hand dropping to my side. "Claribel, you don't understand. I *can't* do this. I'll play with the dogs. I'll hold them. I'll tell everyone how great they are—"

"It's in your contract, Ryan," she replies, dropping her gaze back to her phone. "Poppy says 'jump,' it's your contractual obligation to ask 'how high?' Right now, Poppy says 'hold a dog and read the card.'"

My anxiety mounts as I watch Morrow give a winning performance, the happy puppy wiggling in his arms. It's so easy for him, so effortless. The media, the attention, the distractions.

But I'm not like him. This shit isn't easy for me. I'm usually so good at avoiding it. And Poppy doesn't usually corner us like this. She only snagged me because I was standing there looking like I had nothing to do.

Rule number freaking one: always look like you have something to do!

"Claribel, please," I beg, trying to hand her the card again. "Get someone else."

She slowly raises her gaze again, studying my face. "What's your problem? Why is this such an issue for you?"

"It's not—"

"What, did a dog bite you once?"

"No."

"You afraid of cats?"

"No," I reply with a roll of my eyes. "It's not about the animals—"

"Oh, so you're opposed to charities?"

"No," I say, frustration rising.

"Then I don't see the big deal. Just hold the leash, read the card, and earn your enormous paycheck. Stop being such a drama king." Not waiting for my response, she stalks off.

Drama king? This is such fucking bullshit. My job shouldn't depend on me doing shit like this without warning or time to prep or anything.

Ilmari shuffles past in his full goalie kit, helmet tucked under his arm.

"Mars," I hiss, keeping my voice low.

He pauses, one brow raised at me.

I'm usually scared of this guy and would never normally approach him, but right now, I'm fucking desperate. "I need you to take over for me here."

His brows narrow. "No," he says, shrugging past.

"Mars, please." I grab his arm, pulling on him.

"What the hell is your problem?" he growls, jerking his arm free of my hold.

"Mars, *please* do this for me. I can't do it. I can't—fuck," I groan, dragging a hand through my hair. "Do it *with* me," I offer. "I'll hold the cat and play with it, and you read the card. The fans will love seeing both of us. Come on, please."

He goes impossibly still, surveying me. Slowly, he glances over my shoulder, watching for a moment as Novy chats to the camera, pretending he gives a shit about the weird alien dog in his arms.

"I wouldn't ask if this wasn't serious," I admit. If there was one person I can trust with this, it's Mars. He's a total vault, nothing in or out. "I—fuck," I groan again. "I need help, Mars."

His gaze shifts back to me, studying me.

I let him look. I let him see my fear and panic as I hold out the card again. "Help me."

He glances from me to the card.

"Okay, Ryan, you're up," Poppy calls. "Did you pick your animal? Let's go, honeybun. We don't have all morning."

I wince, eyes shutting tight as I pray this will all be over soon. "Please," I whisper again. "Please, Mars."

Slowly, he reaches out and takes the card from me.

I let out a heavy breath of relief and nod. "Yeah?"

"Yeah," he replies.

"Ryan!"

"We're coming," I shout, spinning around. "Mars and I are gonna shoot the spot together."

"Oh—" Poppy glances between us, eyes wide with surprise. Like me, I think she's a little afraid of the surly Finn. He gets out of everything unpleasant with just a glare. "Oh, that's so wonderful," she cries, clapping her hands.

"No dogs," Mars says behind me. "Pick a cat."

"Sure thing," I say, hurrying over to the carrier holding the little grey and white kitten.

If Mars is helping me, he gets whatever he wants. I'll hold a cat or a python or one of those weird naked mole rat things. Hell, I'd wrestle an alligator on camera if it means Mars reads the damn card.

"Oh my goodness, that kitten is double cute," Poppy cries, hearts in her eyes as she watches me snuggle it. "You're just the sweetest thing," she coos. "Yes, you are. Yes, you are." She ducks down, giving the little kitten kisses, her hands holding to my folded arms.

From behind her, Novy and Morrow glare at me, still holding their squirming dogs. Shit, the looks they're giving me could peel paint.

"Uhh, Pop?" I say, shifting away from her.

"Oh," she says with a laugh, dropping her hands away from me, totally oblivious to this new tension. "Are we ready then, gentlemen?" She glances to Mars. "You got the card?"

"Got it," he says, holding it up.

"What's the kitten's name?" she asks, leading the way over to the cameras.

Mars glances down at the card with a frown. Then he sighs. "Miss Princess," he mutters.

Poppy squeals. "Oh, it's perfect! She is such a little princess."

Mars and I both lean away from her exuberance. Over by the camera, Claribel just shakes her head.

"You owe me for this," Mars say only loud enough for me to hear.

I give Miss Princess a little pat on the head. "Totally," I say with a smile. My heart rate returns to a normal rhythm as we take our places in front of the camera.

40

Tess

Shelby's birthday party is chaos. I feel like I'm back in college at a frat party. Music pumps through the house sound system, with people dancing and mingling in every room. There's a ton of food, even more alcohol, and a present table stacked with gifts. My meager offering of chocolate chunk oatmeal cookies will go unnoticed next to this mountain.

Every Ray seems to be here, and most of them brought wives or dates. I'm casually keeping an eye out for Ryan, but it may be hard to track him down. If we're both circling around, we could go from room to room missing each other. And, like an idiot, I left my phone in the car. There was nowhere to put it in this damn costume.

I've spent the last hour mixing and mingling with this eclectic group of NHL stars and the people who populate Shelby and Josh's life. I've probably met at least thirty people who are church friends, neighbors, or parents from their kids' schools.

It turns out Josh and Shelby are *those* people. The people-pleasing social butterflies. They give and give everything to everyone all the time, leaving nothing for themselves. It means that their home is a mess, and their life is chaotic, but they have a hundred people ready to drop everything and dress up to celebrate a birthday.

It's kind of nice when I think about it. As a Gemini, I can socialize in my sleep. I'm the queen of hosting a great party. But I have an off switch. I need to retreat. I need the quiet. I'm actually deeply private, and I don't make friends easily.

Troy carries some of the blame for that too. It's a narcissist's M.O. to separate and isolate their loved ones from other people who can be critical or voice a second opinion. It took me ten freaking years to realize how effectively he'd removed all my friends from my life.

It started with little things, like he thought my college friend Kelly had an annoying laugh. He worked slowly from there, sowing the seeds of criticism. Her laugh was annoying . . . then it was her jokes that were annoying . . . then *she* was annoying. Then the requests started that we not hang out with her anymore. After a while, I stopped taking her calls, never noticing that it wasn't my idea.

Yeah, that was a whopper to unpack in therapy.

I resent myself so much that I fell for it. How could I not see what he was doing? How did I not see the way I was changing? But I guess, over time, it's like all these little pieces of yourself get chipped away. Like a piece of glass, tumbling along the bottom of the sea floor, you change. You get harder, you close yourself off. What once shined with brilliance becomes dull.

And then it's ten years later and you suddenly realize you don't laugh anymore. You stopped telling jokes because he never liked that you were funnier than him. And you wanted him to feel good, feel like the man. Funniest one in the room. But the joke's on you both, because he's not funny, so neither of you laugh.

And god, but I really love to laugh.

There's definitely nothing funny about the man you once loved harassing you and calling you a whore for daring to move on.

Tears sting my eyes, and I want to scream. Damn it, I am *not* going to cry over Troy while dressed as a sexy devil at Shelby's birthday party. I step away from the circle of people I'm chatting with, making some muttered excuse. I find my way outside, looking for a quiet place to collect my thoughts. Following along the back wall of the house, I keep walking until I see a door. Trying the handle, I pull it open to reveal a dark, three-car garage.

I hold back the sob that wants so desperately to break free, ducking inside. I shut the door, leaning against it. "Fuck," I cry, pounding the door with my fist. A tear slips down my cheek just as the door to the house swings open. I gasp, wiping the tear away as the lights flick on.

Shelby comes walking in wearing her adorable Evy O'Connell costume from *The Mummy*, complete with little round librarian glasses. Somewhere Josh is running around dressed as her dashing Rick.

"Oh, Tess," she cries, one hand fluttering to her heart. "You scared the bejesus out of me!"

"I'm sorry," I reply, forcing a smile as I blink back my tears.

She shuts the door, immediately muffling the music coming from inside the house, and glances around the garage. "Are you out here all alone?"

"Yeah," I reply. "I was just uhh . . . getting more ice." I gesture to the fridge in the corner. "Are there any ice bags in there?"

"No," she says slowly. "All the ice is already outside."

"Oh. Well, then I'll go out there," I say lamely, reaching for the door handle.

"Or—maybe you could help me," she calls as I turn away.

I glance back over my shoulder.

"I came out here to get more soda." She points to a stack of boxes on the floor. "Want to help me get them out to the coolers?"

"Sure." I cross the garage over to her. "I like your Evy costume by the way. I love *The Mummy*."

She beams at me. "Thank you. What's not to love, right?"

I flash her a weak smile.

"Do you want to talk about it?"

"No," I reply, ducking down to grab a case of Coca-Cola.

"Do you *need* to talk about it?" she clarifies.

I go still, holding tight to the box. "Probably," I admit. "At this point, I've kept my shrink gainfully employed for years talking about all my bullshit. Single mom who never loved me, flighty family, abandonment issues, toxic ex, blah, blah. It's pretty boring stuff."

"I don't think it's boring," she replies. "And you don't need to deflect all the time, you know. You can let people know what's troubling you. It doesn't make you weak to admit it. And it doesn't open a door to them weaponizing that knowledge against you. Some people are good, Tess. Some people genuinely want to help. You don't have to keep running."

"Whoa," I say with a huff. "What made you say all that?"

"Because I'm a shrink too. Well, I'm a child psychologist," she clarifies. "I work mainly with kids in the foster system. A lot of those kids are runners too. I see the signs in you."

"Well . . . great." I hoist the case of soda under my arm. "Glad to know I'm so transparent. You know, the great cosmic joke is that I fucking hate running."

She laughs, but then her smile falls. "We all do what we need to do to survive. Can I ask who you're running from?"

"My ex," I reply. "I'm finally pushing him for a divorce after three years of separation and he's not too happy about it."

"I can imagine. Is he threatening you?"

"With fire and brimstone." I gesture to my devil costume in another lame attempt at humor.

She doesn't laugh.

"It's nothing I can't handle," I add quickly.

"Are there kids involved?"

"No."

"Property? Business assets?"

"Both," I reply.

"What are they worth to you?"

I hold her gaze, feeling so completely seen. She may look like Candace, but the voice is so different, the mannerisms, the warmth of feeling in her expressions. I set all my hesitation aside and give her my truth. "Not more than my life."

She nods. "Good. Let them go, Tess. Things are replaceable. Job skills are transferable. Your life and your well-being are the *only* things that matter. Let everything else go."

I tip my head, surveying her. "You're not just a shrink, are you? You lived through this too."

Now it's her turn to shrug. "Josh is my second husband. He came along shortly after Addie and I got out of our last situation. He's our hero," she says with tears in her eyes. "Our guardian angel. He's the one I was meant to find, you know? He's the father my children were meant to have."

"I'm happy for you," I say. "And hey, about the other day when I was so rude—"

"Nope." She raises a hand. "Don't even go there. It's forgotten."

I sigh, leaning my hip against the chrome utility bench. "You know, you're pretty cool."

She smiles again. "I have a feeling so are you. Hey, do you like karaoke?"

"Am I singing or mocking those who sing?"

"Either," she says with a laugh. "Both. We all go out to karaoke over at Rip's on Thursday nights. You should come next week. I promise I won't give you any more unsolicited life advice."

I shift the soda box under my arm. "Sure. Maybe I'll check it out."

She grabs a box as well and gestures for me to lead the way out to the backyard.

As I get to the door, I feel her hand brush my shoulder. "Hey . . . can I ask you for a favor? Are we friends enough for me to do that?"

I raise a brow at her. "What's the favor?"

Her gaze softens as she searches my face. "Be gentle with Langley," she says at last. "He's my not-so-secret favorite, and he's crazy about you. He's one of the good ones, Tess. Maybe even the best one. Just . . . don't hurt him, okay?"

"Yeah," I say, giving her a nod. "Okay."

Langley is crazy about me? Well, that's pretty convenient, because I think I'm crazy about him too.

41
Ryan

Cars already line the block when Novy pulls up at Sully's house a little after 8:00 p.m. The birthday party is in full swing. We're fashionably late, of course. Lukas Novikov doesn't know any other way to be.

After our morning spent shooting spots for the Humane Society, we all went out to lunch and then to the beach. The guys played a little sand volleyball, but I just watched. No way am I torquing this knee again.

"Hey man, you want me to drop you at the end of the driveway?" he calls from the front seat.

"I can walk just fine, asshole," I shout back over the loud music.

He parallel parks half a block down and we all get out. Morrow and I coordinated our costumes. I smirk as I watch him walk in front of me, joining up with Novy on the sidewalk. We're all in jeans and white T-shirts wearing *SOA* black leather motorcycle cuts.

Am I playing fair dressing up as Jax Teller? Hell, no. Fuck fair. I want Tess, and I want her to want me. If giving her a little taste of her favorite fantasy earns me any points, I'll never take this damn costume off.

"Jesus," Morrow cries, nearly jumping on top of me. "Dude, what the fuck?"

Novy and I both look to see a grim reaper wandering across the dark front lawn.

"Who the fuck is that?" Morrow shouts, clearly rattled. "Who are you?"

"Dude, chill," comes a deep, muffled voice. "It's me." Davidson pulls his hood back, revealing his face. "Pretty cool, huh?" he says, gesturing to himself.

"It's not a haunted house, asshole," Morrow snaps. "It's a birthday party."

"Yeah, but this was left over from Halloween," he explains. "I wasn't going shopping for a new costume just for this party."

"Whatever, man," Morrow replies. "Scare me like that again, and I'll knock out all your jibs. Fucking shadow of death creeping on me in the darkness," he says, crossing himself.

"Come on," says Novy. "Let's go."

We all make it to the front door and let ourselves in. The house is packed, dance music playing over the speakers. The first people we see are J-Lo and Lauren. He's wearing long black robes like a toga, and his hair is hidden under a crazy blue wig.

"Whoa, cool costume, J," says Novy, taking them both in. "Hades, right?"

"And his darling wife, Persephone," says Lauren, already tipsy as she throws an arm around J-Lo's shoulder. She went all out in this crazy floral headdress and a pink flower gown.

"You both look great," I add, giving them a smile. Then I snort as I see Teddy the PT intern saunter past with both his fists full of beers. "Who are you supposed to be?" I call after him.

He spins around, totally drunk. He's wearing a blue bathrobe and a long white beard. "I'm Merlin, duh," he slurs. "Aw, damn. Where's my hat? It makes more sense with the hat."

Novy slips a beer out of his grip, handing it to me. Then he takes one for himself before Teddy goes stumbling off. "This party is gonna get messy," Novy says, taking a swig of his pilfered beer.

We move towards the kitchen, in search of the party hosts, Novy and Morrow walking ahead of me. I run right into their backs when they both suddenly stop. "Guys—what?"

I glance between their shoulders to see a wide-eyed Poppy. She's looking up at them, holding tight to her red Solo cup. I don't know what her costume is. She's wearing some kind of prairie dress and a bonnet thing with her hair done up in curls around her face.

Novy glares at her. "You said you weren't coming."

Squaring her shoulders at him, she juts out her chin. "Well, obviously I changed my mind."

Novy is so tense, it's making me tense. "But you said—"

"Cool it," Morrow says, placing a hand on Novy's arm. "Not here."

I glance between them. Something is definitely going on. They were all so irritable at the pet adoption thing. I know Novy drives Poppy crazy, but today felt different. "Guys, what's up?" I say from behind them.

Novy and Morrow immediately split, turning their bodies to reveal me to Poppy.

Her eyes go wide again. "Oh—hi, Ryan," she says sweetly. "Nice costumes." She hides her forced smile behind her Solo cup, taking a sip of her fruity drink.

"Hey, Poppy," I reply, still trying to puzzle out what has them all acting so weird. "Who are you supposed to be?"

She sighs. "Honestly, I should have just made a sign and worn it around my neck. I'm Elizabeth Bennett," she adds, gesturing at herself with a flourish.

The three of us share a glance.

"Elizabeth Bennett?" she huffs, one hand on her hip. "Only one of the greatest romantic heroines of all time? From *Pride & Prejudice*?"

"That's . . . a movie?" Morrow asks with a raised brow.

"This is why you boys only attract the likes of puck bunnies," she cries. "'Cause any woman of class, taste, and sense knows to steer clear!" With tears in her eyes, she pushes between us, stomping away.

"Ignore her," Novy mutters. "She's just upset because she couldn't adopt that cat." He keeps walking in the direction of the kitchen.

Morrow lingers, his gaze still locked on where Poppy just disappeared.

"You okay, man?" I say, putting my hand on his shoulder.

He glances down at my hand, then up to my face. "No."

"Wanna talk about it?"

He holds my gaze and, for a moment, I really think he's about to say yes.

"Guys, I found Shelbs," Novy calls.

Morrow blinks, his expression shuttering. He shifts out from under my hold. "Come on. Let's go see the birthday girl."

"Novy!" A very tipsy Shelby cries, raising her wine glass in the air. "Josh, baby, look. More boys are here!" She takes in our costumes. "Wow, you guys look hot. Like, capital H-O-T."

We all laugh.

"Happy Birthday, Shelby," says Novy, giving her a quick hug.

"Hey, Shelbs. Happy Birthday," adds Morrow.

I'm in her arms when Sully comes up and slaps my shoulder. "Hey, watch those hands, man."

I jerk back and he laughs, slinging his arm around her shoulders.

"Who are you guys supposed to be?" says Novy, taking in her weird combo of button up shirt, bowtie, and long librarian-looking skirt. Meanwhile, Sully has his hair slicked back and he's wearing khakis, a white shirt, and these leather suspenders with a gun holster.

"Hey," I say with a grin. "You're Rick and Evy. From *The Mummy*."

"Yes!" Shelby squeals, launching forward to give me another hug and kiss my cheek. "I knew you were my favorite for a reason."

"Hey, I thought I was your favorite," Sully pouts.

"Mmm, you know you're my main macho man," she purrs, spinning around to wrap herself up in his arms.

"Okay, gross," says Morrow, shielding his gaze. "It feels like watching my parents make out."

"Parents fuck too, Cole," she teases.

"And on that note, I'm gonna go get drunk." He wanders off and Novy follows, leaving me with the O'Sullivans.

"Food is set up over in the dining room," Sully explains, pointing that way. "All the soda and beer are in coolers outside."

"Thanks," I reply, glancing around the room. "Hey, are the Prices here yet?"

I assume wherever Rachel is, Tess will probably be nearby. I haven't seen her all day. I sent her a couple voice memos, but she didn't respond. I want her. And not just because I want to see her reaction to my costume. I just . . . want her.

"Yeah, they're all here somewhere," Sully replies, glancing over his shoulder. "Maybe check outside. Or we've got some games going upstairs."

I slip past them with promises to Shelby that I'll try the Southwest egg rolls. I'm blocked from reaching the dining room by a gaggle of rookies, including Flash, who is very disappointingly dressed as Superman, and Patty, who is dressed as a gladiator.

It's only as he turns that I take in the full picture. A girl presses herself back against his chest. She's dressed in a sexy Cleopatra costume with dramatic makeup, plunging cleavage on full display. Patty has his hands all over her. One is actually slipped inside her costume, stroking her boob.

"Ohmygosh, you look so hot," she says at me, taking me in from head to toe.

"Thanks," I say. "'Scuse me."

"You look just like Jax Teller," she goes on, touching my arm as I try to move past.

"Yeah, well, that was the idea," I reply, shifting away.

"You're a starter, aren't you?" she says, sizing me up again.

I nod, which means Patty may as well have just morphed into a potted plant. He glares at me like it's my fault his date is pawing at me. I glare right back. I'm not above putting a rookie in his place. If he can't keep this girl's attention, that's not my fault.

"Can you guess who I am?" his date asks, showing off her glittery costume.

I take a sip of my beer. "I thought the party theme was fictional characters."

"Yeah, I'm Cleopatra," she replies, brushing her hands down her sides.

Patty snakes his arm around her, pulling her against his chest. Over her head, he keeps glaring at me.

"Hence my confusion," I reply at her.

She blinks up at me. "What?"

"Cleopatra was a real person. She's not fictional. Neither was Caesar," I add at Patty with a smirk.

"She's not real," his date replies with a laugh. "It's from that HBO show."

"Wow." I glance up at Patty. "You two will have very beautiful children."

Before he can respond, I spin around and move back the other way. Nothing is worth spending another second trapped in Rookie

Wasteland, not when I know Tess is here. I step outside and nearly walk right into Mars.

"Whoa, sorry man," I say, putting a hand on his shoulder to steady myself.

He glances over his shoulder at me, taking me in, his body stiff under my hand.

I do the same. "What the fuck are you wearing? Who are you supposed to be?"

"No idea," he replies with an indifferent shrug.

He's wearing a red beanie with a pompom, a blue and white striped shirt, and these bright aqua board shorts. "I don't—" That's when I see the rest of them. Standing not ten feet away over by the coolers are Doc, Jake, and Sanny. And then I'm laughing. "Dude, they made you Smee?"

Mars just glares at me.

Rachel is dressed in a flirty Tinker Bell costume, her hair up in her usual bun. Sanny stands with his arm around her dressed as Peter Pan. Jake is living it up in a ridiculous Captain Hook costume, complete with shiny hook. Even the dog is here. Poseidon darts past in a crocodile costume, chasing after Sully's dog.

"You must really love them," I tease Mars, feasting my eyes on this vision of him in that stupid hat.

"Something like that."

We stand there, watching the other party guests laugh and chat. He was so cool this morning, taking the card and quietly reading it while I held the kitten. He didn't ask any questions, just handed me the card and walked off.

"So . . . are you gonna ask me about it?" I say, taking a sip of my beer.

"Ask you about what?"

I huff, turning to face him. "You know what, man. You can ask if you want," I offer. "I trust you to know. You won't say anything."

Weirdly, I almost *want* him to ask. More than that, I want to tell him. I want to trust him. I know I'll feel better letting someone in on this secret with me. It's such a heavy fucking burden to bear. I do my best in the day to day, but sometimes I'm tired, sometimes I slip up, sometimes I get dragged into filming pet adoption promo spots.

On all my past teams, I had someone who knew, someone who could help me out. Everything has been so crazy since joining the Rays that I haven't really settled into a groove yet. Aside from management like Vicki, I haven't felt ready to trust any of the guys and open up.

Mars glances my way, brows narrowed. "Does anyone on the team know?"

I shake my head, taking another swig of this crappy IPA.

"Why not?"

"I figured you of all people would get it," I reply. "We don't all want our private lives out in the open."

"But you want me to know," he intuits. "You want someone to confide in."

Slowly, I nod. "Yeah, I think I do."

"And Tess? Does she know?"

My heart drops out at the very idea. "Hell no. No way."

He sighs. "Don't be childish, Langley."

I bristle. "Childish?"

"I'm not blind. I see how badly you want her. If you mean to keep her, you must tell her all your truths, even the difficult ones—especially the difficult ones."

We're saved the awkwardness of a deeper conversation when Tess herself comes sweeping around the corner. She's walking arm-in-arm with Shelby. Since when did these two become friends? She throws her head back, laughing at something Shelby says.

My heart fucking stops. I can't breathe. Can't move. My Tess is dressed like a sexy devil, with a red leather skirt, fishnet stockings, and a lacy red corset that makes her breasts look immaculate. A pair of little black horns peek out the top of her auburn curls.

Forget Mars and secrets. Forget everything. Forget my own damn name. This woman is the only thing that matters.

42
Tess

"But if you really want quality karaoke chaos, you gotta get Lukas Novikov up on that stage," Shelby says as we both crack up.

"Wait, Novikov's the broody one with the scar on his face, right? He likes to sing?" I can't reconcile the two images in my mind.

"At this point, I think I've heard him sing the entire George Michael catalog," she replies with a solemn nod.

"No," I cry with another laugh. "Not George Michael."

"You haven't lived until you hear him sing 'Careless Whisper,'" she teases.

Before I can reply, a new voice stops me in my tracks. "Hey, sexy devil."

All my breath leaves my body as I turn, seeking out that voice. Ryan is here. Fuck, I didn't realize how much I missed him until now. He's standing next to Mars, nursing a beer . . . and he's dressed as Jax Teller.

Oh, holy fucking fuck.

I take him in from his mussed blond curls to those broad shoulders filling out his white T-shirt, to the ripped jeans and chunky boots. My attention settles on his black leather cut, complete with *SOA* patches.

"Oh my god." I lift my gaze back to his face, taking in the apple green of his eyes and the curve of his smirk as he pins me in place with a look of open wanting.

Ryan.

Seeing him again, feeling his energy calling out to mine, a truth settles deep inside me: Ryan likes it when I laugh. From the moment we met, he's spent all his energy trying to draw the sound from my lips. Lying in his bed late at night, pretending I'm helping him fall asleep, I'll laugh at something he says, and he'll brush a finger up the column of my throat, tracing the path of the sound. To him, my laugh is music. To him, my laugh is magic.

My Ryan.

I swallow down my nerves, holding his gaze. I'm having this man tonight.

43
Ryan

"Hey everyone," Shelby sings, walking up with Tess. "Having a good time?"

"We're having a great time," Doc replies.

"I love your costumes by the way," Shelby adds. "So clever. Who thought of it?"

"Jake," Sanny and Doc say at the same time.

Behind them, the man himself enters the circle. "That would be me," he calls. "Pretty awesome, right? At first, I wanted to do *Jungle Book* and make Mars be the bear, but Cay refused to put on the red speedo—well, he refused to wear it in public," he adds with a wink.

Sanny glares at his partner. "You know I can withhold sex from you, right?"

"Yeah, but you won't," Jake replies, slinging an arm around his shoulders. "You like it too much. And I don't blame you. I'm pretty great in bed," he says at me.

"I don't need to know any of this," I mutter.

"Are they always like this?" Shelby asks with a giggle, looking at Tess.

"Um, this is actually pretty tame, honestly," she replies. Her cheeks are flushing pink. She's trying not to look at me. Trying not to think about me.

Good luck, sexy devil. Before I'm done with you, I'll be the only thing on your mind.

If I stare at her a moment longer, I may just self-combust. "Well, I'm gonna go get some food," I say to the group. "I made Shelby an oath to try her Southwest egg rolls."

"Yesss," she slurs, saluting me with her wine glass. "And don't forget about the chipotle mayo dipping sauce!"

I nod and bow out, not sparing Tess another look. I duck through the kitchen, exchanging the beer I don't want for a bottled water. Then I pass into the dining room. I'm not hungry; I'm just trying to distract myself. I'm maintaining forward motion. A shark always has to keep swimming, right? If I stop moving, I'll think about Tess. And if I think about Tess in those black fishnet stockings, I'll get hard. And if I get hard, I'll scare the rookies.

I'm turning the corner into the front hall when I feel a tug at my hand. Eagerly, I spin around, ready to pull Tess into my arms. I stop short when a girl in a bedazzled black wig steps into my space.

"There you are," Cleopatra says. "Come dance with me." She presses in, her body rubbing against mine.

"Whoa, I think you might be lost, sweetheart," I say, trying to take her hands off me. But she has two and I only have one. The other is holding my water bottle. Just as I bat one of her hands down, she puts the other one on me.

"I waited and waited for you," she whimpers. "I want you so bad."

"Unlikely, as I've been here all of fifteen minutes," I reply. "Okay—*fuck*—" I drop the water bottle to the floor, grabbing her with both hands. Gently as I can, I spin her around.

She's still wiggling, pressing in at me with her ass. "I just wanna dance—"

"No, no, no." I bend away from her. Fuck, she's drunk. She doesn't know what she's doing at this point. "You know what I think we should do? Get an Uber and go to your house."

"My house?"

"Yeah, let's blow this party. Do you know where your house is?"

"Yeah, but I'm allowed to stay out all night," she says, trying to put her arms around me again. "We can go to your house. I promise it's okay."

I groan. "Jesus, how old are you?" If Patty brought an underage girl to Shelby's birthday party, I'm gonna cross check him to death.

"Nineteen."

Thank God.

"Come on," I grunt, trying to get her to walk in front of me without our bodies touching. "Fuck—*stop*—"

"Ryan?"

I go still, glancing over my shoulder to see Tess looking at me, her eyes wide. Actually, she's not looking at me, she's looking at *us*—me and Cleopatra, my hands clinging to her as she pushes her ass against me, wiggling like a fish. I say the only thing I can think to say. "Help me."

She blinks. In moments, her look of hurt surprise vanishes and she's rushing forward. "What's wrong?"

"She's just drunk," I say, grateful that she's not questioning me. "She showed up with Patty. I don't know where the hell he is. If you see a tall, blond gladiator, punch him in the face."

"Will do." She steps around to my other side and places a hand under Cleopatra's chin. "Hey, honey. I'm Tess. What's your name?"

"Tegan," the girl replies.

"How you feeling, Tegan?"

"Tired," she slurs. "And bloaty. God, why won't he just fuck me already?" she whines.

"Oh, sorry, honey. This one's taken," Tess replies.

"What?" Tegan whines again. "Noooo. But I want him."

"I know," Tess says, patting the girl's shoulder. "But in love, as in life, sometimes there are great disappointments."

"We need to get her out of here," I say over the girl's head. "I was trying to ask for her address to put her in an Uber."

"I don't know if we can trust anything she says at this point," Tess replies. "Do you think Shelby will mind if we put her in a room upstairs?"

"Goddamn it. If she pukes all over the place, Shelbs will make me pay for it."

"Make Patty McHotAbs pay for it," Tess says with a glare. "If he's her date, he needed to take better care of her. She's completely toasted."

"Oh, he'll pay for it in more ways than one," I assure her. Nothing that a few sets of suicide sprints won't fix. He'll be puking up his breakfast at next practice.

"Let's get her upstairs," Tess says. "Can you carry her with your knee—"

"I got it." I scoop Cleopatra up in my arms and move towards the stairs.

Tess follows behind, snatching my discarded water off the floor.

The stairs open to a large game room area where some of the guys are playing video games. No one pays us any mind as Tess and I cut left towards the hallway that leads to the bedrooms.

"I stayed here once," I say over my shoulder. "This is a guest room," I say nodding at a door.

Tess slips between me and the door as she opens it. "Whoa—ohmygod," she cries, throwing a hand up over her eyes.

I peer over her head to see a half-dressed Novy and Morrow spit-roasting some blonde girl. Novy is closer, his back to us. They both turn to the door at the same time, eyes wide.

"Get the fuck out," Novy barks, still thrusting into the girl from behind. His toned ass is on display, pants around his thighs.

The girl between them pops off Morrow's dick. I think my brain explodes when Poppy turns to face us, eyes wide, those tight blonde curls now disheveled. "Ohmygod," she shrieks, a look of horror on her face as she locks eyes with me.

"Oh *my* god," I bellow back as Tess pulls the door shut with a quick, "Sorry, carry on!"

I just stare at the closed door as I digest this new information. All the pieces snap into place: Novy and Morrow's shitty attitudes over the past few weeks, their weird vibes of being in a lover's tiff. It all makes sense. They've been fighting over the same woman . . . and that woman is Poppy Fucking St. James, our public relations manager.

But . . . how? I mean, Morrow is a super nice guy, so that tracks. But Novy and Poppy *hate* each other. They're like cats in a bag. Half of our media training sessions are the result of Novy doing something to piss her off. I guess it's true what they say about love and hate being a thin fucking line—

"Ryan . . . " Tess brushes her fingers down my arm.

I shake my head, trying to clear it. "Right. Fuck." I shift my hold on Drunk Cleopatra and move down the hallway. "Come on, over here."

"But these are the kids' rooms—"

"The kids aren't here," I reply. "They're all over at Shelby's mom's house tonight. Just open this door before I drop the Queen of the Nile."

She hesitantly opens the door, peering inside. "Empty," she says with relief.

We step inside Addie's bedroom, and I move over to the pink princess twin bed, dropping Cleopatra down onto it. She groans, immediately curling on her side into the fetal position, her wig askew.

Tess takes charge. "Here, honey. I'm putting a trash can beside the bed, and there's a water on the nightstand."

Cleopatra just groans.

"She'll be out soon."

"Yeah, and then she'll be hurting in the morning," Tess says at my side.

"I'll have Josh and Shelbs check on her," I assure her.

Tess shakes her head.

"What?"

"It's just so reckless, you know? What if she had done her little bump and grind trick on someone other than you? What if they weren't as noble?"

"She's safe here," I say, putting my hand on her shoulder. "Shelby and Josh won't let anything happen to her."

And just like that, my sexy she-devil is crying. All the distracting thoughts of my defensemen double-teaming our PR manager disappear in a flash.

"Hey, hey, what is this?" I say, pulling her into my arms. "Why are you crying?"

She presses her face into my chest, her arms holding tight to my hips. "God, it's nothing—it's—I'm just being ridiculous. I'm—it was a hard day and—it's nothing." She shakes her head, trying to pull away from me. "God, I fucking hate crying. Lately it feels like it's all I do."

"Whoa, hey. Stay. Tell me." I place my hand under her chin and tip her face up. "Tess, look at me. What happened?"

She shakes her head again, eyes closed. "I don't—Ryan, don't. Let's not talk about it. I can't talk about it, okay? Not tonight. Not here. Not now."

And now I know it has to do with Troy. Man, fuck that asshole. I fucking hate him. I hate the hold he still has on her. I just want her to be free of him.

"I just really missed you," she admits, and my heart does a somersault. "I needed you today. I'm starting to feel like I need you, Ryan, and I think that's scaring me a little. I don't really have anyone else here except Rachel, and you've been such a good friend, but I can't put that on you. I can't burden you."

Friend, she calls me. Not lover. Not boyfriend. I'm just her friend. Ryan Puppy Langley, the nice friend she's casually deep throating. It's better than nothing.

"Hey," I say, cupping her face. "Look at me."

She takes a deep breath before tipping her face up. She's so beautiful. She's got thick black eye makeup on tonight, and those bright red lips could stop traffic. Pair that with the horns and this lacy red bra thing, and I'm ready to get on my knees and beg.

But that's not what she needs right now. She needs comfort and reassurance. She needs her friend. "You're safe with me," I tell her. "Cleopatra is safe, and you're safe too. Nothing will touch you when you're in my arms, I swear to God."

Her hands that were clinging to my hips soften. Slowly, she brushes them up my sides and under my leather cut to splay over my chest. She drops her gaze, watching where her hands touch me. My body heats all over, loving the feel of her closeness. I want her. I *crave* her. But I'm going to respect her boundaries and move at her speed.

"Ryan." Her hands smooth over the planes of my chest.

"What do you need?" I say, voice low.

Her hands go still as she looks up into my eyes. Parting her lips, she says the word that is music to my ears. "You."

44
Tess

"Ryan, please," I murmur, my hands going up to his nape, fingers brushing his hair, as I step in closer. "I need you."

"What do you need?" he says again. His hands are at my waist, smoothing over the leather of my skirt. "Tell me what you need."

I'm not good at being vulnerable. I'm not good at letting people in. I'd rather walk around the world stark naked than walk around admitting to having faults and feelings and insecurities.

And boy, has this man seen me naked. Maybe that's why everything has been so topsy-turvy with us. We started with me naked. No walls, no hiding. Just me, exactly as I am, with curves and freckles and sunburned shoulders.

He's known what I am, *all* that I am, from day freaking one. Now the question becomes: Will I let him know *who* I am? Will I let him in?

Taking a deep breath, I look in his eyes. For him, I'm willing to try. "I want this, Ryan," I say. "I want you inside me. I want you to fuck me. Here. Now."

His energy darkens as he smooths a thumb over my cheek. "Tess—"

"Wait." I lift my hand to cover his on my cheek. "I want to let you in—I—god, I'm gonna try to let you in, okay? But my head can be a crazy place sometimes," I warn, dropping my hand away.

"I've noticed," he says with a smirk. His hand lowers, too, his thumb brushing along the curve of my shoulder.

I shiver, loving the feel of his gentle touch. Centering myself in that feeling, I give him my vulnerability. "Ryan, the last man who touched me did so in anger. I think it's making me afraid to take this step with you. I'm afraid of the surrender, of the loss of control."

He goes still, holding his breath as his eyes flash.

"I want you to help me reclaim it."

He raises a brow. "Your control?"

"And my consent," I say with a nod. "Both."

"How do we do that?" he asks, searching my eyes.

"We fuck," I reply. "And we hold nothing back. I want to give myself to you, Ryan. I want to trust that you won't hurt me, that you'll only bring me pleasure."

"Jesus, Tess." He drops his hands away.

My heart flutters in nervous anticipation. "You don't want that?"

He groans. "Well—fuck, I can't have this conversation in front of Drunk Cleopatra," he says, waving his hand over at the bed where poor Tegan is softly snoring.

I stifle a laugh, taking his hand. "Come on."

"Wait—"

I pull him from the room, glancing right towards the crowded game area before moving left.

"Tess, what are you doing?"

My heart races as I open the next door, peeking in to see a bathroom. No way. I am not fucking this man next to a toilet. Shutting the door, I move down and open the next.

"Tess—"

"In here," I say, pulling him into the dark, empty nursery. It's cute, decorated in soft blues and greys. There's a crib along the far wall, framed in by book and toy shelves. A loveseat is situated under a big window, gauzy curtains drawn to only let in the light from an outside streetlamp.

Ryan steps into the middle of the room and slowly turns to face me. "Seriously? Baby Josh's room?"

I shut the door and lock it, leaning against it. "I don't think he'll mind. And unless you wanted to stay in there with Drunk Cleopatra . . . or join the Eiffel Tower crew—"

"No," he says, eyes narrowed.

"You make me feel good, Ryan," I say, cutting to the chase. "You make me feel safe. And our chemistry is off the freaking charts. I know you feel it too. I think you'll make me a fantastic lover, and if you want it, I'm saying yes."

"Tess . . . " His heated gaze is locked on me.

I push off the locked door, walking towards him. "You can have all of me . . . any way you want me. You can be gentle . . . or you can be rough." I pause, just within arm's reach of him. "I consent—"

And then I'm in his arms. He pulls me to him, kissing me with all the passion I know he feels for me. We melt into each other, our hands clinging as we sigh our relief into each other's mouths that we're finally kissing, touching, sharing air. Why do we ever stop kissing when it feels this good?

His lips are soft, even as his kisses are urgent. He opens me up with his teasing tongue and I let him in, loving the feel of him against my lips. Our hands work feverishly, desperate for this moment of reconnection. I'm slowly learning his body, memorizing the planes of his chest, the muscled cording of his arms. I slip my hands inside his leather cut, smoothing my hands down over his ribs.

"You think you're so cute wearing this, don't you," I tease, nipping his bottom lip. "Trying to drive me crazy?"

"Cute isn't the word I'd use," he replies, his hands flipping up my leather skirt until he's palming my ass, pulling me against his erection. "But it's just a costume. If that's the reason we're about to fuck—"

Silencing him with my tongue in his mouth, I jerk the cut off his shoulders, dragging it down his arms, and drop it to the floor. "I want *you*," I pant against his lips. "There is only you. Fuck me, Ryan. Take control—"

He silences me with another kiss, his hands dropping to his shirt. He jerks it off, only breaking our kiss for a moment before he's opening his pants. "Touch me," he orders, grabbing my hand and slipping it inside his boxers, holding tight to my wrist as I palm his hard dick. His hold softens, sliding down until his hand is wrapped around mine.

I gasp, breaking our kiss as I look down, watching as our hands stroke him together. Precum leaks from his tip. I brush my thumb over it, desperate for a taste. He groans, his free hand going to my shoulder. Then he's cupping my cheek, tipping my face up.

"Oh—" I say on a laugh, taking in the bright smear of red across his lips. "I made a mess of you." I lift my free hand, ready to rub the color off his bottom lip. "Here—"

"Leave it," he says, jerking his head away. "I want it there. I want that devil red lipstick painted all over my dick too. Get on your knees and suck it." He grabs my jaw, squeezing hard enough to make me gasp. "Then I'll fuck you 'til your legs give out. Before I'm done, the only word spoken from these lips will be my name."

"Oh, thank God," I whimper, my body turning to jelly as I drop eagerly to my knees. I grab him by the hips and pull him closer, working him out of his boxers. I'm about to put him in my mouth when he suddenly pulls away from me. "Ryan, what—"

He steps back several feet until his hip hits the dresser. Then he braces his hands to either side, gripping the dark wood, and glares down at me, his gaze molten.

I don't let myself shrink under his stare. I want him looking at me. I'm on my knees in this sexy devil costume, red-painted lips smeared by his kisses. Feeling empowered by the hunger in his eyes, I lift my hands to the top of my red lace bustier. Fingers gripping the cups, I pull them down, letting my breast fall loose over the corset.

A muscle in his jaw twitches, and his hands grip tighter to the dresser. "Crawl."

My pussy clenches. "What?"

"Crawl to me," he repeats. "You want this dick? You want me to make you come? Make you scream? Take control?"

"Yes," I beg, swallowing my nerves.

"Yes, what?" he says with a raised brow.

Oh, my sweet puppy did not come to play. I knew I sensed a hunger for domination in him. I don't think Ryan has ever let himself explore his sexuality. He's unsure of his likes, his cravings. Each time I've said or done something he reacts to, I've taken note. In this moment, I know exactly what he wants.

Holding his gaze, I lift my hands to my breasts, pinching my nipples until I gasp, the rush of pleasure echoing in my aching clit. "Yes, sir." I watch him shiver with need at my words and it makes me tremble too. I love this side of him. I want to draw it out.

Play with me, baby.

"Then work for it," he growls, those pretty green eyes blown black with desire. "Crawl to me, Tess."

Yes, sir.

He looks like pure sin in this light, the shadows playing off the cut of his muscles. His arms flex as he grips the wood of the dresser, his pants open and sitting low on his hips. I can't stand this distance between us for another second. Dropping down to my hands, my breasts spilling out over the top of my bustier, I crawl to him. I hold his gaze, heart hammering in my chest. I'm so turned on, I could scream. I may be the one on my knees, but he's looking at me like I'm a goddess.

He watches me every second, not daring to look away. When he reaches out a hand, I take it. Holding tight to me, he reels me in. "Such a good fucking girl," he says, his other hand brushing over my hair. "So beautiful on your knees for me."

I hold in a whimper, biting my bottom lip.

"Look at me, Tess."

I glance up, my gaze sweeping over his bare chest to hold his gaze.

"Do you like when I call you a good girl?" He's genuinely curious. He wants to know. He wants this to be good for me too. God, he's getting me so hot. My sweet consent king with a sneaky dom side. I'm dead.

I nod. "Yes, sir."

"But you're not a good girl, are you?" he teases, his thumb tracing down my jaw.

"I try," I admit, leaning into his touch.

"Bullshit," he says with a smirk. "You don't know the meaning of the word. Not when it comes to sex. You're pure devil. Look at you," he adds, raising his hand to give my little devil horns a tug. "At least mine was a costume."

I smile up at him, batting my lashes. "Even devils can be good sometimes."

"Yeah, when they want something," he replies. "Tell me what you want."

I reach out with both hands, brushing them over his jeans, up his thighs. Slowly, I tug at his jeans and briefs, pulling them down his hips. "I want my mark on you," I admit, gazing up at him. "I want you claimed, Ryan. I saw you with your hands on that sexy Cleopatra, and I wanted to rip her fucking wig off."

His smile falls as he gazes down at me, a curl of his blond hair sweeping across his brow. He cups my jaw, demanding my attention, his pretty green eyes dark and needy. "Do you really think I would ever look sideways at another woman when I have this goddess at my feet?"

His words strike a chord deep in my trauma-addled soul.

Pretty words. It's just something men say, but never mean. He won't be faithful. They never are—

"Tess," he soothes, both hands cupping my cheeks. It's like he knows what I'm thinking. A shiver goes through me as he brushes those gentle thumbs over my freckles. "Look at me, beautiful."

I peer up at him through my lashes.

"There is no one else," he says, his gaze open and honest. "So long as you give me the time of fucking day, there won't be. I am so hung up on you, it's not even funny. When that drunk girl grabbed my hand, I turned around, desperate to see that it was *you*. I wanted it to be you who came to me—"

"I *was* coming for you," I admit, my hands smoothing over his bare hips. "Ryan, I followed you inside. I wanted to find you, be near you. I just want to be where you are." My gaze darkens as I glare up at him, letting my jealousy loose. "And then I saw her in your arms, and I wanted to fuck you right there in the hallway. I didn't care who watched."

His gaze is triumphant. "And what do you want now, pretty devil? Say it out loud."

I jerk his pants down to his knees, freeing his cock. It bobs in my face, hard and ready for me. I wrap my hand around it, loving the way he tenses, one hand going to my hair. I gaze up at him. "I'm putting my mark on you tonight. You are not a free dick anymore, Ryan. This is mine 'til I say otherwise."

His hand tightens in my hair. "Do it. Claim me."

I lean in, lips parting to taste him, when he pulls on my hair tipping my head back.

"But just know this goes both ways," he warns. "Unlike the idiot twins down the hall, I don't fucking share. It's not in my nature. If my dick is yours, that pussy is mine. We can still be friends who fuck, but I'll be the only one you're fucking. Understood?"

I nod, heart racing.

"Speak."

"Yes, sir."

"Good girl." He lets go of my hair, dropping his hand back to grip the dresser. "Now get on my dick."

Okay, my pussy is officially fanning herself with anticipation.

Dom Ryan might be my new favorite. Wasting no more time, my mouth closes around his tip and I suck, wanting my saliva to make it messy. He groans again, his hands going to my shoulders as I slide my painted lips up and down his shaft, stroking him with my tongue.

"So fucking good," he says, hand tightening in my hair.

I pop off and glance up at him through my dramatic fake lashes. "Like what you see?"

He looks down at me again, his gaze molten as he takes in my devil costume and his dick in my hand, painted red by my lipstick. "Perfect," he says, grabbing for my shoulders. "Up. Get up."

I let him pull me to my feet, and then he's grabbing me, spinning me around and pressing me against the dresser so hard it rattles. He grabs the cups of my lacy bustier and jerks them down harder, fully freeing my breasts. I gasp, loving the tight pinch of the fabric as it bends to his will. He drops his face, peppering my breasts with fevered kisses. Taking one in each hand, he presses his face in at their crease, swiping up my breastbone with his tongue, his breath hot on my skin.

"Oh god," I whimper, one hand in his hair. I fling the other hand back, feeling the soft velvet of a baby changing table against my palm. I tip my head back too, letting loose a laugh. If I'm going to hell for fucking this man in a baby's nursery, at least I'm dressed for the occasion.

"Lick my pussy," I pant. "Ryan, please—need your tongue—*yes*—" I shower him with soft praise as he drops down to his good knee, jerking my leather skirt up over my curvy thighs until it's bunched at my hips. I can only imagine what I look like with the girls spilling out and my ass on display. In this moment, I'm too blissed out to care.

Ryan runs his hands up my calves to my thighs, over the black fishnets. "These are fucking killing me," he says, pressing his face to my thigh to breathe me in. Then he drags his tongue over the stocking, tasting my skin.

I moan with pleasure, both hands dropping back to the dresser as I adjust my stance. "That feels good."

Leaning back to look at me, Ryan slides both hands up to the top of my black lace panties. "Can I see what's mine?"

Heart in my throat, I nod. "Yes, sir."

Holding my gaze, he drags them slowly down my thighs, exposing my pussy. I fight a shiver, my core squeezing on nothing as I wait, desperate for him to give me what I need. He stops the panties halfway down my thighs, keeping my legs pinned together. Then he drops his face forward, grabbing me by the hips as he presses his face to my bare pussy, his warm breath heating my skin as he takes in my essence, peppering my sensitive skin with soft kisses.

"You smell so fucking good," he says, kissing across to my hip bone. "I love the smell of this pussy. Love the taste." To prove his point, he flicks open my pussy lips with two fingers and swipes across my clit with his tongue.

My body spasms as I grab for his hair, my other hand holding tight to the dresser.

"You're gonna come in my mouth," he orders. "Here. *Now*. Fast as you can. Get yourself there. This isn't a marathon, it's a sprint. Run with me, Tess. Fucking fly."

His words spin me up and I'm already aching as he descends, devouring me with all the skill of a man who was born to please a woman, a man who craves control. And I want to give it to him. In this moment, I want to be what he needs. This is what I love about sex with an attentive partner—their pleasure becomes your pleasure, and yours becomes theirs.

"Yes," I pant, rocking my hips against him as I chase my orgasm.

He works with his fingers and his tongue, fucking me like a dream. Pulling his mouth away, he takes two fingers and rubs them over my clit, applying exquisite pressure—soft then hard, working me in small circles. "Tess, look at me," he orders.

Forcing my eyes to open, I look down my body at him. His lips aren't stained quite so red now. There's so much heat in his eyes, mirrored by open honesty. He's looking at me like he *knows* me, like he knows what I need. I think maybe he does.

"Come for me, devil. This one's not for you, it's for me. I fucking own this one. Give it to me."

I'm shocked as hell when I realize I'm right fucking there. I want to give him this. I'll give him my most vulnerable self. I'll give him my orgasm. I tip my head back, eyes shut tight as I come. My body is wracked with trembling as my clit suddenly develops a heartbeat, pulsing and throbbing, echoing out in waves.

Ryan drops his fingers away and replaces them with his hungry mouth. He sucks on my clit, humming and flicking with his tongue, giving me heat, vibration, and pressure in one. I fall completely apart, body shaking as I cling to the dresser, knees giving out.

"Stop—stop," I cry, my hand digging into his hair as I pull him off. "Oh my god, I'm gonna pass out."

He stands, boxing me in with his height and his towering presence. "You did so good," he says, tipping my face up to kiss my lips. "My sexy fucking devil. My perfect good girl."

I'm learning this is what he likes. Once he's had a taste of me, he likes to share it. He wants my taste on my mouth too. He wants all parts of me to taste like my most primal self, and I'm fucking here for it.

I dive in with my tongue, claiming all of his kisses as my body recovers from the shock of such a fierce orgasm. Once I've caught my breath, I drop my hands down to the top of his pants, ready for him to feel as good as I feel. "Fuck me, Ryan. Please, I can't wait any longer. I need you inside me."

He rocks into my hand, letting me wrap my fingers around his shaft. I work him slow, dropping my hand down to cup his balls. Beyond the walls of this room, the party pulses on—loud music, laughter, the thump of stereo speakers. In this room, it's just the two of us. I want him. I *need* him—

"Tess—wait," he says, breaking our kiss. "Fuck. Shit."

"What?" I pant, gazing up at him.

He groans, dragging a hand through his hair. "I don't have a condom," he admits. "I have them back at the house. I really didn't think I'd need one here," he adds, gesturing around the dark nursery.

I nod, knowing what he's asking without asking. "I haven't been with anyone in months and I'm on the pill—but you have to do what makes you feel comfortable," I quickly add. "We can wait. We can go back to the house—"

He kisses me, silencing my offers. Pulling back, he cups my face with both hands. "I've never been with a woman without a condom."

I nod, heart in my throat. "Can I ask why?"

He shrugs. "Call it trauma from growing up as the kid of an ER nurse. She had me convinced pretty much anything would lead to my dick turning colors and falling off."

I laugh, my hands wrapping around his wrists.

"What?" he says.

"Look down."

He glances down and I know he sees it when he laughs too. His hard dick is currently painted red with my lipstick. "I don't think this is what she meant," he says with a smirk, pecking my lips with another kiss.

"I won't pressure you. Sex is about trust and connection, at least it is for me. And we can always do other things."

"I want this," he admits. "I've never really had a connection with a partner before. Sex was always just something I did to . . . get by, I guess," he explains with a shrug. "I mean, I enjoyed it when it happened. But it wasn't really about enjoyment if that makes sense. Everything was wrapped, everything was clinical and safe. It was just about satisfying a need. And then I could refocus on my game."

"You're a hard worker. You're committed to your sport."

"But there is also more to life," he replies. "I'm not blind to living, Tess," he adds, kissing me again. "Exploring sex with you has been so much fun. You talk of trusting me? Well, I wanna trust you too. Will you be my first?"

"Are you sure?"

He takes my hand, palming it over his hard erection, and smiles. "This dick is yours 'til you say otherwise. Take it, sexy devil. Ruin me for all other women."

I mirror his smile as I take his free hand with mine and trail his fingers over my sternum, between my breasts and down, until he's cupping my needy pussy. "And this is all yours." I press myself against him. "I'm aching to have you inside me—"

He silences me with a kiss, and I wrap both my arms around his neck. We're a stumbling mess as he walks backwards across the room, stopping when he hits the loveseat. He sinks down onto it, and a loud squeak shatters the silence.

I gasp as he reaches a hand under his ass and pulls out a velvety elephant stuffed animal. We both look at it in horror before he tosses it aside with another soft squeak.

"I'll buy him a new one," he says, reaching for the panties still twisted around my thighs.

"And a new love seat," I tease, shifting my weight as I step out of them, leaving me bare assed and dripping for him.

"New curtains." He pulls me down to straddle his lap. His hands go to the fishnets, his fingers teasing as he runs them up my legs, ending at my thighs.

"New dresser," I moan, my head tipping back as I grip to his shoulders, my wet pussy gliding against his hard cock.

"I'm gonna buy you things too," he pants, his hands palming my breasts as I move on top of him.

"Ryan—"

"Friends buy friends presents," he counters before I can articulate a protest. His mouth closes around my tit and I moan with relief, desperate to feel us connected. His gentle sucking lights me up, sending a wave of pleasure over my body and straight to my clit. He switches sides and I dig my hands in his hair, holding him to my flesh as I grind against him.

"I need more. Please, baby. Please fuck me. I need you inside me. Don't make me wait any longer—"

We're grinding in a frenzy as he silences me with his mouth, his hips moving with mine. Dropping a hand down between us, I lift my hips off him, losing that heat of connection, But I know it's only temporary. I hold his dick by the base, angling him up as I relax my hips, desperate to take him.

"It's yours," Ryan whispers, his breath warm at my neck, his hands cradling my hips. "Take it, it's yours."

On a breathless whimper, I tease his tip at my entrance, feeling him start to slide in.

"Fucking do it." His left hand tightens in my hair. "Take all of me in your greedy fucking cunt. Be my devil and own me like you—"

We both cry out as I press down with my hips, his length filling me. Dropping forward, I brace with one hand against the loveseat, the other on his shoulder. I work my hips, exhaling as I take him all the way to the hilt. My ass settles against his thighs and we both groan, adjusting to this feeling of connection.

"You feel amazing. Ride me, baby. You're so tight, so beautiful like this. Your pussy is gripping me like a fist—*Jesus*—you're a queen on her fucking throne."

His dirty talk washes over me as I begin to move, loving the feel of him filling me. I work my hips, trying to find the best angle to give my clit friction too.

"You need more, don't you?" His hands cup my breasts as I bounce, chasing my pleasure.

"Yes," I beg. "Please—"

"Please what?" he teases, bending forward to suck my breast again.

"Mark me, Ryan. Mark me so I know I'm yours."

Shifting his hold on me, he drops his mouth back down to the swell of my left breast. He places an open-mouthed kiss against my skin. Then he sucks. He marks my flesh as I ride his dick, my orgasm spiraling tighter.

In moments, he breaks away, gasping for air, and I look down to see the red mark on my breast. It turns me all the way on. He wraps his arms around me, holding me to him as we both move our hips, finding a new rhythm. His cock is the perfect size to give me what I need. My orgasm builds inside me, pressure and heat mounting, unfurling outwards, growing deeper, rooting itself in me like a tree.

"I'm close." I shut my eyes tight as I chase this feeling.

"Tell me when," he groans, his hands sliding down to grip my ass. "Tess—tell me—"

"Not yet," I cry, knowing he's holding back. "God, keep going—"

"Sit back." He pushes on my shoulders. "Baby, sit back and work your clit. We don't stop 'til you scream."

I shove off his chest, keeping myself impaled on his dick as I change angles, all my weight now balanced over my hips as I bounce on his thighs. He holds my weight easily, meeting me thrust for thrust.

"You're so fucking beautiful," he groans, his eyes locked on me as I move on top of him.

I feel all of me swaying and vibrating in this primal dance. I'm on fire with the need to come.

"Touch your clit," he demands again. "I wanna watch you come on my dick."

I drop my hand between us and work my clit, my orgasm burning in my core, moments from bursting outwards. I feel the tingle curling my toes, and I know I'm about to lose all control. "Now," I moan, my hand going slack on my clit as I just apply steady pressure.

Ryan takes over from below, hands on my hips as he hammers

into me, fucking me senseless. My body is frozen as I tip my head back and let out a breathless scream. Beneath me, Ryan's hips grind, losing all rhythm as he chases his release, spilling into me.

Oh god, I can feel it. I feel the moment he releases inside me. It sends my core quivering, and then it's like I'm pulling him in deeper. There's no barrier between us and I take it all, my pussy gripping tight to him as we ride out our orgasms.

The euphoria only lasts moments. Then it just feels like I have nothing left. Emptiness. Perfect emptiness. I'm carved out and hollow. I sink forward, not even recognizing the whimpering noise that escapes me when I press myself against his naked chest.

His arms go around me as our faces swim in a sea of my red curls. He brushes them back, kissing my sweaty forehead as we both find our breath again. After a moment, I lift off him, body still shaking. The loss of him inside me feels devastating. The moment he's gone, I want him back. I feel his cum between my thighs, warm and wet. I flop down next to him on the love seat, clenching my thighs together, holding him in. We're seated side by side, only our hands touching. Slowly, I turn my head, and he does the same. We breathe in sync as we come down from our high.

"That was amazing," he says, still breathless.

I nod, holding his gaze. It *was* amazing. Ryan Langley is amazing. Kind and thoughtful, beautiful inside and out. Generous. Strong.

Fuck, I am in so much trouble.

"I've never—" He goes quiet, looking away.

"What?" I whisper, my hand brushing his thigh.

"It's nothing," he says, leaning forward, his elbows on his knees.

"Tell me."

He glances over his shoulder at me. "The day we met . . . in Jake's kitchen?"

"I remember," I say with a smile, giving his thigh a gentle squeeze.

He nods, his gaze heating as his eyes trail down to the mark he left on my chest.

My hand flutters on instinct, my fingers brushing over it, knowing exactly where it is on the swell of my breast.

"I've never wanted anyone as much as I wanted you in that moment," he admits, his voice soft.

"I remember," I say again.

His gaze locks back on me and the intensity of it has my smile falling. "You want us to just be friends . . . friends who fuck."

My heart stops. "Ryan—"

"And I'll play along," he says quickly. "I'll be your friend, Tess. And I'll gladly fuck you again. You say the word, and this can all happen again," he goes on, gesturing between us. "I want you to feel good. I want to be the *reason* you feel good. And I want you to know that no one has ever made me feel as good as you make me feel. I want this, Tess. I'm afraid of how much I want it," he admits. "But no matter what else happens, we're friends, yeah?"

I nod, trying to will my heart to beat. How is vulnerability so easy for him? He makes it seem so effortless to just say exactly what he's thinking. No games, no tricks. Meanwhile, I'm a mess. Now that the sex is over, my walls are rebuilding fast.

"We can't stay in here," I say at last, shifting away. "People will come looking for us." I'm not sure how I'll sneak past an entire house of people and have no one notice that I'm freshly fucked. I don't even have a lipstick with me to try and touch this up.

Ryan stands with a tired groan, awkwardly trying to shimmy back into his boxers and jeans, tucking his dick away.

I'm slipping my breasts back inside my bustier, adjusting them so they sit right, when something catches my eyes. "Ryan," I murmur, heart in my throat.

"Hmm?" He snatches his shirt up off the floor, slipping it back on.

"Ryan," I say again, panic rising.

"Are these mine or yours?" he teases, dangling my panties on his pinkie. "I think this is a case of finders keepers—"

"Ryan," I cry.

He finally turns my way, his hand already stuffing the panties in his pocket. "What?" He takes in my expression, and then he's reaching for me, dropping back down next to me on the love seat. "Oh—baby, what is it? I'm sorry. I didn't mean to upset you with all my blabbing about Jake's kitchen and—Tess, what—"

I point up to the device with the glowing red light mounted at the corner of the wall. "There's a camera in here."

45
Tess

I slam the door of my car and rush up the driveway in the rain, trying not to spill my coffee or slip and bust my ass. Panting as I reach the front porch, I flip back the hood of my jacket, dancing in place to shake off some of the rain.

I've been up since 5:00 a.m., too wired to sleep—which is crazy because, by all rights, I should be dead to the world. Alcohol and orgasms are a heady combination. Enough to knock me out cold after three rounds last night—twice at the party and once in the shower when we got home.

Apparently, they're just not enough to *keep* me asleep. Not when the sky is falling, and I may lose my title as an honorary Ray.

I slipped naked out of Ryan's bed, threw on some workout clothes, and high-tailed it over here. I need answers. And advice. And to be talked off this ledge . . . or maybe pushed. No one is better at talking me off ledges than Rachel.

I dig in the pocket of my raincoat, fishing out my keys, and let myself into the house. It's the work of moments to pop in the code to disable their alarm system. Then I'm rushing up the stairs, determined to do a proper freakout session with my best friend.

The dog barks, meeting me in the hallway with alarm that quickly morphs into delight. I march right past all the closed bedroom doors, heading straight for the master bedroom.

"Rach, girl, I need to talk to you," I cry, pushing on the half-open door.

Jake and Rachel are curled up together at one end of their double king bed. He's on the end, facing in towards her, being the big spoon.

Ilmari is stretched out across the other king. Caleb is nowhere to be found.

"Rach," I say again. "I need you."

Jake bolts up in the bed. "Tess?" he says, his voice scratchy.

"I need to talk to Rachel," I say, shucking off my wet raincoat and dropping it to the floor.

Ilmari groans something in Finnish, rolling to his side.

"What time is it?" Rachel asks.

"Early," I reply, kicking off my shoes. "Like, not even 7:00 a.m."

Rachel grabs Jake's arm, checking the time on his Apple watch. She whimpers, pressing her face deeper into the pillow. "Tess, no. My alarm was going off in fifteen minutes."

"Everything okay?" Jake says at me, rubbing a tired hand over his face.

Rachel elbows him. "Don't ask her that. Now we'll never get her out of here."

"Hey, it could be important," he counters.

"No, it's about sex," she replies. "Frantic texts and phone calls are for work emergencies. Late-night whine and cheese sessions are for family stuff. Early morning freak-outs are only ever about Tess thinking with her vagina instead of her head."

"Rude," I say at her, one hand on my hip. "Don't act like you know me."

She sighs, sitting up in the bed, propped against her pillows. She's wearing a cute little silk nightie, blue with pink lace. "Tell me I'm wrong," she says through a yawn, her fingers brushing Jake's hair back from his brow. "Is this or is this not about your greedy little kitty scratching up the wrong tree last night?"

"Rakas, take her downstairs," Ilmari mutters, his face still buried under a pillow.

"No, it's cold down there," I say, hurrying over to his side of the bed. Grabbing the covers, I flip them back to expose his freaking awesome back tattoo and his pearly white derrière. "Mars, scooch ov—mygod! Why are you naked?"

Mars snatches the blankets as Jake and Rachel laugh. "It's my bed," he barks.

"God, I'm not getting under there with you naked," I huff.

"Good."

I snatch the little knit throw blanket off the end of the bed and use that to cover my legs as I take up the spot next to Mars on top of the covers. "Where's Caleb?" I say, glancing around.

"He wanders in and out," Rachel says with another yawn.

"How did you even get in here?" Mars asks.

"I used my key," I reply setting my coffee down on the side table.

"And how did you get a key?"

"Because I gave it to her, remember?" Rachel replies, her hand reaching out to pet his hair too.

He scoots closer to her. "How did she disable the alarm—"

"Oh my god, officer, I confess, alright?" I say, throwing up both hands in mock surrender. "I broke in through a window, ducked the net of laser beams, and disabled the alarm by cutting the blue wire."

"Hey, I've seen that movie," Jake teases.

"What the hell is going on in here?"

We all turn to see a very naked Caleb standing in the doorway.

"God," I cry, my hand going up to cover my eyes. "Do none of you have clothes?"

He saunters up to the other side of the bed, leaning down to kiss Jake, then across him to kiss Rachel. "What is Tess doing here at 6:30 a.m.?"

"Girl gossip," Jake replies as Rachel says, "Vagina monologues."

Jake tosses him a pillow and he casually holds it in front of his naked lower half. "I need to get ready for work," he says at his partners.

"Mars and I don't need to be in until nine," Jake replies.

"I'm going in at eight," Rachel adds.

"That doesn't mean I need to suck my own dick in there, does it?" Caleb replies, gesturing to the bathroom.

Rachel just sighs. "Seriously, Cay?" At the same time, I cry, "God, I'm sitting right here."

"Well, I'm interested," Jake says, his tone brightening. "But . . . " He glances dramatically from me back to Caleb.

"I'm sure Tess won't mind if I fuck my husband in my own shower, in my own house, behind a closed door," Caleb replies with a roll of his eyes.

"No, I'm interested in her vagina monologue," Jake admits.

Rachel laughs and it's my turn to roll my eyes. "You can feel free to leave at any time," I say at them both. "I really only need Rachel here to witness my humiliation."

"Well, now I'm definitely not leaving," Jake replies, tugging Caleb down onto the bed next to him.

"I have to get ready," Caleb huffs at him.

"Five minutes, and then we'll do a speed round," Jake tosses out as a compromise. "Tess, you've got five minutes. Go."

Rachel, Jake, and Cay all look to me.

"I—can't—Rach, I need to know how well you know Shelby," I get out at last.

"Pretty well, I guess," she says with a shrug. Then she flashes me a look of horror. "Wait—ohmygod, what did you do?"

"What?" I cry, feigning indignation.

"You only do morning freak outs when you're regretting last night. I know you fucked someone inappropriate, and now you're asking me about Shelby and—oh, holy fuck, was it Sully?"

"No," Jake gasps dramatically, his hand going over his mouth.

Rachel looks ready to implode. "Tess, I swear to God—"

"Ew, *gross*," I shout over her. "No! He's like obnoxiously happily married *and* he wears socks with sandals. Are you kidding me?"

"Hey, I wear socks with sandals," Jake counters.

"We all do," Caleb adds.

"If you need a reason to hate him, how about because his favorite ice cream flavor is Rocky Road?" Jake offers. "I mean, honestly, it's criminal."

But Rachel is looking at me. "If not Sully, then who did you—"

"She fucked Langers," Caleb says, his eyes on Jake's phone.

It's my turn to gasp, peering around the other two at him. "How did you know?"

"Because your mutual attraction is as subtle as a goal horn," Ilmari says next to me, his face still buried in the pillows by Rachel's side. He's shifted a little so now he has a large arm slung over her hips.

"Hooooly shit," Jake says. "Tess, do you have a thing going with Langley? Isn't he like ten years younger than you?"

"Age is just a number," Caleb replies. "He's hot and she's horny."

"And *you* can go drown in the shower," I snap at him.

"They've had a thing since beach day, way back before you and I were even a thing," Rachel says at Mars, still petting his hair.

He just makes a grunt sound, curling in closer to her.

"Wait, now I'm confused," says Jake. "What does Shelbs have to do with any of this?"

I groan, giving Rachel a sheepish look.

Her smile falls, replaced with resignation. "Oh, seriously, what the fuck did you do?"

"Nothing . . . too terribly bad," I hedge. "I just need to know if you'll ask Shelby a favor for me."

"Tess, just spit it out," she replies.

"Yeah, I'm losing interest in this fast," Jake mutters.

"We could already be fucking," Caleb says at him. "You have no one to blame but yourself."

"Fine," Jake huffs. "Tess, tell us what you did last night, or I'm gonna give Cay a handy right here on the bed."

Taking a deep breath, I look to Rachel and try to get it all out in one go. "I need you to ask Shelby if the camera in the nursery records, or if it's just live action. And if it *is* recording, I need you to ask her to just go ahead and erase everything from last night without watching any of it. Okay? Cool. Bye."

I try to launch off the side of the bed, but Rachel throws herself over Ilmari, snatching at my arm. "Oh, no you don't," she cries, jerking me back.

"Ouch—shit—"

Beneath us, Ilmari grunts.

"In the nursery, Tess?" Jake says, his tone laced with disappointment. "Where Baby Josh sleeps?"

"Hey, he wasn't in there," I huff. "And it was either that or we do it in the little girl's room where Drunk Cleopatra was already passed out, or in the guest room where two of your teammates were Eiffel towering your—" My words stop as I realize I was about to give away one of their colleagues.

Jake looks shocked. "How did I miss all this?"

"Because you were too busy outside playing with your hook," Caleb deadpans from his side.

"Oh, right."

"Who did you say was Eiffel towering whom?" Caleb asks, moderately curious now.

But Rachel sits forward, saving me from answering. "Wait . . . Tess," she says in warning. "Langley? You really went there with him?"

I shrug. "Yeah, I think we were kind of inevitable, you know? Our chemistry is great—"

"*Tess*," Rachel says again. "Have you at least told him everything? Does he know about Troy and the pictures and all of it?"

"He knows everything," I reply with a solemn nod. "I couldn't lie to him, Rach. I couldn't hide it. He deserved to know."

"And he's . . . okay with it all?" she asks, one dark brow raised.

"Langers is cool," Caleb replies for me. "He's not the kind of guy to let a little psycho ex drama stand in his way."

"Yeah, he may be a forward, but he's got the heart of a defenseman," Jake adds. "In fact, I think he played D for a while in Junior League."

"If you came here expecting me to play the Tess card, I'm not gonna do it," Rachel says, crossing her arms in defiance.

"Wait, what's the Tess card?" Jake asks, glancing between us.

"It's where Tess makes me channel all her nastiest thoughts and spit them out at her like some kind of mean, painfully poignant truth-teller," she replies.

"Rach, you're my mirror," I beg. "I need you to give me the hard truths. It's the only way I can keep perspective."

"No, it's the only way you keep yourself locked into this delusion that you only deserve shitty things," she counters. "And I'm not doing it."

"I feel like I'm missing so much right now," says Jake, his gaze darting between us.

"Tess's brain is at war with her heart, which has been hijacked by her vagina," Caleb summarizes for him. "She wants Rachel to dunk her heart and her vagina in an ice bath so her brain can take charge again."

Rachel snorts. "Honestly, I think I prefer his way. We've got bags of ice and a tub big enough to dunk you. Wanna try that?"

"No thanks," I mutter, crossing my arms. "Come on, please," I beg. "Just a taste. I'm free-falling over here."

"No," she says more vehemently this time. "I'm not going to hurt your feelings and make you question things with Langley. You two are good together—"

"God, you're useless," I cry, slipping off the side of the bed. "The one time I need you to catch me as I fall, and you're just gonna cross your arms and watch me go splat?"

"Falling for a guy and falling to your death are not the same things," she counters. "That the sensations are similar for you is what we called trauma, Tess. If you're not ready to be with Ryan, be a big enough person to tell him that. I really don't want to see either of you get hurt."

I stare at her wide-eyed before I slowly shake my head. "Who are you, and what have you done with Rachel Price?"

She just shrugs, a little smile on her face. "I did my own free-falling recently . . . or hadn't you noticed," she adds, gesturing to the pile of men around her.

"Married happy Rachel is a total buzz kill," I say, snatching my coffee off the side table. "I'm leaving before whatever infection you have spreads to me."

"Wait—what do you want me to do about Shelby?" she calls.

"Umm, nothing." I slip on my shoes. "Forget about it. I'll take care of it."

"Tess . . . "

"Really, it's fine," I say, ducking down to pick up my rain jacket. "Lots to do today. See you later Price family—"

"Tess," Ilmari calls softly, stopping me in my tracks as I reach the door.

I turn and glance over my shoulder, one hand braced against the doorway.

He's sitting up in the bed now, naked to his waist, his blond hair a mess around his shoulders. He holds my gaze, those steely blue eyes boring into me. "You came here looking for advice. Will you hear mine?"

I hold my breath, hand holding tight to the door. His partners all look to him too, waiting for him to speak. Moments tick by as he just looks at me. Finally, I raise a brow at him and nod.

"Life is short."

I wait for him to say more, but he doesn't. As per usual, he doesn't need to. "Right. Thanks, Mars," I say, tears in my eyes.

I turn away from the vision of all four Prices happy in their marriage bed. Life is short, and they're choosing to live it to the fullest. But I don't have Rachel's strength . . . and she doesn't have my baggage.

I know what my advice is, even if Rachel won't say it for me. My advice is that I should let Ryan go. My advice is that my life is messy and complicated and Ryan deserves better. My advice is good. My advice keeps me safe. I know it's my advice I should take.

So you tell me why I'm marching out of this house, phone in hand, ready to dial Ryan and tell him to be naked and waiting in the shower by the time I get home. Life is short, and I feel like doing some more free-falling before it ends.

46
Ryan

"Holy god," I groan, rolling to my side away from Tess. I'm a sweating, panting mess, and I feel like all my essence has been sucked out of my dick. I'm nothing but an empty shell now, the chalk outline form of Ryan Langley. "Babe, I can't," I mutter, eyes shut tight. "No more. I'm dead."

The vibe she was using drops to the bed, buzzing between us as she giggles. "Poor puppy, did I wear you out?"

I just groan.

She showed up like a spinning tornado, busting into the house at 7:30 a.m. having already been out to the coffee shop. Then she dragged me into her shower where we fucked like animals, her hands pressed against the tiles while I hammered into her from behind. Her pussy squeezed my dick so hard, I saw stars. It was fucking epic. Best wakeup ever.

We somehow found our way back to my room, and we've spent the last hour naked. She made me come again when she slipped a buzzing cock ring on me that made me feel like my dick was zapped by lightning. My jizz spilled all over my stomach, and I practically squealed like a girl trying to get it off when I reached that point of oversensitivity.

Then my red-headed devil licked me clean while she fucked herself with a two-pronged toy she calls her 'rabbit.' She straddled my legs as she rode the toy, her beautiful body moving on top of me as she came again, calling my name.

Now she thinks I can try for round three, and I have to end this while my heart still beats. I'm convinced: Sex with Tess is gonna kill me . . . and I'll gladly thank her for it as my soul ascends.

An hour later, I arrive at the Rays gym to see quite a few guys going through their reps with the strength and conditioning team. Metal music plays through the speakers loud enough to get the blood pumping. I walk past the row of exercise bikes where a few of the defensemen are cycling.

"There he is," Jake calls, waving me down.

As I move towards him, he hops off his bike, sweat pouring down his face.

"Hey, man. What's up—*ouch*—" I cry, reeling from a hard slap to the back of the head. "What the fuck was that for?" I say, glaring at him.

Jake gets right up in my face. "What part of 'be her friend' did your dick translate to 'insert here?'"

I go still staring at him, momentarily speechless. "What—how do you know about that?" I cry, eyes wide.

He just points over my shoulder.

I spin around to see Doc glaring at me. She leans against her open office door, arms crossed. I turn back around to see Jake has been joined by a very large, very broody Mars.

"When did she tell you?" I blurt, my mind reeling.

"This morning," Mars replies. "We all woke to her panicking in our bed."

"Panicking?" I repeat, glancing between them.

"Yeah, apparently she deflowered you in a nursery," Jake teases.

"On camera," Mars adds.

"I wasn't deflowered," I snap at Jake. "It wasn't my first time, asshole."

"It was your first time with Tess, and that's what matters to us," he counters.

I go still, my gaze darting between them. Shit, what did she tell them?

"It wasn't their first time," says Sanford, waltzing between them with that hitch in his step.

"What?" Jake cries, spinning to face him. "How do you know?"

"It's written all over his face," he replies. "I bet they're doing it all over that bungalow."

"Mitä helvettiä," Mars curses in Finnish. "Did you two fuck in my sauna?"

I glance at Mars. Yeah, I'm not answering that. I like my teeth right where they are, thank you very much.

"What the hell did you two do last night?" Sanny teases.

"Nothing," I cry, my gaze darting between them.

Sanny smirks. "Look at you, wild stallion."

"Well, I'm not gonna kiss and tell," I huff, crossing my arms.

"Kiss and tell?" Jake echoes. "Jeezus, Langers. Is this grade school? Are we twelve?"

"We already know you fucked last night," says Sanford. "She told us."

"Yeah, in a nursery, which is fucking weird," Jake adds. "Baby Josh sleeps in there."

"Well, let's not split hairs," Sanford says with a hand on his shoulder. "You blew me in a Baskin-Robbins bathroom last week."

Jake laughs. "Oh yeah. Totally worth it."

"What we need to know is what happens now," says Mars, holding up a hand to silence them. "She's ours to protect."

"Yeah, she's Rachel's family," adds Sanny. "Which makes her *our* family."

"You're in sister-fucking territory right now, asshole," says Jake. "Which is against, like, every code in the hockey bro handbook. No moms, no sisters. You're lucky we don't have you in a headlock on the floor."

"Damage that knee, and you'll all be sleeping out on the deck chairs tonight," Doc calls from her office doorway.

"Will you call them off?" I shout over my shoulder.

"No."

"Answer the question, tough guy," says Jake, giving my shoulder a shove. "What is this between you two? Is she nothing but a puck bunny to you?"

"No," I reply.

"A convenient fuck?" jabs Sanford. "A distraction? A fun trip to cougar town?"

"No—"

"Are you gonna break her heart?" Jake snaps, shoving my shoulder again.

"Guys, I don't even—"

"Love 'em and leave 'em? Eh, Langers?" Sanford says. "Is that your M.O.?"

"No," I growl.

"Then what is she—"

"She's everything!"

All four of them have their eyes locked on me, and my heart is suddenly racing a mile a minute. We're doing this. Right here. Right now.

I glare around at each of them. "She's fucking everything, alright? I'm fucking—I'm obsessed with her." I groan, dragging both my hands through my hair.

"Oh, shit." Jake's eyes are wide as he takes me in.

"I'm not sleeping," I admit. "I'm not eating. I'm distracted on and off the ice. Since the moment I saw her standing in those waves on beach day, it's like . . . " I try to think of the right words to explain it. "It's like pieces of me are getting chipped away and replaced with her."

"Shit," Sanford says, glancing between his partners. "Guys, this is bad."

"Yeah, abort mission," says Jake, taking a step back, his hand on Sanny's tattooed arm.

"You assholes wanna know how this fucking happened?" I say, gesturing to my knee. "I lost concentration on the ice for a split second. I let my eyes drift up to that crowd, and I thought I saw her standing there. One second too long of wishing it was her watching me, and then that winger took me out at the knees."

Jake winces, glancing over his shoulder. "Babe, I think he's serious."

"Of course, I'm fucking serious." I give him a shove. "You asked me what happens now, huh?" I turn around to face Doc. "Listen, Hades. You need to call off your three-headed guard dog," I say, pointing a finger at her.

"Point at my wife again, and lose the finger," Jake warns.

I drop my hand, not breaking eye contact with Doc. "I know you're just trying to be her friend right now and protect her. I know you're scared for her. I'm fucking scared too. What she's going through is scary. But I'm not going anywhere, okay? Fuck being friends. I am crazy about that woman, so just back the fuck off. All of you," I add, glaring at her men.

"Look at the balls on this kid," Sanny says, arms still crossed as he measures me up.

"Hades," Jake snorts. "Sorry, babe, but that's totally gonna stick."

"I'm making us Team Cerberus shirts," says Sanford.

"Ohmygod, can you imagine? I want them in black with like a big three-headed dog on the front. It would be cool, right, Mars?" Jake says, looking to the quiet Finn.

"Leave me out of it," he says.

"Don't worry, Metaphor. We'll make yours a crop top," Sanford teases.

I just shake my head, glancing between them. "You guys are fucking crazy."

Jake laughs. "Are we done here, Hades?" he calls over his shoulder. "You hear what you needed to hear?"

Slowly, Doc nods.

"Sorry, Langers," he says at me. "We had to bring down the heavy on you. We needed to know where you stand. In case you're worried, you passed the test."

"With flying colors," Sanny adds.

"Well, thank God for small fucking mercies." I slip around her guys and head her way. "I've got PT with Brady for the next forty-five minutes. And then I'm coming back over here, and as punishment for Jake hitting me, you're gonna tell me how I can get in good with Tess. I am not messing this up, alright?"

"I thought you just told me to back the fuck off?" she replies coolly.

"Look, I don't need any help running her off. That woman was born with a pair of Nike Airs strapped to her feet."

That earns me a smirk, which I'm gonna call progress.

I step closer, gazing down at her. "Give me something. Doc. One thing I can use to reach her and show her that I mean to stick around. That I'm good for—well, that I'm good for more than just being friends."

She sighs, leaning against the doorframe. "You really like her?"

"I think I'm falling in love with her," I admit. My eyes go wide to mirror hers, and I realize too late my mistake. "Oh—please, God, don't tell her. Please—*fuck*—I know you have your girl code that you have to share everything, but Doc, *please*. She'll run so fucking fast. She's not ready. She—"

"*Ryan,*" she says with a soft laugh, placing her hand on my arm and giving it a reassuring squeeze. "I won't tell her, okay? You're right.

If you tell her that right now, we'll be repairing a Tess-shaped hole in Ilmari's wall."

"So, what do I do?" I press, searching her face. "How do I reach her?"

She gives me another long look, like she's measuring me up. Finally, her shoulders relax a little, and I know I've passed some important best friend test. I drop my hands back to my sides. "For as much as that girl loves to talk, her love language is action."

"Her—what?"

"Service, Ryan," she clarifies. "Acts of service. You can't tell Tess you love her and make her believe you. She won't. It's not in her nature. Your best chance is to show her."

I clap my hands together, brain whirring. "Right, show her. I can do that. Wait—how do you show someone you love them? Flowers? Chocolates?"

She smirks. "Is this a Hallmark movie? Are you gonna teach her the true meaning of Christmas, too, Langley?"

"Well, fuck, I don't know," I cry, my frustration rising. "I've never done this before. I've never tried to show a woman I love her."

"Honestly, that will probably help. Don't think about what you *should* do or what others have done. You need to do what feels right and natural to you. You're a smart guy, Langley. I'm sure you can figure this out."

I nod, my brain still working in overdrive as I turn away.

"Hey, Ryan," Doc calls, breaking my concentration.

I glance over my shoulder, glaring when I see the set of hers. "What now? You gonna threaten me again? List the ways you'll hurt me if I hurt her?"

"No. I'll leave the threats to my three-headed guard dog," she adds with a smirk.

I roll my eyes.

"I was just going to say I think she has a volunteer training event over at Mickler's Beach today."

"Yeah, I know. What do you—" And then I go still, my brain crunching on this new information. "Ohhh . . . and that would?"

"Never know until you try," she replies. Turning away, she disappears inside her office.

47
Tess

"Right, well, I think everyone's here, duchess," Joey calls over at me, checking the names on his phone.

All the volunteers are chatting around the picnic table, cups of coffee and reusable water bottles in hand. It's a warm day for January, and half of us are in our T-shirts and sunglasses. We put out a small spread of fresh fruit and donuts, and it's all pretty much gone.

Nancy and Cheryl are here, though they're already certified. Cheryl chats with the Scoutmaster from Ponte Vedra who brought over five Boy Scouts. The boys are all sitting at the table on their phones looking bored. Aside from the Scout troop, there's an older couple who are friends of the Lemmings and also live at the beach, two college girls looking for summer volunteer hours, and an adorable mother-son duo wearing shirts that say, 'What the shell?'

I hurry over to where Nancy is helping our rep from the FWC get set up under the picnic pavilion. "We about ready to get started?"

"Absolutely," Nancy chimes, tucking some loose strands of her dark hair behind her ear. "John says everyone gets a packet to take home, and we'll just talk through some of the ground rules here before we hit the beach."

John, the Florida Wildlife Commission rep, towers over tiny Nancy. He looks like an ex-football player with his massive chest and shoulders tucked inside his park ranger shirt. There's not a single hair on his shiny, bald head. "Everyone signed their release forms?"

"Yep," I say, holding out the stack of papers in my hands.

He takes them, stuffing them in a folder. "Then we're good to go."

I spin around clapping my hands. "Alright, everyone! John says we're ready to get started."

As one, the group starts to move. I hurry back over to the picnic table, helping Cheryl collect the trash from the donuts and fruit.

"Whoa, cool car," the freckle-faced Boy Scout next to me says.

I glance over my shoulder, and my heart freaking stops. I know that little red sports car. Ryan pulls up and parks right next to the picnic pavilion. What the hell is he doing here? He slips out of the car, his mess of blond curls getting tousled by the wind. He looks like he came straight from the gym. He's still in his Rays tech shirt and shorts. Seeing me, he gives me a wave, that All-American smile melting me.

Goddamn it, girl. Get yourself together.

I huff, dropping the biodegradable plates I'm holding into the trash can, and march over to him. "Are you lost?" I call.

He glances around, shrugging himself into a grey half-zip fleece. "Mickler's Landing, right? You're here, which must be a pretty good sign." He slips on his Ray-Bans, and the kitty is officially purring at the image of this sexy Ken doll smiling at me like I'm where his world stops.

Oh, I am in so much trouble.

"Ryan, what are you doing here?" I press.

"I'm getting certified," he says with a shrug. "Shit, is it too late to sign up?"

"Yes," I say, as behind me Joey says, "No."

Ryan turns to him, flashing him that winning smile. "Hey, I'm Ryan. Nice to meet you."

"Joey Ford, Volunteer Coordinator." Joey shakes his hand. Two blond beach boys with curls and charm for days.

Goddamn it.

"You're just in time," Joey says. "All you gotta do is fill out the release for the FWC, and then we're cookin' with avocado oil."

"Perfect," Ryan replies, glancing down at the form. He screws up his eyes like he needs reading glasses. "Whoa, that's a lot of fine print. Where do I sign, chief?"

"Just put your name here, phone number here, and address here," says Joey, pointing at the blank spots on the form. "And then the John Hancock goes right here," he adds, tapping the bottom of the form.

Ryan flashes me a smile and then starts filling out the form, dramatically turning his back as if it's private information. "Don't want you knowing where I live," he teases.

I huff, turning away too. I don't know why I'm so annoyed. It's not like I wasn't talking it up to him. We fell asleep last night with me walking through my to-do list for the day.

The truth is that I don't think I am annoyed. In fact, I'm annoyed at myself for *not* being annoyed. I like that he's here. I like that he's smiling at me and flirting with me and following me like the sweet puppy that he is.

"Hey," says the lanky Boy Scout with dark hair, eyes wide as he takes in Ryan. "Dude, you're Ryan Langley. You're like—awesome! I saw you play the Lightning last month over in Tampa. You got a goal *and* an assist."

Ryan smiles at him, handing the clipboard over to Joey. "Yeah, that was a fun night. What's your name?"

The kid stumbles all over himself in his rush to get closer. "Uhh—Tyler. My name's Tyler."

"And I'm Evan," says Freckles, hurrying forward too.

Pretty soon, Ryan is surrounded by the Boy Scouts, laughing and taking selfies with them. All the volunteers inch closer, drawn by his charm. My stupid heart beats faster as he takes a picture between the cute, blonde college girls with a smile only for me.

"Okay," I call after a minute, clapping my hands again. "We really need to get started. We don't want to waste any of Ranger John's valuable time."

"Hey, Tess," Ryan calls over at me, his arm still on the shoulder of the kid wearing the sea turtle shirt. "What kind of photos does a turtle take?" he asks with a big grin. "Shell-fies," he replies before I can open my mouth.

I roll my eyes at his lame joke, but the kids crack up as he leads the way over to the pavilion.

"Let's do this thing," he says, giving me a flirty wink. "I'm turtle-y ready to go."

"Oh, you're shell-arious," I deadpan, and he laughs out loud, sauntering off to take his place at the picnic table by Ranger John.

This is fine. He can have his little surprises and his punny jokes. I may be losing my heart to this blond hockey boy, but I'm not about to lose my head. Tess is still firmly in control.

48
Tess

Volunteer day was a huge success, mainly because Ryan stole the freaking show. He was so helpful. He kept all the kids interested and asked insightful questions of Ranger John. He carried equipment, assisted with demonstrations, and at the end of the afternoon, he had everyone pose in a picture that he posted to his Instagram account. The boys flipped when he handed them his phone and let them tag themselves in it.

Then Nancy and Cheryl invited the Out of the Net team out for appetizers and Ryan declared himself my plus one. The bar is packed for happy hour with live music set up in the front. The walls hum with vibrations as they do a cover of Prince's "Nothing Compares to You."

Meanwhile, Ryan and I are in the gender-neutral bathroom with the door locked, his hand pressed over my mouth, my back pressed up against the graffitied wall, as his dick pounds into my slick pussy. How we got here, I have no idea. I blame the chardonnay . . . okay, and the fact that I spent a whole afternoon with this handsome, attentive man looking at me like I was his sunrise.

Everyone else was there for the turtles. Ryan was there for *me*.

"Come for me," he says, his breath hot in my ear as he holds me pinned to the wall.

I ride the high of this feeling. Life pulses just outside the door, a world of people laughing and drinking, oblivious to the fact that Ryan and I are locked in this room, bodies trembling as we chase our releases.

"Oh my god," I moan against his hand.

"If you think you're gonna walk out of here without coming on my dick—" His threat falls away as he pulls out, leaving me gasping.

"No, don't stop," I pant.

"Turn around," he growls. "Hands on the sink. Bend the fuck over."

My greedy pussy does a little dance as I realize exactly what he intends to do next. He threatened to do it on our first date. It turned me all the way on that night too. "Do it," I say, dropping my hands down to grip either side of the sink.

My leggings and undies have already been ripped down my legs so I could spread them. I've got them twisted around my left ankle, my ass and pussy bare for him.

His hand smooths over the curve of my butt as he groans. I watch him in the mirror, looking down at me with such open hunger in his eyes. Watching him look at me like this is gonna make me shatter without a touch.

"Ryan . . . "

He looks up, blinking as he sees us in the mirror. Our reflections hold eye contact as he simmers with need.

"Do it," I say again.

Bringing his hand away, he gives me a sharp slap.

I gasp, biting my lip as the delicious sting rockets from my ass straight to my clit. I groan, wiggling my hips a little as his hand drops down and smooths over the spot.

"Again," I say, watching his reflection in the mirror.

He slaps me again, and we're both groaning now. Dropping to one knee, he peppers kisses over the spot, soothing the burn with his tongue. Then he's back on his feet.

Slap.

"Oh, god," I whimper, loving that I get to watch the motion of his hand in the mirror. I can't take much more teasing, though. My pussy is dripping. I need to come. "Fuck me, Ryan," I beg. "Please, baby, please—"

He grabs me tight by the hips, one hand smoothing up my lower back, under my shirt, as he shoves his other hand between my thighs. His fingers open me up, then the head of his dick is there and I'm sinking back against him, hungry for that feeling of fullness.

God, I've missed fucking with real dicks. And Ryan's is so pretty and long, and he knows just what to do with it. He gets himself in position, the tip of his dick sitting right where I want it. He looks up in the mirror, eyes dark, and nods. Holding each other's gaze, I push, and he pulls, and I take him to the freaking hilt on a silent scream. The moment I feel his hips pressing against my ass, there comes a loud knock, ratting the metal door.

Bang. Bang.

I swallow my shriek, my thighs clenching around Ryan's dick as he barks out, "In a minute!"

I tremble with a silent laugh, my hands still gripping tight to the sink.

"Hurry up in there," the guy shouts back.

Ryan folds himself around me, his hands joining mine on the sink. "You heard him," he says, playfully nipping my neck. "Hurry up and come before you get us thrown out."

"Come with me," I beg, holding his gaze in the mirror.

"Watch me. Keep your eyes on me. Don't look away."

"Oh god," I whimper again, my lips parted as I breathe out. This is so erotic, so raw. I've never held this kind of eye contact with another person during sex before. I've never been able to see so much before. I can see him moving against me—my naked flesh, his grasping hands, my trembling shoulders.

He rocks his hips against my ass, his dick filling me so full. I hold tight to the sink, mesmerized as I watch him worship me. I meet him thrust for thrust, the flames of my orgasm burning hotter, spreading outwards.

"You're so beautiful. You ride my dick like a queen. God—you're all fucking mine—"

I tip my head back, fighting the urge to close my eyes, as his hand snakes around and begins teasing my clit. "Yes—*yes*—I'm so close—right there—" My words choke off on a squeak as I swallow a scream.

"Come," he commands. "Finish with me."

I shut my eyes, unable to take another second of this vulnerability, this connectivity. I let my every sense latch onto the physical as I shatter, undone by the way he makes me feel. I come so hard, my pussy clenching down tight on his dick as his hips stutter and he collapses over my back, coming inside me. His hands cover mine on the sink as he looks for something to hold on to, something to anchor him as he comes apart. Someone.

Me.

He's holding on to me. We're holding on to each other. The terrifying truth hits me as our eyes connect in the mirror again and I see that perfectly sated look on his face. He's happy. He's so goddamn content. He's here for me. He wants me.

But this can't last. This *won't* last. Nothing ever does. I'm broken, and I break things. We're holding on to each other so tight because we know this ship is already sinking. And I'm the iceberg. It's always me.

The clock is ticking. It pulses in my ears to the rhythm of the Prince cover band playing not twenty feet away from us on the other side of that locked door. *Tick, tick, tick.*

How soon before he lets go?

How soon before I'm back to saving myself?

It's time to do what I do best. It's time to let go first.

49
Ryan

"Wait, say that again," I say, heart in my throat.

Doc Brady just laughs. "You heard me, Langley."

I grin ear to ear, swinging my legs off the PT table. "Yeah, but I'm gonna need you to say it again."

"You're cleared, Langley. You can start skating again," he repeats.

My heart does a double flip. "Doc, I'm gonna kiss you on the lips," I tease, hopping off the table and holding my arms open.

He laughs and steps back. "I think my fiancé will object. He's very territorial."

I drop my hands. "Yeah, he'd probably kill me."

"No lie," he says with a satisfied smirk, his eyes back on his tablet.

Doc Brady's fella is an MMA fighter or something like that. I met him last week. He's tattooed and burly with a mafia vibe and a lip piercing. He clashes spectacularly with Brady's clean-cut, nerdy look, but who am I to judge when opposites attract?

Brady glances over the rim of his square-framed glasses at me. "We're gonna keep you in the compression sleeve for a bit yet, just to give the knee some added stability."

"Yeah, cool," I say with a nod.

"And I want you sticking to the ice routine morning and night. And you said you've been using the sauna to help with inflammation?"

I bite back my smirk. Sure, we'll go with that. "Yeah, saunas. I'm a recent convert. Highly restorative."

"Well, good. Keep it up. Your range of motion is great. Strength and conditioning team are all pleased. Scans look good. Pain and inflammation are managed. At this point, if I keep you off the ice any longer, you're liable to cause a new injury out of sheer boredom. Am I right?"

"Doc, I'm climbing the damn walls," I reply earnestly.

He laughs, giving my shoulder a pat. "Then get out of here, Langley. Go join practice."

"And I'm cleared for the game this Saturday?"

"So long as you make it through practice in one piece, I don't see why not," he replies.

I practically fly out of the physical therapy center and through the gym, pulling my phone from my pocket. I instantly dial Tess, holding the phone up to my ear.

She answers on the second ring. "Hey—"

"Babe, I'm cleared," I say with a huge grin.

"Oh—" I hear the sound of a shuffle. "Hold on—"

I keep moving down the hallway towards the locker room as she goes quiet on her end. She's back in moments.

"Ry, that's wonderful news," she says. "Did Rachel clear you?"

"Well, Brady did, but yeah," I reply.

"That's so great. I'm so happy for you."

Her voice is like a shot of serotonin straight to my chest. I keep smiling as I hurry down the hallway. "Yeah. I'm cleared for Saturday's game, and I want you to go. Tess, I want you there."

"You want me to go to your game?" she says, and I know she's looking for an exit.

Fuck.

She's been doing this all damn week. It's like, when we're together, everything is perfect. She's present and loving and so much damn fun. We laugh together and talk. It's never been so easy for me to just *be* with someone. Last night, she even let me walk her through the basics of Mario Kart. She was bored for every second of it, but then as a tease she blew me while I tried to play a round. I lost. Fucking worth it.

When we're together, we don't feel like two people at different stages of life who want different things. Nothing feels awkward or forced or rushed. She's cool and funny, and she's so sexy it will quite literally kill me.

I just want a chance. I want her to stop thinking about life as a chase where she's perpetually on the run. What is it gonna take to let me catch her?

"I'm not sure tomorrow will work," she says. "I've got a lot of planning to do for the gala next week."

"Well, that works perfectly," I reply, forcing my tone to stay bright. "Because tomorrow is Friday. You can work tomorrow and come have fun at the game Saturday."

"Ryan—"

"There are hotdogs, Tess. And churros . . . and popsicles," I tease.

She sighs. "Puppy, why are you only naming the phallic-shaped snacks?"

"Because I want a mental picture of you deep throating a churro in the stands while I'm out on that ice," I reply. "We both know you'll be pretending it's me."

She laughs, and I breathe a sigh of relief. Humor is the only thing I've found to rein her back in when she starts going to the dark place.

"And hey, are we still on for karaoke tonight?"

"Umm . . . "

Now it's me laughing. "Tess, I told you we're in the clear. If Shelbs and Sully were sitting on a sex tape, we'd know it by now. The camera didn't record anything. Now, if you *want* to record a session sometime, that can be arranged—"

"Ryan," she cries.

"What?" I say, still laughing. "You're telling me you've never thought about it? How the hell else am I supposed to survive the away games?"

"You're incorrigible, and I'm hanging up."

"I'm enchanting, and I'm hanging up first," I tease. I'm right outside the locker room. If I go in there talking to my girl with this sappy look on my face, I'll get ribbed for a week. "Wait—so I'll see you later, right?"

"Bye, Ryan." She hangs up.

Yeah, I'll see her later. Tess Owens is it for me. I intend to keep seeing her for the rest of my forever.

50
Tess

I walk into Riptide's Bar and Grill and glance around. It's a typical Americana-style bar with a mess of stuff on the walls and a menu too thick to be of any quality. Never trust a place that offers gator bites and quesadillas *and* pasta carbonara. They can do one of those things well, certainly not all three.

A pretty, college-aged girl in a Rip's baseball shirt and cutoff jean shorts shows me outside. There are tons of picnic tables, both covered and uncovered. A stage area is set up off to the left. A central bar stands covered with stools all the way around it.

It's nearly 7:00 p.m., which means a dusting of clouds makes for a pink and purple cotton candy-colored sunset over the grey ocean. It's chilly too. I'm glad I have my sweater layered over my dress. The seating area is dotted every few feet with domed space heaters.

"Tess!"

I turn to see Rachel standing at the end of a table with a beer in her hand, laughing and waving me over. It looks like half the Rays are already here. I see Jean-Luc and his wife Lauren and their kids, Walsh and his girlfriend Amber, Novy and Morrow. Caleb and Jake are sitting with Ryan. His back is turned, and in all the commotion, he hasn't noticed me yet.

"Well, well, well . . ."

I spin around to see Shelby standing right behind me with a little mini version of Josh balanced on her hip. He's adorable, with dark hair, big dark eyes, and pouty pink baby lips. "Hi Shelb—"

"Nuh-uh," she says, wagging a finger in my face. "If you think I don't know what you did—"

"Shhh," I cry, pulling her away from the rest of the group. "Ohmygod, it's been days. Why the hell didn't you say anything?"

"Why didn't *you* say anything?" she counters with a false whisper, eyes narrowed at me.

"Because—well, what was I gonna say?" I huff. "'Hey Shelby, check your nanny cam if you want a shot of me crawling in a devil costume to suck Ryan's dick.'"

She chokes on a laugh. "Oh god, I didn't actually see that part."

"I—wait, what?" I blink at her, heart racing.

"Yeah, the camera angle isn't great, so I really only saw the stuff that happened in the middle of the room," she replies. "The stuff against the changing table was out of shot. But thanks for the visual—"

"What do I need to say or do for this to never be mentioned again?" I say, gripping her arm.

Baby Josh reaches out a chubby hand, putting it on my wrist.

Shelby considers for a moment, her caramel brown eyes searching my face. "You can sing 'Careless Whisper.' Now. Open the show."

Oh my god. Of all the possible punishments, she has to pick this one? I'm an only-sings-in-the-shower kind of girl for a reason. I can't carry a tune to save my life. "Pick something else," I plead. "Anything else."

Her eyes narrow as she surveys me. "No."

I drop my hands away from her. "You're a monster."

She doesn't back down. "And you fucked a Ray on my baby's stuffed animals while dressed as the literal devil. So . . . "

I bite my lip, tears of mirth stinging my eyes. Oh, this is going to be god-awful. And she'll have only herself to blame. "Fine. Any other requests?"

She considers. "Yeah, actually, I'd love it if you could throw a little Shania in there too."

"Late '90s or early 2000s?"

She puts a finger under her chin, bobbing the squirmy baby on her hip. "Hmm . . . late '90s, I think."

"Consider it done," I reply. Then I lean in. "And then we are *never* discussing this again."

Smiling, she nods and walks past me to go find her seat.

Well . . . fuck. What happens when you get booed off a karaoke stage? Do you have to leave the establishment? Does your name go up on a wall of offenders inside the restaurant?

"Hey, gorgeous."

Ryan comes up behind me, his hands brushing my shoulders. Leaning in, he kisses the back of my head, and I fight the urge to lean into him. Remembering where we are, I go stiff and pull away, turning in his arms to break our connection.

"Ryan . . . "

He sighs, dropping his hands away. "Seriously? Are we still pretending to be just friends? Babe, the team doesn't care—"

"We *are* just friends," I reply. "Friends who fuck to feel good. That was the rule. That was *your* rule," I add, giving him a firm look.

I don't know why I'm trying to pick a fight with him. This just feels too public. And everything is still too unsettled. *I'm* unsettled. I haven't heard a word from Troy in days, but I know he's still having me followed. I've had the feeling of being watched when I walk in to work, when I go to the coffee shop down the street from the bungalow. There's a grayish-black SUV that I see around all the time.

And the last thing I want to do is hurt Ryan or involve him any deeper in my mess. He doesn't even know about the shredded documents hiding in my closet. He doesn't know about the harassment or the stalking. I don't want him to know. I want us to stay in our shiny pink bubble of privacy and orgasms and feeling good.

Which is probably about to pop anyway once he hears me sing.

He searches my face, actively fighting the urge to reach out and touch me. "What is it? What's wrong?"

I do what I do best and deflect. "The camera records. Shelby knows what we did."

"Oh . . . shit." He lets out a little laugh and glances over his shoulder to where Shelby and Josh have just taken their seats. "Umm, well, I'll talk to them—"

"No need," I reply with a weak smile. "She already exacted her revenge on me. It's done."

"Wait—revenge?" His eyes go wide. "Tess, what—"

"I have to go."

"Tess—"

"Go find your seat," I say, giving his hand a squeeze. "You wanted something to record to take with you to your away games, right? Well, this is as good as you're gonna get."

Ignoring his confused protests, I slip past him and make my way to the stage.

AS it happens, belting out god-awful renditions of 'Careless Whisper' and 'Any Man Of Mine' to a generous crowd is a great way to flip that 'fuck it' switch. By the time I sing my last note and the crowd goes crazy, I beeline straight for Ryan, determined to get drunk.

"That was amazing," he calls, waving his phone. "I got it all recorded."

I just roll my eyes. Of course, he finds my utter lack of singing talent charming.

"Add it to the collection," Shelby teases from across the table.

I glare at her, hands on my hips. "Now, is that *never* talking about it again?"

She just laughs and mimes zipping her lips shut as she moves off to go say hi to the new arrivals.

I sit down at the picnic table between Ryan and Caleb, and Cay slides me a hard cider.

"Peach?" I say, sniffing the glass.

"Strawberry," he replies.

"Mmm." I take a sip, delighting in the taste. I like my beers the same way I like my desserts: sweet and fruity. And Caleb may not drink, but he's a whizz at ordering them for me. I think he used to be a bartender during his dark days.

Ryan watches us, one brow raised.

"Oh," I say with a laugh, patting Caleb's shoulder. "It's our weird friend thing. Mars and I have sea turtles, Cay and I have fruity beer, and Jake and I are actually friends."

He just shrugs, checking out the menu.

We all settle in as a pair of ladies not affiliated with the Rays take the mic to perform a Streisand ballad. The cute hostess is actually a waitress, too. She leans her hip against the edge of the tables, laughing and flirting with the unmarried guys as she takes orders, flicking that black ponytail over her shoulder whenever she thinks Novy is looking.

"Here you go, honey," the waitress says at Ryan over the opening notes of a second show tune. She bats her lashes as she slides him his beer. "Can I get you anything else?"

Let's be clear, she's *only* asking Ryan. Cay, with his shiny wedding ring and handsy husband, may as well be invisible. And I'm most definitely the competition. I have a feeling we'll have to smash our own tomatoes if we want ketchup tonight. Either that or Ryan can pull some out of her shirt later.

"Nah, I'm all good for now, Cami, thanks," he says, totally oblivious. "Hey, they're actually pretty good," he says, his eyes locked on the ladies in sequined shirts trading melodies.

Cami is still just standing there, waiting to see if she'll get a look or a word. I raise a brow at her, and she casts me a simpering smile before she saunters off.

The ladies at the mic finish their stirring rendition of 'The Way We Were,' and everyone claps as they take their seats. When Morrow is called up to sing, the crowd goes wild. Even more than the Rays home crowd is the table in the back corner of screaming women. Their hair is cut and styled similarly, their makeup effortlessly contoured, and all of them are wearing cleavage-bearing shirts and jeans and skirts so tight they probably had to be sewn into them.

I peer around Caleb to get a better look. "Umm . . . guys? What's with the Morrow fan section? Is he that much of a ladies' man?"

Ryan and Caleb both follow the line of my gaze. Ryan groans as Caleb rolls his eyes.

"What?" I say, glancing between them.

"Those are the puck bunnies," Caleb replies.

"Really?" I look again, curious. Rachel told me about this phenomenon. Apparently, it happens across pretty much all the major sports. Women will form fan clubs and haunt all the local favorites of the team—restaurants, coffee shops, clubs. "Isn't it possible that they're just actual fans of the sport?" I say with a shrug.

"Do you see any of us playing hockey right now?" Josh asks from across the table, balancing his son on his knee.

"Fans we like," Jake adds from the other side of Cay. "You know, I think I actually have the most interesting conversations with female fans." He turns to Caleb. "Remember that stats chick in college who did a paper on your shooting ratios?"

Caleb nods. "Her research got me a hat trick in my next game."

"Yeah, fans like that we like," Jake says again.

"So, you wouldn't call the bunnies fans of the sport?" I ask.

"Oh, they're fans of something," Josh says.

"Well, what do they think is going to happen from sitting way over there?" I say, casting my eye back to the corner. "If they're looking for a date or a hookup, why don't they actually try talking to you guys?"

Caleb groans as Josh snorts into his beer.

"They're not allowed over here," Ryan replies.

I turn to face him. "What?"

He just shrugs. "Rip's house rule. Puck bunnies sit over there, away from the WAGs and kids. If a Ray wants one, he has to go to them."

"You can thank Lauren for that particular rule," says Shelby, returning to the table.

"Uh-oh," I laugh. "What happened?"

"When the Rays first got to Jax, let's just say the bunnies were a little overzealous," Shelby explains. "One actually sat on J-Lo's lap. He tried to be nice about it and pushed her off. But then she plopped herself right back down, laughing like she thought he was a chair. So, he let Lauren handle it. She was sitting with me and the girls at the next table over . . . "

"Oh god," I say, glancing down the table. Lauren Gerard is a beautiful, leggy blonde with the face and temper of an angel. I can only imagine what she looks like when she's defending her man. "I bet she turned into a total banshee," I tease.

"It was scary," Josh says.

"J-Lo paid for all the bunnies' dinners for how bad Lauren made them cry," Shelby adds with a satisfied smirk.

"Noted. No sitting on Gerard's lap," I laugh, taking another sip of my beer.

The crowd cheers again as Morrow steps up to the mic. The band strikes up, and we all start to cheer as he belts out a pretty good rendition of "Can't Have You" by the Jonas Brothers.

"You know, you can sit on *my* lap," Ryan leans in to say in my ear.

I lean away, setting my beer down. "So, how often do you go bunny shopping?"

He looks at me, one brow raised. "What?"

"Come on, they can't all not know how chairs work," I tease. "Surely one has figured it out."

He just shakes his head. "Tess . . . "

"What? I bet I could find you a good one. I'm an excellent wing woman. Cay, tell him," I shout over at Caleb. "You can't judge me by any previous failures I've had with Rachel. She's impossible to shop for."

"Facts," Caleb says from my other side.

"Honestly, I feel a little vindicated now that I could never find her a good match," I admit. "I was trying to narrow it down to one when that's clearly not her style," I tease at Caleb.

"It's not mine either," he says, slinging an arm around a distracted Jake and kissing him.

"Well, it's my style," Ryan says from my other side. "I'm a one-woman kind of man."

"Would you ever let me wing woman for you?" I ask. "I bet we could find someone sweet and funny, maybe at the coffee shop or the beach? There's still time to find you a cute date for the gala next week."

He slow turns to glare at me. I know what I'm doing and so does he. "You wanna patrol the local beaches and coffee shops with me trying to find me a hot date for your gala?"

"You have a plus one invitation," I reply with a shrug.

"Hey, Ryan, I've got your chicken wings here," says Cami, stepping around the back of us. Is there a reason she needs to touch him? I don't fucking think so. I narrow my eyes at the point where her hand rests on his shoulder. She carefully takes his order off the tray, placing it all in front of him. Another guy behind her is carrying a large tray. She's too busy getting Ryan extra napkins, so that leaves the guy alone, handing out the rest of the food for our table.

The lights flash green and blue as Morrow sings his heart out at the chorus. The bunnies are all on their feet, cheering and screaming, their pomegranate martinis sloshing around.

I'm feeling sensory overload as the music pulses, the lights flash, and Cami is suddenly back, offering Ryan extra bleu cheese he didn't ask for. Her breasts brush against his arm as she leans over to set it down, saying something I can't hear over the music that makes him laugh. She's quickly called away to another table, and Ryan watches me watch her leave.

"What about Cami?" he says, his smile falling the moment she's gone.

"What about her?" I say, heart in my throat.

"She's young and cute and clearly knows how chairs work," he deadpans. "I think she'd make a great date for the gala. Should I ask her?"

The Rays around us all cheer as Morrow finishes his song, but Ryan and I may as well be alone in this crowded room. He's all I see.

"Feel free," I reply, knowing he's just trying to get a rise out of me because I hurt his feelings. But no one hates me more than me right now, so he can spare me the hurt puppy look.

"You know what, maybe she's free tonight," he says, slapping his napkin down. "Hell, maybe she's free right now. Why don't I go ask her?"

"Ryan—" I reach for him as he gets up, but he shrugs away from me, passing Morrow as he saunters past the bunnies, moving quickly towards the doors.

I sit there, staring down at the food I can't bear to eat. I'm not hungry anymore. I'm not anything.

"Jesus. That was worse than watching a car crash," Caleb says. "You're a fucking mess, Tess."

I blink away my tears, glaring at him. "Says the guy who loved his best friend for ten years and did nothing about it."

"Yeah, and if you used half the cells in that ginormous brain of yours—better yet, if you used half the sense of feeling in that bleeding heart you hold in your chest, you'd know not to make the same mistakes I did," he snaps at me.

A tear slips down my cheek and I quickly wipe it away. "I don't know what to do, Cay. Everything is so . . . broken."

He sighs. "You're not broken, Tess. You're scared. What did Mars say the other day?"

I close my eyes and repeat the words. "Life is short."

"Damn fucking right," he replies. "Life is short. Do you really want to spend the whole of it running? Or would you like to slow things down and live a little?"

His words pierce me like an arrow through the chest. "I wanna live." I drop my face into my hands and groan, elbows on the table. "Oh god, I'm so tired of running."

"Then go home to that sweet idiot who loves you," he says, his voice in my ear as the music gets louder. Shelby is on the stage now, ready to belt out some Kesha.

I glance up, meeting his dark gaze.

"Stop living life like you're fucking scared of it. I lived that way for ten years. I'll never get those ten years back. *Go.*" He shoves my food away from me and points over his shoulder towards the doors. "Go home, Tess."

Home.

I've never had a home. My mother's apartment certainly wasn't a home. Neither were any of the half-dozen guest rooms and couches I drifted around as a kid. And even as I was madly in love with Troy, our home never felt like a space I defined. We lived in his family's property, using their decorators, mirroring their tastes.

The closest I've ever felt to feeling like I had a home was when I lived with Rachel. But even then, the apartment itself never felt like home. We made it homey with our decorations and the smells of our cooking and baking, the sound of our laughter. *She* was my home.

Go home.

Now Rachel has a new home and he's sitting right next to me. Caleb is her home. Caleb and Jake and Ilmari. Maybe that's why she and I get along so well. We don't find our home in places or things. We find them in people. For however brief a time, Rachel was my home. Now, we both need to move on.

Go home to Ryan.

That's what Caleb is implying—that despite all the odds, despite all the feelings of insecurity I have, telling me I don't deserve this, I have a home again. It's not Ilmari's bungalow. It's the man sharing it with me. The sweet, twenty-two-year-old man who plays hockey and loves Mario Kart and can never answer a single text message. The man who always puts the oven on the wrong setting even though you tell him three times. The man who needs a haircut and fucks me like a god. The man who makes me laugh and listens when I speak and holds me when I cry. The man who's been showing me every day since the day we met how he intends to put me first.

Ryan Langley.

My Ryan.

My home.

"Tess?" Caleb says, a dark brow raised.

I turn to face him, fresh tears in my eyes.

He looks at me, his gaze darting left then right. Then he smiles, just the corner of his mouth lifting, satisfied with what he sees. "There she is. Hey, stranger."

I smile, swallowing back the emotion thick in my throat. "Tell Rachel I went home?"

He nods, patting my thigh. "You got it."

Shoving myself up from the picnic table, I hurry after Ryan, not bothering to look back.

51
Tess

I stand outside the front door of the bungalow. Ryan's car sits in the driveway. I thought about what I want to say to him the whole drive home, how I want to apologize, what pieces of me I want to offer to him. He needs my vulnerability. He deserves it. I can't keep holding back from him if I want to see where this could go.

Vulnerability. Great, my favorite thing.

I could stand out here all night, freezing my butt off, or I could go inside and face the freaking music.

Big girl panties, Tess.

Taking a deep breath, I slip my key into the lock and turn it, letting the door creak softly open. The living room lamps are on, letting off a warm glow. The TV is on too. I can hear the telltale sounds of Mario Kart. Hurt Ryan came home to play video games, taking comfort in the familiar. Is his heart aching like mine?

I step inside the door, shutting it softly, and lean against it.

You made it inside the house.

Now I just need to walk down the hall.

"She's not here," he calls after a minute.

I grip tighter to my keys. "What?"

"Cami," he calls. "She's not here. You don't have to hide by the door, Tess. It's just me."

I will my body to move, walking down the little hallway. I pause at the end, peering around.

Ryan sits alone on the middle of the couch, game controller in hand. He glances over at me, his hurt expression tearing me apart. The Mario Kart theme music is the soundtrack for the heavy silence hanging between us. I'm convinced those repetitive, high-pitched jingles will play over the sound system when I eventually arrive in hell.

Feeling too anxious to just start blurting out all my thoughts and feelings, I cross over into the kitchen, dropping my purse and backpack down on the counter. And because I'm a mess who always has to do something with her hands, I jerk open the fridge and snatch up a bottle of water.

Letting the door shut, I slowly turn. "Ryan, I—"

"We can't keep doing this," he says, tossing the game controller down. The motion freezes the screen, and the music—thank fucking God.

"Doing what?"

He slings an arm over the back of the couch, looking intently at me. "You can't keep pushing me away. I know you've been hurt before, but any man who would cheat on you is a fucking idiot. I'm not that man, Tess. So, stop testing me."

"Wait—this isn't about Troy being a cheater," I say, setting the bottle of water down. "Is that really what you think?"

"Why else would you be trying to shove me at Cami to see if I stick? You thought the same thing about Drunk Cleopatra, remember? Tess, I'm not that guy."

God, how did this all get so inside-out?

"I know Troy's cheating wasn't about me, Ryan. He cheated because he was weak and lonely and desperate for external validation. He's always needed other people to build him up and make him feel like the man. And I know you're not a cheater. I know you're not Troy."

He launches off the couch. "Then what is this about? If I'm not in your arms, and if we're not fucking, then you shut me out and shut me down. It's like we don't exist outside of these four walls," he says, gesturing around the room.

"I swear, I'm not trying to push you away," I say. "I'm just . . . succeeding."

"Tess, *talk* to me," he presses. "What is this about—"

"It's about *you*," I cry. "It's about me trying to stop you from throwing your life away, waiting on me to give you something when I've told you I never can!"

"Jesus, fuck." He drags both hands through his hair. "Is this about what you said to me at the wedding last month? That bullshit about me wanting to marry you?"

"Ryan—"

"Have I *ever* asked you to marry me?" he shouts. "Have the words 'Marry me, Tess' ever left my mouth in the form of a question?"

"No—"

"Have you ever even asked me my views on the subject?" he says, crossing his arms.

"No."

"No, you haven't," he snaps. "Because you've been too busy running scared, right? Poor Tess can't plan for the future. All she can think about is running from her past. Well, let me enlighten you. I don't give a shit about marrying you. Why would I?" he adds with a shrug. "Neither of us are religious, and we're both U.S. citizens. I don't need the tax benefits and, frankly, I'd rather keep my finances separate from my partner—not because I intend to withhold from her, but because my taxes are a fucking mess."

Of course, my calculating Virgo has thought it all out. "Ryan—"

"That is all to say *nothing* about how unnecessary I see the institution to be," he says over me. "Love is love, right? Look at Doc and her guys. Just look at the bullshit they're having to deal with, picking who gets to be married and who gets a commitment ceremony. And what are they gonna do when they have kids? Who gets to be the father? It's fucking bullshit."

"And then look at you," he says, waving a hand at me. "All you want is out of a marriage that no longer works for you, and yet you're trapped. It's been three fucking years, and you can't break free of that asshole. It's madness."

I hold back my tears as he paces away from me with a muttered curse.

Then he's closing the space between us, taking me by the shoulders and holding my gaze. "If it will stop you running scared, I'll make you this vow right here, right fucking now: Tess Owens, I will *never* ask you to marry me. Those words will never pass my lips, okay?"

Our bodies hum with electricity at being so close. It's like mine knows to crave him. It knows he's nearby. Does he feel the same? The tremble in his fingers makes me think he does.

"But let's not for one more second distract ourselves with talk of a marriage neither of us want or need," he says, still holding tight to me. "This isn't about that. Just admit it: You're terrified."

I gasp, leaning away from him. My resolve hardens at the look in his eyes. "I'm not afraid of anything," I say, heart racing.

"Liar." His hands slide up my shoulders to grip my face. "You're terrified of this. You're terrified of me, of what you feel for me."

I huff, the sound catching in my throat. "You think you know me?"

"I do."

"Why would I be afraid of you?"

"You're afraid of what I can offer you," he replies. "You're afraid of what I represent."

"And what is that?" I say, trying to ignore the way my body lights up at his touch, the way I'm leaning closer to him even now.

"Hope," he murmurs, his lips inches from mine.

I close my eyes tight.

Hope. That word is dangerous. That word builds you up and tears you down, leaving nothing left but a charred and broken mess. Hope that my mother could change, that she could learn to stay. Hope that someone could want me. Hope that Troy was the one, that we would be happy. Hope that his family would accept me. Hope that we'd find a way through, that he could learn to love me again.

"No. I don't have hope—"

"Yes, you *do*," he presses, his hands drifting down my shoulders. "You're protecting yourself with this bullshit about living in the now. But I see you, Tess. You have hope hidden away that you deserve more than what you've settled for in the past."

How does he know me like this? He doesn't get to know me. I can't let him in.

"No one has ever put you first, Tess. Not your family, not Troy, not even Rachel." He says the words so casually, tearing me open. "She has her own life, her own priorities. I give you hope that you deserve to come first."

"I know what I deserve," I say, my walls hardening as I fight him even now.

"Then *tell* me," he challenges, his gaze fierce and direct. He's not backing down. "Tell me what you deserve. Say it out loud."

I lean away, my hands going to his wrists as I try to pull him off me, break our connection.

He huffs, watching me squirm, even as his hold on me is gentle. "You talk a big game, Tess. You're larger than life—your opinions, your ambitions. And you put on such a good act for everyone. Laughing Tess. Fun Tess. Flirty Tess. You wear those labels like they're party masks, floating through life just hoping people won't actually try and see who dwells underneath."

"I know who I am," I counter, knowing it's bullshit. So does he. For better or worse, Ryan *knows* me. It's barely been a few months, but he knows me. Certainly, better than Troy ever did.

"Scared Tess," he presses, keeping me captive with the truth. "Lonely Tess. Angry Tess who just wants to feel something, right? How many times have you said it to me? We're friends who fuck to feel good. But you don't want mindless orgasms. And I don't want anything Cami or Cleopatra or any other woman has to offer. How could I when *you* exist?"

"Ryan, please . . . " He's still looking at me like I'm his world. It's overwhelming and humbling and I don't know how I deserve it. I don't know how to earn it.

"You deserve a second chance, Tess," he says, reading me like a goddamn book. "At everything—love, adventure. I want to help you." He brushes my hair back, tucking it behind my ear. "You're my dream girl. So long as you're on this earth and breathing, I know what I want. I know what I'm working towards."

And now I'm clinging to him, words failing me. I need him to see me. I need him to understand how my vulnerability works. Sometimes I can't speak. Sometimes I can only do. I gaze up at him, reaching out with my soul, begging him to catch me as I fall. Begging him to let us fall together.

Stepping in, his left arm wraps around my waist as he cups my cheek with his right and tips my face up, searching my lost expression. "You're not ready to tell me how you feel, and that's fine. But Tess, you are gonna *show* me."

"How?" I say, willing to try. "What can I do?"

"Show me how you feel. We're done fucking without feelings. We have been for a while. So, take off your panties and put them on the counter. Now."

My insides flutter with need and anticipation. "Ryan—"

"Don't say another word," he says, his fingers pressing against my lips. "You're gonna show me how you feel about me, Tess." He releases me, stripping out of his T-shirt and dropping it to the kitchen floor. "We're fucking with feelings. All of them. Every single one. Give me your rage and your passion, all your broken fucking dreams. Show me how much you care."

Oh, thank God.

I don't have to say it. Our communication goes so much deeper. Souls can speak with more than words, and mine is crying out for him. It's almost like I can hear his, too, calling to me, begging me to come home. Come find him. Come set his world back on its proper axis.

"Show me," he pleads again, kicking off his shoes.

I lift my shaking hands to the opening of my long, white sweater and peel it off my shoulders, dropping it to the floor. He takes me in, standing in the middle of the kitchen in my simple wrap dress. It's black with little red and white flowers dotting the fabric. Slowly, I lift my hands and undo the tie at my waist, tugging the front open until I can drop the dress to the floor.

Now I'm standing in the kitchen in my plain white bra and blue cotton panties. But Ryan is looking at me like I'm wearing the finest La Perla. He steps in, shirtless, and grabs me by the face, pressing his lips to mine, savoring my kiss. It's fast and hard and then he's pulling back, his fingers digging into the skin of my back, unhooking the clasps of my bra. Gently, he drags the straps from my shoulders, tossing the useless bra to the floor.

"Show me the way you ache for me," he commands. "Show me the way your body craves mine like a drug."

I nod once, reaching out for him.

But he leans away. "Your panties, Tess. I told you to take them off." He shucks his athletic pants to the floor, stepping out of them, his hand palming the bulge in his grey boxer briefs. "Then put your hands on the counter and bend over."

Usually, our lovemaking is like a dance. He's fun and playful, letting me tease him and domme him and devastate him with my toys. His energy tonight is different. He needs something different. My insensitivity at Rip's has him spinning. He's craving control. And he wants me to cede my own. I have a choice here. Am I willing to let go?

Holding his gaze, I hook my fingers into the top hem of my panties and shimmy my hips, dropping them to my feet. Stepping out of them, I give him a slow turn before I bend over, ass just in reach of his hands. Picking up the panties with one finger, I drop them down to the countertop. Then, without looking back at him, I place both hands on the counter's edge and bend at the waist, submitting to his will.

52
Tess

My heart races out of control as Ryan steps in behind me, his hands smoothing over my hips, up the curves of my back to my shoulders. I fight a shiver as he presses in, the hard length of his erection still trapped inside his boxer briefs as he leans over me.

"I'm only going to say this once," he says, his fingers brushing up the column of my throat. "*Look* at me."

I gasp as his right hand reaches around to cup my chin and he jerks my face back, twisting my neck. My gaze trails down the length of his arm to his face. It blazes with passion and pain. I hurt him tonight with my dismissal, my feigned disinterest. I see it etched on every line of his handsome face.

"You will never push me at another woman again," he declares. "Say it."

Tears sting my eyes as my heart squeezes tight. "I'll never push you at another woman again."

"I decide who I bring into my bed."

I nod once and he lets me go, his hands smoothing back over my neck and shoulders, down my arms, memorizing my body.

"I decide who I kiss," he adds, bending over to brush his lips against my shoulder, his breath warm on my skin.

I hold back a whimper, loving the feel of him so close, his undivided attention unraveling me.

"I decide who I worship," he goes on, his hands reaching around to cup my breasts, his fingers finding my nipples and giving them each a twist.

I hiss, arching my back as I press my hips against him. My eyes are shut tight as I just feel him all around me.

"I decide who I fuck," he says, his right hand drifting down until he's cupping my pussy, his fingers spreading me open as he drags two through my wetness, circling my clit.

Heat burns through me, spreading across my hips, burrowing straight to my core. I'm on fire for this man, ready to melt. I need more than this soft teasing, but if I ask for it, I'm afraid he'll stop. He's in charge right now.

We both groan as he sinks those fingers inside me, lifting me up on my toes as I arch into his touch. "I decide who I covet, Tess," he declares, kissing my back as he teases my pussy, his free hand snaking around to gently cup my neck.

I tip my chin up, giving him more of me to hold. I love his hand at my throat. I love knowing that it's him. I love knowing he'll never hurt me. "Ryan, please," I beg, unable to keep the words mere thoughts.

"This pussy is *mine*," he growls, spearing me with his fingers again.

I whimper, holding back the orgasm desperate to break free.

"*This* is what I want," he goes on, his breath hot against my skin as he teases me with tongue and teeth. "This body. This woman with these perfect fucking curves. I want all of you. Every hour. Every day. No other woman compares to you. Fuck, you kill me, Tess. I can't breathe when you look at me, and I die when you look away. Tell me I can have you."

"Ryan—"

"Tell me you're mine," he begs, his voice hoarse with command. "Not just your pussy. Not your body. We're not friends who fuck to feel good tonight. We're more than that. God, just say that you're mine."

"I'm yours," I pant, my neck craning so I can look at him. I need him to see in my eyes. I wrap my hand around his at my throat, holding his gaze. "I'm yours," I say again. "Kiss me and fuck me. Worship me, Ryan."

His eyes go dark, and then he unleashes. Jerking his fingers out of my pussy, his other hand drops away from my throat and he leaves me gasping, holding to the counter. Then he drops to his knees behind me. "Spread your legs. Wider. Bend over more."

I barely begin to bend, my feet shifting wider on the cold tile floor, when his hands smooth over my ass and his fingers delve between my cheeks. He starts working my pussy again, his thumb pressing in at my entrance as his fingers circle my clit, spinning me up. I'm slick and warm and I know what he wants. I lift my right leg, angling my hip out as my toes grip to the bottom handle of a pull-out drawer.

With a groan, he crawls between my legs, twisting himself around to face me, nearly tipping me over as he latches on with his mouth, the back of his head hitting the cabinet.

"Ohmygod," I cry, holding to the counter with everything I have as he eats me out from his knees, my thighs practically riding his shoulders as my pussy buries his face. "Fuck—I'm gonna come," I squeal, my legs already trembling.

His arms wrap around my thighs, his hands gripping my ass cheeks hard enough to bruise as he takes my weight, working me with his mouth, his groans creating a delicious vibration that has me seeing stars.

"You're *mine*," he says, his greedy mouth sucking me. His left hand loosens, and then he's smacking my ass. The sting spreads like fire across my skin, and I whimper with need.

"Again," I beg, moving my hips against his chin, chasing my release.

He slaps me again, his hand rubbing away the sting. "Come for me," he commands. "Make me drown."

"Ohhhh god—" I slur over the words as I clench his face with my thighs, riding out my orgasm against his hot and hungry mouth. It hits me in waves. I rock against him, my arms pushing against the counter as I let it take me. With a shriek, I push off the counter, practically doing a pirouette as I try to escape the stimulation without stepping on him. "I can't," I cry, my voice a broken whimper.

He scrambles to his feet, the lower half of his face wet with my release as he chases after me, wrapping me in his arms. "Taste yourself," he demands, his hands holding firm to my shoulders. "Taste the way your body craves mine. She doesn't hide from me. She doesn't push me away. Taste her truth."

I'm still breathless as I cup his face and pull him to me like a starving animal, my lips parted, ready and waiting for that first taste. We both groan as our lips collide, our tongues flicking as we cling to each other.

Then he's breaking the kiss, leaving me desperate for more.

Grabbing me by the hips, he spins me back around to face the counter. I catch myself, hands splayed against the cold granite as he steps in behind me.

"Bend over, baby. Up on your toes."

He finally drops his briefs, dick in hand, as he presses between my thighs, seeking entrance.

I widen my stance as best I can, balancing up on my toes to help correct our height difference. He still has to bend at the knees, the backs of my thighs practically riding him as he finds my center and presses in with his tip.

We're both panting as he drops his hand away, grabbing me by the hips. "Do it," he orders, and I sink back, dropping down his length and pressing with my hips as he guides me back.

"Oh god," I cry out again. He whispers a soft curse, both of us shaking as we connect. I feel him inside me, filling me. My core heats as my pussy flutters around him, welcoming him home. "Please, baby, please," I beg, holding my hips still. I need him to stay in charge. I need him owning me, owning my body.

"Is this what you need?" he says, thrusting into me. The sound of our naked flesh slapping together echoes in my ears as he grabs a fistful of my hair, jerking my head back. "Is this what you need?" he repeats, his voice a growl as he scrapes his teeth along my neck.

"Yes." I don't bother holding back my moan, my back arching as I melt against him. I love the sting at my scalp from his strong grip. With each tug, he lights a fire in me, burning brighter. I'm going to come again. "Don't stop," I pant. "Ryan, please—fuck me. Never stop."

Never stop trying to get closer to me.

Never stop breaking down my walls.

Never stop saying I'm yours.

Please, God, just never stop.

He cries out, hammering into me from behind. Then he suddenly lets go of my hair, and it leaves me feeling weightless. I'm reeling, my hands searching for a better grip. The hand that was in my hair snakes around my neck, and again, my orgasm flickers hotter and stronger. I'm right fucking there. I just need a little more . . .

"Do it," I beg, rocking my hips against him. I drop a hand down to my clit, working the sensitive bud as his fingers tighten at my throat. "Do it," I say again. "Ryan, squeeze. Choke me, baby. I want you to—"

"Oh, fuck," he groans behind me, both hands going to my neck as he gently squeezes.

Our hips slam together, and I work my clit, centering all my feeling on his hands at my throat, restricting my air supply. "More," I rasp. "Please—*God*—"

His hands tighten as he cries out in agony and ecstasy, trying to hold back his orgasm.

"Hold on," I gasp. "Not yet—"

His body folds over mine, losing all sense of rhythm as he teeters on that edge, waiting to fall. "Please, Tess. God, baby, please—I'm dying—"

"Now," I cry.

He drops his hands away from my throat and they grip the counter to either side of my hands. He pounds into me once, twice more, and then he's crying out, coming inside me. I'm already there, my whole body wracked with trembling as my pussy holds him like a vise. It's tearing through me, leaving me breathless and weak, standing here on shaky legs.

As soon as the high crests, I begin the fall, tumbling down off orgasm mountain into serenity sea. I don't even realize I'm crying until Ryan is bent over me, soothing me with his hands and his kisses. "I will never hurt you," he says between kisses, his fingers ghosting over the place he was just squeezing tight. "Tess, I want you. I only want you." He says it over and over again. "There is no one else. Only you. God, just let me want you."

I lie there, my chest pressed against the counter, my sweaty cheek resting on the cool granite. His warm, naked body surrounds me as he whispers sweet nothings, his hands touching every part of me he can reach. So gentle. So tender.

He wants me. He worships me. I think he might love me.

I give him the truth I denied him earlier, the truth our moment of joining has revealed. It's plain as day for anyone to see, but it deserves to be said all the same. Linking his fingers with mine, I bring his hand to my lips, kissing his knuckles. "I want you too. Ryan, I want you."

53
Tess

"So, how did you two meet exactly?"

I glance sharply across the table at Rachel. She's wedged into the booth between Ilmari and Jake. I'm in the corner on our side, Ryan next to me, and Caleb on the end. It's Friday and we're all enjoying a decadent sushi lunch before the guys have to report downtown for some media event arranged by Poppy.

Ryan asked the question. In his defense, Rachel left the door wide open by cracking a joke about the time we were kicked out of a spin class for hacking the Bluetooth speaker and changing the teacher's god-awful techno music.

Rachel snatches up her Diet Coke. "Umm . . . in Cincinnati."

"Duh, we all know that, Seattle," Jake teases, taking the last salmon nigiri off the sushi boat with his chopsticks. "He asked *how* you met. Not where."

"She knows exactly what he asked," Caleb says from the table's end, grabbing the last soft-shell crab roll. "She's deflecting," he adds, dipping it in soy sauce.

"Thank you, Captain Obvious," I say.

Ryan glances between us. "What am I missing? Is it a state secret or something?"

"It's not a secret," I reply, taking a sip of my iced tea. "It's just a little embarrassing."

"It's not embarrassing," Rachel counters.

I set my drink down. "I was stumbling drunk in a gutter, okay? Rachel literally pulled me up out of the gutter, like I was a stray cat."

Around the table, the guys all go still.

"It wasn't quite as dramatic as that," Rachel says.

"It was," I press. "It was like that scene out of *Breakfast at Tiffany's* where she chases after the cat in the rain. Rachel appeared looking like . . . well, her," I say with a wave across the table. "I think you were even wearing the black dress and the pearl earrings. Meanwhile, I was the stinky, wet cat hiding in the gutter."

"Why were you in a gutter?" Jake asks, his kind eyes locked on me.

I purse my lips, trying to suppress the memories of what is arguably one of the worst nights of my life. No such luck. Opening that mental door has it all sweeping back in. I can almost feel the cold rain on my skin.

"It was my birthday," I begin. "I was supposed to be at my not-so-surprise party, but I chose to get drunk and stumble down the streets of Cincinnati instead."

"It was my first night in the city," Rachel adds. "The sport clinic took all the new residents out for dinner, hence my fancy duds."

"Why didn't you want to go to your birthday party?" Ryan asks, giving me his full attention.

I clear my throat, unabashedly holding his gaze. "Well, seeing as earlier that afternoon I caught my husband with his pants down in his office, choking his secretary with his dick, I wasn't feeling in all that festive of a mood. Especially not once I got to the surprise party and saw her blowing on a noisemaker with the same lips she used to blow my husband. So yeah, I bailed through the bathroom window and took myself drinking instead."

"Jesus." With a glare, Jake glances around the table at his partners. "If any of you ever do that to me, I'm just setting the building on fire. You've been fucking warned."

"I'm sorry, Tess," Ryan says, his hand brushing my thigh.

I shift away, snatching for my drink again. "It all worked out in the end," I say, going for a casual tone. "Rachel took me back to her hotel, dried me off, and tucked me in on her very uncomfortable sofa. I think I cried in her arms for two hours, threw up in the bathtub, and in the morning, we ate our weight in French toast. We've been best friends ever since."

Rachel gives me a weak smile. It's hard to think about where we started and not feel haunted by that most broken version of myself. That was Tess Owens at rock-freaking-bottom. Hopeless, joyless, friendless. I was too angry and embarrassed to go crawling back to Troy, back to the house that never felt like a home. I was ready to freeze in the gutter instead. I really did feel lower than a cold, wet alley cat.

But then Rachel was there, smiling down at me like a dark-haired angel. She held out her hand and literally pulled me from my misery. She took all those shattered, broken pieces of me and helped me hold them together with tape and glue. We moved in together, we cooked together, shopped for furniture and groceries. We made margaritas in our underwear and danced in the kitchen. And god but we laughed.

She's a doctor, right? She knows how to diagnose a patient and prescribe the proper medicine. In my case, the cure to the bottomless shame and despair I felt over my failed marriage was rib-cracking, spleen-rupturing levels of uncontrollable laughter.

And meaningless sex with hot women.

Oh, and copious amounts of Thai food.

"You've come so far, Tess," Rachel says from across the table. "I haven't seen you this happy in a long time," she adds with a smile at Ryan. "Jacksonville is good for you."

"So is sex with hunky hockey players," Caleb teases. "Ouch—" He hisses, glaring at Mars, who probably just kicked him under the table.

"Yeah, well you would know," Rachel teases him right back.

Across from me, Jake laughs. "Dude, did you just call Langers hunky?"

"Shit, guys, it's almost 1:00 p.m.," Caleb says, ignoring his partners as he glances down at his phone.

Collective groans go up around the table. None of them want to go to the media event today.

They all slide out of the booth, Rachel's guys each giving her a kiss in parting. Ryan and I drove together and I'm suddenly realizing that if he's leaving—

"Here," he says, holding out his keys.

I glance up. "I can't take your car."

"I'm riding with the guys. They'll drop me off later."

"But—"

"Relax," he says with a smile. "It's a set of keys, not a diamond ring. You just need a way home." And then, as if we're making it a freaking habit, he leans in and kisses me right in front of Rachel, dropping the keys in my open palm. "See you later, beautiful," he says against my lips.

And just like that, he slips out of the booth, taking all my air with him. The guys all shuffle away, leaving Rachel and I alone at the table. I glare across the empty sushi boat at her. Sharing sushi with four hockey players means there's literally nothing left, not even the ginger garnish.

"Why are you all being so cool about this?" I say, arms crossed as I stare her down.

"What do you mean?" she asks, taking a sip of her Diet Coke.

"I mean why aren't you threatening him or making him miserable with invasive questions and best friend attempts to protect my virtue? Where's the righteous indignation?"

She smirks. "What makes you think we haven't tried that already and it just didn't work?"

I roll my eyes.

"Besides, do you really need me to protect your virtue?"

"You've never liked anyone that I've dated," I press, my glare deepening.

She meets me stare for stare. "Is that what you're doing, Tess? Are you and Langley dating?"

I lean across the table. "What are you up to, Rachel Price? You always hate my partners."

"Because you always date losers who are no good for you," she replies.

I huff, leaning away. "Erica was an art historian with a degree from Brown. She played the viola *and* she spoke four languages. You're calling her a loser?"

"She was an emotional leech who bored you to death," she counters, not missing a beat. "And the sex was middling at best, you told me yourself. She wasn't a good match for you, Tess. You need . . . more. You need competence and confidence. You need excitement and playful curiosity. And you need someone who can call you on your shit," she adds with a pointed look.

"Oh, and you think a twenty-two-year-old hockey boy is all those things?"

"Tell me he's not," she parries. "Tess, I have never seen you light up the way you do around Ryan. You're comfortable with him. You're . . . *you*. What is it about him that has you so hooked? What happened?"

"I *told* you what happened," I reply, my voice lowering. "We had *sex*," I say, mouthing the last word.

She rolls her eyes, speaking at a normal volume. "I know you're having sex. That's what happened *this* week. I'm talking about before."

"Before when?"

"Before *before*," she presses. "You two have been keeping dirty little secrets for weeks. Hell, I'm pretty sure it's been months. Otherwise, how did you get so hung up on him so fast?"

"I—fuck—it was beach day, okay? We shared a sort of kismet moment."

"Yeah, the soccer ball to the head," she replies. "I was standing right there."

"No, this was after."

"After what?"

"After the beach."

Her eyes narrow. "You just said it was *on* beach day."

"It was after I left the beach," I explain. "I went back to Jake's to get ready for my dinner date with Charity and I may have slipped out of my suit and tossed it in the washing machine. And then I may have . . . wandered around naked a little."

"Oh, Tess." Rachel shakes her head, a smile quirking her lips.

"Yes, okay? He saw me naked on beach day. He was in the pantry, digging around like a raccoon, looking for more chips, and I didn't see him in there."

"And you gave him more to look at," she teases. "So, that's the big secret? He saw you naked on beach day?"

I glance back up at her.

She goes still, her smiling falling. "Oh, what the hell did you do? Did you fuck Ryan on beach day? Is that when this all began—"

"No," I rasp. "And *shush*. Do we need this whole restaurant to know our business?"

"Will you just tell me what happened—"

"We kissed, alright?" I say over her. "We—well, we shared a perfect fucking moment if you must know. He was flirty and sweet and attentive, and we kissed, and I was naked, and it was magical. And I didn't tell you because I didn't want you giving me judgy eyes or unsolicited advice—or worse, looking at me like *that*," I say, pointing at her face.

"Like what?" she replies, eyes wide.

"Like you see hope for His & Hers towels in our future," I hiss.

It's her turn to glare. "You know I would *never* give you monogramed towels as a wedding present. Is that really what you think of me?"

"This is so not about the towels. Why are you so okay with me dating Ryan?"

"Because he's good for you and he's good to you. What else could I possibly want for you in a partner?" she replies. "I'm just terrified that you're not in the right place to receive his love, and you're both gonna end up hurt. And I don't know how to talk to you about it without making you bolt even faster."

"Do you see me bolting?"

"Your running shoes are on, and you're waiting for the sound of that starter pistol," she replies honestly. "You always are, honey. And Ryan doesn't deserve that. Frankly, neither do you. We all just want you both happy. If your best happiness comes from being together, that's what we want."

I suck in a breath. "Rachel . . . "

"That sweet man is not gonna bolt," she says, pointing her finger in the direction of the restaurant windows. "Ryan Langley stays. If you want him, he's yours for the taking. If you don't, let him down gently . . . and soon. Because he is crazy about you, honey. He's in this. He's sticking. Let him stick . . . or let him go."

"I can't give him what he wants," I whisper, tears burning in my eyes.

"He wants you," she replies. "Correct me if I'm wrong, but you're the only person who can give him that."

"He wants a version of me that I don't know if I'm ready to be," I explain.

"And what version is that?"

I swallow down the emotion sitting thick in my throat. "Wild Tess," I whisper. "The Tess who laughs and dances in her underwear. Free Tess who says what she thinks and takes what she wants. Fun Tess who plays with toys and fucks with joyful abandon."

"He wants *you* then," she says with a soft smile. "The woman you just described is the Tess I know and love. He sees you too, doesn't he?"

I nod, glancing down at the empty sushi boat. "Yeah, I think he does."

"And you're terrified of being seen," she summarizes.

I nod again.

"I'm sorry," she says after a quiet minute. "I want to be there for you, but I don't always get it right. I think it's time that I settle for being your friend, not your partner or your guardian, certainly not your parent. Tess, I'm sorry. If I've ever overstepped or gotten in the way, I'm really sorry."

I glance across the table. "Where is this coming from?"

She smirks. "Ryan might have yelled at me the other day."

I gasp. "He did? Oh god, what did he say?"

Her smile widens. "He called me Hades . . . and he called my guys Cerberus . . . before he told us all to back the fuck off and leave you two alone. He seems to think he can take better care of you than I can."

I laugh, picturing it in my mind. "Hades? Girl, that's probably gonna stick."

"I know. For a sweet puppy he's got some bark," she teases. "And a little bite."

I groan, wiping my tear away with a frustrated flick of my finger. "Fuck, I cannot fall for a Virgo right now. He's too centered for me, too uncomplicated."

"He's perfect for you," she counters. "You need centered and uncomplicated. Does he call you out on your crap?"

"Yes. All the freaking time. It's like I can't get anything past him."

Her smile widens. "Good. Is the sex any good?"

I glance up, letting her read my expression, and her smile turns into a laugh. Pretty soon we're both laughing, holding our sides with tears in our eyes.

"Oh, you are in so much trouble," she says with a slow shake of her head. "These Rays are something else, huh?"

"Says the woman who snagged not one but three," I reply.

"Right?" She laughs. "You're talking to the expert."

"So, what do I do, oh wise one?" I tease. "Teach me the ways of the Rays Whisperer."

She's somber for a minute, her smile falling as her tone turns serious. "Don't worry about Ryan or who you think he wants you to be. If you want to be fun Tess again, be her for yourself. Dance in your underwear, eat whipped cream from the can. Wild Tess is yours before she belongs to anyone else."

Her words coil deep in my heart, settling in my soul. Wild Tess is mine. Wild Tess is me.

54
Ryan

Jake and Caleb got a ride home with Doc from the practice arena, meaning I'm alone in the truck with Mars as he drives me back to the bungalow. I've never been alone with Mars before. It's weird. What do you say to a guy who doesn't talk? I sit in the passenger seat, gazing out the window as the palm trees pass by overhead.

"So uhh . . . how do you like living in Florida," I say, trying to break the silence.

"It's too hot," he replies, his eyes locked on the road.

"Yeah, it's hot near the equator," I mumble, feeling like an epic douche. "I mean, not that we're that close to the equator here. But like, closer than Finland or—"

"Langley?"

"Hmm?" I say, glancing over at him.

"You don't have to fill the silence."

"The awkward silence," I say under my breath.

"Silence doesn't have to be awkward. You Americans all think all silence must be an awkward silence. But two people can sit, not speaking, and simply enjoy each other's company."

I raise a brow at him. "You enjoy my company?"

He just shrugs, still not looking at me.

"That's glowing praise coming from you," I say with a smirk. "You're gonna make me blush over here."

The corner of his mouth tips up and, goddamn it, I feel like a puppy wagging his tail. I don't know why I so desperately want his validation, but I do.

"So, is that what you and Jake do together?" I tease. "You're telling me you sit in silence with him? That's like, a thing he does?"

"I don't discuss my partners or our life together," he replies.

Well, shit. Now I feel like a puppy who's just been whapped on the nose with a rolled-up newspaper.

"I know people are curious about us," he says more gently. "But there's no reason to be. We're just four people living our lives. We've chosen to live them together. Who we are to each other, and how we live, is no one's business but our own."

"Well, and Tess's," I tease. "Seeing as you entertain her in your bed. What's the deal with you two?" I add, glancing his way again.

That earns me a glance back. "Who?"

"You and Tess. Is it a friends thing? A coworkers thing?"

His mouth sets in a firm line. "Are you threatened by me, Langley?"

It's my turn to shrug. "I think any man with two cents worth of sense would feel threatened by you—as an athlete, as a man, likely as a lover. I've seen the heat you pack," I add. "I bet you keep your partners well satisfied."

"I've heard no complaints," he replies.

"And Tess?" I say again.

"She is my wife's closest friend, which must make her my friend. I will care for her and protect her as I would Rachel."

"But you don't . . . with Tess, you've never . . . "

"The only woman I have been with in the last four years is my wife," he admits.

"But . . . you've only been with Doc for like half a year," I reply. "So, you—oooh," I say, eyes wide. "You were celibate for three freaking years? How . . . why? Mars, you could have anyone you want. You're like Jason Momoa-level hot. You could literally have anyone."

"I'm picky," he says with a shrug.

His confession doesn't surprise me. "Yeah, I am too, actually," I admit. "How did you know Doc was the one?"

He turns, glaring at me. "Did I not just say I don't discuss my partners? I spoke English, yes?"

I huff. "Jeez, it was just a question. Could you not just person with me for like three minutes? I promise, I'll jump out while the truck is still moving if it'll make you feel better."

Then he shocks the hell out of me by laughing. It's deep and baritone, coming from his chest. His shoulders shake with it.

"What's so funny?" I say, eyes wide.

"Rakas said something similar to me once," he says. "On the plane. She threatened to jump out the side without a parachute."

I smirk. I can practically hear Doc's voice saying the words. "So, how did you know she's the one?" I ask again.

He considers for a moment. "It was her eyes," he says at last. "She doesn't look, she sees. From the first moment we met, she saw me. She saw what I was hiding, she saw what I needed. She sees me."

I nod, my mind wandering to Tess. I think of the way she is when all her defenses are down—when she's naked in my arms, or right on the edge of sleep. I think of our natural give and take, the easy flow of our conversations, the comfort of our silences.

"How did you know Tess was the one?" he asks, breaking my concentration.

I go still, heart racing. "Umm . . . I don't—I never said—"

"Relax," he says with a soft chuckle. "She's not here, Langley. It's just me."

"What makes you think I think she's the one?" I parry, glancing his way.

He glares at me. "Just answer the question."

He already knows half my secrets, why not know this one too? "It was her laugh," I admit. "That's what hooked me at first. And then I saw her face, and I watched the sound come out of her mouth. She was standing in the surf, the ocean a bright blue behind her. She wore those big sunglasses and the red bikini . . . " I sigh, rubbing my chest. "She laughs with her whole body."

"I've noticed," Mars replies.

"She doesn't laugh enough," I add.

"Then you must give her more reasons to do so," he replies, his tone solemn.

He makes the last turn onto Harbor Way, stopping outside the drive for unit 1006. *His* unit. I'm squatting in his house, and I never even asked.

"Hey man, about the house," I say, unbuckling my seatbelt and turning his way.

"Don't," he says, raising a hand.

"But I never asked you—"

"Stay as long as you need," he replies. "Stay for Tess. Stay for yourself. Go make her laugh."

I narrow my eyes at him. "Why are you so okay with all this? Barely a week ago, you were warning me away from her. Now, you're telling me I can keep crashing in your pad and chasing after her. Why?"

He jerks the truck into park and glances my way. "Because life is short, Ryan. Life is beautiful and short, and you only get one. Live it on purpose."

I make my way into the bungalow through the unlocked front door, and I'm instantly greeted by the sound of the blasting sound system. Dua Lipa's "Pretty Please" is playing, and I can't contain my smile.

"Hey," I call out, slipping my shoes off. "Tess?"

At that moment, the blender strikes up, adding to the chaos. I step around the corner and stop, heart swelling tight in my chest. Tess is wearing a pair of cheeky black undies and a baby pink bra, her hair down. Those auburn curls bounce around her shoulders as she dances to the beat, hips swaying. She's got a wine glass full of crushed ice in one hand, the finger of her other hand pulsing the blender in time with the music.

I lean against the wall, arms crossed as I watch her bounce on her tiptoes, singing off key. Fuck, she's the most beautiful thing I've ever seen. Mars's parting words echo in my mind. *Life is beautiful. Life is short. Live it on purpose.*

Stepping forward, I cross the kitchen towards her, shucking my shirt as I go. She sees my reflection in the microwave and gasps, spinning around.

"Ry, you scared me—"

I silence her protest with my mouth, wrapping her in my arms as we kiss. She sucks in a breath against my lips, letting out a little squeak that turns into a moan as she sinks against me. The wine glass full of crushed ice brushes against my shoulder and I hiss, flinching away. My body is on fire for her, and the chill of the glass is so cold.

"Oh—sorry," she says with a bubbly laugh, setting the glass down behind her.

It gives me an idea. With a grin, I fish my fingers inside the glass pulling out a piece of ice. She watches, eyes wide, as I pop it in my mouth.

"Oh, sweet puppy, what are you doing?" she teases, her hands brushing over my bare chest.

The heat in her eyes is fueling my fire. My dick twitches as I suck on the ice, letting it chill my tongue. I grab her face, my fingers firm on her jaw as I tip her head back, my intention clear.

She grips my shoulders as she parts her lips, her eyes lost to lust.

Leaning my face closer to hers, I dribble some of the icy water into her open mouth. She gasps, closing her lips as she swallows, some of the water dripping down her chin. I chase the water with another kiss, burying my tongue in her mouth. Hers is so warm and mine is cooled by the ice. It doesn't last long before my mouth is just as hot as hers and we're pawing at each other, desperate for more.

I shove her up against the counter, my fingers digging back inside the top of her glass. "Take your bra off."

She doesn't hesitate, jerking the straps off her shoulders to let her beautiful breasts hang loose and free. The freckled skin of her chest is flushed pink, as are her cheeks. I look down, loving the way her nipples are peaked and needy, waiting for me.

The ice drips in my hand as I lift it up, letting a few droplets fall onto her breast. I repeat the motion on the other side, cupping her with my icy palm.

"Oh god," she cries out, arching into me as her skin pebbles over with goosebumps.

Once again, I chase the cold with heat, covering her nipple with my mouth, sucking the icy water off her skin. She tastes like heaven.

Her hands dig into my hair, pulling me back as she searches my face. Her dance music still pulses all around us. "What happened to you today?" she says, her tone gentle, curious.

"Life is short, Tess. Wanna live a little with me?"

She smiles, her eyes twinkling. "You spoke to Mars."

"Yeah, can we not talk about him while we're half naked?"

"Are you jealous of Mars, sweet puppy?" she teases, her hands roving. "Are you worried I'll leave you for his surly sourpuss glares and his steamed salmon dinners?"

I cup her ass, pulling her against me so she feels how much I want her. "Never," I reply, knowing it's the truth. Mars isn't my competition. I have no competition because Tess isn't a game or a prize to be won. She said it herself the night we danced at the Price wedding. If she wanted to be anywhere else, she would be. She wants to be here. She wants to be with me.

The thought burns in my chest, fanning the flames of my need for her. "I like being your sweet puppy," I admit, my hands slipping behind her back to work loose the clasp of her bra. "I like when you pet my hair and fetch me water and get me berries for my morning oatmeal." The bra comes loose, and I drop it to the floor. "I spend so much of my life taking care of everything and everyone else. So, I like being sweet, and I like when you're sweet to me."

She smiles, her hand cupping my cheek. "I like being sweet to you."

I turn into her hand, kissing her palm. But then I grab her wrist tight, jerking her hand down as I step in, my hips pressing hers into the counter.

She gasps, looking up at me, our naked chests pressed together, hearts beating fast.

"But I am not just sweet." I cup her breasts as I lean in, nipping her bottom lip.

"Ryan—"

"I can be gentle, and I can do as I'm told . . . but I like control too." I fist her hair, jerking her head back.

She hisses, letting me do it, a sexy smile pursing her lips as she gazes up at me, her eyes dancing with excitement. "I know you do," she says, her hands flat on my chest.

"I want you to know me, Tess. I want you to know all of me. Life is too short to settle for anything less than everything. You deserve to have everything you want, but I do too."

"And what do you want?" she whispers.

I smile down at her, my hand loosening in her hair. "In this moment?"

She nods.

"I want to lay you out on the bed, tie your hands to the headboard, and fuck you in the ass 'til you scream."

"Ryan," she whimpers, her gaze molten as she literally melts into me.

"I want you," I say, dropping my mouth to hers. "Tess, I want you," I say again, my lips pressed against hers. "Please, say yes. Please, let me have you."

She clings to my hips, her body leaning against mine. "Yes," she whispers, her voice barely audible over the loud party music. "Ryan, yes. Take me. I'm yours. Any hole. Ryan, I'm yours—"

I silence her with a kiss, demanding entrance with tongue and lips, claiming her mouth. The heated press of our kisses helps the fire spread as our hands move. Everywhere she touches me gives me a shock of pleasure. It warms and crackles like electricity, racing across my skin.

I drop my hands to her hips. "Jump."

She gasps, leaning away. "Ry—what—"

"You heard me," I say. Grabbing two fistfuls of her ass, I pull on her, lifting her off the floor.

She shrieks, pressing up with her toes just enough that I hitch my arms around her thighs, pressing her pussy against my erection.

"Hold on," I say, spinning around and carrying her out of the kitchen.

"My margarita," she squeals, laughter caught in her throat as I use her body to shove open her bedroom door.

I walk straight across the room and drop her down on the end of the bed. She shrieks again, her hair flopping around her face in a mess of curls as she drops back to her elbows. I swoop down, kissing both her breasts before I claim her lips. "I'll make you a thousand margaritas once we're done," I vow.

She laughs again, her hands brushing over my shoulders and down my arms.

I pull away and she pouts, reaching for me.

"Get those panties off and crawl up the bed," I say. "I'll be right back."

Not waiting for her response, I hurry across the hallway into my dark bedroom and snatch up a bag from the top drawer of my dresser. I grab the lube from the side table and hurry back across the hall to find her naked in the middle of the bed, legs spread, fingering her own clit.

I go still, watching her play. Her chest is flushed a deeper pink, her cheeks too. "Like what you see, puppy?" she teases.

I groan, dropping the bag onto the end of the bed. "I'm not puppy tonight."

She dips two fingers inside her pussy, giving them a little twist that has her biting her bottom lip like a red-haired siren. "Who are you then?"

Reaching into the black shopping bag, I pull out a pair of pink fuzzy handcuffs.

She gasps, dropping her hand away from her clit as she sits up. "Ryan, tell me you didn't go to a sex shop with Mars Price today!"

I blink. "What—no," I cry. "No, I bought these online. You think I would brave a sex shop without you, are you kidding?"

She crawls down to the end of the bed, taking the handcuffs from me, eyes wide. "These are so cute, I wanna die," she coos, rubbing the pink fur against her cheek. "Ohmygosh, they're so soft—"

I snatch them out of her hand with a glare. "They're not supposed to be cute. They're handcuffs, Tess. This is serious."

She smirks. "Then why didn't you get like, black leather, or just plain metal?"

I pout, feeling a little defeated as I glance down at them. "I didn't want them to hurt you." Her breath catches and I look up to see tears spring to her eyes. I reach for her, my hand brushing her cheek. "Tess, what—"

But she shakes her head, moving away from my hand with a soft laugh. "Nope, I'm fine. Ryan, you're so sweet." She pulls me in, one hand brushing over mine on the cuffs as she cups the back of my neck with the other and pulls me down for a kiss. "You're so good to me," she whispers against my lips. "Good for me."

I smile, heart racing as she lets her walls down.

"I want you to fuck me," she commands. "Put those pink cuffs on me and tear me apart."

I pull away, glancing from her to the bag. "I—there's more," I admit.

She snatches up the bag, the plastic rustling as she pulls out a looped length of simple black rope. "Ohmygod, what the fuck are you gonna do with this?" she whispers, gazing up at me.

I shrug, suddenly feeling self-conscious. "I thought . . . maybe I might, like, loop it through the cuffs . . . and then loop it through the eye hook on the bed frame to sort of...tie you down . . . or something like that," I finish lamely.

Exactly like that. I want to tie her down. Don't make me explain why, but my dick is literally ready to explode at the very idea. Looking at her holding the rope? I'm already dead.

"What eye hook?" she says, glancing over her shoulder.

I huff. "Babe, I'm pretty sure this is a sex bed."

"What?" she cries, her gaze darting back to me.

"Yeah, there are eye hooks all along the base for tying someone up. You never noticed?"

"Ohmygod," she shrieks again. Tossing the rope down onto the bed, she scrambles over to the side and drops down, bare ass in the air, inspecting the thick wooden frame of the bed. "Are you kidding me?" comes her muffled cry. "How did you find these?"

"I dropped my phone the other night while we were watching TV in here," I reply. "Had to sorta crawl under to get it. Remember?"

"And you didn't say anything then?" she cries. "Ohmygod, the hooks go all the way around!"

I stifle a laugh. "You really didn't know you were sleeping in Mars Price's rope sex bed?"

She sits upright, her curls a mess as she flops down onto her butt. "Those kinky fuckers. Rachel has never said a word about rope play!"

My eyes go wide. "Wait—you talk to her about that stuff? Like, you talk to her about sex? Will you talk to her about this?"

She laughs. "This part, yeah. I won't rest until I throw Mars's rope bunny sex bed in her face the next time I see her."

"Hey, babe?" I pick up the rope off the end of the bed.

She glances back at me. "Yeah?"

"Can we stop talking about them now?"

She smiles and nods.

"Good, 'cause I really wanna fuck you in this rope sex bed. Is that cool with you?"

She giggles, her cheeks flushing a brighter pink as she crawls over to me, her arms wrapping around my shoulders. "It's so cool with me," she teases. "I want you, Ryan." She kisses me with those pouty lips, playful and light, even as her words are anything but. "I want you to fuck me." Kiss. "Take my ass and bury your cock in me." Kiss. "And tie me up, Daddy. Stretch me out—"

"I don't like Daddy," I say, leaning away with a frown.

She grins, dropping her hand to cup my hard erection. "Can I call you 'sir' again? Or maybe master? My lord?"

I raise a brow at her, still frowning. "I'm not into role play where I'm a knight and you're a princess in a tower. So, you can drop the 'my lord' crap."

"Sir it is then," she replies, her hand still smoothing up and down my hard dick over my pants. "Take me, sir. Tie me up and fuck me. Fill my ass with your cum."

"Are you gonna be my good girl?" My free hand smooths down her arm to grip her wrist. "Will you do as you're told?"

She nods, biting that bottom lip. "Yes, sir. I'll do anything you say."

I groan. Her submission hits like a jolt to the dick. "Fuck, you are so much trouble."

She leans forward, licking my nipple with a flick of her tongue. I gasp, jerking back and she just laughs, the sound soft and sweet. Gripping her wrist, I lift the furry pink cuff and latch it on, clicking it shut.

"Is it weird that I'm nervous," she admits, her gaze earnest as she looks up at me. "I can't remember the last time I felt nervous during sex."

I gently lift her other wrist, closing the cuff around it. Then I lean down and kiss her lips. "Pick a safe word."

She smiles, looking up at me, her hands bound by the pink, fuzzy cuffs. "A safe word?"

I nod. "Say it, and everything stops."

She thinks for a moment, her smile spreading. "Hmm . . . Bowser," she says at last.

I laugh. "Fuck, seriously? Your safe word for handcuffed, tied down anal sex is gonna be Bowser?"

She laughs too. "Yours is still Yoshi, right? I just want us to match."

"Fine," I say, giving her ass a swat. "Go pick your favorite dildo and bring it to me."

She slips off the bed, a bounce in her step as she reaches for her bag of tricks and pulls out a bright pink dildo. "It matches the cuffs," she teases, handing it to me.

I kiss her again, tossing it down to the bed. I pick up the rope instead, unwinding the end. "Do you trust me, Tess?"

She glances up at me, eyes wide. Slowly, she nods, her smile spreading.

I smile too. "Gimme your hands."

She holds them out, looking up at me with such earnest excitement.

I slip the rope through the middle ring of the cuffs and loop it through, handing her the small coil. "Get on the bed," I command, "Lie on your back, hands above your head."

"Yes, sir," she says, tipping up on her toes to kiss my chin. Then she's turning around and dropping onto the bed, crawling up to the head with her round ass in my face. Once she reaches the middle, she flips to her back, stretching out like a cat with her arms above her head, the furry cuffs holding her wrists together.

She peers down her body at me, parting her legs again.

I don't even bother shucking my pants. I'm not ready for that yet. I just step around the side of the bed, bending over her to kiss her lips as I take the rope from her hands. I have to climb on with one knee, taking the double loop of rope and pulling it through the eye hook drilled into the middle of the frame. Feeding the rope ends through, I pull them tight, giving her arms a little stretch that has her gasping, back arching. "Too much?"

"Not enough," she replies, her voice breathless.

I leave the rope tied off, keeping her arms in place, as I crawl onto the bed, moving myself in between her spread legs. She shifts her hips wide, opening herself to me, her head tipped back as she waits for the moment we connect.

Her pink pussy lips are parted, glistening with her arousal. A little lower, I see the darker pink of her asshole. I groan, desperate for this view once I'm filling both her holes. But I know I won't get it. I have to appreciate it now.

I drop down to my elbows and seal my mouth onto her pussy. That first taste has me feeling out of control. I work her with my lips and tongue, humming against her clit, winding her up, flicking that little bud until she's squirming underneath me.

"Oh god," she cries, her legs clasping around my head. The handcuffs rattle as she changes her position, gripping the rope.

I smooth my hands down her thighs, willing her body to relax as I keep eating her out. I let my fingers play too, getting them wet by dipping them in her entrance. With my mouth sucking her clit, I trail a finger down, circling the rosy bud of her asshole. She tenses again, panting as I rim her with my finger, pressing the tip gently in.

"Oh fuck," she whimpers. "That feels amazing. I'm gonna—"

I lift my mouth away, blowing air on her clit through pursed lips. She shivers, moaning as her legs fall open. I sink my finger in deeper, stretching her out. "You like this?" I drop my mouth lower to tease her pussy. I flick with my tongue, sinking it into the wet heat of her opening, my finger pressing deeper into her ass.

"Yes," she cries, her hips moving against my mouth.

"Yes, what?" I tease.

"Yes, sir," she pants. "I want more. Baby, please, fuck me. Please, Ryan—sir—I need it."

Begging Tess is now one of my new favorite sounds. Laughing Tess makes my heart stop, but Begging Tess makes me fucking feral. I work a second finger inside her ass, dropping spit down onto my fingers to ease their passage in and out. I suck and tease her clit again, letting go of the rope to grasp blindly for the bright pink dildo.

My hand closes around it and I prod her pussy with the tip. She cries out, turned on by my three-way claiming—mouth on her clit, dildo in her pussy, fingers in her ass. I work the toy in nice and slow, giving it a little twist, working it in rhythm with my fingers.

Her thighs tremble, a whimper her only sound as she pulls on the rope, whimpering when she can't get her hands loose. "I wanna touch you," she whines. "Baby, please—"

"Lie back and take it," I say, giving the pink toy a little slap.

She gasps, clenching around it.

I press the toy all the way in, sucking hard on her clit, curling my fingers up and in.

She tips her head back and screams. "Yes—*yes*—ohmygooood—Ryan—"

I pump the dildo twice more and she shrieks, her thighs clamping around my face, her body bowing off the bed as she comes. I feel the flutter of it as her hole clenches tighter around my fingers. I groan, my dick leaking precum into my boxers as I shift my weight, trying to give it some goddamn relief.

"So good," she whimpers, the cuffs rattling as she relaxes. "That was perfect." She's breathless, chest heaving as she laughs, breasts jiggling.

I pull my fingers slowly out of her ass, leaving the dildo pressed up inside her. Crawling up between her legs, I fold myself over her, teasing her nipples with my teeth and tongue. She sighs with contentment, arching into me, flexing against the rope's hold on her.

I pop off her tit and smile, loving the look of bliss on her face.

"Turn over, baby. We're not done yet." I give her hip a little slap as I lean back, giving her room.

With a whimper, she does as she's told. I help guide her legs as she gets on all fours, her cuffed hands pressed flat to the mattress. Seeing her like this, bound and dripping for me . . . I'm already so fucking turned on. I don't know how I'll last once I get inside her.

I've only done anal once before. I'm nervous too, but I won't tell her that. Sex with her is so fun. Exploring what I like is fun too. I want this. I want to feel confident and in charge. I want this control. I want to take her just like this, claiming all her pretty pink holes.

Reaching between her legs, I give the dildo a wiggle. She hums, shifting her hips, letting me sink it in a little deeper. "Do you want me in this ass?" I murmur, my hand smoothing over her rounded cheek.

"Yes, sir," she replies, glancing over her shoulder at me, flashing me a look at those pretty forest green eyes. "You'll have to take your pants off first," she teases.

I mutter a curse, slipping off the end of the bed to finally lose my athletic pants. I snatch up the small bottle of lube, squirting some in my hand. I wrap my slick hand around my dick and groan, my eyes locked on the vision of Tess ready and waiting for me on the bed. She glances over her shoulder again, watching me fuck my own hand.

"You're so beautiful," she says. "So powerful."

Her words of affirmation kill me. I want her to keep going, even as I need her to stop. I take a deep breath, letting it out as I climb back on the bed and inch towards her.

"Are you sure your knee can take the strain—*ah*—" She squeals as I give her ass a smack.

"No talking about my knee when I'm lubed up and about to fuck your ass," I command.

"Yes, sir," she replies. And then, because she's my she-devil, she gives those hips a little sway for me.

I groan, crawling in behind her, both hands smoothing up her thighs and over her hips. "Are you ready for me, baby? You want to take two dicks at once?"

She nods. "I'm ready. Take me, Ryan."

I grab her hips, giving her a little tug towards me.

She gasps, her arms stretched taut by the tied cuffs. "Oh god—"

"Who am I?" I challenge, swatting her ass again.

"You're my sir," she says as I smooth my palm over her skin. "You're mine. Take me—*ah*—"

I tug her hips again. "You're terrible at bottoming," I tease. "Stop telling me what to do, Tess."

"Yes, sir," she replies, her tone laced with mirth.

Yeah, we both know she'll be bossing me again any minute.

Holding her hip steady with my left hand, I grip my lubed dick with my right, guiding it towards her tight little hole. A flash of the bright pink dildo is visible between her thighs. I'm already aching, anticipating the tight fit. "Tell me if I hurt you," I say, my hand soft on her hip. "You have your safe word?"

"Ryan?"

"Hmm?"

"Fuck my ass . . . please . . . sir."

We both laugh and then I'm pressing in, working the tip past her tight ring of muscle.

"Mmm . . . slow." Her body is fighting it at first. "Slow and easy," she instructs. "Wait 'til I relax a little—there," she says on a soft sigh. "Now."

I tease the tip, lubing her hole as I work my way in. "Like that?" I whisper.

"Yeah . . . feels good," she pants, moving her hips against me, ready to take more.

It's a sight to behold, watching my hard length sink inside her. I love this angle. I love seeing her stretched out for me, her hands gripping to the rope in their fuzzy pink cuffs. Fuck, this woman is so fucking perfect for me—adventurous and dominant, caring, thoughtful.

"Ooooh, Ryan," she cries, moving her hips as I sink in deeper. "Yes—baby, please—"

"Like that?"

"Yeah."

"I'm almost there." I sink in until I settle against the curve of her hips. "You're so goddamn tight," I hear myself say, my tone almost reverent.

"I love it," she pants. "Ryan, please baby, move. Fuck me. Don't hold back."

I grunt, repositioning my hands. I tease my length in and out, trying a few short fast thrusts, then one long pull, slamming back in. We both cry out and I feel my release coil tight in my gut and burn up my lower back. My balls feel so heavy and full.

"This feels amazing," she whimpers. "Baby, I feel so full."

"You are full," I tease, dropping my free hand down and around to work the toy as I thrust into her tight ass. She moans, back arching, ass jiggling like a fucking dream as she starts meeting me thrust for thrust, slamming her hips back against me.

"Oh, god," I groan, my rhythm slipping as I feel my release barreling towards me. "I'm gonna come—baby—Tess—I'm coming—"

I pull her towards me until she's all but flat against the mattress, the angle of her hips changing to accommodate being tied to the bed frame. Her hips shift, and my angle of penetration changes too. She screams, her whole body going tight, as her ass and pussy grip me like a vise. I know her pussy is clenching on the toy, but I can feel it too. I feel the pulse of it as she comes, her body trembling on one long moan.

Her orgasm triggers mine. I cry out a string of curses as I drop my hands to either side of her ribs and slam home once, twice more. My release surges like a supernova, blasting outwards, and then I'm shattering. It's the only word to explain it. White spots dance in my vision, and then I quite literally come apart.

"Oh my god," she murmurs over and over again. Her body is shaking. She's slicked in sweat.

My senses clear and I groan, sliding out of her ass.

She gasps, her cheeks clenching at my absence. I'm gentle as I pull the dildo free, tossing it down on the bed, glistening with her release. Her shaking intensifies and then I hear the soft sob.

I crawl over her leg and drop down to the bed at her side, stretching myself out. "Hey, hey . . . are you crying? Baby, come here." Heart in my throat, I turn her face to look at me.

"I'm okay," she whimpers. "Really, it's okay. I'm fine."

"You're shivering." I work quick, clicking the release on the handcuffs, freeing her hands.

She immediately drops them down, crying as she wraps herself up in me. Our arms and legs tangle until we're pressed together from shoulder to toes.

"Talk to me," I say, one hand brushing the curls back from her face. "Are you okay? Was that too much?"

She shakes her head, nuzzling her face against my chest. "I'm fine," she says again. "That was just really intense."

"It was too much," I say, frustration at myself building.

"No," she says quickly, looking up at me, her hand cupping my cheek. "No, it was perfect. Ryan, look at me."

I look down, meeting her forest green gaze.

"It was perfect. I loved it. It was just a lot."

"What do you need?"

"Just hold me for a minute," she says, burying her face back against the sweat of my chest. "I'll be alright in a minute."

"Okay," I say, my hand cupping the back of her head. At this angle, the floral fruitiness of her shampoo wafts into my nose. "This smell is going to haunt me," I say, my hand smoothing down her mussed curls.

"My shampoo?"

"Mhmm."

She nestles closer, trying to share my skin. "Why?"

"Because it's locked in with that first memory I have of you," I reply. "That kiss on beach day . . . I could smell your shampoo when we kissed. Like a tropical sunrise."

She laughs. "A tropical sunrise?"

"Tease me, and I'll pour your margarita in the pool," I warn.

I feel her smile against my chest. "Are you really gonna make me a margarita?"

"Sure," I reply, dropping my hand to rub up and down her back, relieved that the shivering has stopped. "That was the deal, right? I get tied up anal sex, you get a margarita. Even Steven."

She laughs again, looking up at me. "Please don't say 'Even Steven' while I'm wearing your cum in my ass."

I smirk, brushing my fingers through her hair again. "Okie dokie, Smokie."

She shakes her head. "I hate you."

"No, you don't," I reply, rolling on my back and pulling her with me, her hair spilling over my chest.

"No," she says after a moment, her fatigue setting in as the last of her adrenaline leaves her body. "I really don't."

55
Tess

The sound of my alarm wakes me, and my eyes flutter open to see Ryan stretched out naked on my bed. He's on his stomach, his head buried under the pillow. A stream of sunlight peeks through a crack in the curtains, shining across his back, giving his tanned skin a golden glow. The sheet barely covers his perky hockey butt.

I can't help but smile. He's finally ditched the clunky knee brace for sleeping, so now he can stretch out on the bed like the puppy he is, all arms and legs. He looks so peaceful.

It's Saturday. Game day for Ryan. Gala prep day for me.

Last night was a dream. After our epic fuzzy handcuff sex, we showered. Then Ryan made us margaritas and I made us dinner and we sat out on the patio by the fire table. We laughed and talked for hours, eventually stumbling our way back into bed, falling asleep in each other's arms.

Now I'm awake and he's still here. A beautiful, thoughtful, very naked boy is in my bed. Trying not to disturb him, I inch towards the side of the bed. As soon as I flip the sheet back, his hand darts out and wraps around my wrist. He muffles something I don't hear.

"What's that, puppy?" I tease.

Pulling on my wrist, he rolls to his side and peeks his head out from under the pillow. He blinks in the bright light, his tousled blond hair a mess. "I said, where do you think you're going?"

I laugh as he pulls me down, wrapping his arms and legs around me like a giant squid, burying his face at my neck and peppering me with kisses.

"I have to get up," I say after a minute. "I have a ton of stuff to do today."

"There's always tomorrow," he replies, his hands roaming as he wakes my body up. He cups my breast, teasing my nipple until I'm arching into him. I turn and he lets me, wiggling against him until we're a pair of spoons. He flicks my hair back, exposing my shoulder, his warm lips teasing my skin as his hands roam, lovingly touching me all over, memorizing my shape.

After a minute or two, I heave a frustrated sigh. I don't want him to stop. I want to lay in this bed with him in our pink bubble of happiness and never leave. But there are still jobs to do. For both of us.

"It's stuff for the gala," I say. "And if I'm losing tonight to go to your game, then it's now or never."

He sighs, going still behind me, his erection pressing against my hip. "I don't want you to leave this bed," he admits, saying out loud what I'm feeling. "It feels too soon."

"It's after 8:00 a.m.," I tease, but I know exactly what he means. It's too soon for us to separate. This thing between us is too fragile. We can only nurture it if we're together, laughing and fucking and ignoring the rest of the world.

"Tell me you feel this too," he says, his hand brushing a curl off my shoulder.

I shift in his arms, spinning around until our legs entangle and I'm facing him, peering into the apple green of his eyes, framed by dark golden lashes. I brush my fingers down the rigid bone of his sternum. "You know I do. Didn't we settle that the other night? Magnets, you called us."

He nods. "This feels like physics to me, not biology. You pulled me in that day on the beach. I tried to avoid it at first, tried to pretend it was just infatuation or lust. Even when you were in Cincinnati, I could feel it. You know, I asked Doc about you?"

I smile. "Really?"

"Yeah, I was so lame," he says with a laugh. "She saw right through me. She told me about your love of *Sons of Anarchy*."

I gasp. "She did not."

"She did," he says with a smirk. "I think she was trying to warn me away, though. I think she thinks I'm not badass enough for you. She thinks I'll bore you and you'll move on."

"Puppy, you are anything but boring," I reply, making a mental note to tit punch Rachel when I see her.

He smirks, satisfied with my answer. "I still don't know what the hell you're doing with me. I think part of me thought I'd wake, and you'd be gone again. You keep doing that, you know," he adds with an accusing look.

"Doing what?"

"Slipping away," he replies. "Even when you just fall asleep in my bed watching TV, I always wake up to find you gone. You like to leave first, don't you?"

My heart flutters as I take in his full meaning. He's not just talking about slipping out in the morning. "It's my bullshit, self-destructive way of avoiding getting hurt," I admit.

"And does it work?"

A quiet moment stretches between us as he just waits, his gaze slowly tracing the lines of my face. It's like he knows what I was thinking about as I was lying here watching him sleep. "Sometimes," I reply. "But usually, it only works when I was never really interested to begin with."

"And now?" His thumb brushes over my lips. "Shelby says you're gonna break my heart . . . are you?"

"When did she say that?" I whisper.

"The morning you met in the kitchen. She called you a cataclysm. I had to google it," he admits. "It means a life-shattering event, upheaval, ruination."

"I know what it means."

God, is she right? Am I going to ruin him? Troy's threats are still out there. None of this is finished. I'm not free. These shackles I wear can still drag me down to the darkest depths. And not the pink fuzzy kind—

"Hey," he whispers. "For the record, I think she's wrong. I googled words that mean the opposite. You may have ruined me for all other women, but you're not a calamity, Tess. You're a godsend." He kisses the tip of my nose. "A blessing," he adds, kissing my cheek. "A windfall . . . I had to google that one too."

We both laugh as he wraps me in his arms and rolls on top of me, his hips pressing against mine.

"Can we have sex like this? No toys, no mirrors or cameras. No pretzel twists or kissing cobras."

I snort trying to hold in my laugh. "Kissing cobras?"

"I don't fucking know," he says, his hips already moving against mine. "I'm sure it's a thing."

"I'm willing to try the pretzel twist," I tease. "But I don't think I have the right anatomy to play kissing cobras with you."

"Stop talking," he says, leaning down to kiss my lips. It's our first kiss this morning, and it almost surprises me how eager I am for it.

My fingers tangle into his messy hair and I pull him back down to me, kissing him again.

"No distractions is what I mean," he says. "Just you and me. Together."

"You and me," I whisper against his mouth, shifting my hips to part my legs wider for him. We both gasp as we feel him slide against me.

He groans, curling his body over mine, dropping his face to kiss my breasts as a hand slips between us, angling his dick towards my entrance. "Now?" he pants.

I nod, my hands gripping to his shoulders.

He presses in, wetting the tip of his dick. "Fuck, you're tight."

"I'm ready," I whimper, lifting my knee and putting my foot flat on the mattress. "Don't be gentle. Take me. Take—*ahh*—"

He slams in with his hips, sinking inside me. We both tremble at the moment of connection, adjusting our hold on each other before he begins to move again, pressing up and in with his dick, filling me.

I arch my back, raising my hands up over my head. His hands follow, gripping to my wrists as we get tangled in my curls. He holds me like that, grinding against me as we gaze into each other's eyes. I don't want to break this connection we have. Clearly, he doesn't either.

"Look at me," he whispers, his green eyes boring into my soul.

"I am," I reply, panting as I feel my release building inside me. The weight of him on top of me, the feel of him pinning me down, his dick moving inside me—it's all too much. I feel so overwhelmed, my every sense firing.

He's right, playing with toys is fun, and the orgasms we give each other are otherworldly, but this feels divine on a whole different level. This is connection. This is raw intimacy. Who knew good, old-fashioned missionary sex with a boy could have me about to cry?

Tears sting my eyes as he drops one hand between us, working my clit.

"I'm close," I say, my body coming alive at that first touch. Fire races across my skin as electricity hums down my bones, making my toes curl. "Baby, I'm so close—"

"Me too," he groans. "Fuck, I can feel you. You're so tight. Come with me."

I squeeze him, my core aching for release as I hold tight to his shoulders. "Kiss me."

He kisses me, and then we're both coming. His hips jerk against me, and he groans against my lips, chasing his release. I hold tight to his shoulders, feeling my own orgasm tear through me. I cling to him, our naked bodies sheened in sweat as we both fight the urge to tremble.

He sinks his full weight on top of me with a breathless groan. Then he's rolling back to his side, his dick slipping free as he pulls me with him. We catch our breath, cheeks flushed as we just share air. In this moment, things feel perfect. I don't want anything to change.

"Stay," I murmur, ready to cancel all my plans. And I don't just mean for today. "Stay here with me."

He searches my face, brushing my hair back. I can feel his cum leaking out of me. I feel warm and sleepy. I feel cherished. I inch closer, holding his gaze. He licks his lips, and I think I know what he's about to say. My heart is racing. I lean in.

"Tess, I . . . "

I wait, hopeful, expectant. Behind me, my phone rings, making us both jump. It's set to vibrate, too, so it skitters across the side table with each jingling buzz.

"I have to get that. It'll be Cheryl. She's probably waiting for me already."

He nods. "Answer it. I have to shower anyway. Game day starts early."

The phone keeps buzzing.

"You were about to say something," I press, searching his face, but he's already shifting away.

"I'll see you tonight, right? You're coming to my game?"

I nod.

"Good. Then we'll talk again tonight."

Masking my disappointment, I roll over to snatch up my phone. "Hey, Cheryl," I say, my tone all false brightness.

Ryan comes around the side of the bed and bends down to kiss my forehead. I watch him walk away, his naked hockey butt glowing white against the rest of his sun-kissed skin.

"Tess? Hello?"

Shit, Cheryl is talking.

"What? I'm sorry, Cher," I say, swinging my legs off the bed. "Yes, I'm here. I'm running a little late, but I'm on my way."

56

Tess

"And we've had confirmation from the Jacksonville Zoo Animal Ambassador Program," says Cheryl, ticking another thing off her list. "They'll be there to set up at 6:30 p.m., and they'll stay for one hour."

"And they're bringing a gopher tortoise?" I say, tapping out the last line of my email.

"Yes, and his name is Bandit," she replies. "I mean, just look at that face." She flashes me her phone screen over top of my laptop, showing me a video of a large gopher tortoise eating lettuce.

"Ugh, the strong silent type *and* he's health-conscious? Have I just met my soulmate?" I tease.

She laughs, tucking her phone away as she rattles off three more things from her list. We've been like a hive of buzzing bees in the office all day. Joey is over at the venue now, overseeing the DJ delivery and set-up. And Nancy is out haunting all the local party supply shops, trying to get us some emergency cutlery after our order apparently fell off the back of a truck.

I can plan events like this in my sleep, but it's been fun to work with the team. Cheryl and Nancy have great connections in the area, and they're good at networking. We've got several reps from other local nature conservancy groups coming, including our new friends at the FWC, the North Florida Land Trust, and the Duval Audubon Society.

Every Ray on the roster RSVP'd yes, and practically all of them are bringing a plus one. We have a whole range of Jacksonville personalities coming too—city council reps, prominent business owners, even a few other sports celebrities. At last count, I think we had six

Jacksonville Jaguars coming with their wives, even some of the Jumbo Shrimp players. It will be a night by Jacksonville, for Jacksonville, with all the proceeds going to support our local dunes, nesting ground for the sea turtles.

"What did we decide about the balloons?" says Cheryl, still focused on her list.

"We nixed balloons. Environmental scourge, remember?"

"Oh, right," she says with a laugh, shaking her head. "I don't know what I was thinking. Oh—and that box arrived for you while you stepped out for coffee," she adds, pointing to a small box on the corner of her desk.

Her phone rings and she answers it, her voice chipper as she deals with some catering question. In moments, she's pushing her way out of the office, arguing the price of bacon-wrapped dates. She likes to pace when she talks on the phone, and this office is too cramped. At the end of the hall is a terrace meant for smokers. Now it's Cheryl's mobile office. She storms away, leaving the door open.

As soon as she's gone, I pick up the box perched on the edge of her desk. There's no return address label. Again. I bring the box over to my desk. Picking up my letter opener, I slice under the flaps, breaking the tape. Heart in my throat, I drop the little knife with a clatter and peel back the top flaps of the box, peering inside.

"Oh god."

Tears spring to my eyes as I take in the contents: a mess of printed photos, all of Ryan and me. I knew I was being followed, but I typically got the tingling sense when I was walking alone from the coffee shop to my car. Or a few times on the beach, walking with Rachel and her guys. I saw the occasional dark SUV, too, parked down the street. I made notes each time, just like Charlie suggested. But this is . . .

My stomach churns as I pick up a stack of the photos, flipping through them. Ryan going into the house on his crutches. Me coming out, bag over my shoulder, tumbler of iced tea in hand. Ryan and I getting into his car when I'm wearing the cherry dress. Our date night.

I flip through the next few photos. Yep, Ryan and I on our date. The photos are grainy, like they were taken outside through the glass.

We're talking, laughing as I'm leaning in over the table. The photos display a casual intimacy, a comfort.

I want to be sick. It's such a violation.

I glance up sharply, looking around the small office. The photographer brought these here. He dropped them off. He was in this space. He likely watched and waited until I left to go on our coffee run, then brought the box up to Cheryl, posing as a delivery guy. My resolve hardens as I make a mental note. *Install cameras.* I'll pay for them myself if I have to, but first thing Monday morning, I am putting a camera up in this office pointed right at the door.

I keep flipping through the stack in my hands.

Photos of us walking down the boardwalk, arm in arm. It's night, the photos are dark, difficult to see anything. More photos of us at the beach, these in daylight. Ryan stands next to me, looking down at me like I'm his reason, while Ranger John explains how to stake out a nest mound. Fuck, there are children in these photos.

"Oh my god," I say again, hands shaking as I drop the photos to my desk and grab out the next stack.

Ryan and I in the kitchen, taken through the back glass. The creeper got everything. Us arguing, kissing, the shedding of our clothes, us fucking against the counter. Ryan on his knees beneath me, my head tipped back in ecstasy. They're all grainy, the zoom fighting the glare of the glass and the dim lighting, but you can see everything.

I feel numb. This man with the camera watched *everything*. Every moment Ryan and I shared in that kitchen, our walls crumbling, hearts colliding. He witnessed it all. He photographed it all. And he gave all the photos to Troy in exchange for money.

I drop the photos to the desk, and they scatter. Some slide off the edge, tumbling to the floor. I look around for two seconds before I snatch up my wastepaper basket and retch into it. My heart is pounding, pulse racing. I gasp for air, retching again, hands still shaking.

When nothing comes up, I drop the basket to the floor, turning my attention back to the mess on my desk. "Come on." I dive inside the box with both hands, looking for something. Anything. Some heinous note with more cutting words, a list of demands, an envelope with a drop point for where he wants me to leave his blood money.

Because these photos aren't for nothing. They can't be. Troy wants me to know he has them. Why? Proof of an affair? He already had that with the other photos. I don't doubt he can use his power and position to twist HR into firing me. He didn't need more proof. So why do this? Why have these photos taken? Why have me followed?

"Fuck," I cry, tipping all the photos out onto the desk. There's nothing else in the box. No note. No demands.

And that's when it hits me. I know exactly what he wants. And he knows this was the only way to get it. I pick up my phone off my desk, hating myself for walking right into his trap. But this is bigger than me now. These photos are proof of that.

Dialing the number I know by heart, I lift the phone to my ear and wait. The phone rings once, twice. Then it connects.

"This is Troy Owens," comes his voice, deep and smooth through the phone.

Hearing his voice renders me silent. I open my mouth, but no words escape me.

"Hello? Who is this?"

Taking a deep breath, I dive in. "You have to stop."

He sighs into the phone. "Tess. I was wondering when you'd finally call."

"You have to stop," I repeat, my gaze scanning over the mess of photos littering my desk.

"I'm assuming you got my note."

"If by 'note' you mean this heinous box of photos, then yes. You had no right, Troy. This is harassment. And there are children in some of these photos, families—"

"I had *every* right to document evidence of my wife having an affair," he counters. "And those aren't even the only photos I have as evidence."

"Fine. So, you have what you need, then. Divorce me. Take everything, and let's be done with it," I say. "I won't contest. You can name any terms. You want my 401k? Have it. The Reds season tickets? They're yours. I don't even like baseball. I faked it for ten fucking years, much like how I faked most of my orgasms—"

He laughs into the phone, the sound cold and biting. "You think I did all this to divorce you faster? How are you not getting this? I don't want a divorce, Tess. That was never in the cards for me. You've been pushing the divorce, not me. For years, it's been your answer to everything. Too afraid to fight, too afraid to find the solution together. God, you're like a broken fucking record."

"No, what's broken is this marriage," I cry. "Beyond repair!"

"Nothing is ever so broken that it can't be mended," he retorts, and I can practically hear his mother's calm, calculated voice in the words.

"You're delusional. Troy, I am *never* coming back to you. I've moved on. Don't believe me? Just look at the photos your creepy friend took for you. Those smiles? They're genuine, Troy. Those orgasms he gave me in the kitchen? All real. Every one. And he gets me there so easily. I've never come so hard or so fast in my fucking life—"

"If you really cared about this asshole, you would have been more careful," he taunts. "You would have steered well clear of him. But you've always been a stupid—"

"What are you talking about?" I cry, cutting him off.

"I'm talking about the USS Tess, flagship in the fleet for disaster. Only this time, you're dragging your handsome hockey hero down with you."

My heart stops. "Troy, what did you do?"

"You really didn't think this through." He laughs again, and the sound makes my blood run cold. "In your rush to show me what a selfish slut you really are, you pulled him right into the deep end with you. Did you even spare him a thought? No, because you only think about yourself and what *you* want."

"Troy, don't—"

"If you think the PR looks bad for you at our little firm, what will it look like when these photos get blasted all over the tabloids?" he challenges. "How do you think his team will appreciate seeing his name linked with yours in a messy adultery scandal?"

I'm shaking my head in stunned disbelief. He can't be serious. He wouldn't do this. "Troy—"

"And I bet a guy like that has some nice endorsement deals, doesn't he?"

My heart stops.

"Yeah, I looked him up, and he's only on a year-long contract with the Rays. I bet they're making him an offer, right? Some kind of extension option or a fancy new trade deal?" He's fishing, waiting for me to confirm. I say nothing, and he laughs again. "Yeah, that's what I thought. Ours isn't the only family business out there, Tess. The NHL, the Rays, his brand deals—they'll all go running faster than rats on a sinking ship. Where will your sexy boy toy be then? You think he'll still be interested in your stretched out pussy when he's fired for all the bad press you brought him? A lifetime of hard work down the drain over one regrettable lay."

"Don't," I whisper, panic rising.

"Can you imagine?" he teases, twisting the knife. He knows he's got me now. I have to let him make his threats. "And these photos are graphic, Tessy. I particularly like the ones where you're riding his face. Further proof that you're selfish, even in sex. Why don't you get on your knees for once?"

"You wouldn't," I say, trying to call his bluff. "You're not going to put Ryan on blast because that just paints you as the weak man who couldn't keep his woman. You don't want the bad press of this any more than he does—"

"I'm past caring," he shouts. "You don't get to make a fool of me and make demands and just expect me to roll over and take it. That's not how this works."

"Troy, please—"

"We made a vow," he shouts over me. "And I'll be damned if you're gonna waltz away with a flick of your little finger and break it. Who's the weak one here, Tess? The one ready to stand and try and make this work, or the one on the run?"

I shut my eyes, trying to block out his cutting words. The way he oscillates between cutting me down and claiming he wants the marriage to work has my head spinning. I'm dizzy, I'm distracted, which is his whole freaking point. He wants me confused. He wants me upended.

I take hold of the only thing that provides me any point of anchor.

Ryan.

"Troy, you leave him out of this," I demand, knowing my traitor of a voice sounds more like a plea. "He has nothing to do with any of this—"

"That's not the story I'll tell in the press. And that's not the image those pictures will paint," he counters, his self-righteous dominance seeping through the phone. It covers me like a toxic ooze, and I actually feel myself lifting the phone away from my ear. "Keep trying to have your way with me, and I'll ruin you both, I swear to fucking God."

"Leave him alone!"

"Then do as you're fucking told for once in your spoiled goddamn life!"

I close my eyes tight, not letting the tears fall. He's won this round. We both know it. He found my weakness. Love is always a weakness. Caring for other people leaves you open for heartbreak. When am I ever going to learn that lesson? Ryan is my weakness now, and Troy has a knife to his throat. I can't even pretend not to care. Troy will see right through it.

"What are you telling me to do, Troy? What do you want? How do you win?"

"Come home," he replies. "You're done playing turtle rescue. And you're done playing house with that jock asshole. Get on the next plane for Cincinnati. Come home, and we'll discuss the terms of an amicable divorce in person. Two parties, behaving as loving, reasonable adults. Not one reasonable adult and one wild runaway."

"I can't just leave," I cry, glancing around the office. "The fundraiser is tomorrow. I've been working on it for weeks, Troy. I can't abandon it now. I can't do that to Ilmari, to my volunteers. I can't—"

"Fine," he calls over me. "Then first thing Monday morning. Say your goodbyes to Rachel and her pack of assholes, then get on that plane. And don't even think about playing house with your boy toy for another night. That's over. Now. Break it off, or I'll end you both."

It's a lie. I *know* it's all a lie. If I go back to Cincinnati, he'll just find more reasons to stonewall me. He's never going to give me this divorce. The hope of an uncontested settlement is dead, bleeding all over my desk and the floor in the shape of these grainy photographs.

And now he has a hand at Ryan's throat too. I never thought he'd take this step. I wanted to believe he was a coward, too spineless and weak. He's like a boy picking the wings off a dragonfly, only bullying creatures he sees as too weak to fight back.

That's when my heart stops cold.

Troy Owens always does the math. *Always.* He's weighed Ryan and found him wanting too. What else does he have on him? What am I missing? Troy has always had a flair for the dramatic. This isn't his last move. This is merely the setting of the board. His rook is sliding down the squares, boxing me in. The checkmate is yet to come. The thought terrifies me.

"I need your word that you'll leave Ryan out of this," I say, knowing I can't believe him either way. "He's innocent, Troy."

"Don't ask *me* for clemency," he replies. "You're the one with all the power here, Tess. You've always been the one with the power. You'll decide whether he keeps his job or if he becomes tabloid fodder, just another disgraced pro athlete who can't keep his dick in his pants."

"I hate you," I whisper, a tear slipping down my cheek.

"Hate and love are two sides of the same coin, honeybun. I'll see you Monday." Always needing to have the last word, he hangs up, leaving me standing in this mess, alone with my anguish and all my unanswered questions.

57
Ryan

I walk off the ice from pre-game warmup and, I can't explain it, but I feel on edge. I want Tess. I've been here for a few hours now, trying to get my head in the game, but it's not working. The whole time I was on the ice I was watching and waiting for her, but she didn't come.

Now I'm back in the locker room, mechanically taping my sticks. At this point, I could do it with my eyes closed. Rock music pounds through the speakers, rumbling in my chest. Morrow has the aux cord, so it's a Metallica afternoon.

Normally, the music revs me up, building my energy so I can hit the ice hard. But right now, it's grating my last nerve. I can't just sit here, wondering where she is. How many times am I going to check my phone, hoping to get a picture of her in my jersey? I left it wrapped on the bed for her while she was in the shower. I figured she'd put it on and snap a pic, maybe with a wink face or that pouty-lipped smile I love so much. I was going to save it to my home screen.

My Tess. My ginger goddess. Ruler of my fucking universe.

Fuck, I can't sit here. I have to check again. Setting my stick aside, I shove off the bench. I exit the locker room and turn right, trotting down the hall in my skates, thick plastic guards protecting the blades.

"Hey, Mr. Langley," a security guard says with a wave.

"Hey, Ramon. You haven't seen a gorgeous redhead wandering around, have you?"

He just chuckles, the walkie-talkie at his hip buzzing with chatter. "Man, I wish."

"Keep an eye out, will you?" I say over my shoulder.

"Will do," he calls.

Leaving him behind, I peek my head inside the WAG room, peering around with my eagle eyes, ready to stop at the first sight of red hair. The room is full of laughing and chatting women in their bedazzled Rays shirts and jerseys. Kids dart around as a loud cartoon plays on the TV. A long table is set with food—sandwiches, cookies, salad.

But no Tess.

Shelby sees me almost at once and hurries over with Baby Josh balanced on her hip. "I told you I'd send word when she gets here."

I groan, sagging against the doorframe. "Where the hell is she, Shelbs?"

"Traffic?" she says with a shrug. "You know game days can be a mess downtown with parking."

Yeah . . . traffic. I'm not buying it.

I'm trying not to take this so hard, but this is my first game back off my injury, and I wanted my girl here to watch it. I've never been 'that guy' before, even when I was going steady with a girl. But then again, I've never been with Tess before. I just need to know she'll show up for me the way I'll always show up for her.

"Hey," says Shelby, her hand brushing the sleeve of my jersey. "She'll come, okay? She's crazy about you. If you asked her to come, she'll be here."

I nod, wanting to believe her.

"But you should really get out of here," she adds, checking the clock on the wall.

My gaze darts to the wall too. "Fuck—"

"Langley!"

I push off the doorframe and peek back over my shoulder to see Assistant Coach Denison marching towards me.

"What the hell are you doing down here, planning a picnic? Get your ass back in the locker room!" He jerks a thumb over his shoulder, glaring at me.

"Uh-oh," Shelby teases with a smile in her eye.

"Busted," I mutter.

She laughs. "She'll come, Ryan. Go play your game."

I shove off the doorway and start moving back down the hall towards the locker room, passing Denison as I go.

"You boys are gonna give me grey hairs before I'm forty, I swear to God," he says, slapping my shoulder pads as I pass.

Even with Shelby's words of affirmation tumbling through my mind, I still feel unsettled. It's not like I'm fooling myself here. I know what this is about. It was on the tip of my tongue this morning. I wanted to hold her naked in my arms, her defenses down, and I wanted to tell her that I love her.

Because I do. I'm in love with Tess. She's mine and I'm hers. And I think she loves me too. Fuck, I *need* to tell her. I can't focus until the words are out of me.

Focus. Speed. Control.

It's my mantra. It has been since I was twelve. But right now, the mantra I'm chanting over and over is three very different words. I bat them away, searching for my center. Mental performance is just as important as physical performance. I can't play if I can't get my head in the game.

Sully and Walsh cast me a glare as I take my seat between them, snatching up my stick to finish my tape job.

"You alright, Langers?" Sully says. "You seem distracted."

"I'm good. I'm focused."

He just shakes his head, his attention back on his own pregame.

Yeah, I'm focused alright . . . on all the wrong things. I let out a deep breath, trying to clear my head. *Wrap the stick.* Over, under, and over again. Tight lines. Down the blade, heel to toe. Finish the wrap on the backhand side. Then I need to tape the top of the shaft.

I let the rhythm of taping take over me as I sink into my empty headspace. My dead zone. My pregame black out. Nothing can touch me in here. It's just me and my game, the feel of the stick in my hands, the movement of the tape.

But I'm not alone in my head tonight.

Focus.

Focus on Tess—her freckles, those reddish curls framing her face, the satisfied humming sound she makes when she takes her first sip of morning coffee. Focus on her eyes, so green at the edges and golden brown in the middle. Focus on the sway of her hips, the downturn of her bottom lip when she's concentrating on her laptop.

Focus on the sound of her cry as she orgasms, squeezing your dick like a vise. Focus on her words, spoken so softly—*I want you too*.

Speed.

Move fast. You can't be complacent with Tess. She has exactly one speed and it's *GO*. To choose her is to choose a life of endless motion. She's the pace car. Just keep up. Keep running at her speed. Show her you can take it.

Control.

This is the hardest one for me. It's not about controlling Tess. In fact, I'm learning it's the opposite. I can only control myself—my actions, my wishes, my needs. What Tess needs is freedom. That's the only way this works. If I try to take control in this relationship, she'll bolt so far and so fast, I'll never catch up. Worse, I'll never earn back her trust.

Focus. Speed. Control.

I'm in my dead zone, but I can't push her out. She's everywhere. She's everything. This isn't about hockey anymore, even though I'm dressed in my full kit, minutes away from taking to that ice.

Focus. Speed. Control.

But all I can think about are those other words, dying to escape my lips, clouding all my thoughts. Three little words. A new mantra. A new prayer.

I love you.

THE buzzer sounds, ending the second period, and I skate over to the boards, air sharp in my lungs. We're down against the Blue Jackets 2-1. I'm playing like shit tonight. I'm slow on my skates, missing easy passes. I know the guys have noticed. Karlsson had an open shot to pass it to me twice in the second half of the first period, and he kept the puck. Honestly, I don't fucking blame him.

Walsh skates up right behind me, his hip hitting the boards. He's been on line with me all period. "What's wrong with you tonight?" he says, squeezing a water bottle over his sweaty face. The water drips down his neck, inside his shoulder pads. "Is it your knee?" he presses, following after me down the bench towards the locker room.

"My knee is fine."

"Well, you're playing like shit—"

I spin around, glaring in his face. "You wanna say that again, rookie?"

He doesn't back down. His rookie innocence is wearing off now that we're over half a season in. "I don't want a guy on my line who can't carry his weight," he admits, pulling no fucking punches.

"I carry my weight just fine," I reply.

"You're a mess. You've got the next eighteen minutes to get your head on straight—"

"My head *is* on straight—"

"You're distracted," he counters, grabbing me by the jersey and holding me back. The fans pound on the plexiglass by our heads, but they can't hear his words. "You're looking around like you're fucking lost out there. Half the time, it's like you're not even tracking the fucking puck. What the hell is wrong with you?" He gives me a shove, letting me go.

I groan. He's fucking right. I know he is. I'm so distracted. I'm still looking for Tess. I just need to see her once. If she's here, I know she'll wait for me after the game. And if she'll wait for me, I know I can say what I need to say. I can't hold it in any longer.

I push past him along the bench, leading the way towards the locker room. The fans all around us still cheer, trying to get my attention. I tune it all out. White noise.

Walsh follows behind me as we make our way into the locker room. I don't even make it to my stall before Sully is on me.

"Dude, what's up with you tonight?" he says, sweat dripping down his face.

"I'm working on it," I reply, stepping around him to slam my helmet down on the bench.

"This isn't like you. I knew something was wrong during warm-up."

Next to him, Karlsson glances over, munching on a granola bar. He's worried too. I can see it on his face.

"Guys, I'm just having an off night," I say, snatching for my water bottle. "Jeez, you'd think I was out there tryna play with a croquet mallet."

"You don't have off nights," Karlsson says, his voice soft.

"Well, then I'm overdue for one, yeah?" I say, launching to my feet. "So maybe you can all just cut me some fucking slack."

Not waiting for their replies, I push past Sully, marching across the locker room towards the PT room. My eyes scan quickly, locking on my target. "Doc," I call, still fisting my water bottle like I'm trying to choke it.

She wasn't here earlier, otherwise I would have gone straight to the source. And when she did arrive, she avoided me like the plague, sticking to the far end of the bench. I could feel her eyes watching me while I was out on the ice for every shift. My panic spiked higher with each pointed look she gave in the opposite direction. Yeah, she knows something.

She spins around now, her arms full of bananas. She takes one look at my face and her smile falls. Then she's shaking her head, trying to slip past me. "Langley, just don't, okay?"

"Hey—wait," I say, grabbing her arm as she tries to pass.

She goes still, her gaze darting from my sweaty face down to where my hand holds her. "Take your hand off me, Ryan," she says. "Or lose the hand."

I drop my hand away and take a step back. "Is she here?"

"Ryan—"

"Something's fucking wrong," I say, my voice hoarse. "I can feel it in my bones. You keep watching me, but you won't look at me. I'm starting to freak out here. She's supposed to be here but she's not . . . is she?"

She gazes up at me, her expression anguished. "Ryan, she's not coming. I think she just needs some space. She'll be staying with me tonight. Just give her space, okay?"

My heart fucking stops. "Wait—what the fuck happened?"

She groans, turning away. "Ryan—"

"I love her, Rachel. I'm in love with her, and I think she loves me too. I can't breathe—can't fucking *think*—because I need to tell her so badly."

She spins to face me, and I swear I see a small flicker of fear dance inside her eyes. "Ryan, don't." She grabs my sweaty wrist. "Please don't tell her," she says, tears springing to her eyes. "Not now. Not like this. *Please*. You'll make it that much harder for her."

"Harder for her to do what?" I press, my heart racing like I just pulled a double shift. And that's when it hits me. "Oh my god . . . this is about her ex, right? That asshole fucking did something. He threatened her again, didn't he?"

Rachel just shakes her head, holding back the truth I see burning inside her.

"Rachel, *please*—"

"He threatened you."

Rachel gasps, eyes narrowing as I spin to face the new voice. Jake is standing just behind me, his sweaty face solemn.

"Jake, don't," she orders. "Tess doesn't want him hurt, and that's her business—"

"It's *his* business too," Jake counters. "She made *you* promise not to say anything, but I'm under no such gag orders." He looks to me, placing a hand on my shoulder pads. "You love her, man?"

I nod. "I do. So fucking much."

"Then go tell her that—"

"Jake," Rachel cries. "Tess says she has a plan, and we all have to trust her. She knows Troy better than any of us. If she says we step back, I think we all need to listen."

"Will one of you just tell me what the fuck happened?" I beg. "You said he threatened *me*. I've never met the guy. I don't even know what he looks like. What did he do?"

"Check her closet," Jake replies. "Everything you need to know is in there."

Rachel just shakes her head, glaring at her husband. I see through her though. I know she's more scared than angry. What the hell happened today?

I turn away from them both, my shoulder brushing Jake's as I practically run in my skates over to Coach's office. His door connects to the locker room on the other side from PT. The door is open, and I push my way inside. Coach Johnson sits at his desk, eyes glued to a monitor playing game tape from first period. Assistant Coaches Andrews and Denison are here, too, and the goalie coach.

"I need to go," I say to the room.

Three pairs of eyes turn to look at me.

"Langley? What's the problem, son?" says Coach Johnson.

"Family emergency, sir," I reply. "I need to leave. I'm sorry, but I can't finish this game."

"Jesus, what happened?" says Andrews, stepping forward to grip my shoulder pad. "You look white as a sheet—"

"I've never asked for this before, sir," I go on, looking right at Coach. "I've never even missed a practice before my knee. I'm asking now. Let me go take care of my family. I'm no good to you out there tonight anyway," I add, gesturing to the monitor.

They all turn, and we watch as Karlsson shoots me a pass and I miss, out of position and too slow to catch up. That missed pass led to the changeover that led to the Blue Jackets's first goal.

Coach Johnson stands. "You can't tell us what's wrong?"

"I don't know yet, sir. I need to go find out. Until I do, my head's not in this game. I can't play anymore hockey tonight, sir. Fine me, suspend me, do whatever you need to do."

Slowly, he nods, his grey eyes narrowed at me. "Family comes first, Langley," he says at last. "Go. Take care of your business."

I barely get out a 'thank you' before I'm rushing out of the office and over to my stall, ready to rip off this Rays jersey and get home to Tess.

58

Ryan

I pull up to the bungalow to see Tess's rental car parked in the driveway. I slip out of the car and hurry up to the front door, unlocking it. The lights are all off in the living room, but music plays over the speakers. I hear the bridge of "Tolerate It" and my heart sinks. No woman listens to *Evermore* without having thoughts of a love lost.

Tossing my keys down on the side table, I move down the hall. She's not in the living room or the kitchen. I cross the space and move down the dark hallway, glancing between the pair of doors. One is closed, leading to my room. I haven't slept in there for days. The door to her room is open, the golden light warm and welcoming. I knock twice on the open door and wait.

"Tess?" I call.

She doesn't answer.

I step into the room, and my heart, which had already sunk, goes cold as ice. Her big silver suitcase is out on the bed, clothes and dresses and shoes packed neatly inside. The present I left for her is still wrapped, untouched. She just moved it over to the bedside table. The envelope holding her WAG pass rests on top, unopened. More stuff is piled on the chair in the corner. All her toiletries line the top of the dresser.

This is why she wasn't at the game. She was using the time I was away to slip out like a goddamn thief in the night. And she *is* a thief, because when she goes, she'll take my heart away with her. No ransom. No demands.

What I want to know is *why*.

My gaze darts over to the closet. Bracing myself, I step inside, looking around the empty space. Most of her stuff is packed away. A couple sweaters remain on hangers. A few shoes litter the floor. And two small boxes.

I go still. The rotten energy floating off them is palpable. I can practically taste it on my tongue. These are what Jake wants me to find. With a grimace, I bring them out to her bedroom, dropping them on the bed. I open the flaps of the first box and find a bunch of shredded papers inside. There's a note on top as well, but it's written in a tight, slanted cursive handwriting.

I open the other box. Looking inside, I instantly want to feel sick. It's a box of photos. Horrible, grainy, exposing photos of Tess and me. Every moment we've shared has been captured and documented. I get to the stack of kitchen photos and curse, dropping them back into the box as if they burned me.

Someone's been watching us for weeks. Someone violated us, violated Tess. And I didn't protect her. In my defense, I didn't fucking know.

Did *she* know?

This is the big wall I've felt standing between us. That last barrier she just couldn't get over. We're the extrovert and the introvert. The doer and the thinker. The Gemini and the Virgo. We shouldn't work on paper, but we do. We're so damn happy together. And we're good for each other. All I want is to get closer, and yet she's constantly pushing me away. I thought it was her. I thought it was some hang-up she has about commitment and trust. And I think all of that is still true. But now I'm holding the proof of something more. She's been holding back to protect me. She knew someone was watching us. She knew she wasn't safe.

And she didn't tell me.

I swallow my frustration. How hard must it have been for her to keep this from me? Or was it difficult at all? Maybe this level of subterfuge comes easy to her—

Stop.

I fight the urge to crumple the photos in my hands. I'm hurt and confused, but that's no excuse to be unfair to the woman I love. I deserve an explanation just as much as she deserves the chance to give me one. I have to be ready to listen. This can all make sense if I let it.

I already have some of the pieces to this puzzle. Tess holds the rest. I need her to share. We don't stand a fucking chance if she can't trust me with something as big as this.

I glance back down at the photos. The feeling of violation sweeps over me again. My finger brushes over the grainy image of Tess in the kitchen. I'm between her legs, my body out of shot, hidden in shadow. She's all alone, exposed to the lens—her breasts, the arch of her neck, the curve of her hip, the look of wild abandon on her face.

It feels like he stole something from her with the snap of this photo. He took something without asking. I want to beat him with his fucking camera. And then I want to find Troy Owens and beat him too. He's the one that asked for this. He paid someone to do this to us. Why? Does he get off on these? Does he still think of Tess as his?

The thought makes my blood boil. I feel sick. I need to find Tess. If I'm feeling this way about it all, how must she feel? I need to comfort her.

I drop the photos down to the bed, turning my back on them, and head for the door. But I pause in my steps as Tess walks in, juggling a pair of empty moving boxes in her hands. Our eyes meet, and then she's screaming.

"Ohmygod—Ryan!"

Her scream makes me jump.

She drops the moving boxes to her feet, her hands going to clutch at her chest. "Ryan, you scared the pee outta me," she shrieks.

I feel breathless, my heart racing as I take her in at last. It's only been ten fucking hours, but it may as well be ten years. "Tess," I say softly, putting all my feeling into the word.

She stands there in her ratty T-shirt and a pair of leggings, her curly hair up in a high ponytail. She looks so casual, like we're about to flop onto the couch and watch another episode of *Sons*, not pack all her shit to leave. She really meant for me to come home and find her gone? It's an act of cruelty I wouldn't have imagined her capable of.

That's when it hits me: it wasn't her idea. She's acting on orders. Troy's orders. Because he somehow threatened me. How? With the photos? What is he going to do with them? What do they prove other than he's a fucking creeper who should be in jail?

I have to know what the fuck is going on. "Tess, baby—"

"Wait, what time is it? What are you doing here? You're supposed to be at your game for another hour at least. Ryan, why aren't you at your game?"

"I left," I reply, stating the obvious.

"Why would you leave in the middle of a game?"

"Jake said you needed me here, so I left. Now I know why—"

Her anxiety is palpable. "Did anyone see you come in? God, of course they did," she says to herself. "His car is parked out front . . . and so is mine." She glances up, fear in her eyes. "Ryan, you have to go—"

"I'm not going anywhere," I say, standing my ground.

"Ryan," she begs, snatching up one of the moving boxes.

"I told you I would put you first, and I meant it," I say, crossing the room towards her. She goes stiff at my approach, and it breaks my heart. She's so fucking scared. All my anger and bravado melts away. "Oh . . . baby. What did he do to you, huh?"

She blinks back her tears, using the box like a shield to keep me back. "I don't know what you're talking about."

"You don't fucking know?" I counter, my voice rising. "Tess, look around you." I gesture at the chaos on every surface of the room. "You're packing up to run again. I think I deserve to know why. What did he say?"

"It's not your burden to bear," she says. "Ryan, I'm dealing with it. You have to trust that I'll fix this on my own—"

"No," I counter. "Tess, *no*. This isn't love. Hiding all this from me, carrying the weight of it all on your own when I have two strong arms and a strong fucking back to help you—it's not love, Tess. It's control. You're trying to control the outcome for both of us by keeping me in the dark. You need to tell me right now, aside from the photos, what else has he done?"

"What photos?" she dares to say.

I take three steps back and point down at the bed.

She inches closer, needing to see over the large mound of her open suitcase. As soon as her eyes settle on the boxes, I watch the emotion flash across her face—fear, disgust, sadness, anguish. Fresh tears well in her eyes as she looks up at me. "How did you know?"

"Jake," I reply.

She shakes her head, her frustration evident.

"Don't be mad at him. He was just giving me a fighting chance."

"I didn't want you to get dragged into my mess. I—" She sucks in a breath that comes out like a sob. "Oh god—I didn't want to hurt you, but I think I did anyway. Just being near you is hurting you. Even now, he'll know, and he'll use it against us. I never wanted to use you, but that's what he's going to say. He's going to twist this all up and take what we have and ruin it. He's going to take something so beautiful and make it ugly and I can't fucking stand it."

The moving box drops to her feet again, and then I'm rushing forward, wrapping her in my arms. "I'm so sorry," I say into her hair, my hands brushing up and down her back.

She sobs into my shoulder, her entire body trembling as she clings to me for dear life.

"I'm sorry, baby. I'm so sorry," I repeat. "He violated you with those photos. He stole from you. From *us*. Our joy, our happiness. And we have so much of both together, right?" I pull back, tipping her chin up to look in her eyes. I need to see her face. I do better when I can see her.

"I never wanted this," she says, her mascara leaving streaks down her freckled cheeks.

I brush her hair back. "No one wants their privacy violated. Tess, this is a crime," I say as gently as possible, praying she'll hear me this time. "All these photos are evidence of Troy's mounting crimes. Stalking, harassment, blackmail. He's digging his own grave."

"The creep brought them to my work," she whispers. "He watched me leave the office and brought the box to Cheryl. He's been watching me for weeks. He's probably outside even now," she says, glancing around as if he might be peering in through the windows.

My gaze darts over to see the curtains are pulled tight. "Is that why all the lights are off?"

"I didn't want to give him anything else to photograph," she replies with a little nod. "I don't know that I can stay here anymore, even without Troy's demands. This place is tainted for me now." She glances up at me, trying to show me her vulnerability.

"What demands did he make? What's the threat against me that has you running?"

She swallows down the emotion sitting thick in her throat.

"You can tell me. Tess, look at me."

She glances up, her freckled cheeks pink from crying. The mascara stains her upper and lower lids. But she's still so goddamn beautiful. She belongs in the garden of a palace, perched on a marble plinth for all to admire. But I'm selfish. I want to keep her beauty and her smiles. She's mine and I'm hers and no matter what happens next, she's going to know how I feel about her.

"Tess, I love you," I say, my hand cupping her cheek. "Whatever he said to you, whatever leverage you think he has on me—on us—it doesn't matter. Not when we know what we share is genuine. Fuck all the easy criticisms—the age gap and the career differences, us being on different life paths. Age is just a number. And all our careers prove is that we're both driven and hard-working. And sure, you're going through some shit with this divorce, but it's just a life change. Everyone has them. I'm going through one now too—my contract extension, my new endorsement deals. These are once-in-a-career changes and I'm living them now. Did I mention the new one with Bauer?" I add with a smile. "MK sent over the details this afternoon—"

She groans, shaking her head. "God, I fucking *hate* him. I hope Troy falls into a vat of toxic, boiling goo like in that-that movie. You know, the one with Arnold Schwarzenegger. What's it called?" She looks up at me expectantly.

"He's been in a lot of movies, babe."

"Yeah, but there's only one where he's a machine that gets dropped into a lava vat," she cries.

"*Terminator*?" I offer with a confused frown.

"Yes," she says with a snap of her fingers. "That's what I want. I want Troy to stumble off a catwalk into a vat of molten lava, and I want to stir him in with a stick. I don't want him murdered, because I don't believe in that—and I'm not going to kill him, because again, I know that's objectively wrong. But I just need him to trip, you know? I need him to wear his stupid loafers with the tassels that make him look like a trust fund tool, and I need the tassel to get caught in the grate of the catwalk, and I need him to fall into the lava vat."

I just blink, staring down at this woman I love. "That's some dark shit, babe."

"Yeah, well, Troy brings out the fucking worst in me," she snaps. "And he deserves nothing less for what he's trying to do to you."

"What's in this box?" I say, pointing at the smaller one with the note I can't read.

"That was the first present he left me a couple weeks ago," she says, glaring at the box. "My shredded divorce papers. Unsigned, of course."

"And what does he intend to do with all the photos of us?"

"Blast them online," she replies. "He means to paint you as a sex-addled hockey star who can't keep his dick in his pants, fucking anything that moves, even married women."

"Jesus. He doesn't flatter me much, does he?"

"He wants to paint himself as the noble victim in our adulterous affair," she goes on. "Never mind that I left him three fucking years ago after *he* cheated first," she cries. "He started this downward spiral. He broke our vows first, not me. He was cruel and controlling. He lied to me and manipulated me; he got his family to lie and manipulate me. The marriage was broken. It *is* broken. And now look at this mess," she cries, gesturing all around.

"So, he's the cheater and the abuser and the blackmailer, but I'm gonna burn for it?"

She nods. "He knows how temperamental these sports franchises can be. They won't want this bad press. They'll run from you, Ryan. 'Rats on a sinking ship' I believe were his exact words. And I believe him," she adds. "God help me, if he pulls this trigger, it's you who will take the bullet, not me. My life is small, Ryan. My sphere of influence even smaller. I'll lose my job and have to leave Cincinnati, but I was already resigned to that. He knew he couldn't hurt me anymore by attacking me directly—"

"So, he's attacking me," I summarize.

She nods.

"He's hurting me because he knows just how much that will hurt you. Is that it? Do I have all the pieces to the puzzle now?"

"I'm sorry," she says. "I thought I could handle him on my own. I should have assumed he would try to take you from me once he knew I was in lo—"

She catches herself, shutting down, and my gaze locks on her. "Go on."

She bites her bottom lip, her gaze flicking up to mine. "You need to understand that I have monumental abandonment issues, okay? We're talking like, Washington Monument. Or think even bigger, like Mount Rushmore. And those are not to be outdone by my trust issues."

"I get it," I say, heart thumping. "You're Tess the Red-hot Mess. But you were about to say something pretty monumental, and I, for one, am really interested to hear it."

She purses her lips, that little glint in her eyes letting me know my Tess is in there.

Come on, baby, I whisper without words. It's my spirit calling out to hers. I want every piece of this woman—her gorgeous body, her kindness, her clever mind. She's it for me. She's the fucking one. I never believed in the idea of soulmates. But until a few months ago, I had never met Tess. Now the universe is calling me a fool. If my soul ever had a mate, I'd want it to be her. But she has to be brave enough to want me too.

Say it.

She holds my gaze, her expression softening. Her hand reaches out, brushing up my arm as if we're meant to touch. She's where I want to begin and end.

Please, baby. Just say it.

"Ryan Charles Langley," she says, tears in her eyes. "I'm in love with you."

I let out a breath, shoulders sagging. "Oh, thank fuck—wait—" I raise a brow at her. "Charles? Babe, that's not my middle name."

She laughs. "I know, but it felt like a middle name moment, and I don't know your middle name."

I just shake my head, flashing her a smirk as she feeds my line back to me. "All you have to do is ask me."

"I just told you that I love you," she counters. "Me, Tess the

Gemini With Two Dark Sides Owens, just told you, Ryan Puppy Langley, that I'm in love with you, and you have no comment?"

"I told you I love you, like, five minutes ago, and your only comment was to go on a rant about boiling Troy in a vat of lava."

She gasps. "You did not."

I stare down at her as I run the tape back in my mind. "Babe, *yes,* I did. I told you I loved you, and I made a whole speech about how we're fucking made for each other."

"No, we were talking about his leverage—"

"Yeah, and then *I* said—"

"Ohmygod, you said it," she cries, eyes wide as she covers her hand with her mouth. "Wait—you said it and I missed it? You have to say it again."

And now I'm laughing. I can't help it. This woman is going to be the death of me, whether through soul-shattering sex or these circular conversations.

"Ryan," she huffs, slapping my arm. "*Please*. Say it again."

"Why bother? You clearly don't listen," I reply, feigning hurt feelings as I cross my arms.

"I was distraught," she cries, tugging on my arms and trying to weasel her way closer. "I was thinking about how I'd already lost you, and how I couldn't fucking bear it, and how lonely I was without you. I thought I had to do this on my own, like I was fucking cursed to be alone. So, my heart was breaking, and I couldn't hear you beyond the sound of my own agony."

We both go still as I gaze down at her. She's clinging to me with both hands, gripping tight to my forearms. Her freckled cheeks are flushed red, her chest heaving with the exertion of unloading so much emotional baggage at once. I peer into her eyes and smile. My Tess is back. She's in control. The scared creature she was when I first arrived is gone, banished. Tess the Mess, queen of my fucking heart, is here now and I mean to make her stay.

I cup her face. "You look at me right now, you wild creature. Are you looking at me?"

She nods.

"Tess, can you hear me?"

"Yes," she says with a roll of her eyes.

"Do that again, and I'll take you over my knee and spank your ass raw," I warn.

She twitches in my hold, her gaze going molten as she looks up at me. "Ryan—"

"No speaking," I say over her. "It's the Virgo's turn. Tess With Two Dark Sides can have her turn when I'm done, agreed?"

She nods, lifting her hands to wrap around my wrists.

"Tess Owens, I love you," I say, trying to keep my voice from trembling. "I'm in love with you. Did you hear me that time?"

She nods again, happy tears filling her eyes.

"I don't give a fuck what happened in your past," I go on. "We all have one. The only thing I care about is that your past brought you to me. Your past is the story you've already written. You have to let it stay there, okay? We're on a new page together, you and me. I'm your future, Tess. Say it."

"You're my future," she says.

"The past doesn't control your present," I intone.

She repeats me, her voice soft. But I can tell she's not quite convinced. It's okay. I hold enough conviction for the both of us.

"You aren't alone anymore, do you hear me? The only person who can keep you from me is *you*. In that sense, He Who Must Trip on a Shoe Tassel and Boil in Lava is right. You *are* in control, Tess. You're in control of *this*," I say, taking her hand and splaying it over my heart. "You're in control of us. If you walk away, that will be your choice. If you stay, that will be your choice too. The door to my heart will always be open, and I will never seek to control you—"

"But you're in control too," she says. "You could walk away. You could shut me out."

I just laugh. "Have you seen you, Tess? Have you seen these lips?" I brush my fingers over her mouth. "Have you heard your laugh? It stops me dead in my tracks every time."

Her gaze softens as her body sinks into me, craving my closeness.

"Have you watched the way you cross a room in a pair of heels?" I bend lower to brush a kiss against her temple, my hands smoothing down her arms. "Have you ever felt what it is to hold all your attention?" My hands graze over her breasts, and I love the feel of her nipples hard against my palms.

The energy between us turns on a dime, and now I know my Tess is fully here, ready to put her crown back on. She's ready to fucking own me.

And I'm ready to let her.

Inching away from her, I drop my hands to the hem of my Rays tech shirt and jerk it off, dropping it to the floor.

"What are you doing?" Her heated gaze takes me in. Oh, yeah, my sweet devil loves my body. She loves to tease it. Loves to wind me up and make me moan. She needs to feel in control right now? Fine. My Tess gets whatever she wants.

"Tess, I'm yours," I say, taking her hands by the wrists and placing them palm-flat on my chest. "I'm yours. There will never be anyone else. Take me."

She steps in, her hands smoothing over the hard planes of my chest, down my ribs.

I want her so goddamn much. My dick is twitching in my pants, turned on by her presence as much by her beauty or her touch. The truth is that I breathe easier just being in the same room. "I'm yours," I say again, shucking my pants down my hips to the floor.

She looks at me, eyes wide, watching as I strip. "Puppy, what are you doing?"

"I'm giving myself to you."

I step out of my pants, my dick hardening as her hungry gaze devours me. I love her eyes on me. I never want her to look away. I wiggle my toes at each heel, slipping out of my thin athletic socks, until I'm standing before the woman I love, naked except for my neoprene knee brace.

"I'm yours," I say again, feeling the hold on my own control slipping away. I'm giving it all to her, every piece of me. I'm safe with her. All she has to do is hold out her hands and take me. "I want you to be the wild, happy Tess I met on the beach, all curls and confidence and killer curves for days. I want you to be powerful and free. That's all I want."

"I want that too," she admits, her voice soft.

"Then be free with me," I beg. "Tess, baby, I choose you. You're my one. My only one."

Her gaze takes me in, and I feel my body heat all over.

Slowly, I drop to my knees, gazing up at her, begging her with every piece of my soul. "If you want me, Tess, take me. Make me yours."

I watch the column of her throat as she swallows. Then she takes a small step closer on bare feet, her hand reaching out for me. I lean into it like I did on my first night here, chasing her touch. She brushes her fingers through my hair, cupping the side of my head. I don't bother holding back my groan.

"You want me to take you?" Her thumb brushes my temple.

I nod, turning my face to kiss her palm.

"Tell me what you want, Ryan."

Reaching out, I take gentle hold of her hips. "My entire life revolves around me holding onto control—my diet, my exercise, the game, the puck. It's not easy for me to let go."

She nods, understanding in her eyes.

"But with you, it feels so easy," I admit. "I trust you, Tess. I love you and I'm yours. Please, just end my agony and say you'll be mine." I say these last words as I sink forward, my face pressing against her stomach, my hands sliding down her hips to grip her thighs.

"Do you want to be my sweet boy?" Her fingers tease as they dance across my skin. "Do you want to know what it feels like to be claimed?"

I nod, words failing me as I watch her strip out of her T-shirt. She's so goddamn beautiful.

"Speak, Ryan," she says, shimmying out of her leggings and kicking them aside. She stands in front of me wholly naked, wholly mine. "Tell me what you want from me."

I meet her eyes, losing myself in the forest greens and golds. "I want you to fuck me," I reply. "Tess, please, baby. Show me I'm yours."

59
Tess

Ryan kneels in front of me naked, his heart in his hands, giving me all his vulnerability. "Fuck me," he says again. "I want you to do it. I want to be yours in all ways. I trust you. Tess, I love you—"

I silence his words with my mouth. Holding his face, I bend down and take what I need, kissing him with everything I have. I just spent one of the worst days of my life sneaking around trying to find a way to get out of the house without making a tearful goodbye. I was packing to leave. Troy had won. I would never do a thing to hurt Ryan. If that means I let him go, that's what I was ready to do.

But Ryan is right. He deserves for me to be strong. He deserves for me to stop running, stop hiding from a man I left in all but name over three years ago. Troy can bring on the rain. He can drown me for all I care. I'm a good swimmer. And with Ryan holding my hand, I've already found a safer shore.

As usual, Ryan holds nothing back, kissing me with all his pent-up passion and need. He's ravenous, devouring my kisses, his hands roving my naked body. I've never felt more loved than when this man's hands are on me. He's so gentle, even as he takes what he wants. He guides me to my pleasure every time, joyfully claiming his own. I'm safe in his arms, wild and free. He brings out the best in me.

"I love you," I say against his mouth. "Ryan, I love you."

"Thank fucking God," he groans, his teeth nipping my bottom lip as he stands. Our angle changes, and now he's pressing in, our warm flesh fitting perfectly together. "I love you too," he says against my lips. "I've been dying to say it for days. I looked for you at my game. I wanted you there so badly. I wanted to tell you with my jersey on your back."

I lean away, breaking our kiss. "Your jersey?"

He nods, biting his bottom lip in that adorable way he does when he's nervous. "Yeah, I uhh . . . left you that stuff earlier," he says, pointing to the nightstand.

I glance over my shoulder, my heart twisting in a little knot. I meant to open it before the game, but then I got the box from Troy, and it felt too painful to know what sweet, thoughtful thing Ryan left for me. "What is it?" I say.

"Tickets to the game," he replies. "A parking pass and a WAG room pass."

"What's the other thing?"

His hands give my hips a little push. "Open it."

Turning away from him, I pad on bare feet over to the side table, pretty sure I already know what this will be. I unwrap the tissue paper and hold up a Rays home game jersey. It's a pretty aqua blue with thick black, white, and brick red stripes on the sleeves and along the bottom. The stingray logo rests large on the front, a few brand logos stitched to the chest, including a patch for the Winter Classic. A number 20 is stitched on both shoulders. I flip it around to see the big number 20 on the back, framed above by his name: Langley.

"Is this your actual jersey?" I say over my shoulder. "Like, the one you wear during the game?"

He nods.

I turn around, holding it up to my frame, my hand smoothing over the fabric. "Am I even allowed to have this?"

He laughs, flicking my hair off my shoulder and replacing it with his warm lips. "Yeah, I wore that one during the Winter Classic."

My blood goes cold, my fingers holding tight to the jersey. "You wore it when you hurt your knee."

"I wore it when I was looking for *you*," he corrects.

"What?"

He steps in, the jersey pinned between us. "You were so in my head already," he admits, his thumb brushing my cheek. "I had a split moment on the ice when I looked up through the glass, and I swear to God I thought I saw you standing there."

"Me?"

He nods. "Yeah, you were watching me, cheering for me, and I thought my heart was gonna burst. I wanted it to be you . . . which means I didn't see the hit coming." He leans in, placing a gentle kiss to my lips. "Baby, I never saw you coming," he whispers against my lips. "This is yours now," he adds, his hand closing around the fabric. "No one can wear this but you."

"Wow. This is pretty serious, Ryan."

He nods again, his hands smoothing up my forearms.

"I admit, I don't know a lot about hockey, but this is basically you asking me to go steady, right? Isn't this like the sporty version of becoming your old lady?"

"Well, you are ten years older—*ouch*—" He laughs, rubbing the spot on his arm where I just punched him. "Tess, do you want to be my sporty old lady?" he teases. "You wanna ride my dick and cheer for my team and wear my jersey to my games?"

I'm still shaking my head at his low blow, but then I'm smiling and saying, "Yes."

"You know what else wearing this jersey means, right?" he says, his face turning serious.

I raise a brow in question.

"It means we go public. The only person who wears my jersey is *my* person. You're mine and I'm yours and we're together. Everyone will know, Tess. The team, our friends, the fans . . . Troy."

I hate the sound of his name spoken from Ryan's lips. I send up a silent prayer that it's the last time he ever says it.

"Whatever happens, we face it together, yeah? Good press, bad press, and all the press in between," he goes on. "You handle your ex. If you want me to stay out of it, I will. But running and hiding from him are off the fucking table. If you're mine, you stand and fight. We don't hide from our pasts, and we don't keep secrets. Truth and trust. No more working alone, alright?"

I nod again. It's scary for me with all my baggage, but I want this. I want Ryan and the uncomplicated happiness he's offering me. I want to leave my past behind and move forward. I want to trust him. He's holding out a hand like a lifeline, and I'm taking it.

"You're mine," I say, the jersey pinned between our naked bodies as I brush a hand down his chest, over his abs. With a smile, I palm his dick, stroking along his shaft with my fingers until he twitches in my hand.

"I'm dying, Tess," he says with a soft groan. "If this is a tease—"

I cup him tight, and he gasps, his hands going to my shoulders. Stepping into my power, I hold his gaze. "Outside these walls, I'll be Langley's girl. I'll go to your games and wear your number and cheer for you. But we both know that inside these walls, you're Tess's boy."

"Fuck," he mutters, his cock twitching in my hand.

"This body is mine," I say, leaning forward to kiss along his chest. "Every inch. I'm gonna put on this jersey, and then I'm taking what belongs to me."

His jaw clenches tight as his pretty green eyes darken. "Do it," he says. "Show me who owns me."

I drop my hand away from him, and he lets out a sharp breath through parted lips. "Get on the bed," I command.

"Put on the jersey," he counters, his eyes narrowing at me.

With a smirk, I break our gaze and focus on the jersey. Flipping it around, I stuff my hands inside it, raising it up over my head. I tug it down, my head popping out through the open "V." A few loose curls fall in my eyes, framing my face, and I let out a little laugh, watching the way his eyes light up.

Oh, this is just too easy.

I tug the jersey down over the girls. It's a snug fit, but it works. The bottom of the jersey sits tight around my hips. The sleeves are too long, practically covering my hands. "Well?" I say, lifting my hands to the side and doing a little turn for him. I'm sure I look ridiculous wearing just the jersey and nothing else, my pussy and dimpled booty on full display.

"Fucking perfect," he says with stars in his eyes.

My smile widens as my heart beats a little faster. "You like what you see, hockey boy?"

"So fucking much," he replies. He wraps an eager hand around his hard dick and gives it a few slow pulls. "I'm finding it very hard not to pin you to the bed and fuck you 'til you scream," he admits, his voice low.

"But that's not the game we're playing tonight," I tease. "I'm in charge, remember?"

He drops his hand away from his dick, taking a deep breath, shoulders squared at me. "I'm yours. Fuck me 'til there's nothing left."

We collide, bodies crashing together as we reach for each other, unable to hold back a moment longer. His hands reel me in, and we sink down on the bed, right on top of the spread of disgusting photos meant to tear us apart.

I climb onto his lap, my bare pussy resting over his hard dick. We both gasp, his hand dipping between us to adjust so I can grind along his shaft, my wetness making it slick and warm.

"Fuck." His hands grip my lower back as we move together.

I cup his face, my fingers brushing the stubble of his cheeks. He's got a few days of growth. The blond stubble does little to mask his beautiful, youthful face. I tip his chin up, claiming his lips as I grind on him.

"I missed you all day," he says against my lips, his hands drifting down to grip my bare ass as we move our hips, our skin heating from the friction. "Ten hours is too fucking long. You're mine," he groans, shoving his hand up under his jersey to play with my tits.

I break our kiss, arching back as I let my body feel his hands on me, smoothing over my skin. His hands are calloused from years of gripping a wooden stick. The pads of his fingers are rough. I fucking love it. I love the way his palms scratch even as they soothe.

I drag my fingers through his hair, holding onto him as he drops a hand between us. I think he's going for my clit, but then he's wrapping his hand around his dick.

"Just a taste," he murmurs. "Please, baby. Just one taste. Then I want you to own me."

I gasp, lifting up on my hips as he positions himself at my entrance. At the first feel of him prodding, I lower my hips, sinking down to claim his tip. A shiver shoots up my spine, and I grip tighter to his hair, jerking his head back to make him look at me rather than where we're joining.

"Look at me," I command. "Look in my eyes as I take you."

He holds my gaze, the green rim of his irises framing the black of his pupils. His lips are parted, his breath coming out in short pants as I sink lower down his shaft.

"You're so beautiful." I smooth my hands over his blond curls.

"You're so gentle, so kind. I don't deserve it," I admit, letting my own vulnerability free.

His grip tightens on my hips. "Don't you fucking dare," he says, his jaw clenching tight as he pulls on my hips, sheathing me to the hilt. "My Tess will never say that again. You're in my jersey, riding my dick. You're gonna treat yourself the way I treat you. You are a fucking queen. *Say* it."

I drop my hands to his shoulders, grinding my hips, moving with him so deep inside me. "I'm a queen," I pant.

"You're the beginning."

"I'm the beginning," I whisper, my core burning with need.

His arms move off my hips to brush over my shoulders. Then he's cupping my face, pulling me down for a kiss. "You're the end," he whispers against my lips. "Tess, you're my end."

"And you're mine," I reply.

We kiss, mouths opening, claiming the other's essence. God, he's such a good kisser. I could just do this all night and be satisfied. But we both need more. I need to feel in control, and he needs to let go. I can count on one hand the number of men I would ever trust to be this vulnerable with me. Now that Ryan's in my life, the list is only him.

Just thinking about how much I love him, my orgasm is about to crash through me. I cry out, shoving off him. I lift my hips, freeing myself from his dick. We both groan at the sudden loss. I want him inside me. I want his come in me.

There's always later.

I scramble to my feet, panting for air, my pussy's wetness warm between my thighs. "Get on your hands and knees," I command. "Show me what's mine."

With a hungry groan he attempts to turn over, only to be met by the boxes and my half-packed suitcase. Even now, his weight crushes some of the photographs—all proof of what we're determined to overcome together.

I watch all the muscles in his back tense as he makes a dramatic sweep with both arms, sending the suitcase and the boxes crashing to the floor. The smaller box overturns and my unsigned divorce papers rain down like snow, covering the braided rug.

Watching them fall, the truth hits me: I don't care if Troy ever signs the fucking papers. Either way, I'm free.

Ryan crawls on the bed, not caring that it's still littered with clandestine photographs of our entire relationship. He glances over his shoulder at me. "I've never done this before," he admits.

Ignoring the chaos all around us, I focus all my attention on him. There is only Ryan. I step in behind him, smoothing my hands up his thighs and over his toned ass. "I'll make this so good for you." I say, my voice soft. "You trust me?"

He nods, and I flash him a smile. "I want this, Tess. I want you."

"As I want you," I reply.

Leaving him on the bed, I move around to the end and fish my bag of toys out of my upturned suitcase. Tossing the bag on the end of the bed, I open it, taking out my favorite strapless strap-on. It's a purple "L" shape, with the long end shaped like a dildo. The shorter end is thicker, more bulbous like a butt plug, easier to fit and hold in my pussy. My favorite feature is the pair of bunny ears that stimulate my clit.

I hold up the toy and his eyes go wide.

"What is that?" he says.

"A strapless strap-on."

He studies it. "You don't need like, a harness or something? A jock or . . . "

I smirk. "Has eager puppy been doing his research? Do you want me to use a strap? I have one—"

"No," he says quickly. "I—I trust you."

I smile. "This toy will bring us both to screaming orgasms. Did I mention it vibrates?" I press the button to send it buzzing in my hand.

"Don't all your toys?" he replies with a grin.

"Most. Not all. Do you consent, Ryan? Can I ride you with this?"

"Yes," he says, his voice breathless. "Anything. I'm yours."

I snatch up the lube and move around the side of the bed towards him. Setting the toy down, I squeeze some lube onto my fingers. "I'm going to prep you, okay? Deep breaths. When you're ready, you'll push against my fingers, and it will almost feel like you're pulling me in. It can hurt if you don't relax. Trust me?"

He nods, a few curls framing his brow. "I trust you."

I smooth my left hand over his rounded ass, letting my lubed right hand trail between his cheeks, my finger teasing his tight hole.

He gasps, cheeks clenching on instinct.

My hand soothes him along with my voice. "Just relax, baby. I have you. I'm gonna make you come so hard, you'll see stars."

He groans, relaxing against my touch as I tease him, working my finger in and out, opening him up.

"How does it feel?" I murmur, leaning over him to press kisses to his back.

"Good," he grunts out, his hips moving against my hand as his fingers splay on the bed. "I wanna touch my dick," he groans, his head sagging between his shoulders.

"Not yet." I pull my finger out of his ass. Before he can reply, I press in with two, stretching him wider.

"Oh, fuck."

"Down on your elbows," I order. "Spread your legs wider for me."

He does as he's told, and I feel it like a slap to the clit. My body purrs with his acquiescence. "Such a good boy," I praise, marveling at the image of him on his knees for me in total submission.

He rocks back against my hand as I fuck him. "Please," he says after a few moments. "Tess, baby, I need you."

I need him too. He's ready. "Turn around," I say, pulling my fingers free.

He flips onto his butt, legs dangling off the edge of the bed, and I hand him the toy and the lube. "Get both ends ready."

"Which end goes in me?" He inspects the toy like it's a curious new invention.

"The longer end," I reply with a smirk.

I hold the lube for him, watching him prep both ends of the toy. Once it's ready, I toss the lube aside. "Take the strap-on by the longer end. You're going to put the short end inside me," I direct, my hands at my hips.

With an eager smile, he fists the front of his jersey and pulls me closer, teasing the toy between my legs. I widen my stance for him, holding his gaze as he slips the toy in, burying it inside my aching pussy.

"Mmm, that's good," I murmur, wiggling my hips to adjust to the fit. The little bunny part hugs my pussy, the ears riding against my clit.

We both look down to see the five inches of purple dildo protruding from my hips. I feel powerful like this. It's filling me as I'm about to be filling him. We'll ride our orgasms out together, the vibrations connecting us as we fall blissfully apart.

"Fuck," he groans, his hands smoothing over my hips as he looks at the toy. Slowly, his chin lifts and his gaze sweeps up my body to my face. "Take it off," he says.

"The jersey?" I run my hands over it. "Won't that ruin the fantasy?"

"You're the fantasy," he replies. "I want you. Only you. No barriers. Take it off."

Smiling down at him, I strip out of his Langley jersey, tossing it on the bed. Now I'm wearing nothing but my strapless strap-on. Reaching down for the toy, I press the little round button at the base. It buzzes to life, the vibrations hitting me deep.

His eyes go wide as he watches me shimmying, adjusting to the new sensation. "And it can stay in like that?"

"Mhmm," I reply, my hands going to his shoulders. "My pussy has a very firm grip . . . or had you forgotten?"

"How could I?" he teases back, his gaze still caught on the length of the purple dildo. "She's all I think about these days."

"Well, she's going to take very good care of you." I reply. "Lie back on the bed. I want to take you facing me. I want you looking in my eyes."

He inches back, sweeping photos aside as he moves towards the middle of the bed.

I follow him, crawling onto the edge between his spread knees. I smooth my hands up his calves, over his knees, pulling them wider apart. "Feet flat, relax your hips."

"Oh god," he whispers, his head dropping back as he does as I say.

I drop down between his open thighs, licking along his hard shaft from root to tip. Circling his head with my tongue, I suck him into my mouth, humming my pleasure as the change in angle has the toy buzzing against my G-spot.

His hand fists my hair, his hips rocking with the motion of my mouth as I tease him to full hardness. His precum coats my tongue and I moan for him, creating my own vibrations as I devour the taste.

In moments, his hand tightens in my hair, and he's pulling me off with a breathless laugh. "Baby, you keep doing that, I'll blow in your mouth."

"Promises," I tease, nipping his sensitive inner thigh with my teeth.

He hisses, giving my hair another tug.

I wince, loving the little bite of pain. "Are you ready for me, hockey boy? You want me to ride you into paradise?"

"Yes," he begs, his hand softening in my hair as he fists the comforter.

I crawl between his spread legs, settling myself on my knees. The adjustable pony on this toy means I can get a good angle for both of us. I'm going to be coming in no time flat with the added clitoral stimulation. My every nerve hums with excitement as I look down at him, spread beneath me, prepped and ready for my claiming.

He looks up at me like I'm his everything. "I love you," he says, his features soft in this golden light.

I brace his hips with both hands, holding him open as I squeeze the pony with my pelvic muscles, holding it tight. Then I'm pressing in between his cheeks, moving my hips a bit to rub the vibrating tip of the dildo over his tight hole.

"Oh, fuck," he groans at first contact, trying not to tense.

I use one hand to hold the dildo steady as I breach that tight ring of muscle, opening him up to take just the tip. "Breathe, baby," I soothe. "You're doing so well. Look at you taking my pretty silicone dick. Talk to me. Tell me how you feel."

"Mmph. The vibration . . . feels good."

"Look at me."

His eyes open and we connect, apple green eyes meeting forest green. There is such a burst of feeling there. With a gasp, he grabs my hips and pulls, sinking the dildo in deeper. The motion pushes the pony high and tight in my pussy, those bunny ears humming to either side of my swollen, needy clit.

"Oh—*god*—" I cry out, back arching like I was just zapped with electricity. I drop forward between his spread legs, catching myself with my hands to either side of him.

"Feel good?" he pants, a gleam in his eye. He's loving this. I am too.

"So fucking good," I whimper. "Baby, I need to move. Can I—"

"Do it," he orders, my sweet, impaled puppy topping from the bottom.

Recovering my wits, I tip back on my knees, changing the angle for us both yet again. Then I'm thrusting into him, driving the dildo in deeper.

"Incredible." His voice is breathless as I rut into him with short, quick thrusts.

"Look at me," I say again, needing this moment of vulnerability to be shared.

He gives me what I need, his pretty green eyes locking on mine, pleasure etching every line of his face as he rides out my thrusts, holding tight to me. When he begins moving his hips in tempo with mine, the slap of our skin rings out a primal chorus in my ears, I know he's close. God knows I've been close, too, ready to leap, aching to fall.

"My dick," he pants. "Please, baby. I need—*yes*—"

He doesn't finish the ask before my hand wraps around his shaft, pumping him as I pound home. My breasts give him a show, jiggling and swaying like anything as I fuck my man in his perfect tight ass.

"You're so beautiful like this," he praises. "Such a queen. God, you're mine. Never leave me. Tess, please—"

I chase his words, my orgasm lighting me up inside, spreading from my clit to deep in my core, all the way to my fingertips. "Come with me," I cry, my hips stuttering as the rabbit ears work their magic, sending my orgasm shattering through me. I feel it all the way to my toes. They curl in tight, my leg muscles spasming as I break upon the rocks. My hand on his dick stills and I tip my head back, screaming my release, my pussy gripping tight to the vibrating toy.

Below me, Ryan takes over, slamming his hips against mine a few more times before he loses rhythm, too, his hand pumping mine on his dick. "God—*ahh*—" He cries out, his cum spilling all over our joined hands as he falls apart beneath me.

We're a pair of moaning messes, bodies trembling, our skin flushed and slick with sweat. I gasp as the stimulation becomes too much, grabbing the toy and lifting myself off it. I feel empty in the best way with it gone. Carved out, like a coconut without its water. I'm careful as I pull the shaft from him and turn it off, setting it aside.

He lies there, spread-eagle and breathless, gazing up at me through half-lidded eyes. "Come here, baby."

I crawl over top of him, my weight pressing him down as he wraps me in his arms. We kiss long and deep, taking our time as our bodies stop trembling.

Then he's rolling me to our sides, our legs tangling, before he rolls me to my back. Now it's his weight pressing me down. He kisses down my body, pausing to pay special attention to my breasts. "Someday I wanna fuck these."

I just smile, my hands smoothing through his hair. "Be my guest."

He kisses down my body, over my belly, and around my navel. Then he's between my legs, his shoulders pushing my thighs open as he closes his mouth around my clit, sucking my wet release into his mouth.

I cry out, toes tingling as he licks lower, savoring every drop of me. By the time he's done, I'm even more of a shaking mess.

He pants for breath, crawling back up my body to claim my lips, rolling us back to our sides. "You're mine," he says between kisses. "I love you, Tess."

"Langley's girl," I reply, kissing him back. "I love you, Ryan. I'm yours. No more running. I just want to be yours."

60

Tess

"Wow," I say, eyes wide as I take in Rachel and her guys walking through the doors of the event hall.

Jake is at her left, dressed to kill in a sleek black tux, his dark hair oiled back. "I know, we clean up good, right?" he says with a teasing grin.

Ilmari is on her other side, looking like he's about to go involuntarily donate a kidney. His stupidly handsome bearded face is solemn, his long blond hair combed back into a neat top knot. His tux is charcoal grey and fitted like a dream.

Between them, Rachel flounces up in a slinky black dress with a high neck and a thigh-high slit. Her hair is swept down and to the side in an artful knot, a pair of gorgeous ruby and diamond earrings twinkling in her ears.

"Rach," I gasp, my gaze locking on the jewels. I think in a past life I was a dragon. I am entirely too infatuated with shiny, pretty things.

"You like?" she says with a smile, turning her head left and right. "They were a wedding present from the guys. I was excited to finally have a reason to wear them."

I turn my attention to Ilmari. "You still mad at me about all this?"

He just scowls. "I'm not giving the speech."

"Oh, yes, you are, and it's gonna be great," I counter. "And I'll have you know, we've already had several donations pour in this week by people who can't attend."

"Whoa, how much?" says Jake.

"Almost enough to match Ilmari's initial donation," I reply, hands on my hips.

"You're—oh, shit—seriously?" Jake turns to Ilmari. "Dude, that's fucking amazing. This is gonna work." He spins back to me. "Tess, this was so cool of you to do this for him. This is gonna be great."

"Of course, it is," Rachel says with a confident smile. "It's a Tess event. She doesn't miss."

"The food better be good." Caleb steps around his partners to stand on Ilmari's other side. He must have been parking their car.

I take him in, eyes wide. "Cay, you look . . . well, stop-thinking-words hot," I say with laugh.

He just shrugs. He's wearing a sleek navy suit, fitted to a T, with his hair slicked back too.

I take in the picture of the four of them together. "Okay, this should be illegal," I say, gesturing between them. "This level of hotness in one family is totally unfair to the rest of humanity. We're all out here just doing our best, and then in walk the four of you. It's criminal."

"Can you just imagine how cute our kids are gonna be?" Jake teases.

"I told you, we're not doing child pageants," Caleb says, glaring at his husband.

"We *are* gonna do pageants, and we're putting all the money our babies win into the 'Buy Jake a Sea-Doo' fund."

I laugh. "You guys are multi-millionaires. Just buy the damn Sea-Doo if you want a Sea-Doo."

Both Jake and Caleb give me a confused look. "What's the fun in that?" Jake scoffs.

"Oookay," Rachel says with a laugh, looping her arm in with Jake's. "Let's go find the cocktails, yeah? Tess, I'm leaving this one with you," she adds, tipping up on her toes to kiss Ilmari's bearded cheek. "Behave," she says at him.

He just groans, crossing in front of her to come stand by me.

She, Jake, and Caleb slip past us, heading into the event room.

I look up at Ilmari, giving him a little nudge with my elbow. "Wanna go meet the gopher tortoise?"

AN hour later, I'm trapped in the middle of a nest of vipers, also known as city council members. Ilmari slipped this particular net fifteen minutes ago, and I've just been trapped here with my empty wine glass, pretending to listen as Bill Peterson pulls attention away from tonight's cause yet again and back onto rezoning for a golf course.

This is such bullshit. None of these old turkeys are even going to donate to Out of the Net. They're only here because we need them to be on our side when we introduce our joint proposal with the North Florida Land Trust this summer to expand current preserved land areas near a popular sea turtle nesting site.

We're calling that phase two. Phase one is establishing our organization, building a donor base, and getting our name out there. Phase two is enacting meaningful change and pushing for better protections of sea turtle nesting grounds along the Jacksonville beaches.

But I can kiss ass with the best of them. The Bill Petersons of the world will always stand in the way of progress, so you have to find ways to either charm them or work around them. For now, I'm sticking with charm.

He makes some golf joke that has the other three laughing. I flash the fakest smile you've ever seen, using my empty glass as a cover when I raise it to my lips and say, "Oh—well, will you look at that? Empty." I tap the side of my glass with my manicured fingernail. "Excuse me gentlemen, won't you?"

They release me with polite nods, and I slip away, hurrying off in the direction of the cash bar. The bottom of my dress swishes around my ankles. It's a cute, ocean blue number with off-the-shoulder sleeves and a sweetheart bodice. The dress reaches the floor, with knee-high slits to either side. I've paired the look with my hair up and some fake, chunky emeralds in my ears.

Rachel meets me halfway to the cash bar, a glass of white wine clutched in either hand. She holds one out to me. "I was on my way to rescue you."

"My hero," I sigh, taking a sip of the chilled chardonnay. I glance over my shoulder to make sure I'm far enough away before adding, "Those might be the three dullest men on the planet."

"But they all sit on the city council," she says with a shrug, leading the way over to a standing table where Caleb waits, guarding several small plates of food. "I made him get you one of everything," she says, gesturing at the plates.

"Oh, I can't eat now," I say with a wave of my hand. "I need to mingle—"

"*Tess—*" She grabs my arm to reel me back in. "Look around you, hon. It's a smash hit. People are already saying we should do this again next year. Take a second, take a breath, and eat some food."

I glance down at the rainbow array of appetizers. "Ooo, did you try the mac and cheese?" I snatch up the mini serving, complete with panko breadcrumbs browned on top. I couldn't believe it when the caterer had it on her menu.

"Yeah, it's delicious," Rachel replies.

"I ate, like, six of them," Caleb adds. "What's in it? Crab?"

"Lobster," I say, taking a bite. The white cheddar is melty and warm around the noodles, pairing well with the sweet notes of the lobster meat. "Oh *god,* that's good."

My stomach has been growling for the last thirty minutes, but I've been too busy to eat. I finish my helping of mac and cheese in four bites, then I pop a couple bacon-wrapped dates before munching on the crudités.

"You all good?" Caleb says at Rachel. "Need anything?"

"We're good," she replies, smiling up at him. "Thanks, babe."

He leans over the table, pecking her lips before wandering off in the direction where all the other Rays have congregated. I glance around him to see Ryan mingling in the mix. He's been casting me flirty winks and smiles all evening.

"Cay seems to be settling into married life," I say, nibbling on another carrot stick.

Rachel smiles. "He's my mystery boy. The other two are so easy to figure out. Ilmari because he does exactly what he wants when he wants, and Jake because he has no filter and speaks his every thought and desire out loud. Cay is harder to read. He makes us all work for it."

"But you like a challenge," I say. "If they were all easy to read, you'd get bored."

"True," she says, taking a sip of her wine.

"So . . . that thing about the pageant babies—"

"*Not* pregnant," she says, cutting me off. "Are you kidding me? We only just got married. I have four very big personalities living in one house. Five if we count Poseidon—"

"Which we do," I chime.

"We all need time to settle. I want us to feel like . . . us," she says, not finding a better word. "We need to be us before we can be more."

"But you want more? Eventually, I mean?"

"Oh, yeah," she says with a smile, and my stupid little heart flutters for her. "We all do. And yes, if and when I spawn, I will name you their godmother," she adds.

"They'll need their Auntie Tess," I tease. "Who else will teach them how to throw such a fabulous soirée?"

She just laughs.

I reach across the table, squeezing her hand. "I'm happy for you, Rach."

Before she can respond, Poppy St. James comes breezing up to our table in a flouncy, strapless lilac dress, her hair up in a big, blonde bun. "Hey, y'all, what did I miss? Anything good?" She snatches up a carrot stick off my plate, taking a bite.

I take in her flushed cheeks, her squirrelly behavior, and her messy hair. Usually, Social Media Barbie doesn't have a single hair out of place on her pretty blonde head. The only other time I've seen her looking like this was when . . .

My gaze snaps to Rachel, and I know she's already gotten there too.

"Poppy . . . " she says, a glint in her eye. "Where did you just come from?"

"The bathroom," she replies, but her eyes give her away. Has this woman ever told a lie in her life?

"Don't you lie to me," Rachel presses, seeing right through her too. "Were you just hooking up with someone?"

Poppy huffs, plopping her half-eaten carrot back onto my plate. "Why don't you just scream your foul accusations to the high heavens?"

"You're as bad as this one," I say, jabbing a thumb at Rachel, relieved the secret is out.

"Hey, I've been good all night, I swear," Rachel says, raising one hand in mock oath. "The gala host's wife isn't allowed to sneak off into coat closets, right?"

"I don't know what you two are talking about," Poppy replies. "I stepped out for five minutes to answer the phone and use the bathroom."

As she speaks, Novy walks past our table, straightening his tie with a quick, "Evening, ladies."

Hearing his voice, Poppy goes still, her back so ramrod straight, someone must have just shoved a telephone pole up her booty.

Rachel and I exchange another glance. She waits for Novy to clear our table before she descends. "Poppy," she gasps. "You and Novy—"

"*Shhhh.*" Poppy waves a hand in her face. "Will you hush up?"

"You horny little horndog," I tease. "In front of the turtles, Poppy?"

"Oh, please," she says with a righteous huff. "If you two aren't the pot calling the kettle black. First there's you, Miss I Married *Three* Hockey Players," she tosses at Rachel. "And don't think we don't see the way you look at Langley like you wanna climb him like a tree," she adds at me.

"Actually, it's the other way around," I reply, wholly unashamed. It's not like he's my colleague or my patient. And Ryan and I agreed last night that we're going public. "He was the one climbing *me* when we first got here. I may have given him a lil' taste in the storage room."

Poppy just huffs again, snatching a glass of wine off a passing tray.

Rachel leans in, elbow on the table. "So, uhh, how long have you two been...you know?"

"That is absolutely none of your business," Poppy replies, taking a sip of her wine.

I glance from her to Rachel. "Did you—"

"*Blegh.*" Poppy spits the wine back into her glass. "Will someone take this away from me?" She slaps the glass down and slides it away.

Rachel's eyes go big as saucers, and I'm sure I'm not any better.

"Wait—are you pregnant?" I say.

Color blooms in Poppy's cheeks as tears fill her eyes.

"Oh . . . Pop." Rachel closes a hand around Poppy's, giving it a squeeze. "It's Novy's, isn't it? Does he know?"

"I . . . " Poppy sniffles, her pink lips pursed as she tries not to cry.

Rachel is trying to read her. "Wait . . . it's *not* his?"

"Ohmygod. She's not sure."

Both women glance over sharply at me.

Fuck. I just said that out loud, didn't I? I blame the mac and cheese. "You're not . . . are you? You're not sure."

Slowly, Poppy shakes her head.

"This is a lot of information to digest at the turtle gala," Rachel says, her dark eyes wide. "Well, are you—I mean—is it *two* guys on the team?"

Poppy snatches up the wine glass, ready to take another sip, before she gasps and shoves it away. "Oh, for Pete's sake! No, okay? I don't know who the father is. And yes, they're both on the team. And *yes*, I know I'm a mess. So why don't you just slap the scarlet 'A' on my chest and tie me to the stake already? Because this wanton hussy has *two* gentleman callers. And you know what? I'm not picking. You didn't have to pick so why should I?" She snatches up the wine glass again, realizes it's in her hand and shrieks, shoving it at me. "Gosh darn it!"

My eyes go wide, watching her fall apart as I save the wine glass from her panicked clutches.

"It's Morrow," Rachel says. "You've started something with Novy *and* Morrow. Right?"

"*Please*, Rach, you can't say anything," Poppy pleads, taking her hand. "I'm not ready for people to know. I'm not—we're not like you, okay? We're—this hasn't been easy for us the way it seems so easy for you. The boys are—it's just not easy to fall into something like this . . . " She falls into silence as Rachel squeezes her hand.

"I won't say a word, Pop," she assures her. "It's not my business. It's not anyone's business."

Poppy sniffs back tears. "I just—god, I never meant for any of this to happen," she admits. "And now it just keeps happening. Four months ago, I was arguing with Lukas in an Uber. Now I'm meeting him in empty bathrooms at charity events like we're a pair of horny teenagers. If we're not screamin,' we're screwin,' and I don't know how to stop."

"And Morrow?" Rachel asks.

Poppy just sighs. "I don't know how to stop."

"Geez," I mutter, taking a sip of Poppy's wine. "What's in the water over at that ice rink? First Rach snatching up three in one hand, now you? Should I be worried Ryan is gonna come home with Patty McFlashy Abs next week?"

Before they can reply, Nancy comes hurrying over to the table. "Tess, honey, there's a slight hiccup for tonight's beach walk plans."

"Ugh, don't tell me."

"Yup. Rain," she says with a nod.

I groan. "Damn you, Florida."

"Doppler says it's coming in quick," she adds, flashing me her phone to show me the weather app. "I think we may need to cancel."

This is a huge bummer. I was really looking forward to treating people to a beach walk out on the sand at night. I loved the image of all of us walking in our fancy duds, heels in hand, pretending to be sea turtles as we noticed the effects of light pollution.

"'Scuse me," I say to Rachel and Poppy. The clock never stops, even when there's salacious gossip to be heard. I step away from the table, Nancy following at my side. "How long is the rain supposed to last?" I ask, moving towards the pair of double doors that lead out to the back deck.

"Hard to say. Maybe an hour? But you know—"

"It's Florida," we intone at the same time.

I just sigh, pulling the door open and holding it for her to step through. The chill of the January air actually feels good as it kisses my skin. The wind blows, tugging on the loose tendrils framing my face.

"What if we just went and did it now?" I say, peering out over the railing at the white sand. Not fifty yards away, the ocean rolls in and out. "We could push back Ilmari's speech until after. Heck, he could even give it down on the beach. That could actually be great."

"I can run it by him," Nancy offers.

I huff a laugh. "Oh, no. Mr. Price has me making all executive decisions."

"Yeah . . . about that." She glances up at me sheepishly.

"What?"

"Um, well, Mars actually gave us strict instructions to run all ideas involving him past him first."

I laugh, turning around to lean against the wooden rail. "Well, I'm the Director of Operations for Out of the Net, and I say we're moving the beach walk up, along with his speech."

"And while I do love that idea," she hedges. "He did rather sternly imply that your orders regarding him are not to be followed without his express approval."

I glare down at her, even though I know she's only the messenger. "Seriously?"

"Please don't put me in the middle."

"Oh, trust me, I can handle that broody Finn myself," I say, pushing off the rail. "You're welcome to stand on the sidelines for this one, Nance. Come on, let's go light the torches."

She hurries behind me, both of us shucking our heels as we walk down the short boardwalk leading out to the beach. While the sun was still out, we set up a short row of tiki torches to light up the boardwalk's end and signal for walkers where to return.

"Oh, and a donor keeps asking about you," Nancy says, walking in step behind me. "Says he wants to speak to you about the terms of his donation."

I rack my brain, trying to remember that conversation. "His donation?"

"Yeah, he said you were expecting him, but you hadn't mentioned it to me so . . . "

I glance over my shoulder at her. "What did you say his name was?"

"Umm . . . Troy," she replies, checking the little notebook still in her hand. "A Mr. Troy from PFH Consulting Group. Do you know him?"

61
Ryan

Tonight is going so well. I was a bit anxious at first, thinking this might be a lot of rubbing shoulders with land developers, but I shouldn't have worried. Really, this just feels like one big fancy Rays party. The WAGs love an excuse to get dressed up, the alcohol is flowing, and everyone seems to be in good spirits. I've eaten my weight in appetizers, including, like, eight of those little cups of the lobster mac and cheese. Tess was right, it's goddamn delicious.

Everyone showed up for Mars. And we're all making generous donations. I've spent most of the last half hour laughing in the corner with Sully, Shelby, and Karlsson. Every so often, I let my gaze settle on Tess until she looks my way and I flash her a wink.

She's radiant tonight. She's working the room like a queen without a crown, floating from table to table, laughing and chatting it up. I smirk to myself, watching as she gets pulled away from Rachel and Poppy's table, Nancy hurrying along at her side. She's walking directly away from me. God, do I love this view. Her ass sways as her heels click, the fabric swishing.

In the rush of party set up, I may have pulled her into a coat closet . . . and she may have pushed me to my knees. I focus on the beer in my hand, remembering the feel of that soft fabric bunching around my face. Later tonight, I'll be taking her out of that dress and leaving it on my floor.

I told my coaches about Troy and his threats this morning. Tess was anxious about it, but I knew it was the right thing to do. Coach Johnson had questions, but he was cool. We've got a PR strategy meeting planned with Poppy for tomorrow morning. For tonight, I don't want Tess to worry, and I won't either. We deserve a night of fun with our friends, a night to act like the couple we are where everyone can see.

"So . . . seems like you and Tess are finally official, then?" says Sully, following the direction of my gaze and flashing me a knowing smirk.

I tear my gaze away from her and smile. "Yep. That woman is it for me."

"You work fast," Karlsson says.

"Hey, when you know, you know," I reply.

"And no running?" says Shelby.

"I'm fast," I reply, taking a sip of my beer. "I can keep up."

Sully laughs. "Well, she seems like a great girl to me. When you whacked her in the head with that soccer ball, did you ever think you'd end up here?"

"Did you really think you'd land a girl like Shelbs the first time you met her?" I tease.

"Hell no," Sully replies as we all laugh. "These women are so far out of our league. I'm not questioning it, though. I'm like you, man. She says run, I fucking run."

Shelby smiles up at him. "We like running together, don't we, baby?"

"Yeah, we do," he says, kissing her lips.

Karlsson and I shift awkwardly, flashing each other a shrug before the other two break apart.

"You look happy, Ryan," Shelby says at me. "Really."

"I am. I'm really fucking happy."

"Well, this is dumb, then," says Sully, looking around for a passing waiter. "We need to celebrate. Here—" He passes out fresh drinks to the four of us. "Cheers to Ryan and Tess," he says, holding up his glass. "To running in the same direction."

We all raise our glasses, and I grin like an idiot in love. "Cheers."

"Cheers," says Shelby, clinking her glass with mine.

"Skål," Karlsson intones, raising his glass too.

As I lower my glass, there's a crashing sound behind us that makes us all jump. I turn sharply around to see that a waiter has accidentally bumped one of the standing tables, knocking it to the ground. His hands are full with a heavy tray, so I set my glass down and hurry over.

"Hey—hey, I got it, man," I say, ducking down to right the table for him.

"Thanks," he says, breathless. "Didn't see it there."

"You're all doing great tonight," I tell him. "Food and service are all really great. Good job."

He just nods, hurrying away.

I duck down and pick up the little candle holder thingy that broke in three pieces with the crash. I set it and the flickering electric candle back on top of the little table.

"Ryan Langley?"

I turn around to see a man walking up to me, a smile on his face like we're old friends. Shit, did I already meet him tonight and forget? He's tall, about as tall as me. And he's wearing an expensive looking blue suit with cognac leather belt and shoes. His dark hair is slicked back, dark eyes taking me in.

"Hey," I say, holding out a hand. "Yeah, I'm Ryan."

"Thought that was you," he replies, taking the hand I offer him and shaking it. "I recognize you from the photos."

"Photos?"

"Yeah . . . the Rays post you to their socials all the time," he adds with a laugh, dropping my hand. "Your handsome face is everywhere. They even put you on a billboard. You can see it driving south from the airport."

I force out a laugh too. "Oh . . . yeah, I heard about it, but I haven't seen it." With any luck, I won't. No one needs to see that much of my face.

He slips his hands into his suit pockets, still smiling at me, his gaze taking in my suit before coming back to my face. "NHL star forward, Ryan Langley. You're living the fucking dream, man. When are the Rays gonna wake up and lock you down in a no-trade contract?"

"Trust me, we're working on it. But I leave the contract negotiations to my agent and just focus on the game."

"I bet you do," he says, his smile falling.

"What?"

"And endorsement deals too," he goes on. "You must be making a pretty penny with those. Good to diversify your assets . . . while you can."

"Yeah, I get by," I reply, shifting on my feet as I look around for the quickest exit. I don't like talking money with strangers. And this guy is giving me seriously smarmy investment broker vibes. He's leaning in closer like he's about to make me a sales pitch. Yeah, not happening. "Well, listen, it was great to meet you—"

"Whoa, hold on, there," he says, stepping in closer, his hand going to my shoulder.

I immediately step back, breaking our connection. He's got me in the corner of the room, my back to the wall. I look around, but everyone close has their backs turned so no one is looking this way. We've all perfected the art of the 'mayday' alert. Very useful with clingy bunnies and fans. One flash of it in my eyes at another Ray, and they'll begin Operation Polite Extraction.

I'm not sure what this guy wants, but I'm ready to exit stage fucking left.

"I was actually hoping I'd run into you here," he says, still boxing me in. "I have something I'd love for you to sign." He slips his hand inside his suit coat, and I instinctively lean away. Then he pulls out a paper folded long ways. He holds it out to me with a flourish, like it's the deed to a new car.

I look down to see my hand is already in the air, like it's too damn polite to realize we're trying to get *out* of this conversation. My fingers close around what is actually several papers, stapled in the corner. "You want me to sign this?" I say, looking down at the folded pages. I'm not picky. Fans give you all kinds of weird stuff to sign. I just want him to go away.

"Well, open it first. You should always read something before you sign it. That's some legal advice I'll give you for free."

I glance up at him. "You're a lawyer?"

He nods, his mouth curling into a smirk. "And you've just been served, asshole."

I go still. "What?"

He takes a step closer, his voice lowering as he glares at me, his mask of fake civility dropping away. "Open the fucking document and read it, you ignorant piece of shit."

"Fuck you. I'm not signing anything," I say, trying to hand the papers back to him.

He laughs again. It's a cold, hollow sound that sets my teeth on edge. "You don't actually need to sign them," he says. "The order is going into effect either way."

"What order?" I say, my mind spinning.

"Open it and see," he replies, a self-righteous smirk on his face.

I jerk open the pages, finding the first one, and look down, trying to make sense of the thick block of black text. It looks like a legal document of some kind. It's got a set of tabs sticking out at the bottom, flagging all the lines that need signatures. But he's right, someone has already signed it with blue ink. All the signature lines are signed. "What the fuck is this?"

"You tell me," he jeers. "Any real man would be able to take care of his business. Look at the fucking document and read it, asshole."

Panic lances my chest as I try to make sense of what I'm reading, but the font is impossibly small. I realize with a jolt that this was intentional. This smarmy lawyer guy took a normal document and purposefully shrunk the font. He wanted to come here and give this to me. He wanted to watch me struggle to read it. Why? Who would—

Oh, fuck.

The creeping feeling that's been inching up my neck since this guy first walked up to me suddenly turns to ice. It shoots through my veins as I lower the papers, my gaze settling on the monster in front of me. I know exactly who he is. My hands shake as my pulse races.

"Troy." I spit out his name like the foulest curse.

"In the flesh." He holds out his hand again, as if he really expects me to shake it. "But I prefer the title 'Tess's husband.'"

"Fuck you."

"Careful there, hotshot," he teases, dropping his hand back to his side. "We wouldn't want to make a scene now, would we? Lots of important people here tonight. Coaches and donors, city councilors, the press . . ."

I glance around, and he's right. I'm not ten feet away from Head Coach Johnson and his wife. And we were all warned by Poppy, like, ten times that Press was here. They did a little TV spot earlier with Tess and Mars over by the turtles. My panic starts to build. We don't have a plan yet. Nothing is set. I don't know what I can say or how to make this go away.

"You make a scene now, it'll make the front page," says Troy. "You'll ruin our Tessy's big night . . . and your career . . . and your life."

I'm not buying his bullshit, not with Coach's reassurance that the Rays will take my side. "Get the fuck out of here, Troy."

"Actually, I was invited," he counters, oozing his self-righteous confidence all over me. "I have the invitation in my pocket if you don't believe me. Wanna try reading that instead?"

It's all I can do to keep my cool and not pound him into the floor. My hands shake as I hold up the papers. "What is this?" I say, shaking them in his face. "More empty fucking threats? More blackmail? It's not gonna work. My coaches already know—"

"None of my threats are ever empty," he replies, his fake smile falling.

"Do your worst," I counter. "You've got nothing on us. It won't be bad press when Tess and I explain the truth. And unlike you, I actually have credibility. My team believes me. Tess is gone, and she's never coming back to you."

"That's good," he replies, his voice lowering. "Practice saying it now. It will make it that much easier for you to accept later . . . you know, unless you like the idea of going to jail."

My heart fucking stops. "What the hell are you talking about?"

"I already told you." He taps the papers in my hand. "Ryan Langley, you've been served. I'll go ahead and leave this with you. It's just a copy. The originals have been filed back in Cincinnati. And don't worry, I'll make sure my connection over at Jacksonville PD gets a copy too."

No. This isn't happening. I glance down at the papers again. This can't be what I think it is. How did he pull this off? It has to be a bluff. I square my shoulders at him. "Drop the act and just make your threat, you fucking monster."

He laughs at me. "I already did. You're holding it. Maybe one of your teammates will show you a little mercy and help you sound out the letters. Or your sister. You're putting her through grad school, right?"

I go still, rage coursing through my veins like lava. Not Cassie. How does he fucking know?

"Shame for her to lose everything, too, just because you're a piece of trash that can't find himself a woman who isn't already married," he jabs.

I taste bile in my throat as I hold back from punching his fucking lights out. How is this possible? He knows about me—my life, my secrets, my family. I don't know how he knows, but he does. Of course, he does. He's part fucking demon.

"Troy, what did you do?"

"Ah-ah," he teases, wagging a finger in the air. "It's Tess's husband, remember? And I can't believe she's wasting her time with a loser like you. Trust me when I say it won't last."

He's spinning me up, just trying to get a rise out of me. Does he expect me to wail on him right here in the middle of the gala? Is he trying to pick a fight? I can't fucking think with him up in my face like this.

"You need to leave," I say again. It's a demand and a prayer.

Please, God, just make him leave.

But he leans in closer, his dark eyes narrowing. "You think you can offer her a better life than what she has with me?"

"I *know* I can. I don't fucking cheat on her. I don't make her cry or treat her like trash." My jaw tightens as I add, "And I don't hurt her."

"All you are is hockey," he says, ignoring my accusations. "That's all you have to offer the world. When that's gone, you'll be nothing. One more useless, dumb jock. They wouldn't even hire you to work a donut counter. You're fucking pathetic. And my Tess is going to see right through you in the end. Honestly, I'm doing you a favor with this," he adds, pointing at the documents in my hand. "Consider your relationship over. If you want to keep playing hockey, if you want to keep supporting your family, be the one who walks away first."

"Troy, what did you do?" I say again.

"Remember, I've got my eye on you," he says, tapping his cheek. "I'll love nothing more than to turn you over to the police. It'll be hard to play hockey in a jail cell. Not impossible," he adds with a grin. "But certainly harder. It's such a shame, too, because I really liked that billboard."

He claps me on the shoulder, and I fucking let him. I think I might be in shock.

"Great to meet you, Ryan. You know, your photos don't do you justice. You're much more handsome in person."

This time I know he's talking about the photos in the box in Tess's closet. He's seen them all, and I'm gonna be sick.

"Hey, and good luck against the Wild next week," he says, dropping his hand away from me. "You know, if they let you start . . . and if you're not in jail."

62
Tess

The ocean breeze whips around us. There's sand and surf, music from the party, distant laughter. It all fades to nothing. All I hear is white noise . . . and the panicked beating of my heart.

Troy is here.

Nancy's mouth is still moving. She's talking at me, glancing from her little notebook back to me. Then she's reaching out, her fingers brushing down my arm. I don't even feel it.

"Tess? Honey, are you alright?" Her voice reaches me like she's speaking from the other end of a long tunnel.

No, I'm not fucking alright. Troy is here. As soon as she said the words, I *knew*. It's like I can feel him. Troy is here somewhere, and he's looking for me.

"Tess?" Nancy's dark eyes are wide as she steps in closer. "Honey, you're scaring me a little. Talk to me."

I blink twice, my brain zapping back into focus. All the sounds of the beach come flooding back to me. A chill runs down my arms, raising the fine hairs. I reach out, taking Nancy's free hand. "I need you to go find Ilmari and Ryan."

"Honey—"

"Nancy, I'm fine," I say, forcing a smile. "Listen to me," I press. "Ilmari and Ryan. Find them now. Fast as you can. I'll wait right here."

"Can't you tell me what's really going on? Who is Mr. Troy?"

"I promise, I'll tell you everything, okay? Right now, the only thing that matters is that you find Ryan and Ilmari and send them to me. *Please*, Nancy."

She nods, and I let her go. Asking no more questions, she hurries back up the boardwalk, leaving me alone in the middle of the dunes. In the distance, thunder rumbles and a fork of lightning splits the sky. The storm is rolling closer.

No, the storm is already here.

The thought comes unbidden to my mind, and I clench my hands into tight fists. Troy is the storm, and he's here.

He was never going to wait for me to come back to him. He knows I won't. Even if I left Ryan last night like he asked, this was never going to end with me back in Cincinnati. I would have run again instead. Farther this time. Troy can't lose his chance to hurt me. He's playing the only two cards he has left: hurt Ryan and hurt my friends.

What's his next move? What will he do?

"Tess!"

I spin around to see Ilmari and Jake jogging towards me. Both men look concerned.

"What's wrong?" Jake calls. "Nancy said you were freaking out—"

"Troy is here," I say, cutting right to the chase.

"Oh . . . shit. Well, did you see him? Did you talk to him?"

"No."

"Good. Don't. Tess, fuck that guy. Let's call the police and drag his ass out—"

"No," I say, grabbing his arm. "Jake, no. That will only set him off. He always has a plan. If we do anything that seems expected, he'll be ready to retaliate. He's smart, Jake." I turn to Ilmari, tears in my eyes. "He wants to hurt me."

"And how does he do that?" Ilmari asks.

I swallow the ball of emotion in my throat. "By hurting Ryan . . . and hurting you."

"Me?" he says with a raised brow. "Why does he want to hurt me?"

"Because you're my friend, Mars. I'm not here doing all of this because I'm a bleeding heart for sea turtles and sand dunes. I'm here for *you*. I'm here for Rachel and Jake and Cay. I'm here because you looked at me on Hal Price's back patio with tears in your eyes, and you told me you didn't want to fail. And look, I know you're still mad at me about all this," I say, gesturing around. "And I won't make you give the speech if it really matters that much to you, but I love you, Mars Price. I would do anything for you and your family."

"Why are you saying this?"

"Because you deserve to know," I reply. Then I glance to Jake. "You both deserve to know. I love you, too, Jake. I'm so happy you found my Rachel, and I'm happy you make her so happy."

"Tess, why does this feel like a goodbye?" Jake's face is a mask of anxiety.

"Because Troy is here to test whether you love me too," I reply. "A narcissist can't stand when their victim has attachments outside of them. He wants you to push me away. He wants caring for me and being my friend to be a burden for you—"

"Tess, you aren't a fucking burden," Jake says emphatically. "And if that guy gets close to you, I'll knock him out flat."

"No," I beg. At the same time, Ilmari say, "No violence, Jake."

"Well, then, what's the plan here?" Jake replies. "We need to go get Seattle," he says at Mars. "I don't want him getting close to her either. He touches her, he's fucking dead."

"And Ryan," I say, heart in my throat. "We need to find Ryan. He's who Troy wants most. Troy knows the best way to get to me is to get to him. He can't hurt me anymore, so he's going to hurt Ryan. I told Nancy to find him. He should be back. He should be here—"

"Okay, okay," Jake soothes, stepping in to wrap me in his arms. "Shhh. It's okay."

I don't even realize I'm crying until I hear the sob come from my chest. I cling to Jake, and Ilmari steps in behind me, his hand on my shoulder.

"We need to go back inside," Ilmari says. "I won't leave Rakas alone in there. She is the only other person Troy knows, yes?"

I nod.

"And we'll find Ryan," Jake adds. "Come on, sweetheart." He takes my right hand, weaving our fingers together. "We won't leave you for a second, alright? We've got you, Tess. We love you too. We've said it before, but your name may as well be Price. You're on our 'ride or die' list, okay?"

I nod, blinking back my tears.

Ilmari takes my other hand, leading the way back up the boardwalk.

"What's the ace up his sleeve?" Jake calls from behind me. "How does he want to hurt Ryan?"

"The photographs," I reply. "He wants to flip the script and say I'm the cheater, not him. He wants to tear Ryan down and frame him as an adulterer so the Rays and his endorsement deals will all drop him. He wants to ruin his career with bad press."

"Jesus," Jake mutters. "Fucking diabolical."

"And this is his best plan?" Ilmari asks. "Framing Ryan as your adulterous lover? He has no other cards to play?"

"As far as I know," I admit. "But as Jake says, he's diabolical. I didn't think he was capable of some of the things he's already done."

We step back up onto the deck which is flooded with golden light from the wall of windows. The three of us stand together, hands clasped, gazing through the glass. It's like all our friends are somehow enshrined inside the glass, like a moving portrait. Laughing and smiling faces, light twinkling off glass stemware, the bluesy notes of a Norah Jones song filtering through the speakers.

I have eyes for only one person. "Where is he?" My anxiety mounts as I look for Ryan.

"What does Troy even fucking look like?" Jake says, his gaze darting left and right.

"There's Rakas," Ilmari says, relief in his tone. "Come." He pulls on my hand, and the three of us hurry inside.

"Mars, we need to find Ryan," I say, my neck craning.

"We need to find Troy," Jake counters. "If someone yells 'shark' at the beach, you find the fucking shark first."

But Mars isn't listening. He drags us both over towards the cash bar where Rachel is standing laughing with two players whose names I don't know. She turns at our approach, her smile falling as she takes in our faces.

"What's wrong—"

"Come," Ilmari says, throwing an arm around her shoulder and pulling her away from the others.

"Ilmari, what's wrong—"

"Troy," I answer for him. "He's here, Rach."

"No," she whispers, immediately glancing around. "That's not possible. God, why?"

"Because I broke his rules. He told me to walk away from Ryan and I didn't. He told me to let him go and I can't. I won't. Rach, I love him, and he loves me, and we want to be together, and there is nothing wrong in what we're doing—"

"Oh, honey." She wraps me in a hug, and we cling to each other.

"We need to find Ryan," I say again. "Please, Rach. Help me find him. *Please.*"

She nods, smoothing her hands over my shoulders. "Okay, honey. Yeah, let's—" She goes still as a statue, her concern morphing into silent, quivering rage, and I know there's only one reason why.

I go still, my every sense firing, telling me to be wary of who is approaching. One look in Rachel's eyes, and she gives a curt nod, confirming what I already know. Her men read her, too, because Jake and Ilmari quickly move to either side of their wife, boxing her in, even as they both keep a hand on me.

Slowly, I turn, coming face to face with Troy.

"Hello, Tessy," he says with a cold smile. "Why don't we step outside so we can have a little chat?"

63
Tess

Troy is here. It all feels so surreal. He's not supposed to be *here*. The Rays are not his set of people. He's an 'old money' type. He gives off such an aura of arrogance and condescension. When we were younger, I mistook it for confidence. He has nothing in common with someone like Jake Price, who comes from nothing and worked his way into something through drive and talent.

It took me a long time to see that Troy's upbringing was not so much a blessing as a curse. He doesn't know how to work for things. He doesn't know how to value the things he has. And he doesn't know how to appreciate what it feels like when those things are taken away. In a word, he's spoiled. And he's the worst kind of spoiled: the kind that is fundamentally incapable of admitting it.

That's why he's here now. He doesn't understand that there are things in his life that he can't possess. I am one of those things. Try as he might, he can't control me. He can't make me do as he commands. I center myself in that truth.

I am wild. I am fierce. I am free.

I take him in, from his slicked-back hair to his designer suit and his whiskey-colored loafers.

Next to me, Jake must be doing the same because he scoffs. "Seriously, Tess? *This* guy? He's got fucking tassels on his loafers."

"He was hot in college," I say with a shrug.

Troy levels his gaze at him. "You must be one of the doctor's useless assholes. It takes a special kind of spineless man to lose his woman not once but twice. Well done, there, champ."

"Wow," Jake replies. "That was poetic as fuck. Were you looking in a mirror when you practiced that? 'Cause from where I stand, you're the one who keeps losing his woman." He puts a protective arm around Rachel. "My girl is right here, *asshole*."

"Troy, you need to leave," Rachel says, her hand tight in mine.

"I'm not going anywhere," he replies. "Not until I've spoken to Tess."

"There is nothing you could say that she needs to hear," Rachel replies. "It's over, Troy. She's moved on. She moved on years ago."

Troy glowers at her, his gaze dropping to where our hands meet. Then it trails slowly back up to our faces. "I don't remember asking for your opinion," he says at her. "You've always been a terrible influence on my Tess. I expect nothing less from a rotten gash."

I gasp as I feel both men move around me. Jake lunges, cursing at Troy, but Mars holds him back. "No," Mars growls in his ear, holding him tight, both arms wrapped around his torso.

Jake thrashes. "Let me go. I'll fucking *kill* him—"

"It's what he wants," Mars presses in his ear. "Calm down."

"Angel, don't," Rachel pleads, her hands on Jake's arm. "Ilmari's right. He's not worth it. Jake, *please*. People are watching."

She's right. The people closest to us have all turned, watching us with wide eyes, confused as to what they're seeing. In front of me, Troy just smirks, his eyes twinkling with mirth. Fuck, he's loving this. He knows we can't touch him because he'll just cry 'assault.' We have to stand here and let him spew his poison. My friends and loved ones have to take it on the chin. That's how they prove themselves. They resist his needling.

Or *I* take it on the chin. I agree to speak with him alone and spare them this humiliation. I glance around the room again, looking for Ryan. Where is he? Why isn't he coming to find me?

Jake nods, and Ilmari loosens his hold on him. Jake has eyes only for Troy. "You won't get what you came for. You will *never* speak to Tess alone again. She's done with your sorry ass. Be a man and move on. And if you speak to my wife like that again, I *will* kill you."

Troy crosses his arms. "Unlike you, I'm actually married to my wife," he counters. "All you're doing is playing pretend. When she gets bored of your dick, she'll move on. Women like her always do. He's the one who will suffer," he adds, pointing at Ilmari. "But then, from what I've read about you, people always seem to move on, don't they? Anyone who's ever cared for you has either died or left."

"Suksi vittuun," Ilmari curses.

"Kulta, don't listen to him," Rachel says, tears in her eyes as she puts a hand on Ilmari.

"Troy, stop," I beg, stepping forward. "I'm the one you want. Take your spite out on me."

He holds out his hand. "Let's go somewhere quieter."

I look down at his hand, trying to stop my trembling.

"Tess, don't," Rachel begs. "Stay."

"I'm not leaving until you speak to me," Troy counters, his threat clear: *This doesn't stop until you do.*

"Tess—"

"The deck," I say over Rachel's protests. "That's the only place I'll go with you."

He scoffs. "What, so they can all watch us through the glass like we're animals in a zoo? I don't think so."

"They can see us, but not hear us," I counter. "You can say whatever you need to say . . . you just can't hurt me again. Not without them seeing."

"Jesus." He glances around at all our faces. "Is that what you're telling them, Tess? Is that why everyone is acting so uptight? What, have you been down here saying I beat you all the time? Where's the proof? Where are the medical records? Where are the police reports? I've never touched you. Not in thirteen years—"

"You're lying," I say, tears in my eyes. "We both know you're lying—"

"You're the fucking liar," he snaps. "The cheater, the quitter. God, I can only imagine the lies you've spun to make me look like the villain. Meanwhile, you're the one fucking anything that moves. We all know I've got enough evidence to end your little boy toy's career. You've even had your turn with this one if the papers are to be believed," he adds, gesturing at Jake.

"Those stories were all bullshit, and you know it," I say.

"No, they aren't."

We both turn to look at Jake. "What?" I whisper.

His gaze softens as he looks at me. "Come on, Strawberry. There's no reason to hide what we have. Even a broken clock is right once a day. That's you," he says at Troy. "You're the stupid broken clock. But you're right about Tess and me. We were together, and it was magnificent."

Troy just scoffs. "You're a lousy liar."

"And you're a lousy lay," he counters. "But I'm not lying. Tess and I fucked like rabbits all over my beach house. Sorry, babe, you were at work, and I got horny," he says at Rachel. "And we both know this one is no help in that department," he adds, jabbing a thumb over his shoulder at Ilmari.

"Jake," Ilmari says in warning.

"What?" Jake says at his partner. "Are you seriously upset with this cretin knowing our business? He's a total piece of shit. No one will believe him either way, Mars."

Troy's gaze darts between them.

Ilmari just shakes his head. "He doesn't deserve to know our private business."

"Sure, he does. Clearly, he loves salacious gossip." Jake turns back to Troy, gesturing at Mars. "He only fucks women. Yeah, that's right, I said *women*. Don't even ask me the number of times I've come home from a long day at practice to find these two riding his cock and face. I swear, it's a sight to behold."

Next to me, Rachel clings to my arm. "Oh god," she whispers, her gaze darting between her men and Troy.

My eyes go wide, too, as the pieces of this curious new puzzle click into place. Could this actually work? My relationship with Ryan is the ace up Troy's sleeve. He wants to hurt me by ruining Ryan. How is he supposed to do that if half the Rays on the team boisterously claim we've also had affairs? Jake and Mars are taking Troy's sharpest arrow and burning it to ash.

"This is bullshit," Troy huffs. "You're all a bunch of fucking liars."

"Are we all lying? Or are *you* lying?" Jake presses. "Because these stories just don't add up."

"Mars!"

My hand tightens around Rachel's as Caleb approaches, his dark gaze locked on us. He hurries over, a slight hitch in his step. He looks to Mars as both men put their phones back in their pockets. Apparently, Mars sent on an SOS.

"What's happening?" asks Caleb.

Mars nods at Troy. "This is Troy Owens."

Caleb's face becomes a mask of rage as he slowly turns, taking in Troy for the first time.

"Perfect," Troy huffs. "The gang's all here. You're the washed up one, right? The gimp? You're even more useless than the pretty idiot," he adds, pointing at Jake with a vicious smirk.

Caleb's face becomes unreadable as Rachel and I cease to breathe. He's her mystery boy after all, the unpredictable one. Jake inches closer, his hand going to Caleb's shoulder. "Babe, we've got it handled."

Caleb just shrugs him away, his eyes locked on Troy. "Are you here to be the tough guy? You wanna say some shitty, hateful things, looking to spin us up so we throw the first punch?"

Troy just smirks.

"Yeah, I've known guys like you all my life."

"What, rich guys?" Troy replies, squaring his shoulders at him. "Guys with power and purpose?"

"Don't speak in my wife's presence again," Caleb counters, his expression obsidian. "She doesn't need to suffer the sound of your obnoxious bleating for another second."

Troy glares. "I don't take orders from sorry, washed-up has-beens."

Caleb just nods. "Clearly, you did your homework. You googled some footage of me taking a hit to my knee, yeah? So, like any bully, you think you've found my weakness. I can't take the hits anymore. I have to get others to fight my battles for me. Is that what you think?"

"Let's just say you don't intimidate me the same as your Swedish friend here," Troy replies.

"He's Finnish, asshole," Jake snaps. "Get it right."

Now it's Caleb putting a hand on Jake's shoulder, even as his eyes don't leave Troy's face. "You're right. Ilmari has the look of a Viking god who will snap you in half. And he will if you take even one step closer to our wife. But I am the fucking darkness," he says, stepping closer to Troy. "I am where your nightmares go to multiply. And I am telling you now that if you even look in my wife's direction again, I will knock every single jib from your mouth and make you choke on them."

Troy crosses his arms. "Threatening a lawyer, Mr. Sanford? Bad move."

"It's Price," Caleb corrects. "And I'm threatening a coward and a menace. An abuser of women—"

"Tess is a dirty fucking liar—"

"Tess is *mine*. She left you and found herself a real man. Real *men*. Forget about Langley. He's not your threat. It's me. She's mine now. And unlike you, I don't lose the things that are mine. I protect them. You will not look at Tess, you will not speak to her, you will not so much as breathe her fucking air. I will give you this warning only once: Get lost and stay lost. Forever."

Jake steps in to stand shoulder to shoulder with Caleb. "My husband told you to go. Don't make him say it again."

At the same time, Ilmari steps to the right, placing himself in front of Rachel and me, blocking us from Troy's view. Heart racing, my hand takes hold of Ilmari's arm. Next to me, Rachel does the same. I can't help myself, and I peek around him to look at Troy.

"Tess is ours now," Ilmari intones. "It's time to let go."

After a painfully long moment, Troy huffs a laugh and takes a step back. "You all present a united front. Very impressive." He lifts his hands in surrender and takes another step back. "Tess, I'm going," he says at me, peering around Ilmari to flash me a wink. "I never wanted to see you anyway. That's not why I came tonight."

My heart drops from my chest. "Then why are you here?"

He just smiles. Slipping his hand into his pocket, he pulls out a folded check. "Do I leave the donations with you?"

None of us move.

Stepping forward, he dares to reach out and slip the check into the pocket of Ilmari's tux. Then he gives me one last knowing look. "I'll see you around, Tess."

"No, you won't," I say, finding my voice at last.

His smirk turns into a glower.

"This is the end, Troy. From this moment, I will never see or speak to you again. Even as you stand before me, I do not see you. There is nothing left. Absolutely nothing. Take this as the last word you ever hear from my lips: goodbye."

I've said the words, but I know his narcissism won't let him absorb them. So, I'm not surprised when he just smirks and says, "We'll see."

With that, he turns and walks away, taking all my air with him. He hardly clears the glass doors before Jake lets out an exasperated groan. "Ohmygod, what an awful fucking piece of human garbage! Tess, you're seriously still married to that guy?"

"I have never wanted to kill someone so much in my life," Caleb says, his arms going around Rachel as he pulls her closer. She clings to him, one hand still clasped in Ilmari's large hand.

"Fuck, I know, right?" Jake cries. "We are fixing that pronto. Your divorce is my new life's mission, I swear to fucking God."

Rachel turns to me, slipping away from her men. Hands shaking, she cups my face, tears in her eyes. "Are you okay?"

I just shake my head, holding back my tears. No, I'm not okay. In this moment, okay feels like an impossibility.

"You will be," she says, kissing my cheek. "Tess, he will never hurt you again."

But I don't care about me right now. There's only one person on my mind. "Ryan." I say the word with the only air left in my lungs.

"Yeah, we'll find him. Okay, honey? Right now. We'll all look." She nods at her men, giving them a silent order, and they scatter, set on their mission. "We'll find him," she says again.

But I know the truth. Troy already did.

64
Tess

I stand there in Rachel's arms, heart pounding. Her men are all on the hunt for Ryan. Other Rays in the room have taken notice of us.

Poppy is the first to reach us, placing a hand on Rachel's shoulder. "What just happened? Who was that?"

Novy and Morrow appear suddenly behind her, framing her like two angry gargoyles, their eyes both locked on the door Troy just exited through.

"That was my ex-husband," I reply.

"Oh, heavens. Are you okay?"

"No. I need to find Ryan." I lift my gaze to her, glancing between her and her men. "Have you seen him?"

Poppy shakes her head, but Morrow nods.

"Oh god, when?" I say, taking his hand.

"I saw that guy talking to him over on the other side of the room," he replies. "He handed him something and walked away. I didn't really pay much attention though. That's all I saw."

"Where did Ryan go?"

"I'm sorry, I don't know," he replies.

Just then, Nancy hurries forward. "Tess, I couldn't find Ryan. I swear, I looked everywhere. His car is still here, but the man himself has vanished into thin air."

My heart sinks, but I find her a smile. "It's okay, Nance. Don't worry, I'll find him."

"What else do you need me to do?" she says, dutifully waiting for instruction.

I glance around the room. The people closest to us are still casting wary looks, but in the back of the room, I hear laughing and mingling. Not everyone was pulled under by the Troy Tornado. The alert has clearly gone out across the Rays though. All the players are moving closer, their conversations hushed, their expressions worried.

I turn to Nancy, squeezing her hand. "You and Cheryl hold down the fort, okay? Tell Joey he's giving the speech in fifteen minutes. Keep it short. Nothing more than thanking the donors and guests and wishing everyone a safe drive home."

She nods. "But . . . what do *you* need?"

"I need to find Ryan," I say again.

"Go," says Rachel. "He's here somewhere. He wouldn't leave without you."

"Wouldn't he?" I say, heart in my throat.

"He loves you, Tess," Rachel replies. "Go find him. I'll put all the Rays on alert."

With a nod, I'm off. I slip around the edge of the room, hurrying towards the door that leads into the cloak room where we all stashed our coats and bags. Digging to the bottom of the supply box, I tug out my little clutch and open it, plucking out my phone.

My heart races as I flick my thumb across the lock screen, eager to see if he left me a voice memo. The home screen flashes bright, but there are no messages from Ryan. No texts. No voice memos. No funny GIFs.

I tap his number and put the phone to my ear, praying that the dial tone will connect. It rings once. Twice. Three times. Then his voicemail picks up.

Scrambling to my feet, I leave the closet. "Ryan, baby, where are you? Please call me. Please let me know you're okay. I know Troy talked to you and whatever he said, whatever he did, it doesn't change how I feel about you. I love you. I'm coming to find you, okay? I'm—god, just—I'm coming."

Clutching my phone, I hitch up the bottom of my dress as I search the venue. "Has anyone seen him?" I ask Sully as I pass him in the front hall.

"No," he replies, his expression worried. "We're all looking," he assures me. "He's here somewhere, Tess."

"Please keep looking," I say, dashing away from him.

If I were Ryan, where would I go? I don't leave in my car, but I'm nowhere to be found on the premises. Where am I? Where feels safe?

I stop in my tracks as I look around the kitchen. The confused staff look back at me, packing away their catering equipment. He's not here. God, where would he go? Where would *I* go if I was running from myself? If I was feeling trapped, with nowhere left to run, where would I go? Where would I stand to meet my end?

Spinning on my heel, I hurry out of the kitchen through the side door, the cool January air caressing my fevered skin as I do my least favorite thing on earth. I kick off my heels, hike up the bottom of my dress, and I run. I run to Ryan.

Looping around the back side of the building, I take the stairs up onto the back deck and race across it, heading for the boardwalk. If I was feeling driven to the end of my rope, I would run until there was nowhere left to go. I would run to the water's edge.

My feet pound the boardwalk, and my breath comes out in sharp pants as I crest the dune. I stop at the end of the boardwalk, my naked toes right on the edge. A sea of white sand stretches out before me, ending in the black of the ocean.

"Where are you?" I say, my gaze darting left and right.

The torches remain unlit, but there's enough light pollution even on this stormy night for me to peer down the beach and see a pacing silhouette some hundred yards away.

It's Ryan. He's safe.

I sigh with relief, even as I hitch my dress back up and take to the beach. I run to him, my feet sinking in the deep, cold sand. Beyond us, less than a mile out, the thunderhead rolls in, dark and ominous, the clouds rumbling like the deep belly of a hungry beast.

Ryan stands at the surf's edge in his tuxedo, the water lapping inches from his feet. His phone light glows in the darkness like a beacon, drawing me to him. He holds it up over a clutch of papers in his hand, reading them.

My heart sinks. This is what brought him out here, whatever Troy gave him. "Ryan," I call, needing him to see me.

He spins around, his face cast in darkness by the bright light of his phone. "Don't come any closer!"

I stop on instinct. He's still a good fifteen yards away. "What are you doing out here?"

"Tess, go back," he shouts. "Don't come any closer."

"Ryan—what happened? What did Troy say to you? What did he do?"

"I think he served me a restraining order," he calls.

My heart drops. "What?"

"I think it's for you. Tess, please don't come any closer. I can't—I don't know what this is," he says, his tone anguished.

I try to catch my breath, taking a step closer. "Well, what does it say?"

"I just said I don't fucking know. I'm not a lawyer!"

"If it's a restraining order for me, I don't even think that's legal. What does it say?"

"I just said I don't fucking know," he shouts, his phone glowing over the papers again.

"Well, am I listed as the plaintiff? Are you the defendant?"

"I don't—where would it say that?"

"At the top," I reply, taking another step closer. "Babe, it's the first thing. The top usually lists the court and the district and the case number, along with the plaintiff and defendant."

He looks down at the document again. "Okay . . . so if my name is on the second line, what does that mean?"

I grab my side, holding the stitch as I catch my breath. "Bottom line is usually for the defendant. Does it say 'defendant'? If it's a TRO application, it might say 'applicant' and then list my name, which would mean Troy is doing all kinds of illegal shit. He can't just fill out a TRO on my behalf. But this isn't my area of law," I admit. "I'm only going off what I saw in law school and courtroom dramas."

"It just doesn't make any sense," he says, shining his phone light on it again.

Watching him struggle, a niggling awareness eats at me. "Ryan . . . do you mean you can't understand it . . . or you can't read it?"

"Don't fucking patronize me," he shouts, his hackles raised. He's in defense mode. I've never seen him like this. He's unraveling at the seams.

I take another step closer. Then another. We're within ten feet of each other now, and I can see his features clearly—the stress, the worry.

"I told you to stay back," he says, but the fight is leaving him. He craves my closeness as much as I crave his.

I have to know. I have to ask.

"Ryan . . . baby, can you read?"

"Of course, I can fucking read. I'm not an idiot, Tess."

"Okay . . . then read it out to me. Read the first line. Just the first one."

He groans, looking around hopelessly before he flashes the camera light over at me. "Is . . . do you spell your name T-E-R-E-S-A?"

"Yes," I reply. "Yes, that's Teresa."

His eyes narrow at me. "Teresa?"

"That's my name, Ryan. My legal name is Teresa. Is that the first name listed?"

"Yeah."

Oh, shit. Troy, what the hell did you do?

"And . . . do you see R-Y-A-N—"

"I know how to spell my own name."

"Okay," I say, as gently as possible.

"But this font is—fuck, he did it on purpose. He made the font so fucking small. He shrunk it down so I can't read it. The letters—they all blur together." He looks down at the page again. Then he looks back up at me, his expression anguished. "If I have time, if—I just need to take some time, and I can usually work it out, you know?"

I just nod. "I know, baby."

He shakes the papers in the air. "But that fucking monster knew! He served me this and told me I'll go to fucking jail over it, and I couldn't even argue with him because he knows I can't—" His words stop as he drops the papers to his side. Looking out at the dark surf, he just shakes his head, battered and helpless.

Weeks of missed clues suddenly align themselves in my mind, and I feel like the biggest fool. How did I not see it? How did he hide it from me so well? At the same time, my hatred for Troy grows exponentially. Somehow, he dug deep enough into Ryan's private life to learn this about him, and then he found a way to weaponize it. It's truly the most base, demeaning form of cruelty. I could kill him for it.

And it makes me love Ryan even more. He's strong. He copes. More than that, he thrives. My sweet beach puppy, my valiant protector. God, he's just *mine*. I need to bring him back to me.

"Ryan, honey, are you dyslexic?"

His gaze darts to me and he glares, his walls firmly up. For once in our relationship, he's the one feeling backed into a corner.

"It's okay if you are," I say. "And I'm not angry at you for hiding it from me. I just need to know." I point to the documents in his hand. "If Troy gave you that, we need to be able to read it, so we know what we're dealing with, okay? So . . . are you?"

Slowly, Ryan nods. "Yeah."

"How bad is it?"

"Severe," he admits. "I have dyslexia and dysgraphia. Most days it's so bad I can hardly read anything. My spelling is worse. It's . . . fuck, it's exhausting. And embarrassing," he adds.

I close the space between us, looking up at my handsome hockey boy. The knot of his tie is loosened, the top button undone. His hair is no longer slicked back behind his ears. In his anxiety, he's been fiddling with it. And now the wind from the coming storm whips some of the loose blond strands across his brow.

In his body, I see the man, powerful and strong. Millionaire NHL hotshot Ryan Langley, star forward of the Jacksonville Rays. But in his pretty green eyes I see the boy, lost and embarrassed and coping in a world that has been unkind.

"The oven," I whisper. "Bake and broil. You—"

"The font on those dials is always so damn small," he says. "And I was in a rush and the words look the same. That's why I don't cook. I can never follow the stupid instructions. I always mess it up. I mess everything up."

I nod, more pieces clicking into place. "And the voice memos?"

"Easier than texting."

"Your contracts . . . your finances . . . "

He just shrugs. "Why do it wrong when I can just pay to have someone do it right? MK knows. He's cool about it. He always breaks things down to make sure I understand."

"And the beach? The release form?" I remember he made a joke of turning away, like he was hiding his answers so I didn't cheat.

"I had Joey fill it out when you walked away," he admits. "I said I hit my hand on a weight machine at the gym. He didn't ask questions."

Is it odd to say that I'm impressed? His skill at coping is off the charts. "I didn't see it," I admit. "Ryan, I didn't know."

"That's kind of the point," he replies. "I don't want people knowing this about me, Tess. I don't want them judging me or pitying me or calling me stupid. I'm not stupid, I—" He groans, glancing my way. "I really didn't want you to know."

"Why?"

"Because I didn't want to give you one more reason to think I'm no good for you," he admits.

My heart stops. "Oh . . . Ryan—"

"You know it's true," he snaps, glaring at me. "Tess, you're so fucking smart. You're a lawyer and you run nonprofits." He shakes his head. "I just play hockey—"

"Don't," I say, stepping forward and grabbing his wrist. "Don't say that. There is nothing wrong with you, Ryan. I would never say that. I would never even *think* it. And you don't have to carry this alone," I add. "You don't have to hide or be ashamed or think people would actually choose not to be with you over having a learning difference."

"I've been hiding it for so long," he say, the pain evident in his voice. "I'm so fucking tired. This shit is hard enough for me to deal with every day without other people piling on."

"And Troy piled on, didn't he?"

"He's a fucking asshole." He says the words, and I know they're meant to imply his indifference, but I can see it in his eyes: Ryan is anything but indifferent to the insults Troy flung his way.

"What did he say to you?" I ask, squeezing his wrist.

But Ryan pulls away.

"Ryan—"

"All I am is hockey," he says again. "It's all I have to offer you, Tess. I have no other way to earn a living. My dyslexia is so fucking severe—" He groans, pacing away. Behind him, the thunderhead rolls closer. The static rises in the air, the threat of rain looming.

"I barely made it through school," he goes on. "They passed me through high school on a technicality. I took to the draft the first chance I had because I was never going to survive college. Tess, if I don't have hockey, I have nothing. I have to play and earn and stay on the ice as long as possible. It's not just about me and you and the life I wanna make for us. You know I'm putting Cassie through college too. And I'm hoping my mom will retire this year. It's all on me."

My heart thrums, loving how well he cares for those he loves. "Oh, honey, and no one can take that from you—"

"*This* can," he shouts, shaking the papers at me. "I think this is a restraining order. Which means that if I get close to you, I can go to jail. Dealing with some bad press is one thing. Even with bad press, they'll still let me play. But a criminal record for breaking a restraining order is a total non-fucking-starter. I'll lose everything. My mom—my sister—" He spins away, shoulders heaving with emotion.

After a moment, I hold out my hand. "Give them to me, Ryan."

He doesn't turn around.

"Please," I beg. "You said you trust me, remember? Did you mean it, or has this all been about the thrill of the chase?"

He spins around with a glare. "What the fuck are you talking about?"

"You trust me when we're naked. You trust me with your body. Trust me with your heart too. Trust me, Ryan. I'm not going anywhere. I'm sticking. You're sticking, and I'm sticking too. I can help you. I *will* help you." I hold out my hand again, waiting.

Slowly, he nods and hands the papers over.

I take them, and he holds his phone flashlight over the pages. I squint, trying to make out the text. He's right, it looks like someone reduced the print size to like eight percent. "Babe, I can barely read this either. I don't think you can even file it looking like this. A judge would have a cow." I scan the pages as best I can, checking the signatures. Slowly, I look up, a smile spreading on my face.

Ryan holds his breath. "Wait, Tess—fuck, why are you smiling?"

I drop the papers to my side, breathing a sigh of relief. "Because we've got him," I whisper.

"What?"

I close my eyes, body humming. Oh god, I've got him. In his rush to checkmate me, Troy left himself exposed at last. He's made a critical error. For so long, I've been the one running as he chased me around the board, claiming all my defenses and boxing me in the corner. Now it's my turn to step boldly forward, a queen in her crown. I have everything I need to checkmate *him*. I have everything I need to be free.

Ryan looks down at me, his eyes searching my face. "Tess—"

I step in, wrapping my arms around his neck, the fraudulent restraining order still clutched in my hand. Pulling him down to me, I kiss his parted lips. He's stiff against me, his body still coiled tight by fear. But each kiss softens his hesitation. I press myself against him, willing him to feel how much I need him, how much I love him. His mouth opens, and I flick my tongue between his lips, coaxing him.

Be with me, your goddess, your queen.

"I love you," I whisper against his mouth. "I will never let him hurt you. I'm your goddess, remember? I protect what's mine."

With a groan, Ryan pulls me to him. He wraps me in his arms just as the first drops of rain begin to fall. A flash of lightning sparks overhead and we both gasp, breaking our kiss. I look up into his eyes and the heavens open, freezing cold rain pouring down.

"Come on," he shouts over the din, grabbing my free hand.

"Wait," I cry, anchoring my feet in the sand.

He spins around. "Tess, it's not safe out here—"

"I don't care about our pasts," I call out to him. "I don't care about this," I add, dropping the wet documents into the surf. The tide pulls them back and I lose them in the waves. "Stand here with me and let the rain wash it all away."

He stands with me, our hands clasped together, as the rain pours down. "What are you gonna do now?" he calls over the thunder.

"Now, I make you a vow," I say with a smile. "I am done running."

He stills, the rain drenching his head and shoulders. It drips down his beautiful face. "Say it again."

I step closer, gazing up at him. "All my life, I've been running and searching and looking for that place that feels like home," I say over the rain. "All the while, I've been alone. I thought it was my curse. Poor Tess, destined to be alone forever."

"And now?"

I smile up at him. "And now, tonight, I ran out here to find you. Ryan, I ran to you. I ran home. And now I'm done running."

He cups my face with his hand, our faces inches apart. "That's all I want. I'll be your home, and you'll be mine."

I nod, covering his hand with mine. We lean in to kiss again, but a clap of lightning forks right above us and we duck on instinct, throwing our arms above our heads.

"Tess!"

"Ryan!"

We turn to see a group of people with umbrellas moving down the sand towards us.

"Get outta the rain before you get your crazy asses struck by lightning," Jake shouts.

"Come on," Ryan says, grabbing my hand again.

Hitching up my soaking wet dress, I run at Ryan's side, racing back to where all the Rays wait at the end of the boardwalk. We sink in the deep sand, meeting them at the foot of the dunes.

"What the hell were you two doing out there?" Rachel cries, stepping forward with an umbrella, trying to cover us both.

Karlsson steps up on Ryan's other side, raising his umbrella high.

We're both shivering, wet through to the bone, with lovesick smiles on our faces. I look around and see that everyone is here, all our friends we love like family—Rachel and her guys, Shelby and Josh, Poppy, Novy and Morrow, Cheryl and Nancy and Joey. Everyone was looking for us. Everyone cares.

"Are you okay?" Rachel says.

Ilmari steps around me, wrapping me in his dry tuxedo coat.

"Oh—your speech," I cry. "I ruined it."

He gives my shoulders a gentle squeeze. "There's always next year."

I smile, my shoulders sagging with relief, even as I shiver.

"Troy left," says Caleb, his eyes locked on me. "We watched him get in the Uber."

"What's the plan here, Tess?" says Jake. "That asshole's never gonna stop."

"No more playing defense," Ryan says.

I glance up at him, my hand still clutched in his. "What?"

"I'm a forward," he says at me. "That means I don't sit back and wait to take the hits. I bring the fight to the other team. Let me do this, Tess. Let me help you. We tried your way. Now I want to try mine."

"Let us all help you," Jake adds.

"You're not alone, Tess," says Caleb.

Ilmari's firm hand gives my shoulder another squeeze, and I have to fight back fresh tears.

They're all here. They all care. My team. My family.

"Put us in, Coach," calls Josh from under his umbrella, Shelby on his arm. "Just tell us how we can help."

I look around at everyone, Ryan's hand clasped in mine. Swallowing down my nerves, I clear my throat and shout out to the group, "I want to thank you all. Not just for coming out tonight and supporting our cause but . . . well, for supporting me. From the first moment I met you all, you've been so kind and welcoming." I glance from Poppy to Shelby, who both offer me smiles.

"You took me in and made me feel like family," I add, looking at Rachel and her guys. "Now Ryan *is* my family. Like the sea turtles we all came out tonight to support, Ryan and I are caught in a bit of a tangled net. We ask for your patience and your help as we fight our way free."

"Anything you need," Jake intones.

"Ryan's a Ray and you're with Ryan," Josh adds. "We take care of our own."

I nod, taking a deep breath. No more defense. We're playing offense. We're taking the fight to Troy. I have a plan, and I think it will work. My freedom is so close, I can taste it.

I turn to Ryan, squeezing his hand. "Babe, have you ever been to Cincinnati?"

65
Ryan

I stand in front of the golden elevator doors, watching as the white light flashes across the top, showing an elevator on the move. It's coming down fast. My heart beats in tempo with the lights. Slow and steady.

"Are you ready for this, man?" Novy says at my left, balancing a box in his hands. "You make a good forward, I won't lie. But this feels like an enforcer move. You sure you have what it takes?"

"I'm ready," I reply.

"He's ready," Sully says at my other side, holding the other box.

The elevator dings, and the golden doors slide open, revealing an empty car. We all step in, me, Novy, and Sully to the back. Morrow, Karlsson, and Jake follow.

"We'll catch the next one," Sanford calls.

I nod, taking a deep breath.

"What floor?" says Morrow.

"Seven," I reply.

He jabs the number, and the car rattles to life, rising in the air.

"You've got this," Sully says on my right. "This ends today. Finish strong."

I nod again.

The elevator dings, and the doors slide open once more. The guys and I pile out. I take the lead, glancing around the stylish atrium. A pair of Barbie-looking young women sit at a long reception desk. Their eyes go wide with interest as they take us in. I can only image what they think seeing six professional hockey players flood their lobby.

"Good morning," the blonde on the left chimes. "Welcome to

Powell, Fawcett, and Hughes Consulting Group. What can we do for you to today?"

I give her my most crowd-winning smile. Tess calls it my 'bubblegum ad' smile, all flashy teeth and flirty eyes. "Good morning. We're here to see Mr. Troy Owens. I believe he's expecting us."

"Oh . . . umm . . . " She looks down at her computer screen, tapping a few keys and clicking her mouse. "I don't see any appointments for Mr. Owens this morning."

"Well, that is definitely a mistake," I reply, batting my lashes a bit. "I had to fly on a plane to get here today. I'm sure the date and time are correct."

"Oh, well . . . "

"I don't think I caught your name," I say, leaning my elbow on the desk.

"It's Katie," she says with a smile.

"We're both Katie, actually," the blonde to the right says.

"You two should do a Doublemint commercial," I tease, and they both laugh. Yeah, they can't resist the full Ryan Langley smolder. They're already breaking; I can see it in their eyes.

"Are you guys athletes?" Katie Two says, glancing from me to the others.

"Are we that transparent?" I reply.

"You're looking at the starting line of the Jacksonville Rays NHL team," Novy says, giving her a sexy wink. "And yes, we *are* more handsome in person. Damn cameras always add five pounds."

Both girls giggle.

I lean closer. "Troy is an old friend of ours. We hit the links together. So why don't you go tell him that we're here, and see if he can't fit us into his busy schedule?"

"I'll go," says Katie Two, getting up from her chair.

Katie One nods at her, her cheeks blushing as Jake steps up to my other side. "It'll be even more fun if you just tell him there's a surprise waiting," he calls to Katie Two. "Let's see the look on his face when he sees us all here."

Katie Two flashes him a smile over her shoulder, disappearing down a hallway.

I step back from the desk, taking a breath.

"That was easier than we planned," Sully says.

Behind us, the elevator dings, and the doors open. Out comes Sanny, Mars, and MK.

"Oh, shit. It's showtime," Novy mutters.

I spin around to see Katie Two leading the way back down the hall, Troy at her side. He's dressed to impress in his Brooks Brothers day look, that dark hair slicked back.

"Ta-da," Katie Two says with a wave of her hand, an excited look on her face.

Troy pauses, holding my gaze, a thousand emotions flashing on his face. The one he settles on is rage as he marches forward, pushing past Katie Two. "What the hell are you doing here?" he shouts. "This is my place of business. Get out." He points at the elevators.

The two Katies watch behind the desk with wide eyes. I know, behind me, at least a few of my guys have their phones out, recording everything.

"This is private property," Troy says. "You all need to leave. Now."

"We're not going anywhere," I reply. "And you said all you needed to say in Jacksonville. Now it's my fucking turn."

"Damn right," Sanford says.

"Tell him, Langley," Sully adds at my side.

A few people peek their heads out of the offices.

"Katie, call security," Troy orders.

As one, Novy and Sully step forward and tip their boxes over. The Katies gasp as the floor is littered with a rain of confetti from one box and pictures from the other. The grainy photos of Tess and I from the last several weeks go sliding across the shiny floor. I pulled out all the graphic ones, but the effect is the same.

The Katies both stand, peering over the desk to look at the mess. The people who were peeking out their doors are now moving down the hall, curious to know what's happening. Good. I want an audience for this.

"Recognize your handiwork?" I say, gesturing at the mess. "The divorce papers you shredded and delivered on Tess's doorstep? How about the illegal photos you had taken of us for weeks?"

Troy huffs, arms folded across his chest. "This is all bullshit. We fired Tess for breaking our morality clause. She's a messy whore.

Who's to say where the hell these photos came from?" he says, gesturing at them with a sneer. "You surely can't trace them back to me."

"You think so?" I challenge. "Maybe you haven't heard that we caught your peeping Tom photographer friend yesterday."

Troy blinks, his gaze darting from my face to the guys, looking for confirmation.

I step forward, crossing my arms too. "Yeah, he was set up real cozy in the back bushes, ready to get more shots for you. He sold you out, Troy."

A flicker of worry crosses his face, but he quickly recovers. "You're just trying to entrap me. You want me to admit to something we both know I didn't do."

I flash him an incredulous look. "Entrap you? What, are you some kind of Bond hero now? Troy, you're a third-rate lawyer working at your mommy's firm. You barely close three mil a year in deals. I make that just with my endorsements," I taunt. "You're a shit businessman and an even worse con man. You're pathetic. Is it any wonder she left you?"

Troy simmers with rage now, and I have to admit, this feels kind of good. But he's a narcissist through and through, so this is all fleeting. He'll blink this away and go back to playing the righteous victim within the hour.

"And we can't forget about this," I say, pulling a new copy of the restraining order from my pocket.

He smirks. "And what is that? Why don't you open it and read it out for us."

"You got sloppy," I say, ignoring his jab. "You processed this TRO in Tess's name against me, acting as her legal counsel. You have no proof I was stalking or harassing her, and she's already contesting it. You manipulated your position into getting this approved, didn't you? Does Mommy know you're trading on her name to get judges to approve baseless TROs against the wife you like to batter?"

"You don't know what the hell you're talking about," Troy counters. He glances around, glaring at the faces of his colleagues who all regard him warily. "He's just some dumb hockey player. He doesn't understand anything—"

"I don't," I admit, cutting him off. "But *he* does." I gesture behind me to MK. "Troy, meet my sports agent. He's a lawyer who's actually good at his job."

MK steps forward and gives Troy an awkward wave. "Hiya. Mike Kline, Elite Athlete Management."

"Tell him what you told me," I say.

"Oh, yeah—well, it looks like you committed some pretty serious legal malpractice," MK explains, pushing his glasses up his nose. "Add to that the fact that it was perpetrated against your intimate partner, and there's a history of abusive behavior, they'll likely disbar you. There may even be some jail time if she decides to press charges for the assault . . . which happened here on company property, right?" He looks to me.

"Yeah, it did," I reply.

Behind the desk, the Katies both gasp. Troy's other colleagues are all looking at him with wide eyes.

"That's a fucking lie," Troy declares. "Tess will say anything to undermine me."

"She's telling the truth, and so am I," I counter.

"Is that why you came here? You came to my place of business to try and humiliate me with these lies? Did you bring all these hockey goons to rough me up? Please, make my fucking day. I'd love to see every one of you carted out of here in cuffs for trespassing and assault."

"No one here will harm you. They all just wanted to meet you," I explain. "See, they were all super-curious to put a face to a name, especially when they learned how you like to abuse your partners."

"Fucking lies—"

"They know your face now, asshole. They've got it fucking memorized. Guys, you got him clocked?" I say over my shoulder.

"We got him," says Jake.

"Oh, yeah, I'll never forget that ugly fucking face," Novy says.

Troy scowls at me. "Just tell me why you're here, Langley."

"I'm here to tell you that you picked the wrong fucking one," I reply. "You thought I was easy prey, but you've bitten off way more than you can chew with me. I am not alone in this world. I roll thirty people deep at all fucking times," I say, gesturing over my shoulder to the lobby full of Rays. "I am stronger than you, smarter than you, and people just plain like me better. I am so far out of your fucking league."

Troy just scoffs. "I will take such delight in ruining you."

"You can try," I counter. "Knowing your stupid ass, you will. Come at me all you want. I'm ready for you. My friends, my family, my team, they're ready too. I only came to give you this message: Tess is with me now, and you will *never* see or speak to her again."

"You want that rotten whore, you can have her," Troy shouts. "She's fucking dead to me!"

Behind him, a few people gasp. They glance between each other with horrified looks on their faces. I can only imagine what they think of Tess compared to what they think of the boss's spoiled rotten son.

"I hope you really mean that," I say. "Because if I get even a whiff of your stench within a two-mile radius of her ever again, I will rain fire down on you. And I'm not just talking about the harassment, stalking, and blackmail charges I'll file for myself. You and I both know Tess has everything she needs to get you convicted by any judge or jury. We will fucking end you, Troy. You will be the one who rots . . . in a cell."

"What do you want?" Troy says again, his gaze darting around the room. "I assume you came here to make a deal. You're threatening me with all these lies because you want something."

"I do want something," I reply, slipping my hand into my other back pocket. "I have something here for you to sign." Stepping over to the reception desk, I set the papers down. "Katie, can Mr. Owens borrow a pen?"

She mechanically hands me one, her blue eyes wide.

"Thank you." I turn to Troy. "Sign this, and we leave. Sign, and Tess and I extend you mercy."

Troy crosses over to the desk, snatching up the papers. His gaze darts across the page for all of two seconds before he tips his head back, letting out a wolfish sound that chills me to my bone. "Oh hell, are you kidding me with this? All of that to get me to sign some divorce papers? You could have saved your fucking time."

My heart stops as I glare at him. "Why?"

He shoves the papers back at me, the pen rattling down off the reception desk. "Because I already signed them."

I blink twice, glancing from him to the unsigned papers. "Wait . . . what?"

66
Tess

"Come on, you piece of junk." I tap through the new printer set-up menu for the third time. The stupid thing is supposed to connect to Wi-Fi, but I'll be damned if I can figure out how. I stretch out my arm, reaching for the manual on the edge of my desk while I hold down the reset button. I'm in a full yoga bend, the machine giving me a warning beep as I wiggle the manual closer with my fingers.

I don't want to be dealing with a malfunctioning printer right now, but I can't sit still. At this very moment, Ryan and half the Rays are up in Cincinnati confronting Troy on my behalf. I meant what I said: I will never see or speak to him again. Narcissists only understand boundaries when they're firm. I drew this line in the sand, and I'll be damned if I cross it again.

Troy Owens is nothing but a memory for me now. Someone I used to know.

The printer makes a high-pitched whirring sound and I slap the top with a curse.

A memory he may be, but the fact remains I *need* those damn divorce papers signed. I'm giving Troy this one last chance to sign them uncontested. Otherwise, I'm going full-scorched earth. By going after Ryan, Troy woke the dragon. I won't rest until I'm free, and if he is going to threaten the people I love, I will burn him to ash.

Boundaries, I have them now. Fuck around, and you *will* find out.

In this case, Ryan and his teammates are bringing two boxes full of "find out" straight to Troy's office door. I've been sitting by my phone, waiting impatiently for an update all morning. Not even this printer can prove a good enough distraction.

The beeping continues, and I curse under my breath, holding the stupid reset button down again. For fuck's sake, I have a B.A., an MBA, and a J.D. Surely, I can manage to set up one stupid, freaking—

"Good morning, Tess."

I gasp, nearly toppling out of my warrior pose in my rush to spin around. My heart stops as I see Bea Owens standing in the doorway of my office. She looks as perfect as ever, tall and lithe, with a ballerina's body, all collarbones and angled hips. She's draped in a navy sheath dress, pearls at her ears and neck, with an Hermès Kelly on her arm.

"What are you doing here?" I say, heart racing, crossing my arms.

She's peering around the room, taking in all the improvements I made to the space—two new desks, framed pictures on the wall, stick-on wallpaper to cover the old water stains. It's a far cry from her cherry wood executive office suite, but it's mine.

"So . . . this must be your new office."

"I'm not coming back," I say, fighting my nerves.

Dealing with Troy's drama is one thing. After thirteen years, I'm a master at shoveling his bullshit. But Bea is an entirely different animal. She's been my weakness for so long, a mentor and mother figure in one. I've had her up on a pedestal. Saint Beatrice, patron saint of lost daughters.

Even when she sided with Troy, even when she watched him lie to me and cheat, when she helped him manipulate me . . . god, even then I worshipped her. But all false idols must eventually fall. I used to look at her and see Jackie Kennedy. Now all I see is Troy's mother.

Her inspection of the office complete, she holds my gaze. "I've missed you these last weeks."

"I'm not coming back," I say again. "If you came here to ask me that, you can just go. Cincinnati is done for me, Bea."

"I know," she replies.

I suck in a breath, my eyes narrowing on her as the truth hits me. "I'd say you can have my official two-week notice, but we both know you've let Troy move forward with firing me. Anything to appease him in his time of grief, right?"

She says nothing, and I know I'm right. I just scoff, shaking my head. I was holding out vain hope that she would prove to me my idolization was worth it. Looking at Bea in her Prada and pearls, I see it was all a mirage.

"You know, I've spent the last thirteen years feeling like an imposter," I say, admitting it to myself more than her. "Poor, underprivileged Tess with her loud opinions and her financial aid scholarships. I didn't buy my way into your world, Bea. I *earned* it. I worked hard and got accepted into the Ivy League. Meeting Troy and your family, I felt tapped for greatness. I was finally leaving all the chaos of my old life behind me. I was chosen. I was *in.* I learned the rules, and I let you all chip pieces of me away so I could fit inside your little boxes."

"You talk as though we mutilated you," she says, her face unreadable. "Like it wasn't *you* being the driver of your own fate. You're not a victim, Tess."

"Oh, I know," I reply. "I asked for everything I got. I stayed when I should have run. I sat quiet when I should have shouted from the rooftops that everything around me was artifice and bullshit. I fought so hard, Bea. And for what? What did it earn me in the end? What do I have to show for a decade of living in your illustrious shadow? Here at the end of things, I see the truth: I was never really in . . . was I? Not with him, and certainly not with you."

"I loved you in my way," she says. "And Troy tried—"

"Don't," I say, raising my hand. "No justifications. We're past them. I don't know what you came here for, but I really don't think you'll find it, Bea." I lower my hand back to my side, heart in my throat. "I think you should go," I whisper. "I need you to go."

Behind me the printer lets out another alarming beep. A paper jam or a problem with the alignment tray. I spin away from her, flipping the switch to turn the whole machine off. Once my back is turned, I take a deep breath, gripping the sides of the machine.

"I'm not here to cause you any more heartbreak," she says gently.

I slowly turn back around. "Then why are you here?"

Setting her Hermès Kelly on the desk, she opens it with perfectly manicured nails, her massive, emerald-cut diamond flashing on her finger. She pulls out a blue legal file and hands it out to me. "I came to give you this."

My eyes lock on the document. "And what is that?"

She sets it down on the corner of the desk between us. "Open it and see."

Heart in my throat, I snatch up the file and open it. Tears sting my eyes as I read the bold statement along the top: PETITION FOR DISSOLUTION OF MARRIAGE.

"Oh god," I whisper, my fingers brushing tentatively over the page. It's signed. "How did you . . . "

"My son is an imperfect person, Tess," she admits. "I know this. I have always known this. He is quick to anger and action. He can be obstinate. Lord knows he and I have fought many battles over the long years. You fought your battles too."

We both know that's an understatement. "Why now, Bea? What changed?"

She clears her throat. "Troy is a passionate man, Tess. Sometimes that passion overtakes reason. Without reason, we can make poor decisions. We can take actions that are . . . regrettable."

I narrow my eyes at her, trying to puzzle out the truth. "What are you trying to say?"

She holds my gaze, her eyes sharpening as she lifts her chin. This is corporate mergers and acquisitions Bea, boardroom Bea, "let's make a deal" Bea.

"Oh god," I whisper, letting the truth hit me like a crashing wave. I see the moment her eyes flicker, and she knows I know.

"I need to know it ends here," she says, gesturing to the papers. "You have your freedom. Now you can go . . . and leave Troy in peace."

I hear the words she's not saying: *Now you can go . . . and don't press charges.*

Indignation hardens in my chest. She's not here for me, and these papers are no gift. They're a buyout. A hush payment. She's protecting her son. She will always only *ever* protect Troy. Not me. Never me.

"What finally tipped your scales? You ignored the abuse because he was always careful. There was never any proof, no witnesses. It was my word against his—"

"Tess—"

"So, what changed, Bea?" I press. "Did you find out about the stalking and harassment? Maybe someone tipped you off about the photographer he's had trailing me for weeks."

"I don't know what you're talking about," she replies, every inch the boardroom tiger protecting her wayward cub.

I narrow my eyes, hooking on the truth. "It was the TRO, wasn't it?"

Her eyes flash, and I know I'm right.

"He used your name, didn't he? He roped you in to pull strings with the judge. You're not just protecting him now. You're here protecting yourself . . . aren't you?"

"You have what you wanted," she says, pointing to the papers. "The divorce. That's what you said you wanted, yes? We were generous. It's an even split, per the laws of the state of Ohio. All assets, all properties—"

"I don't care about assets and property." I slap the documents down on the desk. "That's your obsession. *You* care about the look of things. I never did."

"I know," she replies solemnly. "It's how I knew this marriage was doomed to fail."

Her words hit me like a punch to the gut. I drop my hand down to the desk, gripping it tight.

"You were always too headstrong, too uncultured," she goes on. "You fit into our lives like a rusty, broken wheel. I did my best, for Troy's sake. You were what he wanted at the time, and I can deny him nothing." She pauses, her gaze tracing my features.

I lean instinctively away, hating her appraising eyes on me.

"And then I saw how broken you were," she says. "A bird without her feathers, yearning to fly. So, I took you under my wing. I played the part of your doting mother, your business advisor. I taught you to dress and speak and act. All the while I watched as you two pecked at each other. I watched you bring out the worst in my son, and I was helpless to stop it."

"And his worst carved out the best of me," I challenge. "I thought it was gone, lost forever. I thought I would never know that wild, happy Tess again. You call me a rusty, broken wheel. Do you know what Ryan calls me?"

She purses her lips, saying nothing.

"Dream girl," I say, a smile lighting my face. Love for him fills me, lighting me up as I face down my last remaining dragon, sword and shield in hand. "You're right about me, Bea. All my life, I've been a lost bird, looking for a home, somewhere I could feel safe and loved and free to be myself. In my ignorance, I thought maybe money and power could buy those things. I was so wrong. It took me walking away from everything to find that home at last."

"I assume your new home is Jacksonville?" she asks.

"No. My home is *me*. It's been me all along. I am everything I need. I am enough just as I am. I am smart and driven. I'm kind. I'm passionate and funny and sexy as hell." I square my shoulders, confidence flowing through me. "I came to Jacksonville to be closer to Rachel. I thought she was my home. But I was wrong. She's just the first person to hold up a mirror and show me that I'm enough."

"And this new young man?" she presses, one brow raised.

My smile widens. "He's my mirror ball. His every surface reflects my perfections back at me. He loves me for exactly who I am. I'm not too loud for him or too opinionated. He doesn't cringe when I tell jokes because he's worried I'm funnier than him, pulling away his spotlight. He lets my light shine out as brightly as I want, and he shines it all back on me. I have never known a love or an acceptance of self like I have with Ryan."

"Well," she says, emotion thick in her throat. "It sounds like you got everything you always wanted, then."

I nod. "I'm happy now, yes. And I'm free. Even without these," I add, tapping the divorce papers. "I was already free in my heart. These free me on paper, too, the last chains tying me down to the rotting edifice of the life I thought I wanted."

"Rotting edifice?" she says with a raised brow. "Hardly flattering."

"Well, if the Manolo Blahnik leather slingback fits," I reply with a shrug.

She sighs, glancing around the small office as she shifts her Kelly onto her arm. "I need your word it ends here. I need to know you won't retaliate against Troy."

I purse my lips, glancing down at my phone on the desk. No message from Ryan yet. Right now, he's in Cincinnati going to the PFH office, pressing Troy to sign the papers. My window is closing. If ever I wanted to claim something from Bea Owens, now is my chance.

I square my shoulders at her, hands on my hips. "On the phone, I told you I had a plan for how we all walk away clean. You didn't believe me. You sided with Troy. And now you're implicated in his legal malpractice."

"Tess—"

I raise a hand to silence her. "Let's not beat around the bush here. All I have to do is say the word, and my lawyer will come down on you both. I'm the one with the leverage now, not you."

"So, what do you want, Tess?" she says, her words clipped. "How do I make this stop here?"

"You both need to agree to go to therapy," I say without missing a beat.

Her eyes go wide. "Therapy?"

"Troy needs intervention, Bea. He needs help that you can't give him. And you need help too. Because the way you love him is hurting him. He needs to be held accountable for his actions. Set boundaries. Enact consequences. A therapist can give you the tools to better engage with him. He needs you, Bea. You're the only person I think he truly cares about. Help him."

"So . . . what? We go to therapy and send you proof of our sessions?"

I nod. "Yeah—well, no. Don't send the proof to me. After today, I want no contact with either of you. Send it to my lawyer. Biweekly sessions for the next year. Go, learn tools for managing a healthier relationship with your son."

She arches a brow. "And if I say no?"

"Then I press charges."

Her frown deepens as her lips purse. "And if I can't convince him to go as well?"

"Then I press charges," I repeat. "See? Boundaries and consequences."

She considers for a moment. "Fine. Consider it done. Anything else?"

I smile, my eyes locked on the framed sea turtle poster behind her head. "Yeah . . . make a donation to Out of the Net." I let my gaze slide back to her, soaking in her surprised face. "And whatever the number is in your head right now, double it."

"Sea turtles?" She gives a sad little shake of her head. "I can see your time with me has truly taught you nothing. You have a knife to my throat, and your only demand is that I go to therapy and donate to this nonprofit?"

Her words settle deep in my chest, and I realize she's right. Thirteen years in her shadow, and I survived. I'm still me. I wouldn't say she taught me nothing, but her lessons have left only scars. I will heal. I *am* healing.

I beam at her, my heart feeling ten times lighter. "Yep. Make the donation, make it truly outrageous, and I'll even issue a joint statement with Troy that you can share with all your friends and associates. We'll say we parted in friendship and that our families remain close as I move on to pursue new philanthropic endeavors."

She considers. "And the fallout? The press?"

"You can tell everyone about the donation," I reply. "PFH gets the tax break and all the good press, while you avoid the harsh spotlight of a contested divorce. Most importantly for you, Troy avoids disbarment and criminal charges."

"These are all things we get," she says, that eyebrow arching in question. "What do *you* get, Tess?"

I glance down at the signed divorce papers. "I get to be free." Slowly, I look back up at her, meeting her eyes. "And I get to never see you again."

67
Tess

"Wait . . . so that's it? You're just . . . letting him off the hook?" Rachel stands in the surf, her hands tucked in the pockets of her polar fleece.

Poppy stands at her side. Her long blonde ponytail is pulled through the back of her Rays hat. They're both looking at me like I've got snakes for hair.

"Yeah, that's it," I reply, taking a sip of my hot chocolate. The February air carries a chill this morning, biting at my fingertips as I raise the travel mug to my lips. We pretty much have this stretch of beach all to ourselves.

"And you're . . . okay with that?" Shelby presses from Poppy's other side. She's the one who brought us the hot chocolates. Our guys are all still in Cincinnati, helping Ryan pack up the rest of my apartment. They fly back this afternoon.

"I am," I reply with a nod, and I know in my heart that I mean it.

The girls eye me warily, saying nothing as we continue our walk in the surf.

"Look, I *could* press charges," I explain. "I could take Troy to court for the stalking, the harassment. I could air every single piece of dirty laundry we shared over the last decade. But Troy would give as good as he gets. He would drag out every minute of it. He and his mother would try to bury me in delays and legal fees and counter claims. Don't you see? Fighting him in court is just another way I let him win. I'm done letting him take up my time, my joy. He's taken enough from me. They both have. Please, tell me you can understand," I say, reaching for Rachel's arm.

She pauses, slipping her hand out again to take mine. "Oh, honey,

I do," she says, her tone earnest. "I promise, I do. I mean, if it were up to me, I'd go total *Game of Thrones* on his ass. He hurt you, Tess. He hurt my friend. If I had my way, he'd be torn apart by a dragon's talons."

"Or a pack of wild dogs," Poppy adds.

"Hey, what's the myth with the man who has his insides eaten every day by a vulture?" asks Shelby.

"Prometheus," Poppy replies. "And it wasn't a vulture, it was an eagle."

I give them a gentle smile. "I don't know if I can find an eagle to commit to eating his insides every day. That seems like more work than finding a fair judge and jury."

"But you *want* to find a judge and jury?" Rachel nudges. "You want to press charges?"

"No," I admit, giving her my truth. "I'm sorry, but I don't."

"Oh, Tess, don't apologize to me," Rachel says, taking my hand again. "I just want you to be sure. I want you to weigh all your options and make the best choice for you. And I want you to know you *have* choices. Because if it's a matter of paying legal fees or you needing to hire a legal team, you know we would—"

"I know," I say, squeezing her hand. "I know you'd help me without question. I know you'd give me a kidney if I needed it."

She smiles. "Let's hope that doesn't become necessary anytime soon, but yes, I would. At this point, I'll have to fight Jake for the honor," she adds with a laugh. "He's very determined to protect you and make you feel like a Price."

"I may not have a kidney to offer, but you have my support," says Shelby from my other side. "Whatever you decide, whatever feels right to you, we're here, Tess. And just because a court isn't involved, it doesn't mean there's no justice."

"What do you mean?" asks Poppy.

"Well, in my experience, justice looks different to each person," Shelby explains. "For some, justice only comes when they see their abuser behind bars. Others feel justified when their abuser admits to their crimes and seeks forgiveness."

"Troy will never admit he's at fault. Turtles will fly before he ever apologizes to me," I say. "But maybe the therapy will be enlightening.

If not for him, I think Bea isn't beyond reaching. And she holds massive sway in his life. I really think she can help him."

Shelby gives me a sympathetic nod. "In that case, perhaps the sweetest form of justice comes from you boldly moving on. Leave them to each other. We survive, we thrive, and we never give them power over us again."

It's my turn to pause, holding her gentle gaze. I've never mentioned what she admitted to me in the garage. Not to Rachel, not to anyone. Shelby may be a child psychologist who deals with cases like mine in a professional capacity, but she and I both know her experience runs deeper. She bears her own scars.

"Is that what you would do?" I ask.

She smiles, tears in her eyes. "I would want the future too. No more living in the past."

I nod, my heart fluttering with relief at being understood. Next to me, Poppy sucks in a breath that sounds almost like a sob.

"Pop? You okay?" Rachel asks.

"Oh, goodness," she says with a little laugh. "Don't mind me. I'm such a hormonal mess these days."

"What about you?" I say at her. "What would you do?"

She sniffs back her tears, wiping under her nose. "Some days it feels like my past holds more ghosts than the Haunted Mansion." She closes her eyes, taking a deep breath. Slowly, she opens them. "I want the future too," she says, her lips quivering as she places a hand on her little bump. "Heaven help me, I can't keep looking back. I want to look forward. I *need* to look forward."

I nod, giving her shoulder a squeeze.

"Well, here," says Rachel, glancing around the sand at our feet. "Find a shell."

Poppy sniffles. "What?"

"Everyone find a shell," Rachel says again.

Seashells litter this stretch of beach—cockles and whelks, even the occasional conch shell. Most are no bigger than a silver dollar. I find one half-buried in the sand. It's a little scallop shell, orange at the edges and rosy pink at the base.

Next to me, Shelby dusts off a little white shell. "What are we doing with these?" she asks, holding it in her open palm.

"Everyone has one?" Rachel replies, holding a curled black shell in her outstretched hand.

We all show our shells, our fingers dusted with sand.

"Right, so this was something my grandma did with us when we were little," Rachel explains. "You whisper a secret to the shell, a hope, a dream. You give it to the shell to carry, and the ocean keeps it safe."

Poppy raises a skeptical brow. "You want me to tell this shell a secret?"

Rachel smiles. "If you want. Or you can give it your past. Give it your ghosts." She looks to me, her gaze solemn. "Give it your pain, your frustration."

"I'm gonna need a bigger shell," Shelby deadpans.

"Shells are tough," Rachel replies. "They can hold more than you think."

I look down at my shell, noting the thin ridges and the color, rusty like my hair. My heart beats faster as I close my fingers around it, letting those ridges imprint into the meat of my palm.

Rachel stands next to me, her eyes falling shut as she takes a deep breath. "Give the shell whatever you need it to carry for you. And when you're ready . . . let it go."

"Let it go?" Poppy repeats.

Rachel smiles, opening her eyes. "Like this." Giving her shell a little kiss, she cocks her arm back and flings her shell out into the waves, letting the water swallow it. Then she lets out a deep exhale, her shoulder relaxing.

Closing my eyes, I concentrate on the shell in my hand, feeding it my anger and frustration, my fear, my loneliness, my own self-defeat. I am Tess. I am strong and confident. There is no room for shame. I give it to the shell. I am beautiful and kind. There is no room for insecurity. I let the shell have that too. I am powerful. I am wanted. I am loved. There is no room for doubt.

Giving the shell one last squeeze, I open my eyes and gaze out at the water. I watch the waves crash in once, twice, the white caps frothing against the sand as the water laps at my toes. Taking a deep breath, I cock my arm and fling the shell into the air, watching as it sails over the surf to land with a soundless plop in the grayish blue water.

"There." I take Rachel's sandy hand in mine. "It's done."

"It's done," she repeats.

To either side of us, Poppy and Shelby throw their shells into the ocean too. The four of us stand there with tears in our eyes, watching as the waves crash at our ankles.

After a few minutes of reverent silence, Poppy clears her throat. "Anyone up for brunch?"

"God, yes," Shelby replies. "I'm starving."

"Me too," Rachel echoes. "Tess? You in?"

I glance away from the water at the faces of the three women smiling at me, waiting for me, including me. They want me here. I'm wanted. I'm loved. I'm home.

There is no room for doubt.

"Yeah," I say, trying to keep the emotion from my voice. "Yeah, brunch sounds good."

68
Ryan

The sun shines in through the sliding doors of the back patio. I threw them open wide, letting the smell of the sea fill my lungs. It's a perfect February day, cool and dry, not a cloud in the sky. Beyond the whitewashed deck, a little boardwalk leads out over the dune and down to the beach.

I glance around the empty space, letting my eye linger on the open kitchen. The cabinets are white, the style modern, with sleek stainless-steel appliances. I like the hardwood floors. They're a light oak color, giving it a beach house vibe.

Knock, knock.

"Hello?" Tess calls, her voice echoing around the empty space. She sounds hesitant. Of course, she is. I just got back from the airport and wouldn't let her come pick me up. Instead, I told her to meet me at this random address. "Ryan . . . are you in here?"

I spin around with a smile, walking a few paces to the left so she can see me from the entryway. 'Hey, babe," I call.

She steps into the empty living room, and I swear my heart fucking stops. She looks gorgeous in a cropped T-shirt and flowy floral skirt with a slit halfway up her thigh. Her hair is up in a messy bun, big gold hoop earrings almost touching her shoulders.

She flicks her aviators off, tucking them on top of her head as she looks around. "Where are we? Why did you tell me to meet you here?"

She's asking questions, but I can't make sentences right now. I can't talk anymore about Cincinnati or her encounter with the dragon-in-law. I haven't seen my girl in forty-eight hours, and I'm feeling desperate. I rush over to her, wrapping her in my arms. She thinks

I'm going in for a kiss, but I surprise her when I pick her up, hauling her over my shoulder.

"Ryan," she squeals, her arms flailing as her purse slips off her shoulder and hits the floor.

I give her ass a playful swat as I hurry over to the kitchen and drop her right on the island. Stepping in between her legs, I cup her face and kiss her.

She moans against my lips, her body melting against me, her arms around my neck.

"Baby, I missed you," I say, peppering her lips with kisses.

She laughs against my mouth, her hands smoothing over my shoulders. "I missed you too. Fuck, I love you."

"I love you so fucking much." My hands drop down to her thighs. I smooth them up and down, feeling the way she shifts to the edge of the counter. At the first touch of her bare thigh, I know there's no stopping us.

I had a plan, a whole damn speech, but it flew right out the windows, sailing away on the open ocean. Tess is in my arms, and I can't not have her. "I want you," I say, my hand slipping under the slit of her skirt, grazing up her thigh.

"I want you too," she pants, hiking up the skirt.

I help her, the two of us fevered as we pull at our clothes. I jerk her panties down, dropping them to her ankles. She unbuttons my jeans. It's the work of moments before I've got my hard cock in hand, lining myself up at her entrance.

"Please, baby," she whimpers, nodding as she bites her bottom lip, both of us looking down at where we're about to be joined.

I angle the tip of my dick where I want it and look up, holding her gaze as I sink in inch by inch. Her lips part in a breathless moan as she takes me, her long eyelashes fluttering.

"That's it," I soothe, my hand gripping her hip as I make a few short thrusts, working my dick all the way in. "That's my girl. Fuck, you feel so good." She's so warm and tight.

Her hands go to my shoulders as she angles her hips back, opening her channel, easing my thrusts in deeper. We both moan, chests heaving as I rock against her sharp and fast, my bare hips slapping her thighs.

"Oh god, don't stop," she begs, her pussy fluttering around me. "Ryan, please—"

"I had a whole plan," I pant. "Tess—*god*—I had a whole fucking speech. One look at you, and it all went outta my head. I can't think—can't fucking breathe 'til I come inside you—"

"Give me the CliffsNotes version," she says, her lips against mine.

"You're my home," I say, hands shaking as I feel my orgasm building. "You're all I want. You make me so fucking happy."

"*Ahh*—" Her pussy clenches me tighter as she drops one hand from my shoulder, slipping it between us to tease her clit. "Fuck," she screams, head tipping back as she comes.

The walls of her pussy squeeze me like a vise, and we both cry out, our bodies falling together as I lose all sense of rhythm. I'm wrapped around her and in her, my face buried at her neck, as I release. I spill into her, filling her with my cum.

We stay like that, clinging to each other, her ass perched on the edge of the kitchen counter. After a few moments, we loosen our hold on each other. I lean away, keeping my dick inside her as I cup her cheek and sprinkle her face with kisses. "I love you. Love the way you make me feel."

She lets out a deep, shaky breath, and I feel her relax around me. Then she's blinking up at me, the haze of her orgasm lifting as she comes to her senses. She gives me a little push, and I pull out, the warmth of our releases pooling between her legs and on the counter.

With a whimper, she reaches between her thighs, swiping her fingers through our release. Her green eyes are molten as she lifts her fingers to my lips. "Taste."

I suck her fingers into my mouth, groaning at our taste on my tongue. It reminds me of another moment, only a few short months ago, that I had her finger in my mouth.

"Better than frosting?" she teases, reading my damn mind.

I nod, letting her fingers go. And because I can't help myself, I do the same, swiping two fingers from pussy to clit, bringing it to her parted lips. She doesn't hesitate, pulling my fingers into her mouth and teasing them with her tongue as she licks them clean. She lets them go with a pop, and then she's slipping off the counter, ducking down to pull up her panties.

The haze of our joining dissipates, and I find myself standing in the middle of this empty kitchen with my dick wet, my pants around my ankles. The back doors are wide open. With a laugh, I duck down and pull up my pants, tucking myself away.

Fuck, this woman is trouble.

She steps around the island and walks back into the empty living room. "Why did you want me to meet you here?"

"What do you think?" I reply, gesturing around.

She glances from the kitchen to the whitewashed stone fireplace to the large, outdoor deck leading out to the beach. "It's cute. What is it, two bedrooms?"

"Three," I say. "Though the third bedroom is pretty small. The whole place is small, really. It's just a bungalow. But it's a new build, and it's right on the water."

She spins around, her face framed with curly red tendrils. "It's super cute. Are you thinking of renting it?"

"I bought it."

She gasps. "What?"

"Tess, I bought this house. My contracts are all approved. The Nike deal, the new deal with Bauer, my contract extension with the Rays. You're looking at a guy with a twenty-million-dollar four-year contract and a four-mil signing bonus," I say, unable to avoid puffing out my chest a bit.

"Four?" she says, eyes wide. "I thought it was three."

"MK negotiated," I say with a grin.

"Oh—Ryan, that's amazing," she cries, coming around the island to wrap her arms around me.

I let her hug me, taking another shameless hit off her scent. She's all floral and coconutty. I want that scent bottled. I'll wash all my sheets and clothes with it. I want to drown in her. But I know a Tess-scented detergent isn't enough. I want *her*. I want everything.

She lets me go, spinning around again. "When do you move in?"

"Whenever I want," I reply. "It's ready now. Seller was motivated, and so was I."

She smiles. "I'm really happy for you," she says again. "How does it feel?"

I glance around and shrug, slipping my hands in the pockets of my jeans. "Like it's a house."

"And they told me all you hockey boys lack common sense," she teases.

I just smile, watching her fill up this empty space with her light. "It's not a home, Tess."

"Well, not yet. But you gotta give it a fighting chance. At least put down a rug. Maybe a couch here," she says, pointing to a spot on the floor. "Plug in your Nintendo, toss a few boxes of Kraft mac and cheese in the pantry, and you've got yourself a Casa de Ryan."

"That won't make it my home," I reply solemnly.

She turns around, slower this time. "Curtains, then? Maybe something blue. And a dish of seashells. Apparently, no Florida home is complete without a decorative dish with some shells. Oooh, can that be my housewarming gift to you?"

"It's not my home, Tess," I say again.

I can almost see the relief on her face as she lets out a little breath. "Oh, is it like a rental, then? Diversifying your assets?"

"No, I'm gonna live here. This is my house. I'm gonna decorate it top to bottom. I'll work out on my patio in the mornings, do beach walks at night. And yes, I'll make my mac and cheese on the stove and play Mario Kart when I'm bored. But none of that will make this my home. Only one thing can do that."

She goes still, her chest rising and falling as she eyes me warily. "What are you doing?" she finally asks, unable to play dumb a second longer.

"Not proposing," I reply.

The breath she's holding leaves her in a puff through parted lips. "Ohmygod, you were scaring the shit outta me," she says, her hand covering her chest as she takes a deep breath. "Ryan, you said no marriage. You said you don't believe in it—"

"And *you* said no man will cage you," I counter. "You said you'll never be someone's wife again. So, I didn't know how to fucking do this without making it seem like I'm proposing to you when I'm not. 'Cause neither of us want that . . . right?"

She blinks at me, tears in her eyes, saying nothing.

And now my heart has fucking stopped. "Oh . . . fuck."

She steps forward, one hand reaching out to me, whether to pull me closer or push me away, I have no fucking idea. "Ryan—"

"Tess, what the fuck are you doing to me," I cry, dragging both hands through my hair.

"Nothing!"

"You can't stand in the house I bought for you, wearing my cum between your legs, looking at me like that when I ask if you want to get married. I'm gonna freak the fuck out!"

She gasps. "You—what? Ryan, tell me you did *not* buy me this house!"

"Of course, I bought you a house," I shout, gesturing around. "I gave up my death trap apartment weeks ago. And you said you couldn't keep staying in Ilmari's house after all the peeping Tom bullshit. I wanted a place where we could *both* start fresh. New chapter, right?"

Tears sting her eyes as she shakes her head.

"Don't do that," I say, my head mirroring her shake. "Don't close off. Talk to me. Get it out."

"I'm scared," she admits. "This is all moving so fast. Ryan, I'm scared of what I feel for you. I have never loved another person the way I love you. Not as a friend, not as a lover. Not ever—"

"I feel the same way," I say, stepping closer, my hands brushing down her arms. "Tess, I know I teased you and said I don't believe in soulmates and love at first sight and all that stuff. And I'm still not sure I do," I admit, taking her hands in mine. "I'm a rational guy, Tess. I like evidence. I like knowing a thing is real because I see it and feel it. But now, I'm beginning to think I didn't believe in soulmates because I hadn't met mine yet. How can you see and feel what it is for your soul to mate with another's until you find that person meant to be yours?"

"Ryan . . . " she whispers.

"Tell me you don't feel it too," I challenge. "Tell me you don't feel a . . . a rightness in yourself when we're together. At first, I told myself it was lust. I told myself it would fade if I could just scratch that itch. But baby, it's not fading. It just gets stronger. Every day the wanting you gets stronger. Do you not feel it too?"

"I do," she admits, her voice small. It matches her hope. She's not ready to dive in with both feet. Her trust burns like a weak candle on a windy day.

"One step at a time," I say, being the strength I know she needs. "You don't want to live at Ilmari's house anymore, right?"

She shakes her head.

"Good, so move in here. You can have your own room if you want. Or you can sleep in my bed, and I'll worship you like the goddess you are every day of the fucking week. Every night too," I add with a grin. "And I'm thinking of adding a sauna out on the back deck."

She smirks.

I cup her cheek, brushing my thumb along her soft skin. It might just be my favorite point of contact when we're not fucking. I love the softness of her cheek. "We're starting small. Let's live together. No labels, no cages. Just two souls happiest together. Whatever else comes—marriage, babies, life partnerships, or a respectful parting of the ways, that door will always be open," I say, pointing to the front door. "I will never hold you back or hold you down. I don't need any papers or legal proof to mark what we both know is true."

"I know," she says, her hand splaying over my chest.

"I just want to love you," I say. "I want to put you first. I want to see you smile every day and know I'm the reason. I want to be your person. I want to make my home in you, and I want you to make your home in me."

"I want that too," she says. "More than anything."

"I told you I would never ask you to marry me, and I meant it—"

"I'll ask," she says, tipping up on her toes, her hands on my shoulders.

"Wait—what?" I look down at her, eyes wide.

She looks right back up at me, her gaze unwavering. "I'll ask you. Ryan, you deserve to be asked—not right now," she adds quickly, and we both let out a nervous laugh.

"No, yeah," I say, nodding as if she hasn't just punched a hole through my universe.

"My divorce isn't even final yet," she hedges.

"Fair," I say, still reeling.

"And if it's okay with you, I'd like us to just take this slow," she goes on. "I want us to enjoy each other. No cages, no labels, right?"

"Of course," I say, nodding like a bobblehead.

"But I *will* ask you, Ryan," she says again, a smile curling her lips. "If we someday decide that a legal marriage is what we both want, then when I'm ready . . . when *we're* ready . . . I'll ask you to be my husband."

"Are you serious right now?"

She flips my hair off my brow with gentle fingers. "It's like what you said about soulmates. You don't know what it means to have one until you have one. I think perhaps I was too quick to dismiss the labels of husband and wife and what they could mean to me because I hadn't met the person who was meant to carry that title with me." She smiles, dropping her hand away. "Ryan Puppy Langley, you're the best person I know. You're so kind and loving. You're gentle, yet strong. You listen. You learn. You fight and grow. I'm in love with you, and I'd be honored to be your wife . . . someday . . . probably . . . " Her grins widens and there's a twinkle in her eye. "I know that's not the most romantic of not-proposals, but it's as vague as I can make it."

Joy floods through me, and then I have her in my arms. "I'm gonna need you to say that again," I say, my face nuzzling her neck.

"What—the whole thing? Ryan, that was total word salad."

"No, just the last part—or the second to last part—the "L" word part," I clarify.

She laughs, her hands stroking my back. "I love you, Ryan."

I groan. "Again."

"Don't get greedy," she teases.

"Too late," I reply, my hands drifting down to cup her perfect ass. "You know that's my fatal flaw. I'm greedy when it comes to you. I want every kiss . . . " I brush my lips against hers. "Every smile . . . "

"They're yours," she replies, her face glowing with joy.

"Every orgasm," I add with a smirk.

"There I draw the line," she says, pushing against my shoulder. "You know how much I like playing with my toys. And you travel a lot. I can't possibly give them all to you."

I consider for a moment. "That's fair. How about when I'm away, I still get to watch? We haven't experimented with video calls yet. That could be fun."

"Sorry, puppy. This show is live action only," she teases, her strokes shifting from loving to seeking, her hands brushing down my abs and over my hips. "What if I promise to think of you when I come and you're not around?"

I groan, sinking against her as I kiss her neck. "Don't go breaking my heart—"

She stills, pushing me off her gently to hold my gaze. "Don't break mine."

"Never. Tess, I'm gonna be so good to you."

"We'll be good to each other," she replies, kissing up my jaw. Her hands slip under my shirt to stroke the warm skin of my back.

I weave my fingers into the curly hair at her nape and give it a pull, loving the little hiss she does, the way her eyes heat as she gazes up at me like I'm the only thing she sees. Smirking down at her, I add, "And if we ever do get married, we're having mac and cheese at our wedding."

She laughs, her hands slipping down to cup my ass, pulling me tight against her. Then she angles her mouth up and whispers in my ear, "Make it lobster mac and cheese, and I'll even wear white."

It's a gift and a promise. She's offering me hope. I just have to trust her and love her. This woman is mine. My friend, my soulmate. She already wears my jersey and sleeps in my bed. Someday, she may even share my name. As we sink to the floor, unable to wait for more, the name rings true in my mind: *Tess Langley*.

My Tess. The cataclysm that came and shook me up. Now she's mine to love. Mine to cherish. Mine to make happy for the rest of my lucky fucking life. I smile, kissing her perfect lips.

Nothing has ever felt so right.

Epilogue
Ryan

ONE YEAR LATER

My alarm goes off and I groan, rolling to my side. It's too fucking early. But it's game day, and I have to get up. I snatch for my phone, determined to silence it before it wakes Tess.

As soon as my fingers wrap around it, I go still. That's not my alarm sound. It's music. Like a ringtone. I pull my head out from under my pillow, blinking in the semidarkness as I check the screen. It's my phone, and it's definitely an alarm, but it's playing the chorus of 'Marry Me' by Jason Derulo.

Gasping, I shut it off and roll over, totally expecting to see Tess sitting up in the bed like a no-sleep gremlin, holding out a ring box. But she's not there. Her side of the bed is empty.

I drag a tired hand over my face as I sit up.

She's been hinting pretty strong these last few months that she was ready to propose. She's been making a game of it, twisting me up just to wind me back down. I've about reached my fucking limit. I've assured her I'm happy either way. We're a year into this thing, and there's no end in sight. I am so in love with that woman, it's not even funny. Tess is *mine*.

But a promise is a promise. I'm not proposing. Ever. If she wants me, she knows where to find me.

I set my phone down and swing my legs off the side of the bed. The moment my feet touch the floor, I'm wide fucking awake. There's a trail of red rose petals starting under my feet and leading across the bedroom, disappearing down the hall.

"Tess, you better be out there," I shout, tiptoeing through the rose petals.

They go down the stairs and around the corner into the kitchen where—

I stop, eyes wide, looking around as I take in a garden's worth of red roses. "Oh . . . fucking hell."

Vases cover every surface of the kitchen—the counters, the stove, the island. There are more stacked on the dining table. Only one little spot remains cleared away at the end of the table. Tess has prepared my usual game day breakfast bowl of steel cut oats with fresh berries. I just have to add the hot water.

"Tess!" I shout, listening for sounds of her somewhere in the house. She's probably hiding around the corner, snickering into her hand. "Tess!"

But the house is dead quiet.

I huff, turning back to my breakfast. There's a red envelope resting next to my bowl. I snatch it up. She drew a heart on the front with a letter R inside it. I pull out the card and as soon as I open it, the chorus of Taylor Swift's "All of the Girls You Loved Before" starts playing.

Damn it. She knows that's my favorite Swift song. I call it my 'Tess Song.' On a dare, I even sang it to her during karaoke night a few months ago.

I drop the card and pull my phone out of my pajama pants pocket. I call her, one hand on my hip, glaring at my breakfast. The phone rings and rings as the musical card continues to play.

She doesn't answer.

"Fuck!" I shout at literally no one. "I am marrying you so fucking hard! Don't even test me!"

THIRTY minutes later, Jake and Caleb drag me out of the house for our game day morning beach walk. I tried to tell them what was happening, but Jake wasn't having it. He's almost as bad as Mars when it comes to game day rituals.

We stop by the coffee shop on the way. Colby, my favorite barista, passes me my grande iced tea. She's got the perfect tattoo-to-piercing ratio to know you're always going to get a quality product.

"Here you go, Ryan," she chimes. "And hey, guys, good luck tonight!"

"Thanks, Colby Like the Cheese," Jake teases, taking his coffee from her. It's their little joke. That's how she introduced herself on her first day here. Now it's all he calls her.

I lead the way outside where Sanford is waiting with the dog. Jake hands his husband his coffee, and then we all make our way over to the beach.

"So, she's dodging your calls?" says Jake, taking a sip of his coffee.

"Yeah."

"But she left you a garden of roses and singing cards and phone alarms?"

"Yeah," I say again.

"Dude, you're so getting proposed to tonight," Sanford teases.

I pause, stupid smile on my face. "What? Oh god, do you really think so?"

Sanny just shrugs, flipping his aviators down onto his face. "Well, she's already home, so she's gotta go big. What's bigger than seeing 'Will you marry me?' in the flashing lights of the jumbotron?"

"Dude, the guys are gonna lose it," Jake laughs. "You will never, *ever* live this down."

I smirk, glancing from him to Sanford. "I have that stupid beach puppy look on my face, don't I?"

They both nod.

"Yeah, you're embarrassing yourself," Sanny says.

"You're embarrassing *us*," Jake corrects.

I don't even care. I flip my sunglasses down, too, taking a sip of my iced tea.

Sanford and the dog lead the way down to the beach, and we take it slow, just strolling along the surf in our bare feet. It's barely a half-mile between our houses, so Tess and I walk down most mornings, meeting the Prices at the coffee shop on the way.

Then we all pound the sand back in the direction of our house. The Prices drop us off, the guys usually steal some fruit, and then they make their way home. Everyone gets to walk "the circle" as we call it.

The beach is busy for a Saturday morning in February, but the weather has been so great this week. It's sunny and clear, with a good surf. Lots of people are out riding the waves. We pass a small group of women doing yoga and a young couple making out on their tie-dyed beach blanket.

Poseidon zigs and zags all around, chasing the ball we take turns throwing for him. I think I've just about convinced Tess to let us get a dog.

"Oh, shit," Sanny laughs.

I pause, tennis ball in hand, Poseidon dancing at my feet. "What?"

He's standing in the surf, water lapping his bare feet, looking up in the sky.

"No way," Jake cries, one hand over his eyes. "Dude, that is so fucking cool. Marry her or I will."

"You're already married, asshole," Caleb says.

"Technicality," Jake says with a distracted wave of his hand. "Besides, you've never given me a message in skywriting before."

Heart racing, I shade my eyes with my hand, peering up into the sky. One of those little red prop planes is flying past, right along the coastline, trailing a big white banner behind it. "Oh my god. What does it say?"

"It says 'Marry me, Ryan,'" Sanny replies.

I slow turn to face them, my smile fading to a frown. "You two are in on all of this, aren't you?"

"No," Sanny says as Jake laughs and says, "Duh."

Sanford elbows him and they bicker as I look back up at the plane. The words on the banner are in big, bold black letters, but with the fluttering, it's sorta hard for me to read. Just in case, Tess made sure the guys would be here to read it with me.

I smile. My girl thinks of everything.

In the past year, I've come out to the team about my dyslexia. They were super cool about it. Not that I expected any different. I've never felt so at home with a team like I do with the Rays. They're my brothers, my family.

The only real hurdle was Poppy. She cried and told me I was

brave and then I had to talk her down for three whole days because she wanted me to do a big literacy campaign with the local public schools. It's not a never, I assured her. Just a no for now.

I may be a tough guy out on the ice, but my dyslexia is still a vulnerability I don't like sharing. The guys all get it. Tess definitely gets it. Maybe someday I'll put my face on a dyslexia poster. But for now, I'll stick with the stupid billboard out by the airport.

Jake watches me with a big grin. "Dude, this is fucking romantic. *Please* tell me you're saying yes."

Oh, I'm saying yes. It's been a long road for both of us to feel truly ready, but I'm marrying the fuck out of that woman.

I just have to find her first.

I get back to the house, and Tess's car is still gone. I don't even have to go in to know she's not home. She's not nearly finished torturing me today, I just know it. But if this night doesn't end in a proposal, she's gonna be sleeping in a tent on the porch.

I mean, I'll sleep in it too, because I'm not leaving my woman out in the wild where animals could get her. But I have to prove a point, so tent camping it is.

God, I am a whipped fucking asshole.

I smirk, letting myself into the house. I've only got about forty-five minutes before I have to leave for the arena. I hurry through my routines, passing my kitchen full of roses. I shower, shave, and do some stretches while I have a snack.

Meanwhile, Tess maintains total radio silence.

I slip into my suit and head down to the laundry room where I keep my gear bag. I retrofitted a shower and hang-up area for all my stuff. It keeps it from stinking up the rest of our stuff in the main closets.

I grab my backpack, ready to stuff my workout gear, a change of underwear, and some fresh socks inside. I pull the zipper and my eyes immediately narrow. There's something tucked into the front pocket. I widen the zipper and tug out a blue file folder. Flipping it open, I peer down at a legal-looking document. It's an application of some kind, with spots for your name, address, and phone number.

It's been filled out in blue pen. My heart thrums as I work through the first few lines.

"Oh my god." Tears sting my eyes as I trace my finger along the lines, stopping when I see my last name: L-A-N-G-L-E-Y.

Now I'm smiling like a fool. This is a name change application. We talked about doing it a while ago. I had just returned home from an away game and she asked me if she could take my name, even with us not being married.

"Tess Owens is my past," she said over shared cartons of pad Thai. "I want Tess Langley to be my future . . . even without the ring."

Of course, I said yes.

The next day, Doc stopped by with a set of fancy, monogramed towels that had them both laughing for ten minutes straight and ended with them crying and hugging.

That was the last time she mentioned it.

I find the date on the form and my smile spreads. This is dated from over a month ago. These are the copies she already submitted that carry a government seal and signature.

That's when it hits me. She's not *changing* her name. She already *changed* it. I think she changed it the day after we discussed it. She's Teresa Langley now.

Yeah, nothing is going to keep me from getting to this game. And Tess better be there, ready to get on one knee.

"WHAT'S up with you?" Sully says, lacing up his skates. "You're being weird today."

"Leave him alone," Jake shouts from across the locker room. "He's a man in love."

"We know," says Walsh on my other side.

"Yeah, but tonight Tess finally makes an honest man out of him," Jake calls to the room.

Sully looks at me wide-eyed. "Wait, is he serious, Langers? Are you finally joining the Married Men Club?"

"We don't call it that," says Jake.

"Oh, but we should," says J-Lo, stuffing his head inside his jersey. "It's the most exclusive, most elite club."

"How do we know Tess is gonna ask you tonight?" Walsh asks, snagging my stick tape.

"We know," Jake and Sanny say at the same time.

I just roll my eyes, letting the guys tease me as I punch Walsh and steal back my stick tape. I'm halfway down the blade when a very confused looking Teddy comes stumbling in. "Uhh . . . guys? Is this allowed?" He steps back and four men in sparkly red and white striped suits and straw hats come marching in.

"What the fuck is this?" says Novy, getting to his feet.

But I already know what this is.

"Please, God, no," I mutter. "Anything but this."

"Hello," the tall man with the ginger mustache calls out to the room. "We're looking for Ryan."

The whole locker room hoots and hollers as they point me out, because apparently there's no sense of brotherhood left in this damn sport.

I get to my feet, already in my skates. "Listen, you really don't need to—"

"You're Ryan?" Mustache asks.

"Oh, yeah, that's him," says Sully. The asshole is way too gleeful about this.

All around the room, the guys are getting their phones out. My gaze flashes to the corner where Doc is leaning against the wall by Mars, her arms folded. Catching my eye, she winks.

Oh, fuck her. She is so dead.

Mustache blows on some little flute thing. "Ready, boys?"

And then I'm knocked to my ass on the bench as the quartet breaks out in boisterous singing and arm-swinging:

Bum bum bum bum.
Tonight's the night that Tess will get on one knee.
Bum bum bum bum.
And you and she will live oh so happily.
Your hair is blond, your eyes are green, your face is like a dream.
And only you know what to do to make your lover scream.
The question's short but life is long; you know just what to dooooooo.
Just say 'yes' and Tess will make an honest man of yooooou.

The song ends and the locker room erupts. I'm buffeted on all sides as the team rallies around me, cheering and hollering as the quartet tries to make their exit.

"Ohhh, no, you don't," Jake cries, grabbing Mustache by the arm.

And that's how I end up standing half-dressed in the middle of the locker room, a barbershop quartet flanking me on both sides, as the guys and Claribel snap a thousand pictures that will inevitably end up all over social media.

Oh, yeah, I am marrying Tess tonight . . . if I don't kill her first.

BY the time I get out onto the ice for warm-ups, I'm coiled tighter than a fucking spring. I can't even focus on my usual routines. Who cares about stretching hip flexors or practicing my puck handling. If Tess isn't here, I'm burning this barn to the ground.

As I skate around, peering through the plexiglass, I feel a charged energy in the air. The fans are standing. Some are clapping. As I pass along the wall, I notice a lot of yellow. People all up and down the sections are wearing neon yellow T-shirts. A pair of guys sitting right on the ice are both wearing one. They pound the glass as I pass, beers in hand.

I circle back, glaring at them. "What are those shirts?"

They laugh and point. They both have a picture of a smiling Tess silk-screened to their chests.

"Where is she?" I shout.

They both just laugh, making kissing faces at me through the glass. I pass by two more people. One is wearing a neon shirt with my face. The other is a big diamond ring with a question mark. All down the rink, fans are wearing shirts with our faces and diamond rings.

The music changes over the speakers and someone cranks it up louder. My entire body zings alert as the chorus of "Marry You" by Bruno Mars echoes around the frenzied stadium.

Oh god, this is it. It's fucking happening.

I'm like a figure skater out here, breezing around, searching the crowd for her. The jumbotron is locked on me, following me down the ice. The other guys aren't even pretending to warm up as the crowd starts chanting "Marry her."

"Tess!" I shout, knowing she can't hear me.

"Mar-ry her."

"Mar-ry her."

They pound the glass. They do the wave. They blow their stupid plastic horns.

"Tess, I swear to God—"

"Ladies and gentlemen," comes the booming voice of the announcer. "A very special lady has a veeeeery special question to ask one of our Rays."

I slide to a stop, spraying ice, as I glare up at the jumbotron screen. The camera is on me, zooming in on that hopeful, sappy look on my face. The crowd goes wild, so do my teammates. Then the camera changes, and suddenly she's there.

Tess.

She's standing against the glass. Her red hair is half up, half down, curls framing her face. My jersey is on her back and she's holding up a hot pink glitter sign. The sign is the same as the shirts, with pictures of our faces and an engagement ring. It's like an emoji math question. It's *her* question.

Tess + Ryan = Married

The crowd chants "Mar-ry Her! Mar-ry Her!" and I'm turning in circles looking for her in real time.

"Tess!" I shout, willing her to hear me, to call out and guide me home with the sound of her voice.

I finally spot her three sections down from our bench. The cheers of the crowd crescendo as I race towards her. I slide to a stop at the boards, my stick rattling down. Then I'm throwing my gloved hands up against the glass, just wishing I could make it disappear.

She smiles down at me with tears in her eyes, dropping her sparkly pink sign to the floor. Then she does a little turn, showing me the back of her jersey with a flirty wink. It's my name and number on her back, but she added something in front of my name.

I sound it out, smiling ear to ear. Her jersey reads Mrs. Langley.

"You are in so much trouble, Teresa Langley," I shout.

She turns back around, and both her hands go to the glass, pressing in against mine. "So, what do you think?" she calls back. "Shame to waste the name change. Want to make an honest woman of me? Will you marry me, Ryan?"

"Hell, yes," I say, and the fans around her cheer louder. "I'll marry you right fucking now. Get out here."

She shakes her head, beaming at me, nothing but love shining in her eyes. The scared, hopeless Tess from a year ago is gone. Before me stands a fierce lioness, a tower of beauty and strength. And she's mine. She loves *me*. She's choosing me. She's already chosen.

"Nope," she says with a teary smile. "After the playoffs. Turks and Caicos. The whole team is coming. Everything's already planned."

"We'll *renew* our vows in Turks and Caicos," I reply. "But I am marrying you tonight."

I knew this was the night, so you better fucking believe I came prepared. Slipping my hand out of my right glove, I tip it over and shake it, letting her engagement ring drop into my palm.

She gasps, eyes wide as I hold it up at her through the glass. It's a three-carat, round-cut solitaire diamond on a yellow gold band. I bought it the week she moved in with me last year. You know . . . just in case.

My gaze darts left to where arena security is opening the gate for us. I skate down and she shimmies along the row, people moving out of her way to let her pass. I drop my other glove to the ice and pull her to me with my right hand as soon as she passes the last seat. With my left, I hold up the ring. "If you're asking, I'm saying yes."

She smiles, holding out her left hand. "I'm asking."

I take her hand, not caring that we're both trembling as I slip the ring on her finger. Then she wraps her arms around my neck, and I kiss her like she's the only person I'll kiss for the rest of my life.

"Marry me, Ryan," she murmurs against my lips. "I'm asking. Make me the happiest woman in the world."

"Yes," I say with my whole soul.

"Marry me."

"Yes."

All around us, the crowd goes wild.

THE END

BONUS EPILOGUE

EVER wish you'd been there for the day Tess and Ryan tied the knot? Keep reading to find out how it went down in this exclusive bonus epilogue!

TESS

I've never really been much of a sports girlie. In high school, I did marching band, which meant I was at every football game, but only under duress. My girlfriends and I usually sat in the stands exchanging hot takes about CW love interests and post-modern literature, blithely ignoring the boys in tights running up and down the field.

I don't play fantasy football or care about who's going to the Super Bowl. I never watch the Olympics. I don't even think I could name three NBA teams. And don't get me started on golf, which is nothing more than a good walk wasted and an environmental scourge.

Sports and Tess? Yeah, they just don't vibe.

So, you tell me why I'm standing with my hands pressed against the glass of this hockey rink, screaming at the top of my lungs, "Come on, ref! Are you freaking blind? That guy was totally charging!"

Oh yeah, because the guy getting charged just happens to be my fiancé.

Ryan gets to his feet, and I feel like I can breathe again. One of his teammates skates in fast, supporting him with an arm around his waist. That was a hard hit. The other guy came out of nowhere, knocking Ryan down to the ice. He didn't even have the puck. I'm like ninety-percent sure that's called charging.

That's right. I learned the rules of hockey. Who am I, and what have I done with Tess Owens? I smile, glancing down at the sparkly new ring on my finger. What I did was fall head over heels in love with a professional hockey player. Now Tess Owens is officially Tess Langley, and she knows all about icing and high sticking, faceoffs and power plays.

And honestly, aside from the moments of sheer terror when Ryan takes a hit or gets in a fight, I really do like it. I like hockey. It moves fast, has lots of action, the scoring makes sense, and I don't sweat my tits off or get sunburned sitting in the stands.

A sharp whistle blows and the booing in the stands turn to raucous cheers as a fight breaks out on center ice. After seeing the instant replay of the dirty hit, Jake and J-Lo go after the offending player, pounding him down to the ice. The linesmen quickly dive in and pull the players apart.

I ignore the brawl, my eyes locked on Ryan as he gets safely to the bench. Rachel is right behind him in moments, ducking between the players, her hand on his heavily padded shoulder. I breathe a little sigh of relief. Rachel will take care of him. She'll make sure he's not hurt.

There's only like three minutes left in this game, and the Rays are ahead by two. Ryan takes off his helmet and my shoulders relax. He's done for the night. I watch one of the rookies hop the boards to take his place on the ice with a look of glee on his face. Ryan's loss is his gain. He skates around like a circling hawk, ready to dominate in these last few minutes.

My phone buzzes in my pocket and I pull it out, reading the text from Rachel:

RACHEL: Head over to the press area. They wanna interview Ryan about the proposal. Marty will let you down.

I smile, tucking my phone away. People all around the stadium are still wearing the silly T-shirts I had made, decorated with mine and Ryan's faces. Rachel helped me get the staff involved to pass them out at the door.

Snatching up my sparkly pink sign, I tuck it under my arm and trot up the stairs as everyone in my section cheers for me.

"Yeah, go get him, honey!"

"Congratulations!"

"You should get married on center ice!"

"Marry me instead!"

I pant as I reach the stop, hurrying over to the yellow-vested usher. "Hey," I gasp, hand on my chest. "Whew, that's a crap ton of stairs—where's the team press area?"

"Follow the signs around to section 101," she replies, pointing out to the hall. "There's an escalator that'll take you down, but you need a special wrist band to get down there—"

"Got it, thank you," I call over my shoulder, dragging out the "u" sound.

The concourse is already flooding with people. The smell of popcorn and fried food hang heavy in the air. I duck and weave through the exiting crowds, waving where I can and smiling as people recognize me, all the while following the signs for section 101.

Inside the rink, the horn blows, signaling the end of the game, and the crowd cheers. A win on home ice is always cause for celebration. People are queuing to come up the escalator, but I hurry over to the usher blocking the way down.

"Hey," I say, still breathless. "Are you Marty?"

The older gentleman smiles, his cheeks creasing. "Sure am, honey. Are you the lady of the hour?"

I laugh, flicking my unruly curls off my shoulder. "Mr. Marty, I'm the lady of the century. Ryan Langley is the luckiest guy on two skates."

He barks out a laugh. "Oh, I believe it. You go easy on him now. He's a fan favorite."

"He's my favorite too," I say with a wink.

Standing back, he lets me on the escalator, holding an arm out as others press in closer.

I ride the escalator down and weave my way through the crowd. The press is already assembling, setting up their mics and cameras. A press backdrop stretches along the far wall, decorated with the Rays logo and team sponsors.

"Tess, oh my goodness! You're engaged!!" A squealing pair of arms wrap around me from the side as Poppy hugs me. Her shorter frame means she barely reaches my shoulder.

"Yeah, I guess he finally wore me down," I tease.

"Oh, you hush." She laughs, slapping my arm. "We all know you've been smitten as a kitten for Langley since you two first met. It's about time you both made it official."

"I told him about Turks and Caicos, but he says he's marrying me tonight," I confide, my stomach fluttering with butterflies.

A look flashes on her face and I go still. She covers it quickly, giving her long blonde ponytail a flick over her shoulder. "Well, I'm sure I don't know anything about that."

I grab her arm as she tries to walk away. "Poppy St. James, what do you know?"

"Nothing," she cries, feigning shock. "Your business is your own, Tess. I just hope I'm invited either way. You know I love a good wedding."

Before I can press her for more, she's cornered by a camera crew and she takes off to help them. Her moody assistant follows in her wake like a raven.

I'm left waiting around for like twenty minutes, my nerves humming with excitement. I keep checking my phone, but I'm getting nothing from Ryan or Rachel. I shoot off another text to each of them, glancing around.

Fans fill the stands to either side, hanging over the railing to gaze down into the press pit. Some of them have spotted me and cheered or waved. It feels strange to be the center of all this attention, but Ryan deserves it. He's had the patience of a saint, waiting with me and loving me as I've worked through my insecurities. He deserves for me to show him just how committed I am to loving him out loud.

Spending my life with Ryan was never in question. I will never love another person the way I love Ryan Langley. But unpacking a lifetime's worth of trauma around the institution of marriage has left me feeling more anxious than a salmon in a bear hug. It's taken some pretty heavy therapy to get me ready to take this plunge.

And honestly, it took me moving here to Florida and entering the world of the Rays. Meeting Ryan's teammates and their families is the first time I feel like I've ever really seen an example of a good marriage. More than that, the Rays are an expression of good love. The way they care for each other and their partners, their children, their pets. It's community. It's selfless giving. Everyone gets what they need on this team. Everyone is accepted. Everyone is valued.

Watching Rachel and her guys has been so affirming too. They are an example to me every day of the different forms love can take. Across their little unit, they have it all—romantic love, passion verging on obsession, the comforting love of a partner, a friend. I think it took seeing the way their unconventional marriage works for me to understand with total clarity that marriage was never my problem.

It was *who* I married.

I was so young and naïve. Worse than that, I was lonely. I was aching to find somewhere I could belong, determined to believe a family could want me. And yeah, I was ambitious too. Troy said all the right things and had all the right looks. He lured me in like a moth to a flame . . . and then he singed my wings, leaving me flightless on the ground.

Marriage to Ryan doesn't feel like a cage. I'm not afraid of resentment or the growing ache of having no escape. Marrying Ryan is a gift I can give him, a symbol of my love and devotion. And he won't burn me for it. He'll hold me gently in his hands and let me grow wild.

He says he wants to marry me tonight?

Bring it on. I'm more than ready.

"They're coming out," someone in a Rays tech shirt shouts.

The fans hanging over the rails cheer.

The damn butterflies in my chest take flight and I drop my sign to the floor behind me, inching closer. I want Ryan to be able to see me.

Sully is the first Ray to walk out, followed by Jake. Then it's Ryan. His golden hair, still wet from his shower, is tucked under a Rays hat. He's all smiles as he takes a seat at the narrow press table, a pair of mics in his face. All the guys wear matching warmups. The last one out is Head Coach Johnson, still in his sharp navy suit and black tie.

Ryan searches the small crowd as he gets comfortable. Laughing at something Jake says, he finds me. His eyes light up, and I swear I feel like a damn lighting bug, just glowing from the inside out. I smile and wave.

"Hey, baby," he mouths, his gaze darting away as he's distracted by motion behind him.

The press dive right in, asking the coach a few easy questions about the win and his thoughts on the game. Meanwhile, Ryan doesn't take his eyes off me.

Okay, scratch lightning bug. I feel like a volcano under his intense, longing stare. Magma bubbles in my gut, and I start to sweat. I want to barrel through these reporters and climb over the table.

Before I can do something truly outrageous, Poppy's shadow appears at my shoulder.

"Here," says Claribel, holding out a small box. It's barely big enough to hold a gift card.

I take the box, turning it over in my hands. Something rattles inside. "What is this?"

"He says you'll know when to open it." With that, the spooky witch disappears like she's got a freaking invisibility cloak.

I look around. "Wait—what?" She reappears at Poppy's side several feet away. Poppy is smiling from ear to ear as she gives me a thumbs up sign. The tingle of excitement in my tummy sharpens to something heavier.

Oh god, it's happening now, isn't it?

I look from the little box in my hands to Ryan and gasp, heart racing. He's looking right at me. I hold the box up to my ear and rattle it again. He smirks, shaking his head.

Not yet.

Oh my freaking god. What is he doing right now? What did he plan?

I can't say I don't deserve to get edged a little. Planning this day for him has been the most fun I've had in a really long time. I didn't even get to see him react to most of the proposals, but that doesn't matter. The roses, one for every day I've known and loved him. The singing card, the sky writer, the barbershop quartet. Oh god—the guys were live streaming it for me, and I about died watching his face melt off when they started to sing.

He's had all day to come up with something epic. I glance around, ready to see an Elvis minister pop out in sunglasses a bedazzled suit. I can hardly focus as the reporters finally ask Ryan a question. I totally miss the first half.

"—all impressed you managed to keep your head in the game given your little pre-game surprise."

Everyone laughs. Quite a few people whistle and cheer. Several faces turn to me with big grins. Ryan beams, his bubblegum smile on full blast.

"You both must be pretty excited," the reporter goes on. "When's the wedding?"

Ryan leans into the mic, laughing as Jake elbows him. "Yeah, uhh . . . look, I take my job seriously. So, when that puck dropped, it was game time, and I kept my head in the game. A goal and an assist felt good . . ." He looks to me, tearing me apart with his smile. "But nothing feels better than saying 'yes' to my girl."

Everyone cheers again.

"As to your other question," he calls over the crowd, still looking at me. "Tess, baby, if you're game, I'm game."

I gasp, holding his gaze as he gives a little nod. With fumbling fingers, I open the box. Two wedding bands sit nestled inside on a piece of jewelry felt—a large one for him and a slender band of yellow gold with tiny diamonds for me. Tears fill my eyes as the small crowd parts, giving me a clear line of sight to Ryan.

"Tess Langley, make me the happiest man in the world and marry me," he calls out. "Right here, right now. No more waiting, baby."

Half the crowd shrieks before quieting. It's almost eerily silent as they all look to me, waiting. Do they seriously think I'm gonna say no? I smile wide. "Hell, yeah! I'll marry you, Ryan."

The crowd goes wild and the reporters all kind of laugh and shuffle around as the four guys at the table stand up. I guess the press conference is officially over. In moments, I'm surrounded on both sides. Rachel takes one arm and Caleb takes the other.

"Come on, Red. Let's go," he says, giving my arm a squeeze.

"What are you doing?" I cry, glancing over my shoulder, looking for Ryan. But he's gone. "Where are we going?"

"Set change," Caleb says as Rachel pulls me through an open door.

We're suddenly in a small storage room. Random AV equipment mix with stacks of chairs and boxes of electrical cords. "Rach, what—"

Rachel turns, holding out a big white box. Someone taped a label to the top that says "Bride Stuff." She smirks, glancing from Caleb to me, "Okay, so we had like three hours to plan this, so it's not gonna be the most glamorous wedding . . ."

"Like I care," I cry, shoving the little ring box at Caleb. Then I snatch the larger box from her hands. I set it down on the chair and peel off the lid, looking inside. "Oh god."

"You can get married in that jersey if you really want to," she says. "Or . . . okay, so I stole this from your closet a few hours ago." She reaches in, pulling out a cute white sundress. It's got a square bodice and poufy capped sleeves. I think I wore it to a baby shower last year.

I take in my jersey, ripped jeans, and little ankle booties. "Dress, please." I snatch it from her hands. "Eyes closed, Cay."

Caleb dutifully turns around as I strip out of my jersey and jeans and slip on the summery cottage-core dress. It flows down with a flounce around mid-calf.

"And I asked all the WAGs for an emergency veil. You've got four to choose from." She pulls the veils out one at a time. One has a decidedly 80s pouf effect. The other is a single long piece of veil that would trail the ground. Doesn't seem quite fitting for the side of an ice rink. Knowing me, I'll just snag it. "Personally, I think this one is the winner," she says, holding up a delicate birdcage veil with a jewel brooch and clear plastic hair clip.

"Oooh, yes," I gasp. "Oh, it's perfect. Whose is this?"

She smiles, tears in her eyes. "It's Shelby's."

I let that sink in. Aside from Rachel, Shelby is who I'm closest with of the WAGs. She really feels like a soul sister, like she's meant to be in my life. Wearing her veil feels like a gift. Oh god, I'm not gonna make it through this. "Fuck, Rachel, stop," I whine, looking at her teary face. "If you cry, I'm gonna cry, and I can't cry. Get it together and help me."

Caleb chuckles as Rachel sniffs it all back with a nod. Then she helps me tame my curls into a sort of artfully messy chignon and attaches the birdcage veil. It's the work of moments before I'm decked out in all white like a bride.

"Here," says Caleb, pulling something from the box. "This is from us . . . me, Mars, and Jake, I mean."

I take what is obviously a little jewelry box with a trembling hand. Cracking it open, I gasp, tears spilling over. "Cay, no," I cry. Inside is a beautiful pair of stud earrings. My finger brushes them. "Are these sapphires?"

"Something new and blue," he says with a shrug. "It was Jake's idea. He picked them out. I just picked them up."

"Don't you dare pretend this was nothing," I say, glaring at him through my tears. "Will you help me put them on?"

He helps me by holding out his hand, letting me drop the earrings I'm currently wearing into his palm as I exchange them for the sapphire studs. "You know, sapphires are a Gemini birthstone," I say, turning to show Rachel.

"And you're the perfect Gemini to wear them," she replies.

"Thank you, Caleb," I say, kissing his cheek.

"We love you, Tess. Oh . . . fuck." His eyes go wide, and he leans away as I burst fully into tears. No more sniffles. Just loud, ugly, snotty, crying. "Okay, I didn't mean it," he says over my sobs. "Shit—we tolerate you at best. You're just okay—"

"Babe, you can go now," says Rachel, patting his arm. "I think your work here is done."

He makes himself scarce, and it only takes a few minutes for Rachel to help me calm down enough to fix my makeup.

"Okay, your dress is something old, your veil is borrowed, your earrings are new and blue." She ticks each item off on her fingers, giving me a once over. "Dress is gorgeous, veil is attached, makeup looks flawless. I think you're ready." Her gaze settles on my eyes. "Are you ready?"

My shoulders stiffen and I glance over my shoulder toward the door. "Oh god . . . are we doing it right here? Is he out there?"

"Yeah, they timed it this afternoon. They only needed like eight minutes for the set change, and we've been in here for like twelve."

I suck in a deep breath, blinking back my tears. "Ohmygod . . . Rachel, am I about to get married at a hockey rink wearing ankle boots? I have pretzel breath."

She laughs. "Only if you want to, and I think I have some mints in the box. There's no pressure here, Tess. We can walk out the door and I'll have Caleb bring around the getaway car. Langley will understand if you need more time—"

"No," I cry. It's as if hearing his name unlocks a door inside my mind. It's not just his name anymore. It's my name too. I've been Tess Langley in my heart for so long now. I'm ready to tag a "Mrs." to the front of it. "No," I say again. "No, I'm going out there. Wild horses can't stop me. I'm marrying him. I love him, Rachel. I *want* to marry him."

Now she's the weepy one. She wraps her arms around me in a hug, her hands rubbing my back. "I know you do, honey. And I'm so happy for you—"

"Okay, enough of that," I say, pulling away. "This makeup is perfect. We're not messing it up again."

She nods, checking her phone. "Okay, well if you're ready, they're ready. Ilmari is waiting just outside."

"For what?"

She pauses. "Oh, umm . . . well, we thought maybe he could walk you down the aisle. It's not much of an aisle but—oh no—" She grabs me by the shoulders. "Tess, don't you dare cry. Pull yourself together."

I suck in a shaky breath, my bottom lip trembling. My eyes are getting decidedly itchy.

"Breathe through it, soldier. No more tears until we get at least one picture of you looking this gorgeous. Do you want to be puffy and red faced in your wedding photos?"

"Good point."

"Right?"

"Yeah." I take another calming breath. "I'm good."

"You're good?"

"Yeah, totally," I squeak out.

I'm not good. I'm the opposite of good. I'm an emotional freaking mess, but in the best way. All my life, I've waited to find the person or place that felt like home. I've always been searching for *my* people. The people who could know me and love me anyway. The people who would never ask me to compromise my big thoughts and feelings. The people who wouldn't cut me down, taking pieces away until I fit the shapes they made for me.

Coming to Jacksonville, meeting Ryan and the Rays, I finally came home. Nothing is going to stop me from walking out that door to him.

"I'm ready," I say, taking a deep breath.

Behind me, Rachel just did the world's fastest costume change. I turn to see her tucking a pair of gold dangly earrings in her ears. Her Rays polo and athletic pants are on the floor. Now she's wearing a slinky black dress. She grabs a pair of pumps out of her bag, balancing on one foot to slip them on. "Figured you needed a bridesmaid," she says. "I volunteered."

"Of course you're my freaking bridesmaid. Wait—but you can't be my maid of honor. You're what . . . matron, right?"

"Ugh, please don't make me call myself the matron of honor. That makes me feel like an old Regency lady with a wastrel son and a dark secret."

I snort a laugh. "Fine. You can just be my second, like in a duel."

She frowns. "Does that mean I have to marry Langley if you chicken out?"

"I think it means you have to be ready to take on his best man," I reply with a shrug.

"Oh, well his best man is Jake, so no contest there." She brushes her hands down the front of her dress. "Alright, let's do this, Tess Langley. Let's get you married."

We head over to the door, and she slips around me, opening it. Someone set up a room divider thingy in front of the door, so my view is blocked. Mars stands just outside the door, handing a small bouquet of flowers off to his wife with a brush of his lips to her temple. Then he's handing a larger bouquet to me.

"These are beautiful, Mars," I say, taking in the artful spray of roses and greenery.

"I was given one job today," he replies solemnly. He looks like a million bucks. Literally. He's wearing his game day suit. It's a dapper gray with a thin black tie. He offers out his arm to me. "Langley is a lucky man."

Oh shit, I'm definitely not gonna make it. Hearing Mars offer such soft, understated praise? Yeah, someone's gonna have to find a mop. Before I can lose it, Rachel is back at my side, squeezing my arm. "Mind over matter, Tess. Shake it off."

I nod, sniffing back my tears. "Yeah. Right. I'm ready." Reaching out, I take Ilmari's arm.

Rachel gives the signal and the music starts up, something pretty and orchestral and decidedly wedding-y. With a last look to me, she nods and steps around the corner, head held high and shoulders back. She starts walking down what I must assume is the aisle.

"Ready?" Mars places his large hand over mine on his arm. I glance down, taking in the wedding ring glinting on his finger.

I nod again. "I'm ready."

He leads the way, walking me around the corner where Rachel just disappeared. I gasp to see they've transformed this little space. A black movable banner, like the one in front of the door, now stretches in front of the press wall, hiding the sponsor and team logos.

The press cleared out, and the space is packed with chairs, but no one is sitting. It looks like the entire Rays team, their WAGs, and half the support staff are crammed in here. All the remaining fans still hang over the railings, respectfully silent as I step into view.

All the players changed back into their game day suits. The wives are all still in their cute sweaters and boots, and the staff all still wear Rays gear. Everyone is here for us. Everyone loves and supports us.

Mars leads me around the back row of standing Rays to the mini aisle opening. Once I'm at the end, I can finally see Ryan. He's standing not twenty feet away in front of what looks like a white, 80s-style wedding arch that someone decorated with flower garlands and twinkle lights. He's in his navy suit and no tie, the neck open, his blond hair slicked back behind his ears. He's smiling at me like I'm his reason, tears in his eyes.

Mars leads me down the narrow aisle, stopping in front of Ryan.

"God, you look so beautiful, babe," he says, wiping a tear from his eye.

I'm probably crying too. I don't even know. All I know is I want to go to him. But Ilmari keeps a firm hand on me. The music settles, and the crowd behind us sits on their squeaky folding chairs.

Josh O'Sullivan steps up from behind Rachel, smiling at me. "Langley said y'all wanted to make this thing legal tonight. I just happen to be a justice of the peace from when I officiated for my brother last summer. I hope you don't mind that I volunteered."

I let out a laugh. "What? Are you kidding? Josh, that would be amazing. Thank you so much."

"Right then." He turns to a waiting Caleb, who hands him a microphone. "Alright, folks," he says into the mic. "Let's have ourselves a wedding."

Everyone cheers, the team hooting and hollering.

I gasp. "Oh wait—oh no—"

Ryan's eyes go wide as me looks at me. "Tess?"

"The rings," I say in a panic, looking to Rachel. "I don't know where I put them. We went to the room and—"

"I have them right here, babe," Ryan replies, patting his suit jacket pocket.

I blink back tears, heart racing. "You—what?"

"Yeah, Sanny gave them to me just before you came out."

"Dude, you were the ring bearer," Jake teases at his partner.

Caleb just shrugs, standing next to Jake in his equipment manager uniform.

A few of the other guys laugh.

"So . . . are we good?" asks Josh, glancing between us.

I give a fervent nod, my eyes locked on Ryan.

"Yeah, we're good," he replies for both of us.

"Alright then. Well, first I'm going to ask who gives this woman to be married tonight?"

Next to me, Ilmari stands quiet and calm. He's been my friend through so much. He's steady as a rock as he calls out in his deep voice, "I do." Turning to me, he tilts his head down and brushes a kiss to my cheek.

Okay, there's no way I'm making it through this without needing an IV for rapid rehydration.

Guiding me forward, he places my hand in Ryan's. Then he's stepping back to sit in the only empty chair in the front row. Rachel steps in close, tapping my shoulder. "Flowers, honey."

"Oh—" I let out a watery laugh as I turn, handing off my bouquet. With both hands free, I can cling to Ryan, losing myself in his pretty green eyes.

"We're all gathered here tonight to witness the marriage of two amazing people," Josh begins. "Two of the kindest souls, two stars burning bright. It's always a gift of nature when any people who were meant to find each other actually navigate the hurdles of life and make it to their partner's side. Anyone who knows Tess and Ryan separately or together knows they're seeing nature in divine action. Before us are two souls that *belong* together, for it is in sharing of this life together that they both shine their brightest."

Josh turns to Ryan, holding out the mic. "Ryan, do you have anything you'd like to say to Tess?"

Clearing his throat, Ryan squeezes my hands. "Yeah, I do." He lets out a shaky breath. "Tess . . . god, I've thought of so many words for this moment. I planned them all out. You know me, I like to have a plan. I've practiced my vows in the mirror at our house, in hotels when I'm away, even once or twice in an airplane lavatory."

I smile through my tears as the crowd softly laughs.

He swallows the emotion thick in his throat, willing himself to continue. "I practiced because I wanted to be ready. The moment you decided you were ready to marry me, I wanted to be ready to tell you why it was the best damn decision of your life."

The crowd laughs again.

"I was gonna wow you with big statements about our love and the beautiful life we'll have together. I'd thank you for taking a chance on me. Most important, I'd swear to you I'd make it all worth it."

I squeeze his hands, and he squeezes back.

"But now you're standing here, looking so goddamn beautiful, and all the careful speeches I planned are gone," he admits. "I have no speeches. I have no words . . . other than these: Tess, I'm already yours. And that love we could share? It's already timeless. That beautiful life we could live once we're married? We're already living it. You're mine in my heart. You're mine for always. I love you."

A tear slips down my cheek under the birdcage veil as Josh turns to me. "Tess, do you have anything to say to Ryan?"

I nod. Lowering my walls for him, I speak directly from my heart. "Ryan . . . I've known a lot of ugly love in my life—selfish love, one-sided love, love that comes with cruel conditions and cutting ultimatums. From family, from friends, other lovers, I always thought I had to *earn* love. And the fact that I could never keep it meant I didn't deserve it. There was something unlovable about me."

He grimaces, shaking his head in frustration at the very idea. His strength gives me strength. Fighting back my tears, I hold his gaze. "But then I met a pretty boy on the beach," I say with a smile. "You showed me what *kind* love looks like, Ryan—it's in the way you treat your friends, your teammates, your housekeeper, even your accountant. And then there's the way you love me . . ."

I close my eyes, fighting back the surge of feeling roiling inside my chest. He gives my hands a gentle squeeze. I open my eyes and see the tears slipping down his cheeks. "Your love for me is the kindest of all," I manage to get out. "I never really knew selfless love until I met you. I have never felt so completely safe to be me . . . and know you'll love me anyway. I get to be loved by you, and that's really special. I don't have to earn it. It's just . . . mine. It's mine because you want to give it to me, because you think I deserve it, because you know I'm worth it."

"You are," he cuts in, his tone fierce. "You're so fucking worth it, babe."

I smile and nod through my tears. "So, let's just love each other, yeah? Let's just shine this love we share back on each other and be so freaking happy together."

"Yeah. Tess, that's all I want," he says fervently.

"So, marry me," I go on. "I'm not afraid of your love, and I'm definitely not afraid of losing it. Marry me, Ryan Langley. Please, god, don't make me wait any longer."

He laughs through his teary smile. "Babe, that's what we're doing right now."

The crowd around us laughs too.

"Right," I say, glancing to Josh. I forgot I even had a microphone pointed my direction. "Can you hurry this along?" I say at him to more laughter.

"You've got rings, right?" he says with a smile at Ryan.

Ryan lets go of my hands to take out the rings, handing me the larger one meant for him. With trembling fingers, I slip the thick yellow-gold band onto his left ringer finger, slipping it over the knuckle. "You went and got this today?" I say with a raised brow.

He nods. "Yeah, on my way in for morning skate."

I smile, holding out my hand, so he can slip my new wedding band on my finger. It clicks into place next to my sparkly engagement ring. Shortest engagement of the century, and I wouldn't have it any other way. The first thing I'm going to do when this is over is change their positions on my finger. I want the wedding band closer to my heart.

"Well, with the vows being said and the rings exchanged, there's nothing left for me to do but ask you the both the million dollar question," says Josh. We both smile as he turns to Ryan first. "Ryan, do you take Tess to be your wife? Will you love and cherish her so long as you both shall live?"

"I do," he replies confidently.

Josh turns to me. "And Tess, do you take Ryan to be your husband? Will you love and cherish him so long as you both shall live?"

"I do," I reply. "I will. Ryan, baby, I love you so much."

He flashes me his biggest megawatt bubble gum smile. He's practically bouncing on the balls of his feet, looking from me to Josh with an excited glint in his eyes.

Josh smiles back, tipping the mic his way. "Tess and Ryan have vowed their love to each other in front of these witnesses. So, it is my great pleasure to announce them as husband and wife. You may kiss the—"

I don't hear the word "bride" before Ryan is swooping in, his arms going around me to claim me in a fierce kiss. All around us the crowd goes crazy—the players and their wives, the fans hanging off the railings. Everyone claps and cheers as Ryan tips me backward, his arms strong around me as we kiss.

"I love you," he says against my lips. "Tess, I love you so much."

"I love you too," I say through my tears, clinging to him. "Forever, Ryan."

God, please let it be forever.

We break away and Josh is still there, mic in hand. "Ladies and Gentlemen, may I announce for the first time, Mr. and Mrs. Ryan and Tess Langley!"

Thank You

Wow. I wish I had more words or maybe a few better words, but that about sums up how I'm feeling as I type this. Just . . . wow. You all changed my life. I never in my wildest dreams anticipated that *Pucking Around* would receive the reception it did. Now that it has, I am every day overflowing with thankfulness.

I'm going to try and thank some people here, but I'm sure I'll miss a few.

To Ashley, my alpha reader—You were the first person to believe in me and my stories. You've cheered me on every step of the way, and I couldn't be more grateful to have you by my side.

To my beta reader team—Alex, Amanda, Rachel, Mallory, and Nikki, thank you for your unwavering support as you helped me make these characters and their story stronger.

To my ARC team—Your enthusiasm for these characters and this world are the reason this book exists. I wanted to tell this story for you. I wanted to share it with you. And now I have, and I hope you love Tess and Ryan as much as I do.

To my entire support team at Jabberwocky Literary Agency and Penguin Michael Joseph—Thank you for taking a chance on this quirky, queer hockey romance series and helping me get it into more readers' hands.

And to you, my wonderful readers—Thank you for making my life bigger, brighter, and more magical than I could have ever dreamed.

Life is short and we only get one. I'm thankful I have this chance to live it to the fullest.